the

HARSHEST
HOPE

the HARSHEST HOPE

VICTORIA LUM

Cover Design Copyright © 2023 Y'All That Graphic
Editing by Becca Mysoor, Grace Bradley, and Amy Briggs
Proofreading by Virginia Tesi Carey
Formatting by Elaine York, Allusion Publishing (http://www.allusionpublishing.com)

Author's Note: Please note this story may contain areas that may be sensitive to some readers. For a list of potential areas of sensitive content, please visit: https://www.victorialum.com/sensitive-content-information

Also, a few classical music pieces are referenced in the story. For the best reading experience, I'd recommend playing those pieces in the background when they are referenced. Happy reading!

To anyone who has ever felt the rough edges and sharp cuts of hopelessness, may you find the strength to soldier on in the darkness before dawn, because a beau-tiful sunrise awaits you around the corner.

ACT ONE——FIRST LOVE

Hope is a useless, fickle concept.

When she's on your side, it may feel like your future is full of possibilities. When she's not on your side, it feels like a slap to your face. I don't waste my time on hopes and dreams when there's really only one thing I want, something most people take for granted.

Time.

The smell of antiseptic soap and hand sanitizer hits my nostrils as I walk through the hospital doors. My footfalls sound loud on the clean tile floors as I drag myself to the elevators, my body exhausted from less than four hours of sleep, and press the button for the third floor. It's a trip I've completed too many times in the last few years, but lately, the usual nausea in my gut has morphed into a tightness I can't shake, as if I somehow know I won't be walking down these halls much longer.

I attempt to take a deep breath as I stare at the door before me, but it doesn't fully alleviate the heaviness of the lead in my chest. Barbara, the morning charge nurse, passes by and gives me a kind smile, a suffocating sympathy in her brown eyes. I twist my mouth into something I hope resembles polite acknowledgement, turn the doorknob, and enter the room.

The muted, steady beeping of the heart rate monitor echoes in the quiet space—like the ticking of a clock. Resounding. Reminding me time is limited. Jarring florescent lights wash the room in a stark brightness, drawing attention to every sunken dip and sharp angle of my mom. My heart twists and aches, the gnawing pain threatening to take the breath from my lungs. Upright and engrossed in the pages of a well-worn book she's reread many times over the years, *Romeo and Juliet,* my mom adjusts the striped woolen cap covering her head where her thick hair used to be. I bite my bottom lip and force my tense muscles to relax as I approach her. Upon sensing my presence, she sets her book down and looks up, the warmth in her blue gaze shining back at me.

I clear my throat and sweep my hands down my body. "So, how do I look?"

"Adrian, sweetie, look at you. I never thought I'd see you wearing the same uniform I wore all those years ago." Her eyes glisten with tears as she smiles at me.

"I feel ridiculous. I'm a little too old to be playing dress-up." I tug at the worn, faded navy-blue jacket I purchased online that is fraying at the edges. *Gently used, my ass.* I sit down in the chair next to the bed and take her frail hand in mine.

"Pssh. Don't be silly. You just turned nineteen—you have your entire life ahead of you."

My nostrils flare as I bite the inside of my cheek. I let out a chuckle. "As do you, Mom, you still have a lot of time left too."

I don't look into her eyes. I'm good at hiding, but I can't seem to hide from her.

Mom squeezes my hand and lets the comment slip by. We both know time is the one thing she doesn't have. Lymphoma. Terminal stage. Her third bout of this horrific disease. I can feel her slipping away some more each time I visit, and I'm helpless to stop it.

Life is so unfair.

I gnash my teeth together at the thought and force myself to relax, to play pretend.

"So, are you excited about the first day of your new school?"

"Considering it's the middle of the school year of my senior year and I'm older than the rest of my class and wearing this clown outfit, not particularly." I'm switching schools only for her, because I know it's something she always wanted.

"You'll love it. It'll open so many doors for you, even though you're only there for a few months. It's worth the hassle." She pats my hand, forcing me to glance up at her. Mom's lips curve into a smile, her face lighting up with joy. Despite her sunken cheeks and hollowed eyes, Mom still radiates life...or whatever amount of life she has left. "I had some of my most memorable years there, but of course, my best memories are with you, your dad, and Millie."

I nod, smiling at her as I squeeze her fingers gently, a touch of reassurance so she can hopefully worry less about us. I don't tell her how Dad is barely holding it together most days. I also don't tell her how Millie has become more withdrawn these last few weeks. It's as if we all sense the end is near.

"Do tell me about your first day later, okay, sweetie?" Her eyes are unfocused, taking on a faraway look as if she's reminiscing about the long-gone days of her youth before everything happened.

Thump. Thump. Thump.

A series of knocks interrupts our conversation. Moments later, a short man with thick, black glasses and a clipboard walks in. Sweat beads on his forehead and he grimaces.

"Um. Excuse me, ma'am. Is this a good time?"

Mom nods and adjusts the cap on her head.

The man pulls out a few sheets of paper from his clipboard. "We don't normally do this, but we couldn't get a hold of your husband and we've tried a few times already. Um. Your hospital bill is overdue." He glances at me, his hand twitching as he fidgets, and continues, "Perhaps the originals got lost in the mail, so we thought we'd bring copies to you just in case."

Heat rises to my face and washes over my body. He's a debt collector. Dad must have forgotten to settle the last installment payment.

"I-I'm sorry for the delay." Mom retrieves the sheets from him as her head dips. As if she needs to apologize for inconveniencing everyone because she is fucking sick.

Gritting my teeth, I snatch the papers from her. This is the least of her concerns right now. "We'll take care of it." I level a hard stare at the man, who seems to shrink under my gaze, and he stammers a thank you before leaving the room.

Aside from time, I also need money.

Not for cars, or fancy clothes, or taking chicks out on dates, but for the necessities. And apparently to pay the hospital and the doctors for keeping my mom alive while she suffers.

I glance at the figures, and my heart drops to my gut in a swooshing free fall. Fifteen thousand dollars. Shit. I have my job after school. Maybe I can think about cutting out some other expenses or take up my best friend Jack's offer.

"Sweetie, Adrian, Adrian!"

My eyes flicker up at Mom while my brain is working on overdrive on how to earn more money for all these expenditures.

"Yes, Mom?"

"Your dad won't tell me when I ask him. He just says not to worry. Are things going okay at home? We don't have the money, do we?"

I pat her hand and force a reassuring smile on my face, a mask I'm better at wearing when I'm around her these days. "Things are fine. We have this in the budget. Don't you worry about a thing." This should be the least of her concerns. If hopes and wishes do work, I'd wish I were ten years older, with a degree or two, climbing up some corporate ladder, and making enough money so the people I love no longer need to suffer and worry about the necessities.

But we all know hopes and wishes are figments of imagination. Stories we tell little kids.

Reality is far uglier.

I take out a DVD from my backpack, *Romeo and Juliet*, the classic 1968 version, and place it on top of her soft blankets, hoping to cheer her up. "I found this at the grocer's the other day. Your favorite. Maybe you can ask the nurses to play it for you later."

She grips the package tightly and smooths her fingertips on the cover. "My sweet boy. You always know what I like and need. Your dad and I watched this on our first date…" Her voice trails off.

I lean in and wrap her bony body in my arms, careful to not squeeze too hard. Her body trembles, shaking like a leaf under the wind. She seems so fragile and is always in pain. Closing my eyes, I bask in her warmth and am transported to a memory of her wrapping me in a big hug when I was little, remembering how safe I used to feel in her presence.

It's my turn to protect her now. It's my turn to take care of her.

I pull back and say softly, "I'll let you know how things go. Don't worry about me, or Millie, or Dad. I'm taking care of them."

She smiles again, but the warmth doesn't quite reach her eyes. "I know, sweetie. I'm worried about your dad. He told me his job at the bank is precarious at best. There are rumors of a layoff. I'm so sorry to put all this on you. I know you're taking on so much already, far too much for a boy your age. If only—"

"No, I'm happy to. I just want you to focus on getting better."

I glance away and blink my eyes rapidly before the moisture gathers and betrays the turmoil of emotions swirling inside me. I twist my lips into a wider smile. A fake smile. But neither of us comment on that either.

"See you later, Mom."

Exhaling a ragged breath, I close my eyes for a brief respite outside of the door, attempting to calm the tempest swirling inside me, and I swallow the pins and needles in my throat. My hands tighten into fists as I walk away, wanting to punch something. I want to yell, to scream, to ask the higher power why this is happening to us.

But I don't. Instead, I leash down the storm inside me as I always do, and stride toward the exit, a pawn in this cruel game of life.

CHAPTER 2

Adrian

The sun beats down on the windshield of my car as I drive up the winding road to Warwick Academy, a prestigious, private high school perched on a beautiful cliffside in Palos Verdes, a suburbia filled with the rich and famous in LA. The city is situated on a small mountain, which boasts riveting views of the Pacific Ocean with waves crashing against the rocky shores. The magnificent French Baroque-style establishment beckons the attention of passersby, and one can't help but gaze upon the grand structure beyond gold-tipped iron fences. It seems like they modeled the school after the Palace of Versailles. I snort at the over-the-top opulence as I make a turn into the parking lot in my car.

What excess. What waste. What ridiculousness.

The waitlist is miles long, with folks putting their babies on the list before their first steps or words. They say anyone would be lucky to score a spot at the academy, even if it's only for a few months. I can't help but roll my eyes at the rumors. Apparently, with the name of the school on resumes, doors are opened, connections are made. Having attended Warwick meant "you have arrived." I couldn't care less about these so-called superficial accolades or secret handshakes of the rich and famous.

But attending Warwick, even for such a short period of time, has a lesser-known side benefit, one Mom told me about when she insisted I apply. The headmaster here has deep connections with most of the prestigious colleges in the nation and as the head of an Ivy League feeder school, he writes letters and advocates to admissions committees for the school's students during the critical few months when universities sort through the thousands of applications filtering through their system.

And I need the extra boost, the secret handshake.

I need a full-ride scholarship to a good college in order for me to dig our family out of the hole we are in. Plus, it makes Mom happy. It was always one of her bigger regrets that she couldn't give me the same comforts and quality of schooling she had when she was younger. And so, I suck it up.

The engine groans and stutters. Fuck. I'll need to find time and more of the money I don't have to get it checked out. I find an empty spot at the far corner of the parking lot and turn off the engine, bracing myself for the snobbery I'll no doubt face as soon as I walk through those double doors. A slice of dread funnels to my insides, but I shove it away, clenching my muscles, imagining myself in a suit of armor. Impenetrable. I miss my public school down the hill where the normal folks live.

You're doing this for Mom. These people don't matter.

I pull down the rearview mirror and check my appearance. Mid-length dark-brown hair, courtesy of Dad, which needs a haircut. Light-blue eyes from Mom. No stains on my shirt or suit jacket. It'll have to do. I throw on a scarf, the flimsy material doing little to warm me up in the cooler temperatures of January. Cracking the stiff joints on my neck, I take a deep breath and exit the vehicle.

The hairs on my arms stick up, and a jitteriness fills my veins. I hear the whispers and see the finger-pointing from the corner of my eye before I even enter the main building, a towering structure with swiveling colonnades, arched windows, and intricate carvings on the stucco walls. I'm a fish out of water and I definitely don't belong here.

But that doesn't matter. I'm too old for this shit and too tired to care.

These kids may be rich in their wallets, but they're peasants in their life experiences.

"That's our new scholarship kid, huh?"

"Duh. I mean, look at the piece of shit he's driving. Are we accepting the poor now?"

"I hear he's a legacy, though. At least, that's what I overhead in the headmaster's office the other day."

I grind my teeth against each other as I clench my muscles. *Someday, I'll show them. One day, I'll walk amongst them and they'll be clamoring for my attention instead.* Steeling myself, I shove open the two double doors and head into the administration office for my assignments, the curling flames of anger mixing in with the heaviness in my chest.

Fuck them. Fuck them all.

"How may I help you?" A middle-aged woman with curly brown hair and rosy cheeks sits behind a large oak desk.

"It's my first day. I was told to report here."

She glances up at me as recognition dawns in her gaze. No doubt she knows about my family's story and about Mom—I had to provide a family status in my application. "Ah, you must be Adrian Callahan. I'm Doris, the school secretary." A small crease mars the smooth skin on her forehead as her brown eyes stare at me in what I've come to know as one of my most-hated emotions.

Pity.

I give her a terse nod. The emerald tie is choking my airway. The office reeks of the odor of full-grain leather and expensive, upholstered furniture. It smells like everything else in this place.

Rich. Old. Pretentious. Wasteful.

I tap my fingers on the desk in an erratic rhythm as I wait for the lady to return with a slip of paper and a pamphlet.

"Here's your schedule and a map of the campus. Your first class is Shakespearean English Literature in Room 308 with Mr. Nichols. Class is just about to begin."

Retrieving the documents, I dip my head in acknowledgement then turn to walk toward the door.

"Hold on. Our policy is to have someone walk you to your first class on your first day here. A welcome of sorts. I've called another student from your class to come by. Stay put and she'll be here shortly."

She.

Probably another snobby, party girl decked out head-to-toe in expensive jewelry, driving a luxury vehicle purchased with her parents' funds. I resist the urge to roll my eyes at the thought of needing to wait for a spoiled *child* to escort me to class. After all, I'm older than all the students here.

The grandfather clock in the corner of the room chimes a familiar tune in the background—*The Westminster Quarters,* as I've learned from my hours spent studying at the library on the weekends to catch up on coursework I've missed during some especially grueling weekdays. The haunting, beautiful sound echoes in the room. The craftsmanship of the clock is exquisite, with angels and flowers carved deep into the red wood case. The face is enclosed in glass with the minute and hour hands forged from gold, which glint in the lamplight. The copper pendulum, slightly dulled with age, swings to the chimes. I'm momentarily mesmerized by the beauty of the antique and don't hear the door open behind me.

"Hi, Doris. How are you doing? You look wonderful today," a sweet voice says from behind me—a voice radiating warmth, like a cup of steaming, creamy hot chocolate on a freezing winter's day.

I smell a faint scent of lilies before I see her.

My heart picks up in rhythm for no apparent reason as I slowly turn around. My breath catches in my throat as I take in the owner of the dulcet voice in front of me.

Long, sleek hair, the color of espresso beans, streaked with dark-russet strands.

A heart-shaped face with large mocha-brown eyes framed with the thickest of lashes.

Porcelain skin, smooth with only the lightest scattering of freckles.

A small pair of lips currently quirked up in a smile. Two beautiful dimples.

Pocket-sized to my six-foot-two height, with curves in all the right places.

An elf. A fae. A pixie.

"Emily, you smooth talker. I'm doing fine, thank you. How are you doing yourself? How is Jess doing? We miss her around here, you know."

Emily. Her name is Emily.

She gives me a wink and walks up to the desk, propping her arms on the top. The fragrance of lilies is stronger as she stands next to me. The hairs on my arms prickle to attention under the suit jacket and my senses are on alert, as if my body knows something about this person that I don't know. As if this is somehow a turning point in my life.

Shake it off, dude.

"She's doing great. She's at ULA and staying on campus—acing her classes as usual. She even has a boyfriend. I'm happy for her."

"Oh good. I'm glad to hear. We expect nothing less from her." Doris clears her throat and motions to me. "This is Adrian Callahan. Today is his first day. He's in the same Shakespearean Literature class as you. Can you walk him to class and go over how things work here?"

Emily cocks her head to the side and flashes a blinding smile at me. A real one, not the fake ones I'm doling out or the ones I'd expect from the school of snobs. "I'm Emily Kingsley. Welcome to Warwick." She extends her hand toward me. Kingsley. A slither of unease snakes its way through me, but I can't pinpoint the reason.

I clench my hand, quickly wiping my palm on my trousers, and gently clasp her hand in mine. My large palm engulfs her soft one and I could swear I see her quickly intake a breath of air.

"Hi," I murmur, my voice sounding deeper than usual.

The moment passes as quickly as it appeared and I reluctantly drop her hand. She twists her fingers and rubs her palms together, a flush creeping up her slender neck. My fingers twitch with an irrational impulse to trace the pinkness there.

"Come on, follow me. I'll show you the ropes."

I glance back at Doris, only to find her staring at me with the damn pity in her eyes again. I give her a nod and follow Emily out of the office.

"So, Adrian, tell me about yourself. What brings you to Warwick? Are you really older than the rest of us? Is it true your mom went here when she was younger? Where were you studying before? What are your plans after graduation?"

Her low heels make *click, clack* staccato sounds on the marble floors as she walks quickly in front of me, the energy practically radiating from her aura. Her navy-and-green-checkered skirt sways side to side, highlighting her toned legs, currently clad in white, knee-high socks, with a thin green stripe near the top where they meet her smooth skin, and the round curves of her backside. A warm, fluffy scarf is curled around her slender neck.

I may have a different opinion about our uniforms now. I think I like them.

She stops mid-stride and I nearly plow into her. Emily stares at me expectantly, genuine curiosity brimming in her eyes. How refreshing after the chilly reception I experienced outside of the school just now.

"Are you going to ask me for my social security number next and the inseam of my dress pants?"

Her eyes quickly dart to the front of my pants and she looks away, the pinkened cheeks making a reappearance. She resumes walking and tosses her hair back. "I see how it is. You're going to be one of those grumpy boys at school."

"Men."

"Huh?" She glances up at me as I take a few large strides and catch up to her.

"I'm not a boy. Far from it."

The beautiful pink may be a permanent shade on her skin now. I bite the inside of my cheeks to keep from grinning, the burn of anger slowly doused by whatever water magic this curious pixie is inflicting on me.

"Scholarship student. Yes, I'm nineteen. Yes, she graduated from here. Lomita High. Not sure—college, maybe. And no, I'm not a grump. I just don't like to talk a lot."

Emily arches her brow at my quick responses. A small smile graces her lips. "Hmm. Interesting. I'll get more out of you at some point this year."

I let out a deep chuckle, the rough sound seeming foreign to my ears. How long has it been since I truly laughed? Too long. The heaviness, which apparently abated in the last ten minutes, is slowly seeping back into my chest at the thought, slithering back into its familiar home.

"So, the campus is divided into four buildings with a central courtyard. This building is for liberal arts and languages, the one on the other side is for sciences and mathematics. That one way over there is for extracurriculars, including the gym, the pool, art workshops, theater, etcetera. The final building houses the dining hall. Most students end up eating on campus because the food is actually really good here. With the insane cost of tuition," she pauses and rolls her eyes as if recognizing the ridiculousness of this environment, "they've hired a wonderful chef here."

"A chef? Why am I not surprised?"

"I know this all seems very pretentious...and most of the time I'd agree with you, but there are some really wonderful people here. Not everyone comes from affluent backgrounds. The school has a few slots each year for top performers who live in the vicinity. In fact, my sister Jess's best friend, James, was one of them, and he's an awesome person. He's at MIT now. There are also exchange students and scholarship students. I think it's pretty great most of the time. You'll see."

I arch my brow, my expression no doubt dripping in disbelief, and she grins cheekily at me. "Trust me, Adrian, you'll have a good experience here. Emily Kingsley will not lead you astray."

Shaking my head, we round a corner as she points to a closed door on the far right. "That's us. Mr. Nichols is pretty awesome too." She stares at me and arches her brow. "I sense more skepticism radiating from you. Trust me, Emily—"

"Kingsley will not lead me astray," I mutter under my breath, finishing the sentence for her, unable to stifle a smile as I turn the doorknob and let her proceed before me.

Her gaze shines with laughter as she crosses the threshold, her heels accidentally tripping on the raised step in the doorway. She tumbles forward and I quickly curl my arm around her waist to steady her. Her breath quickens as my heart skips another beat and I stare into her widened eyes, noticing the small, golden flecks shimmering against the light. Despite the thick clothing between us, I could somehow feel the heat of her lithe body seeping through the layers of cotton and wool. My fingers tighten and curl reflexively. She gasps, her soft lips parting. My eyes flicker to the movement and liquid heat rushes to my chest.

"T-Thank you. Quick reflexes there," she whispers breathlessly, the apples of her cheeks flushed.

I quickly release her and drag my hand through my hair, my fingers still tingling from the brief moment of contact. I clench and unclench my hand, wanting to release some of the sudden tension there. Someone clears his throat loudly and I feel the heavy weight of someone's stare. Dragging my gaze away from Emily, I survey the classroom for the source of the unease, and locate a hulking jock with gleaming, white-blond hair shooting daggers at me through eyes with barely concealed fury. Frowning, I glance away.

The murmuring in the classroom comes to an abrupt halt. Twenty pairs of eyes track my movements as I amble over to the teacher. Tiny droplets of sweat bead on my forehead, the tie feeling too tight around my neck. I ignore the pointed looks. The damn whispers. My eyes trail over to Emily, who has taken her seat in the third row. She gives me a wink, one dimple forming in her smooth cheek. My lips twitch in the smallest of grins.

"Thank you, Ms. Kingsley, and you must be Mr. Callahan." A lanky man, probably five years or so older than me, walks over and shakes my hand. "I'm Mr. Nichols. Your desk is that one, fourth row down. Please take a seat."

Ignoring the soft murmurs in the classroom, I stride over to the empty desk behind Emily, my eyes trailing over her features. She gives me a nod of encouragement. Someone coughs again.

"Loser."

The rest of the class snickers.

My head whips toward the offender, the blond jock from earlier, who is smirking at me while his group of hooligans cackles beside him. "What are you looking at, scholarship kid?"

I crack my neck and clench my hands in tight fists as a burning fire unfurls from my abdomen, threatening to break free. My lips twist in a snarl and I take a deep breath. *I'm not here to make trouble. Six months, then I'm out of here.*

"Ryan, what the heck was that?" Emily whispers to the blond jock, her brows furrowing.

"Just coughing. The stench of trash is so strong, I can't help it. But don't you worry about me, darling."

"Ugh. I'm not your darling. Will you just drop it already? And stop being such an asshole." Emily turns around as I settle in behind her. *Sorry,* she mouths.

I shake my head as I tamp down the heat of anger swirling inside me. She gives me a sad smile and turns toward the front of the classroom. Ryan flips me the middle finger. I clench my jaw.

Fuck. This is going to be the longest six months ever.

CHAPTER 3

Adrian

"**C**ome on, Millie, go change your clothes and wash your hands. I'll fix us some food for dinner before I head out." I usher my seven-year-old sister into our cramped apartment. My parents used to tell me Millie was a wonderful "oopsie" surprise. Because of our age gap and the current situation at home, sometimes I feel more like a father figure to her than just being her older brother.

Looking at my wrist, I check my watch. Four-thirty p.m. I have an hour before I need to head to Grocery for Less for work. Dad should be home by then.

I hope he has some time and energy to spend with Millie today.

I hope he isn't going to numb his mind with the contents of the alcohol cabinet again.

I hope—

Fuck hope. It's never done shit for me, anyway.

Millie pouts at me as she narrows her eyes. Strands of her dark-brown hair are falling out of her ponytail. "You don't need to remind me. I know the routine already. I'm not a baby anymore."

I let out a deep sigh as she stomps toward her bedroom. Stifling a yawn, I quickly set her backpack down, take out her folders, and go over her papers, searching to see if she has any homework due tomorrow, any permission slips to sign, or anything else of importance. It looks like she has some math homework due. I make a mental note to check her work when I get home from my shift tonight.

The florescent lights flicker on and off after I flip the switch by the kitchen door. Faded cabinets with paint chips flaking at the corners, linoleum countertops peeling on the sides from years of use—home, sweet home. Someday, I'll be able to move my family to a better place. Millie would never want for anything anymore. We would be able to afford new clothes, meals out, all the normal things other people enjoy. Dad wouldn't have to feel so pressured at work. Mom wouldn't—

She wouldn't be here.

I bite down hard on my bottom lip, relishing in the brief flash of pain that is punishment for thinking this way…for accepting this harsh reality.

There are some things money can't fix or buy after all.

The burning heat of anger always simmering inside me flashes to the forefront, the flames scorching me as I struggle to tamp down the fire. I force a ragged inhale, a breath which doesn't quite reach my lungs.

My sister needs me.

After washing my hands, I open the refrigerator and take out the corned beef and sauerkraut casserole I prepared over the weekend and defrosted this morning. Cracking my knuckles to release a pop of tension, I slide the dish into the oven and set a timer for half an hour. I wash and dry Millie's lunch box then fill it with a simple turkey sandwich and some grapes for tomorrow. The more I accomplish now, the less I need to do when I get home around midnight. I can then use the quiet hours to finish my coursework and hopefully have time to catch a few hours of sleep before another day begins.

I'm stuck in this hamster wheel of life with dread and gloom-filled days and I can't escape. God, I want to escape, to run away, to live the day of a regular guy my age, going to parties, picking up chicks, worrying about something as mundane as exams. But I'm shackled by responsibility.

Millie saunters out and sits at the small, circular dining table and begins her homework. We have two small bedrooms in this tight space, and they still charge us an arm and a leg for it. My parents—well, Dad now—sleeps in one room while Millie takes the other. I sleep on a pull-out futon in the living room. I don't mind. They need their rooms more than I do. I'm rarely at home, anyway.

"I saw Mom today after I dropped you off at school." I put the lunch box in the refrigerator and proceed to make a quick salad for dinner. Tomatoes, lettuce, onions, a few olives. Dice, dice, dice. Add dressing. Mix ingredients. The familiar routine soothes me, temporarily distracting me from my hopeless thoughts. These fresh ingredients are part of the perks of me working at the grocery store. Sometimes, when they have a surplus of food that is close to its expiration, they allow me to take some home.

Lower grocery costs while getting paid. Two wins in my book.

The sounds of pencil scribbling on paper stop. I glance up, finding Millie staring intently at the paper in front of her. "How is Mommy doing?" she whispers.

I clear my throat and attempt to sound normal. "She's doing well. She misses you. Make sure you go visit her with Dad next time, okay?"

More silence.

Her sniffling fills the air. Millie shakes in her chair as tears roll down her face, the chubby face which has slimmed down the last few years as she blossoms from a toddler to a little kid—most of which Mom missed because of her stays at the hospital. The heaviness in my heart spreads to my lungs and I feel like I'm suffocating again.

Setting down the knife, I walk over to the table and wrap Millie in my arms.

"Shhh...everything is okay. I'm here."

"I-I'm scared of seeing Mommy at the hospital." The sobs are louder now.

"Why?"

"It's a scary place. The beeping and the machines. The smells. S-She doesn't look like Mommy anymore. She's so skinny—I can see her bones. What if one day she d-disappears?"

My heart twists inside of my chest as wetness prickles my eyes. I swallow the thickness in my throat. "She's still our mommy, even if she looks different now. She still loves us very much. She's being brave and fighting the disease. So, we need to be brave and fight for her, okay? We should spend our extra time with her, cheering on the sidelines for her. Like you see people doing at the races on TV."

The oven soon dings as the smell of salty beef fills the small space.

"That smells so good, Adrian." She pulls back and wipes her eyes with her sleeve and scrunches her nose dramatically.

"I know. It's your favorite. I'm going to put it on the counter so you and Dad can help yourself and if he doesn't—"

"I'll make sure Daddy eats some dinner. I don't want him to get sick. Don't worry."

The pit in my stomach grows bigger. Millie is only seven years old—she shouldn't be worried about such things. She should be thinking about rainbows and unicorns and concerning herself with whom to play with on the playground. I ruffle her hair and walk back into the kitchen to cut a slice of the casserole for myself so I can fill my stomach before spending the next few hours restocking shelves and completing stock counts.

As much as I have a disdain for the rich people who turn their noses up at us, I desperately wish I had their resources so I could take care of our financial troubles. A sticky sense of shame washes through me with this frank realization. I'm a hypocrite. I hate the people who have what I don't have.

With Mom's hospital bills the last several years piling up, in addition to the one we received this morning, and Dad barely pulling through work each day, to say our wallets are tight is an understatement. The part-time income I earn at the grocery store and the lower cost of food helps a little but barely makes a dent in the bigger picture. Desperation floods me as I recall the look on her face when the man handed her the bill. She must realize we don't have enough money to pay it off.

Some people say money can't buy happiness. Money isn't everything.

I call bullshit.

I have a love-hate relationship with it, but deep down inside, I wish I had enough of it. Maybe some of our worries would go away then.

Resolution fills me and I know what I need to do—I'll talk to Jack tonight.

The doorknob rattles and the creak of the front door indicates Dad is home. I turn my head toward him as I swallow a bite of the food. Dad staggers in, a heaviness in his gait. His tall frame is slightly hunched over, as if he can't find the energy to straighten up and face the world. His dark hair is speckled with gray now and dark circles rim his eyes.

"Son." He smiles at me, a fake one, since it looks exactly like the ones I give out. I nod and return one of my own.

He walks into the living room and I hear a faint murmuring of "Daddy."

A few moments later, he slumps toward the kitchen and grabs a plate of casserole. "How was your first day?" He doesn't ask me about Mom. He knows I saw her this morning, but I think deep down, he doesn't want to talk about her condition and how rapidly it has been deteriorating lately. Perhaps if we don't talk about it, we can pretend it doesn't exist.

"Fine. Things are fine." I finish my meal and wash my plate and utensils in the sink. "Millie has homework due tomorrow. Can you look over her work?"

He nods and walks over to the one place I don't want him near. The liquor cabinet. He pours amber liquid into a large glass. The first glass of what will most likely be multiple glasses tonight. It looks like I'll need to check on Millie's homework myself.

"I'll look into it."

"How's work?"

The silence seems loud in this tiny space. I know he's been having problems at work, but maybe things are worse than I thought. Dad stops at the threshold of the kitchen door and turns around. His eyes are red and glistening with unshed tears. "Son, I-I'm failing you and your sister. I failed your mother."

He chokes up, his voice laden with guilt. "When we eloped all those years ago, I promised her she would never want for anything. I promised her I'd take care of her and our family no matter what hardships we encounter. Us against the world. We are poor in money but rich in life. B-But when it comes down to it, I'm not strong enough. I'm not strong enough to w-watch her wither away. I'm not strong enough to be there for you and Millie. I-I'm sorry, son." He takes a big gulp of the alcohol.

The plate in my hand shakes as I grip it tightly. *What about me, Dad? I don't have the fucking option to "not be strong enough." Someone has to keep things afloat. Why does it have to be me?* I keep the steel-tipped whip of my thoughts leashed inside me because I know Millie will cry if she hears us argue.

Instead, I reply, "It's okay, Dad."

There's nothing more I can say, because things aren't okay. They're all lies we tell ourselves.

He lets out a big sigh and trudges away. I quickly finish my chores and go into the bathroom to change into casual wear for work, a plain black shirt, and dark blue jeans. I shrug on a cargo jacket and walk back into the living room. Millie is almost done with her food and is scribbling quietly on her homework. Dad set his dinner plate on the coffee table, his casserole mostly untouched, but his glass is empty of the alcohol. Alcohol we can't afford, but he still brings home irresponsibly. He is staring at the photo album in front of him, his wedding album, a regular routine now. He exhales deeply as he flips a page.

My parents love each other. So much they dismissed the concerns of everyone around them and eloped all those years ago. Before Mom got sick, our apartment used to be filled with laughter. There were lots of hugs and snuggles, kisses and dancing. Their story was supposed to be a fairytale. Except, now it seems like their ending isn't a happily-ever-after. It's a sluggish and agonizing train wreck to the death-do-us-part with me and Millie being casualties. It's a slow-burning fire that leaves him a husk of the man he used to be. It's as if his soul is deteriorating with her health.

If this is what love does to you, then I want no part of it.

Grabbing my keys from the dining table, I announce, "I'm heading off to work. Millie, be good. Dad, I'll be back around midnight."

Millie waves at me, her lips quirking into a sweet smile. Dad glances up from the photo album. "Drive safe, son."

I step outside and close the door behind me, finally able to breathe outside of the suffocating room.

"What are the two stages of photosynthesis and where do they take place?" Jack scratches his head as he looks at the flashcards in his hand. "What is this shit?"

"Light-dependent reactions, which take place in thylakoid membranes, and the Calvin Cycle, which takes place in the stroma. It's AP biology. Didn't you take this last year?"

He snorts. "Please, like I remember anything I read last year. Senior year, baby, my body may have physically been at school, but my mind definitely wasn't there." Jack Szeto is my best friend from my old high school and currently a freshman at a local college, something I would've been doing if I wasn't held back a year for missing too many days of school last year. He flips the card around. "And you'd be right. I don't know how you remember this shit."

I take a sip of water from my water bottle and smirk. "It's not my fault I'm a genius...and failure isn't an option." If I want a shot at making something of myself.

"Clean up on aisle sixteen," the intercom announces as Jack and I both groan. The cooking oil aisle. This will be a fucking mess to deal with.

"Dude, it's your turn. I took the spoiled cheese fiasco last month." Jack shrugs and crosses his muscular arms, leaning back against the wall next to the bathrooms of Grocery for Less. He grins and winks at a female customer walking by. She blushes and enters the women's room. Only Casanova Jack can look good carrying a mop with an apron tied around his waist. His longish jet-black hair falls over his face and his small lip ring glints in the harsh light.

"Shit."

He snorts. "Shit is right. Glad to see you at work today. I thought for sure you'd quit after you stepped foot into that fancy prep school."

I walk over to the closet housing the cleaning supplies I'll need for the spill. "I wish. It'd be my dream not to see your ugly-ass face every day," I toss back as Jack bursts out in laughter behind me. "You know why I'm still here in this dump."

"Have you given what I told you some more thought? It pays well—all cash, under the table."

"I'll do it."

Jack grins and slaps his hand on my back. "Attaboy. I knew you'd come around. With your boxing lessons when you were younger, you'd be a favorite in the ring—I just know it. And I'd get to earn a few bucks on the side with my referral. Free fight night is tonight. It's quiet tonight, so the boss will let us leave earlier. Let's go after work."

There's an underground boxing ring at Jack's college. It's illegal and frankly the main reason I haven't said yes to his offer to fight in it for so long. But now, with our bills piling up to the sky, I don't have a choice. And fuck if I don't also want to punch someone and let out some steam.

Jack whistles as a group of girls pass by. They giggle as they walk away.

"Dude, stop that. You'll get yourself fired someday."

"It's only a problem if the ladies don't like it...and look at them blushing. This is consensual flirting. College is where we fuck and party, live life to the fullest, man. You could do it too, with your fucking dark-hair, blue-eyed thing you got going on. I see how the girls look at you."

Pushing my cart of cleaning supplies past him, I stroll toward aisle sixteen. "No time for that shit. You know what I'm dealing with at home."

"No one is telling you to start a relationship. Just have fun. Let out some of that pent-up anger you got goin' in there."

"Been there, done that. Not interested." Tried the one-night stand thing twice and while it was briefly satisfying, the girls were stage-five clingers and too much trouble. Frankly, if I had time, I'd much rather catch a few extra hours of sleep.

We reach the dreaded aisle and lo and behold, a huge, oily mess is all over the floor and one of the lower shelves. Some idiot must have dropped the plastic carton of cooking oil, cracked the container, and then put it back on the shelf instead of letting us know. I sigh and squat down with my paper towels and start to blot out the mess.

"Oh hey, look who's here. It's the new loser in class."

I stiffen, recognizing the grating voice of my new classmate, Brian or Ryan or whatever. I roll out my shoulders and continue wiping down the floor, pretending I don't hear him.

"Who are you calling a loser?" Jack questions, the menace seeping through his voice.

Fuck. If I don't stop this, Jack will get into a fight and will really get fired, and he needs this job as much as I do. Taking a deep breath, I rise to my feet and turn around to find a red-faced Jack glaring at the smug bastard from school and his three goons. They're decked out in navy-and-green letterman jackets and dark, tearaway basketball pants.

"Ignore them, Jack." I hold my hand out to block my friend from advancing toward the basketball asshole.

"What, loser? You have something to say?"

Jack moves to step forward, but I hold him back as the pulse riots inside me and my muscles lock up in tension. *Don't fucking engage, Adrian. Step. Back.* A muscle tics in my jaw as I let out a ragged breath, my patience as precarious as acrobats on a tight-rope.

"Heard your mom is in the hospital and your dad is a drunk. Even your family members are losers."

I freeze, the blood in my veins turning ice cold.

My heartbeat thuds against my ears, an internal roar threatening to break free.

My nostrils flare as my top lip twitches in fury.

Curling my hands into tight fists, I turn around and stare at the asshole in the eye for the first time tonight.

"What? Nothing I'm saying isn't the truth." His thin lips turn up at the corners in an ugly sneer.

I take a step toward him.

And another.

And another.

A brief flicker of fear flashes in his eyes as he lets out a half-hearted chuckle and looks at his friends next to him, who have slowly stepped back, probably because of whatever expression they see on my face.

I'm exhausted. I'm hungry. I'm furious at the world. I'm in so much goddamn pain that my heart is numb to it. But now, the anger which has been percolating in the background seeps through my pores, and a red haze fills my vision.

No one talks shit about the people I love.

I catalog his features for the first time. Around my height, maybe a few inches taller. Two hundred pounds, give or take. Favors his right hand and right leg. A straight-lined scar on his kneecap. Most likely surgical. He may be bigger than me, but that doesn't mean everything in fighting. My reflexes are faster. Shallow breathing means he is nervous as fuck.

I curl my hands around the lapels of his jacket and lean in, my voice barely above a whisper. "You can talk shit about me. I *don't* give a fuck. But talk shit about my family, and that's the last thing you'll be saying out of your mouth in a long time."

Holding my gaze to his, I observe the changes in his pallor, my mind clear and laser-focused as my senses stand on alert. A dark-red flush creeps up his neck as he glances at his friends again. He bares his teeth and shoves my chest.

I may not be a jock, but I work out at school during my lunch hour and I have my reflexes from my younger days of boxing before everything happened. He barely makes me move an inch. *Go ahead and hit me. Hit me and see what'll happen. As Jack said, I have a lot of pent-up anger I need to let out, anyway.*

"What are you going to do about it, loser? If I want to talk shit, I'm going to talk shit."

I cock my head to the side and stare at him, my voice even. "You can try and watch me start by busting open your right knee-cap, which you've had surgery on, right? Or what about that smooth face of yours, pretty boy?" I rasp as I step closer to him, daring him to take it a step further. Taunting him. My body burns for a fight—something to relieve the pain I'm feeling inside every day.

We stare at each other. An impasse. The blood roars in my ears as my nostrils flare. The sounds of customers and the dings of the cash registers fade to the background. Jack steps to my side as we face off these punks in a united front.

"Ryan? Adrian? What's going on?"

A sweet voice slices through the tense atmosphere.

I look beyond Ryan and see Emily and a reddish-blonde haired girl, both dressed in cheerleading outfits, carrying a few packages in their arms. Emily slowly walks toward us with a frown on her pixie face, her ruby-red lips pursed in concern. Cracking my neck, I step back slowly, my eyes glued to Ryan's brown stare, communicating my message silently.

Fuck you. Don't fucking test me. I'll show you who the true loser is. You don't want to experience the wrath of someone who has nothing to lose.

He gulps visibly, most likely belatedly knowing he crossed a line. "Nothing's going on, Emmie. Just bumped into our new classmate over here."

"I told you not to call me Emmie."

"You know you like it, darling." My heart constricts at the endearment.

Emily's eyes narrow into slits as she marches up to us. "Save it, Ryan. I'll never be your darling, or your whatever. And I *real-*

ly hate that nickname." Her chocolate gaze darts to mine as her tongue dips out to wet her lips. My eyes zero in on the movement and the blood pulses in my veins. "Everything okay, Adrian?"

The scent of lilies hits my nose, and my fists slowly unfurl. I take in her appearance in detail. The knitted, long-sleeve white-and-green top clings to her tight curves. The hem of the sweater is cropped right above her belly button. Her smooth skin is beckoning me to touch, to trace. A short skirt completes her uniform, highlighting yet again her toned legs. I swallow, willing my galloping pulse to slow down.

"Don't spend your energy worried about loser over here. I was just telling him I can give him some of my old uniforms so he doesn't need to wear those rags at school."

The blood rushes in my ears and my face heats up. I clench my hands into tight fists and gnash my teeth together. I look away from Emily, not wanting to see the pity in her eyes, but I can still feel the weight of her stare on me.

"It really won't hurt you to shut up for once, Ryan," Emily says as I stare at the shelves behind her and focus on my breathing. "Your old uniforms are disgusting, and I'd bet the pants size is too small for Adrian, especially in that...area."

Ryan's hooligans snicker and my eyes dart to Emily, finding her doling out a very on point "I'm not impressed" look at a red-faced Ryan, her hand waving in the vicinity of his groin.

A twitch of amusement seeps through the anger and I snort.

"Adrian?"

My lips tilt up in acknowledgement. "We're fine. I think Ryan and I have just come to an agreement on some things."

She quirks her brow and looks back at Ryan. His goons are silently staring at him, no doubt waiting for his response. Pathetic lemmings.

"Whatever." Ryan shrugs and turns to Emily, apparently dismissing me and Jack as inconsequential. "You guys got what you need?"

Emily nods, barely acknowledging him. "Why don't you guys go and pay for the stuff? I'll be right there." The queen dismisses her subjects. Somehow, I find the thought amusing. Ryan and his lemmings huff and grab the items from the girls and head to the register.

The girls wait until they're out of earshot when Emily quips, "They said something stupid and regretted it, didn't they?"

Jack snickers. "Well, aren't you cute?" He brushes his thick, black hair to the side and flashes one of his trademark smiles he claims melts panties. "I'm Jack, and who might you be?"

Emily blinks and stares at him. She quirks a sardonic brow. Her friend laughs. "Please don't try that on her. It doesn't work."

Jack's attention flickers to Emily's friend. "Oh hello, beautiful. I love your orange hair. Reminds me of the most beautiful of sunsets."

I shake my head and stare incredulously at Jack, who is wagging his brows at her. "Ladies, meet my friend Jack, who's mostly harmless. Jack, this is Emily and her friend..."

"Sarah. We're obviously cheerleaders. The basketball team was playing a game around here and we just stopped by to pick up some snacks and stuff." Sarah completely ignores Jack as if he doesn't exist. "It's strawberry-blonde, dumbass," she mutters under her breath.

Interesting.

"I'm not living up to my word, am I?" Emily furrows her brows.

"What do you mean?"

"I promised you'll have a good experience at Warwick and jackass is not leaving a good impression. I don't know what's wrong with him. He's ridiculous, but usually not this horrible."

I have a feeling I know why Ryan is pissed at me, but I don't give a shit. She brushes a few silky strands of hair that have slipped out of her high ponytail. Now, in addition to the frown between her brows, her forehead is scrunched up as if she's deep in thought. My fingers want to smooth out the creases on her face.

"Don't worry. I don't care about him. And I still believe that Emily Kingsley..." I crack a small smile and bite my bottom lip.

She snorts, an unladylike sound that is very cute coming from her. "Will not lead you astray," she finishes as she quirks her lips to the side, a deep dimple making an appearance on her cheek.

"Emily! Sarah! You guys ready yet?" Ryan hollers from the end of the aisle.

The girls glance back and Emily grins at us. "See you tomorrow, Adrian... Nice to meet you, Jack." With a grin, she turns away and the girls link arms and rejoin the guys.

The scent of lilies lingers in the air and oddly enough, the earlier tension and anger have completely disappeared from my body.

My eyes trail their retreating figures. Just as they reach the exit, Emily turns back and flashes me a bright smile before shyly glancing away and leaving the store. My heart gallops in my chest, the palpitations not due to anger this time. I clutch the paper towels tightly into a ball.

My mind wanders to the fairytales Millie reads. Isn't there a story about a princess and a pauper? Or is it the other way around?

"Holy shit," Jack murmurs next to me.

"What?"

"You're so fucked, dude."

I ignore his comment. It's just adrenaline and misplaced emotions, that's all.

"**O**kay, let's call it a day. We'll try the move again at our next practice," Coach calls out as I grab a water bottle and drink a few large sips to quench my thirst after the thirtieth failed attempt at this new maneuver I'm trying out, something called the basket toss with a double full twist. A cool, wintery breeze brushes by, kicking up the freshly cut blades of grass on the football field. Winter in LA is never too cold, so it's refreshing to be practicing out in the open as opposed to inside the gym.

"I'm so beat. I think being tossed up and falling so many times takes a piece of your soul with you. Thank goodness the guys were there to catch me," I say to Sarah, who's wiping the sweat off her forehead with a small towel.

"It's one of the most difficult stunts, don't be so hard on yourself."

"Ha. I guess being tiny helps—getting tossed around in the air is probably less effort for everyone else involved." I grin at my ride-or-die bestie.

Sarah laughs and throws her strawberry-blonde hair—the color of the fall leaves—over her shoulder. "I don't know what you're talking about, you're still heavy, which I'd know since I had to lift you for all those tries—"

I shove her gently. "Hey!"

"Fine, fine, fine. You're tiny and weightless like a feather. Happy now? And you know what I always say. Weight and height are just numbers. Being healthy is number one."

"Yes, Mom." I stifle another smile. As much as I say so otherwise, I have absolutely no problem being the tiny but mighty height of five-foot-one. My mother may give me grief otherwise about my weight and height, but I couldn't care less. She's tougher with my sister than me usually...probably because I don't pay attention to her insane comments about everything under the sun. And frankly, there's a bit of freedom being the middle child. The focus is usually on the eldest or the youngest.

"Can you believe it? Last few months of senior year, then we're going to be out of here." She breathes out as anticipation sizzles through the air.

"I'm so excited. The next few months will be a breeze—waiting for college acceptance letters, senior prom, graduation..." I can't wait to move out of the house and see what my future holds, to be able to be me without my parents looking over my shoulder.

Sarah rubs her pale hands together as she contemplates my answer. "You know you're on the shortlist for prom queen. Have you given some thought about what you're going to wear? If you want to get something made, I hear the designers are all booked up months in advance."

I let out an exhale, a small billow of air fogging up in front of me. "I'll figure something out." Part of me just wants to grab something off the rack, but I know Mother will probably have my head for it if I decide to go with outfits that "commoners" wear. It's totally ridiculous. Glancing sideways at her, I ask, "What about you? Are you already planning for prom?"

"Hey, girls, are we going out to Ryan's party tonight?" Chelsea, another girl in our squad, throws her arms around our shoulders.

I shake my head. I see enough of Ryan and his gang of troublemakers as is anyway, since our families are longtime friends. I don't need to see him on my own time. But people seem to love him. His family is extremely well-off, even for Warwick standards, and he has reached the mythical "popular" status here. "You guys have fun without me. This is a party I'm definitely passing on."

"He's going to be so disappointed, you know. He's been carrying a torch for you as long as I've known him." Chelsea trots by our side as we head toward the locker rooms.

"He better get used to it, because my feelings toward him are as frigid as the Arctic. Not going to happen. Nothing is alive. Even the smallest fires can't be sparked."

"Ouch. That's a burn."

Sarah chimes in, "Chelsea, I'll go with you. I don't have anything better to do anyway tonight. And let's give Ems a break. Ryan has been especially insufferable these days." She sends a warm look of sympathy to me with her big eyes.

Just as we approach the entrance to the building housing the locker rooms, I spot an imposing figure clad in our spring uniform sitting on the top corner of the bleachers next to the doors. My pulse speeds up slightly, and I bite my bottom lip to keep from smiling.

"Hey, you girls head in first. I'll join you later." I keep my eyes on Adrian, who has one hand curled around a lock of his thick, brown hair, so dark it almost appears black in the shadows. His other hand cradles a large textbook in his lap. A pencil is perched between his teeth. A cut appears on the side of his face with a fresh bruise blooming around it. I frown, my insides pinching at his appearance. He didn't have this the other day.

Sarah follows my gaze and her eyes widen with recognition. "The new guy from the other night, huh? Whoa, what happened to him?"

"What new guy?" Chelsea stares in the same direction as her mouth opens to form a small, comical "O." She blinks a few times and adds in a hushed tone, "You know his mother graduated from here, right? Her family cast her out when she married this poor guy with no money to his name. Everyone's talking about him. I don't know what I was expecting…but nothing like *that*. He's totally delicious and has this broody vibe and bad-boy streak about him.

That bruise totally looks hot on him." She pulls back and arches her brow knowingly. "I see why Ryan doesn't interest you, Ems."

I roll my eyes and refrain from responding, because, frankly, I don't know how to explain this magnetized curiosity I have toward Adrian. I still remember the moment I saw him in the office the first day. It was as if everything happened in slow motion.

"Hi, Doris. How are you doing? You look wonderful today." I smile at the secretary, my gaze flickering to the strong backside of the tall guy standing in front of her desk. His back is bent as he drums a steady rhythm on the wood with his hands. His large hands.

Mystery guy slowly turns around. I'm not usually a girl who pines for princes and romance, or believes in silly fancies like love at first sight, or even love in general, but I swear the air gets sucked out of the room...or perhaps out of my lungs when he fully faces me. His light-blue eyes meet mine. A mesmerizing blue. The color of the early morning sky on a sunny day...but with the intensity of...of something darker. The hard glint in his eyes tells me he has seen things in life...experienced the rougher edges of the tapestry, something you don't usually see in the students here. He towers over me by at least one foot. The school uniform hangs slightly loosely on him, as if it were a little big for his frame, but he's not skinny. His body is coiled in tension, a predator lurking in the background, preparing to strike when the victim isn't looking.

Doris says something to me and I barely hear her but manage to respond—Kingsley-bred manners after all.

My heart thuds loudly in my chest and I could've sworn the beats were more deafening than chimes of Mini Ben, the antique grandfather clock standing in the corner of the room. I wink at him in an attempt to dispel this weird tension in the air and his eyes widen by the smallest fraction.

Doris clears her throat and motions to the mystery man. "This is Adrian Callahan. Today is his first day. He's in the same Shakespearean Literature class as you. Can you walk him to class and go over how things work here?"

Adrian. His name is Adrian.

My gaze is drawn back to the enigmatic, brooding guy standing next to me. With his chiseled jawline, the slight cleft in his chin, he looks like one of those actors playing high schoolers on television.

Completely out of place. Impossible to ignore.

The girls' giggles draw my attention back to them as they stare at me with teasing glints in their eyes.

"Oh, shut up. I'm just curious about our new classmate." There's something unique about him and I want to peel back the layers to see what's hiding between the rough around the edges yet quiet exterior. Heat creeps up my face as I wave them away, my body already angling toward the bleachers.

"Ha. *Curious.* Yeah right. You need to tell me all the details later," Sarah hollers as she and Chelsea walk inside the building, their arms hooked around each other.

Shaking my head, I climb the steps quietly, wanting a few more moments to gaze at this intriguing person in front of me. Adrian flips a page, his lips pursed as if he's deep in thought. He takes out the pencil from between his teeth and scribbles something in the margins. The morning breeze flutters by, carrying moisture from the marine layer and I shudder, my body having cooled down from the exertion earlier.

"Like what you see?" his deep voice rings through the air, shocking me into immobility.

Adrian looks up, his startling blue gaze locks on to mine. The wind ruffles his hair, but he doesn't appear to notice. His fingers grip the pencil as he swallows, the Adam's apple bobbing in the strong column of his throat.

Heat crawls up my face at being caught ogling him. Biting my bottom lip, I lift my hand tentatively and give a small wave. "Hi there," I call out.

Blinking his eyes a few times, he shakes his head subtly before lifting his fingers in a small wave, a tiny smile gracing his face. He keeps his gaze on mine as I slowly make my way up the steps to him. There's a unique calmness to his being—a stillness, as if he's an immovable boulder in the middle of harsh currents, and no matter what nature throws at him, he stands there unapologetically and unyielding, providing a place of rest to the weary in rough waters.

I plop down on the icy-cold bench next to him and shiver once more. Dang it, I forgot my coat in the locker room.

He shrugs off his jacket, his muscular arms flexing in the morning light as he gently places it on my shoulders. His white dress shirt and green tie appear too flimsy for comfort. I frown and move to take off the jacket to give it back to him, but he stills my hands with his fingers.

"Don't. I'm used to the cold. You just exercised and cooled down. You need the jacket more than me." The rough timbre in his voice, like a brief caress, sends renewed shivers inside me. He spares a glance my way. The intensity in his baby blues nearly takes my breath away. "Mom always told me the mark of a man is not his money or his worth, but how he treats other people."

My breath catches in my throat as I cocoon myself in his warm blazer, surrounded with the remnants of his body heat and the lingering scent of mint.

"T-Thank you."

His lips twitch up into another half smile and he turns his attention back to his book. Ah, *Shakespearean Theory and Modern Literature*. We went through that last semester. He must be playing catch-up.

"What happened to your face?" I couldn't help myself.

He spares me a glance before smirking and glancing back to the pages. "Wouldn't you like to know."

I do. That's why I'm asking. A weird silence settles between us. Apparently, that's all I'm getting out of him on the topic.

"So, you saw me practicing?" Keep chipping away at the block of ice and eventually I'll get a sculpture out of it.

His hand stills momentarily on the page before he replies, "It's impossible not to notice..." My pulse rushes in my ears. "With all the yelling and flailing." My stomach deflates, and his lips quirk into a grin, as if he senses my disappointment.

"You never did tell me why you're older and still in high school."

"You never asked."

"It was implied when I asked for your age."

He chuckles and faces me. "I just turned nineteen on Christmas, so I used to be a year behind everyone else anyway because I was born late in the year. Then, last year, I missed too many days in school, so they wanted me to stay behind for a year."

"Oh. That actually makes sense."

"You were expecting something more dramatic?"

"I don't know...maybe you're a secret undercover reporter looking to write an exposé on posh, rich high school kids...or you are a secret drug dealer who is tired of the underworld and wants to turn a new leaf? The possibilities are endless." I waggle my brows at him.

He busts out in laughter, his voice rough but warm. Adrian's eyes widen in apparent surprise. "Pixie," he mutters, shaking his head.

"What?"

"I can't remember how long it's been since I laughed like that. You're *something else*...all right."

"Are you allergic to laughing?" I stare at him quizzically.

He arches his brow, his dark locks falling across his forehead. I want to reach up and brush it off his face. I wonder what his hair will feel like against my fingers. "There aren't usually many things in life worth laughing about anymore," he murmurs. The creases in the corners of his eyes soften as his smile fades into a frown. He looks down at his textbook, but his gaze appears unfocused.

My heart twists inside my chest at the solemn statement. "I heard your mom is sick. Is she doing okay?"

Adrian rolls his lips, releasing them on an exhale. "S-She's not doing well. The doctors aren't optimistic." He stares into the distance, his shoulders tense.

Unbidden, I reach out and clasp his hand in mine, wanting to somehow give him some of my energy, some of my strength, to let him know he's not alone. He freezes, his body so still I can barely see him breathe. Afraid I crossed a line, I move to draw my hand back from his, but he clutches it tightly. I freeze, trapped in this strange tension between us.

"How are you doing? Is there anything I can do for you?" I whisper, not wanting to disturb the intimate atmosphere.

His palm squeezes mine as his thumb trails small clockwise circles on the back of my hand, but I don't think he even notices. The tiny motion sparks a frisson of awareness through me and goosebumps stand to attention.

"You're the first person to ask me those questions. This...this is enough. Thank you."

His thumb is now rubbing counterclockwise circles. My skin feels like it's on fire. I bite my bottom lip and force myself to relax as flutters percolate in my stomach.

"Is that why you missed so many days last year?"

Adrian nods, still staring into the distance. Students filter out to the football field. Soft laughter and chatter make their way up to where we sit.

A quiet hum, not penetrating the bubble we're in.

"W-Well...I know this is probably stupid and sounds selfish, but...I'm glad you stayed behind one year. T-That way, I was able to meet you..." The words tumble out of me without a filter. "To be your friend, I mean." Using my free hand, I clamp it over my lips, afraid of what crazy sentiments I might spew out next.

Adrian whips his head toward our interlinked hands, pausing as if suddenly realizing he's held on to me this entire time. His eyes slowly trail up to me, the light blue darkening at the edges, bringing out streaks of silver in his irises. With his other hand, he reaches out and slowly pries my hand off my mouth and smiles, showcasing his pearly whites, and my heart skips a few beats. The gash on his face doesn't dim the impact of his dazzling smile. I hold my breath and wet my lips in a nervous tic. His gaze catches on to the movement and the smile slips off his face, gone as quickly as it appeared, and a muscle in his jaw twitches. Returning his gaze back to mine, he gives my hand one last squeeze and lets go.

I curl my palm into a fist, trying to keep the warmth from his hand as long as possible.

What just happened? Is it all in my head?

The bell rings in the distance, signaling the beginning of first period in five minutes.

"Emmie, you coming to class or what?"

I turn my head toward the intruder. Ryan. He's standing at the bottom of the bleachers, and glares at us with contempt. He gives Adrian a once-over, his lips curled in apparent disdain or disgust. I glance back at Adrian, and any emotions on his face just now are wiped clean, replaced with a blank expression.

"You coming?" I ask him.

"You guys go ahead first. I'll pack up and be there shortly."

Nodding, I stand, remove the jacket, and hand it back to him. Slowly, I walk down the stairs.

"I'm thankful I got to meet you too."

His voice was so quiet, the words so soft, I almost didn't hear him. I stop in my tracks and turn around, finding him staring intently at me, his mouth parted in what appears to be surprise, as if he's caught unaware by what he just said.

My mouth splits into a wide smile and I see his chest lift in a quick intake of breath, his eyes darkening in intensity as he pins me in place with his gaze. Heat rushes to my face, and I take a deep breath to calm my rattled nerves. Turning back slowly, I continue my descent.

The butterflies swirl higher and higher inside me.

CHAPTER 6

Emily

"**...D**ebutante ball at the country club and I just don't under-stand why you'd refuse to participate. Emily. Emily, are you listening to me?" Mother's shrill voice interrupts my thoughts of a certain blue-eyed guy from the wrong side of the tracks.

"Huh?" I turn to my mother, who's sitting at our dining room table dressed to the nines for our usual family dinner as Steven, the youngest of the three Kingsley siblings, snickers next to me.

"What am I going to do with you? You're eighteen and about to graduate and leave for college."

"Thank goodness," I mutter under my breath as I shift in the seat.

"What did you say?"

"Nothing. I said nothing. You were saying?" Better to pretend I'm listening and agreeing with her than to argue with her. She never listens to us, anyway.

In Audrey Lee Kingsley's mind, Jess and I should take advantage of college to find a man with the right background—old money, settle down, have kids, and grow the wealth of the family. In a way, she did the same when she was younger. My grandparents were traditional, conservative Chinese immigrants with more wealth than they knew what to do with. They moved to the States when Mother was a baby and she found my father during their years at Yale.

Kingsley is an old, blue-blooded name, but their coffers were empty. It was a perfect business union of sorts—the Kingsley name with the Lee wealth. After marriage, she supported Father as he worked his way up TransAmerica Corporation, an international conglomerate that has their hands in everything from banking to technology. Ironically, or perhaps not surprisingly, the Lees are major shareholders of TransAmerica.

"Mother is reminding you to find the right man and settle down. Someone like Ryan," Steven supplies unhelpfully, his mouth twisting up in a sly grin.

"I'll get you later," I murmur under my breath. My younger brother and I are three years apart, and while I love him to bits, we bicker a lot.

Father sits silently during this entire conversation, yet another normal occurrence, his head buried behind a newspaper. My parents have a formal marriage. I've never seen them fight, raise their voices, or interact with each other with anything resembling deep affection. Despite outward appearances, Mother claims there is love between them.

If this is what "love" and marriage are supposed to be, please count me out.

I set my chopsticks on top of my bowl, careful not to stick it in the middle of the rice since that's a major faux pas in our culture, and glance at Mother, who has her lips pressed firmly together in a thin line. "Mother, I'm full. May I be excused?"

"Emily, why can't you be like Jess? Your sister listens to me, she..." My mind zones out again as I nod periodically, just so she thinks I'm listening.

But I never do. I've perfected the art of conscious daydreaming.

Steven kicks me under the chair with his gangly leg. He's experiencing a growth spurt and is more limbs than body these days.

I kick him back, relishing the *oomph* I get out of him. Emily one, Steven zero.

Finally, Mother stops her nagging and changes the topic to Father's work, where he's apparently dealing with a fiasco at the banking division, a suspected embezzlement.

"Why haven't you fired him yet?"

"We're looking into it, Audrey, just to be sure. Perhaps there are reasons we aren't aware of."

"Criminals are criminals, no excuses."

I clasp my hands in front of me. A perfect imitation of my poised older sister. "Mother, I'll be practicing piano in the music room." Practicing piano is always a perfect excuse to leave the table. No card-carrying Asian parent will say no to their kids practicing the piano. The fact I love the music is just a bonus. Letting out an exasperated sigh, Mother waves me away.

I all but skip to the music room on the second floor of our large mansion on the outskirts of Palos Verdes. The house is too enormous, too roomy for my taste, especially with Jess in college now. My precious, beautiful black Steinway & Sons grand piano stands lonely in the middle of the room, with Steven's violin case tucked into a dark corner.

"My baby," I whisper, trailing my finger across the cool surface and slowly lift the fallboard, revealing the immaculate keys, all eighty-eight of them gleaming under the soft light of the sole lamp I just turned on.

I sit down and play a piece from memory. My favorite from Ludwig van Beethoven, the "Piano Sonata No. 14," otherwise known as the "Moonlight Sonata." As my fingers fly over the keys, I'm transported to another world...a world with calm, still waters rippling under the moonlight, haunting melodies of the wind, the gentle lapping of waves along the shores, the highs and lows of yearning, disappointment, love, and all the emotions within the human mind.

Only this time, in the tranquil, solemn peace, there is a boy, teetering at the edge of manhood, who keeps to himself with an invisible shield around him, keeping everyone at arm's length, carrying too much weight on his shoulders. He walks quietly along the shores, the soft wind blowing his dark hair across his face, but he doesn't appear to mind. My fingers dance with the keys as I become one with the music and imagine being in the world with him. Perhaps I can be his spark of light in the darkness of the night.

My eyes gently open as I finish the brooding *Adagio Sostenuto,* the first of the three movements of the sonata. Normally, I would be eager to move on to the lively *Allegretto* movement, the second, less-recognizable part of the musical piece, eager to inject vibrant life into the room. But this time, my mind remains with the image of the lonely boy.

Adrian.

Shaking my head, I attempt to clear my thoughts. I don't know him well enough... Yet, there's something about him that draws one's attention. Despite his faded, secondhand clothing, his lack of material possessions, which appear to be the norm at school, he radiates a simmering intensity so full of passion, full of depth, full of strength. We may be worlds apart, but somehow, my soul seems to be drawn to his.

I move on to another piece of music, eager to dispel these swirling thoughts inside me. Music helps me purge my restlessness, my aimlessness, the hole inside my chest. Even though I'm graduating soon, I have no idea what I'm going to do in the future, who I'm going to be. What drives me and motivates me to get up in the morning? Until I figure that out, I have my music and my daydreams.

After practicing piano for an hour or so, I return to my room, a large space probably the size of a studio apartment, with a beautiful en suite bathroom. It's my haven. I've decorated this retreat in lavender and pale greens. My queen-size bed is filled with fluffy, soft pillows and cushions of all sizes. I sit at my desk and finish a few assignments I didn't get a chance to complete earlier in the day. My mind is still whirring, my feet tapping against the floor. *Young ladies shouldn't shake so much. It's bad luck.* Mother's words, a superstition in some Asian cultures, echo in my brain but I shove it away. I tap even harder. Take that.

A melodic chime fills the air. My phone. I look at the caller ID. *Jess.*

"Hey, sis. How are things going for you?" I chirp into the receiver.

"Ems! How are you? Things are fine. Ben went to get us some late-night coffee before we head back to the library for another study session. I just wanted to check in to see how things are going with you? How is Mother?" Concern bleeds through her voice. I think she's afraid Mother will turn her attentions to me now that she's at college and not here to buffer things. Jess is three years older than me and is the sweetest soul I've ever known. It would be easy to be resentful of her, since she is Mother's golden child, but she's never made me feel less than. Instead, she quietly supports me to pursue my interests, which include the desire to rebel against Mother's expectations. She's the type of person to set herself on fire to provide a distraction to the enemies charging in so everyone else can escape. I'm thankful to have her as a big sister.

"Mother is fine. The same ol' same ol'. You know me, I've mastered the art of ignoring her. No need to pay her any attention when I'll never meet her standards, anyway." I don't tell her too much about Mother's nagging because I don't want to worry her. Jess has been taking it extra hard since Nana's passing. She's even started seeing a therapist for anxiety issues.

"You let me know if you need me to come home more often on the weekends, okay? I worry about you and Steven." I have a nagging suspicion she stayed close to home for college because she's concerned about us. The least I can do is not add to her stress. Quiet chatter filters through the phone. I think I hear Ben, her boyfriend. "So, how's school going? Any interesting news? Any boy problems?"

My foot stops its incessant tapping. Adrian. *He's not a boy problem. What are you thinking?* Somehow, I want to keep Adrian to myself for now. A secret just for me.

"The usual at school. Nothing interesting. Don't worry about me."

"Okay... Hey, I have to go. Love you and talk soon?"

"Love you too. Say hi to Ben for me."

I set down my phone on the desk and contemplate my next move. It's almost midnight now. The house is silent as everyone is most likely asleep or getting ready for bed. With my mind made up, I go to my closet and change into a warm pair of sweatpants and a thick sweater. I grab my car keys, my star-shaped glass wishing jar from my bookshelf, and stuff them into a crossbody bag. Then I quietly open the sliding French doors in my room. My eyes squint in the dark as I adjust to the moonlight. I shudder, my heart pounding against my rib cage.

I hate the dark, but it's something I have to overcome.

Closing the door softly behind me, I tiptoe to the balcony and swing my leg over the railing, a move I've done so many times before I can do it in my sleep. My arms reach out to the large oak tree right next to the trellis, and I slowly climb down to the ground below.

Landing softly on the wet grass, I take a deep breath, inhaling the cool night air, before scurrying to the garage, which is thankfully far away from the house, so no one hears me starting the car and driving off. I head to a less-popular beach, which is empty of visitors at this time of the night. I may hate the dark, but I love the beach at night. It's an oxymoron. After parking the car, I walk to the boardwalk, slip off my shoes, and dip my toes into the prickly grains of sand.

The ocean looms ahead of me, the waves crashing against the shores in a constant rhythm, much like music...the music of nature. The air is sticky and salty, smelling of seaweed, marine life, and infinite hopes and wishes. I amble to my usual spot, close enough to the waters but also the streetlights on the pier. Just enough light to curb my panic and keep my fears at bay.

My heart pounds to the rhythm of the waves as I stare into the dark ocean. Being so close to such a vast wonder of nature humbles me. I feel as if the possibilities are endless, the world out there is vast, and somewhere in the great beyond, I'll find my dream, the fire which will light up my soul. The ocean at night is my secret haven, a place where I can truly be me, not the cheerleader at school, not Mother's disappointing daughter, not the eighteen-year-old who has no clue what to do in a few months. I can be myself here. No judgment.

A rustling sound comes up behind me and fear claws my insides as a pounding pulse shoots up in my chest. I reach into my bag for the pepper spray I carry with me and whirl around, searching for the origin of the noise. Blinking a few times, I recognize the person approaching my spot. The lonely silhouette of someone who's entered my life without a notice, and has already left a lasting imprint behind.

"Adrian?" I yell above the roaring sound of the waves.

His head snaps up, and his eyes widen as he stares at me in bewilderment. He's clad in a dark puffer jacket and jeans, a messenger bag strapped across his shoulders, his hair already ruffled by the wind.

"Emily? What are you doing here?"

He walks toward me, kicking up the sand in the process. Reaching me in a few big strides—perks of having long legs—he lifts his hand up in a half wave.

"I could ask you the same thing."

"I just wanted to clear my head. I usually go to one of the beaches around here at night after work and learned about this one at school today, so I thought I'd check it out... What are you doing out here so late at night by yourself? It's dangerous." His deep voice is laced with concern.

Smiling, I plop down onto the sand and pat the spot next to me. He slowly lowers himself. The scent of mint and masculine spice wafts through the air, and I close my eyes. His body heat radiates, and I'm tempted to curl up next to him. I'm sure I'd feel very protected and safe. A welcoming calmness settles over me at his presence. Despite his broodiness and inner tension seeming to coil tightly inside him, I'm not afraid of him.

Instead, I keep my gaze straight ahead at the harsh waves, a glimpse of nature's unpredictable temperament. "This is my routine. I'm here most nights. This is a pretty safe beach—not too many people know about it, and I always have my phone and pepper spray with me."

I can feel his heated gaze on me as I continue, "It's hard to explain, but I'll try, anyway. I'm deathly afraid of the dark. Started when I was about five-years-old and was playing hide and seek with my siblings at night but the power cut out. My house is huge, enormous for a five-year-old, and I couldn't find them. I was afraid to wander around the house in the dark with the large shadows and strange noises, so I stayed hidden in the closet crying myself to sleep. They did find me an hour later, but ever since then, I have a terrible phobia."

"So, why are you out here, then?"

My gaze flickers to him, finding his brows furrowing as he cocks his head, no doubt trying to figure me out.

"I don't like to be afraid of things, and it's not like I can engineer a blackout on a regular basis. My house is a bit stifling...my parents and all. So, one day, I decided to try my hand at something I read online. Exposure therapy. Facing your fears and whatnot. I ended up coming here, and it was utterly terrifying, but I survived. So I did it again. And again. And again. While I'm still afraid of the dark, hence me picking this spot with the pier lights nearby, this is one way for me to take control of my fear. And over time, I fell in love with the ocean at night as well. The beach is so quiet and peaceful. I can think and dream and be myself."

"Hmm..." He hums noncommittally before extending his hand toward me, palm up. A white bandage is wrapped around his fingers. Another mysterious wound.

I glance at him in confusion.

"Your phone, unlock it, please." He extends his hand.

I flip open the newest flip-phone model and enter the world's most unoriginal passcode, my birthday, and hand it to him. He takes it and enters a string of numbers. A moment later, he reaches inside his jeans pocket and pulls out his own phone, which is buzzing.

"I programmed my number in your phone," he begins. "I don't have a text plan, but if you feel scared, or if anything unusual happens, call me. I'll come right away." His light eyes, which appear dark in the dim light, gaze intently at me. "If anything sounds strange or smells funny at night, get out of here and call me. No matter what time."

A warmth travels from my rib cage and spreads to my chest as my heart picks up speed. I can't help but bite my bottom lip to suppress a smile.

"You will, right?" His deep voice, the sound of the lowest notes on the piano, so strong, so beautiful, filters to my ears.

I nod, temporarily rendered speechless by his concern. Apparently mollified, he turns back toward the ocean. Slowly, he opens his messenger bag and retrieves a reading light and a textbook, the familiar blue cover of the series of books used for advanced placement science classes. I peer over his shoulder.

"AP Physics? Aren't you already taking AP Biology?"

"Most of my classes are AP. There are some things I need to catch up on, unique courses like the Shakespearean Literature class we're in, but for the most part, my grades are decent."

He's smart. I don't know why it doesn't surprise me. Perhaps it's the sharpness in his gaze and the way he seems to absorb information in class without having to take many notes. Adrian flips on his reading light and begins scanning the open textbook. I notice some scribbles in the margin where he has a few notes. His eyebrows pinch in concentration.

Smiling at the comfortable atmosphere, I take out my wishing jar from my bag and my hands begin their search in the surrounding sand. My fingers sift through the soft grains, which are mixed with hard pebbles, before they latch on to a prospective target.

"What are you doing?"

I dust off the shell I just found and hand it to him. "I collect seashells. They're for my wishing jar." I motion to the glass jar on my lap. "I find shells at the beach and when I get home, I attach small strips of paper to them. They contain random hopes and dreams I have."

He stares at me incredulously, his eyebrows hiked up. "This is what you do when you come here at night? Collect shells for hopes and dreams?"

I nod vigorously. "What's life without hopes and dreams?"

An unidentifiable emotion flashes in his eyes, gone as quickly as it appeared. His gaze drops to the jar on my lap as he murmurs, "What if they don't come true? Isn't that just disappointment, then?"

Shrugging, I reply, "Some will. Some won't, but the process of dreaming is beautiful. It reminds me life is full of possibilities."

A heaviness settles on his being like an invisible cloak. He stays still, something he's obviously used to doing. I bite my tongue to keep from asking him what's on his mind. He seems like he needs time to think through some things.

"If you could have any dream come true, what would you want?" I ask, unable to resist.

His eyes hold mine as he contemplates his answer. I hold my breath, not knowing why, but I have a feeling this question is not an easy one for him.

"I-I'd wish for the people I love to be happy and healthy," he whispers, his eyes darkening, so much I can't tell where his pupils meet his irises.

He doesn't wish for wealth. He doesn't wish for a bigger house or fancy cars. His wish isn't for himself, it's for others. Somehow, the thought causes my chest to clench in pain.

"May I?" He motions to the jar.

I uncap it, drop in the new shell I just acquired, and hand it to him. "You'll think it's stupid."

"I'm sure I won't."

He gently shakes the container. The clinking of seashells and scraps of paper against glass fills the air, with the sound of the waves a backdrop to the otherwise quiet night. Adrian tips the jar over and a few wishes come tumbling out. Glancing at me, he pauses, as if waiting for permission to peek into my soul. Swallowing the lump in my throat, I nod.

He unfurls one strip of paper attached to a beautiful brown shell. "Playing piano at Carnegie Hall," he murmurs.

I tuck a strand of hair around my ear as heat travels up my neck. There's something extremely vulnerable about your dreams being laid bare in front of someone else.

"Finding a job with meaning," he whispers as he reads another strip.

I bite my cheek. My fingers twitch. Part of me wants to snatch the jar back from him.

"Get my hands on a copy of the *Muller Goldleaf Limited Edition Beethoven Complete Piano Sonatas*." He glances at me. "Can't you just buy that?"

I shake my head. "It's a rare collector's edition. Hard to find and super expensive, even by my family's standards."

He nods as he opens another wish.

"True love's kiss on top of the Empire State Building at the strike of midnight on New Year's Eve." He smirks. "I didn't peg you for a romantic."

Clearing my throat, I blink a few times and reply, "I got inspired by *Sleepless in Seattle*."

"They didn't kiss on top of the Empire State Building in the movie."

My mouth drops open. "You watched it? I thought it's considered a chick flick!"

He shrugs, completely unruffled and nonchalant. "It's a classic."

"That's what I tell people!"

Adrian shakes out another wish. After he unrolls it, moments pass, and he starts chuckling under his breath. He glances at me from the side, his tongue dipping out and wetting his lip as he shakes with mirth.

"What?" Heat rises to my face. A sudden thought occurs to me. *Oh no, please don't tell me it's what I'm thinking of.* I snatch the scrap from him and tilt it toward the moonlight. My face feels hot to the touch now as blood rushes in my ears.

"So, skinny dipping in the ocean, huh? Didn't think you had it in you," he rasps, his voice taking on a gravelly edge.

Images of us swimming in the ocean, our bodies as naked as the day we were born, flash through my mind. Hard muscles, soft skin, and kisses. Curves, moans, and sighs. I snatch the jar and the wishes away from him. "Okay, that's it. No more nosing in my wishes for you. You go find your own hopes and dreams."

He laughs, his voice ringing loud in the intimate space as he bumps his body gently against me. I glance at him and find his eyes twinkling as he grins at me. A beautiful, blinding smile. It transforms his entire face.

My breath catches in my throat and I suddenly find myself wanting to be the one to put this smile on his face, always.

CHAPTER 7

Emily

"**A**s a reminder, the first exam is next Wednesday, and your paper on *Romeo and Juliet* versus modern society is due at the same time." Mr. Nichols's announcement in front of the class is met with a cacophony of groans and complaints just as the bell rings, indicating the end of class. "Mr. Callahan, must I remind you again sleeping is not permitted in class?"

The classroom erupts in laughter and snickering as I hear the squeaking of a chair behind me. I immediately turn around, instinctively worried about Adrian as he has been reprimanded by the teacher a few times this week for dozing off in class.

Some weeks have passed since we first bumped into each other at my beach. Even though Adrian has been acing his coursework in his other classes, from what I overheard in the gossip chain at school, something I'm no longer surprised about after seeing how he seems to study with every free minute he has, whether at night at the beach or in the mornings at the bleachers, I know he was a little worried about this one. The curriculum is also moving pretty quickly and is building on theories from the prior semester, so it's a lot to catch up on.

As if sensing my concern, Adrian pauses in the middle of packing up his books, his hair disheveled as sleep lingers in his eyes. He glances up at me, a small frown forming between his thick brows. A new bruise appears in the corner of his lip. He still doesn't tell me where or how he's getting hurt, and it worries me. I keep wondering if I should tell someone—I haven't figured out who I'd trust with this information yet—but every time I ask him, he insists everything is fine.

"Are you okay, Adrian?" I motion to his mussed hair and his lips, stopping my fingers a few inches from touching the wound on his face. "I-Is there anything I can do for you?"

"I'm fine." His gaze simmers with unspoken words, repressed emotions. Again.

"But, you—"

"Emily," he whispers softly, his deep voice laced with warning, "I have it handled."

My heart flutters in my chest at his unwavering stare. As if sensing my growing discomfort, one corner of his lips twitches up in a half smile, reassuring me.

Letting out a deep breath, I prod, "How are you feeling about this class? I know the coursework is moving pretty quickly, and you seem tired a lot... I have some really good notes from last semester. Mr. Nichols mentioned they may come in handy for this class so I always carry them around. Do you want them?"

At his silence, I bite my lip and rock forward in my chair, nearly tipping myself over. "Not that I think you need it. I mean, you seem like you're catching on really quickly...but I see you studying in the morning at the bleachers and at night at the beach and thought maybe my notes can help. Actually, I'm acing this class. Do you want to study together? That way...I can be there to answer any questions you may have?"

I glance up to find those beautiful eyes, which are shining with laughter, the previous intensity fading into the color of a tranquil lake. "Again, just thought that might be helpful...not that you need it. You probably don't. Actually, why don't I just turn around and we pretend this never—"

"You're rambling. Do I make you nervous?"

My face heats up and I focus on the divot on his chin, which is very close to his beautiful lips. His tongue darts out, wetting the cut on his lip, and I find myself doing the same thing.

"Emmie, my parents want me to remind you we have dinner tonight," Ryan interrupts, shaking me out of my temporary trance as my eyes quickly meet Adrian's, only to find them darkening at the edges as he pins me with his stare.

Not looking away, I reply, "I-I remember."

Ryan lets out a sigh of what sounds like frustration. "Let's go, Emmie. I have something to give you for the Valentine's Day dance coming up."

I wave him away, all the while holding my gaze on Adrian, who is as motionless as a statue, as if he's waiting for my next move. His hands curl into fists, the white of his knuckles showing. Everyone assumes Ryan and I are going to the dance together. Before, I couldn't have cared less whom I go with, since there's no one at school who piques my interest. But now...

The butterflies make a resurgence in my stomach as a lock of hair slips from my French braid.

"I'll meet you at the library," Adrian says, just loud enough for Ryan to hear. "I *definitely* need your help in class. I think we have a free period now, so I'll see you there." He flashes me a brief smile as he reaches out, his rough fingers lightly grazing my cheek before tucking the stray hair behind my ear. My skin sizzles from the contact, and my mouth parts in a gasp. Adrian winks, packs up the rest of his books, and leaves the classroom, his steps silent but resounding.

With my pulse rioting inside me, I turn to Ryan, who is standing there with barely restrained anger, his face mottled and red. "What?" I ask.

"You like him, don't you?"

"It's not any of your business."

"What do you mean? We've always been close—"

I let out an exasperated sigh. "Ryan, our *families* are close. You and I," I motion between the two of us with my fingers, "are just family friends who've grown up together."

"The loser has nothing to offer you. He's so poor, he doesn't even have the money to buy himself a new set of uniforms. He probably can't even afford to go to college. You know why he looks like shit half the time? He fights at an underground boxing ring... for money! That's how poor they are."

"What?" I gasp, my pulse galloping once again. "How do you know?"

"Some of the guys like to go there for fights sometimes and they saw him there on multiple occasions. Stay away from him. He's bad news. He'll just drag you down with him."

I'm barely listening to him anymore. All I can think about is the lonely boy who has been dealt a horrible hand and is now resorting to using his body to scrape together a living for his family, while insisting he has everything handled. A burning sensation prickles my eyes as I'm filled with an irrational impulse to find him and to wrap him in a hug. I stand there silently, my hands clutching my scarf as a way to channel the intense emotions.

"Fuck this shit." Ryan slams something on the table and stalks away. One ticket for the Valentine's dance in two weeks.

I groan, slapping a hand on my forehead. Ryan is prickly and annoying, but I don't want to hurt his feelings. After all, he has always been nice to me. Bemoaning my boy troubles—thank you Jess for jinxing me—I almost collide with Sarah outside the doors of the classroom.

"You guys okay in there? Thought I'd wait out here to see if you want to talk about it," she asks, concern in her soft voice.

I shrug. "I can't seem to get through to Ryan. He just won't take no for an answer."

"But honestly, weren't you thinking of giving him a chance last semester?"

"The thought crossed my mind, but I think it was more because he was convenient. Gosh, I sound like a bitch, don't I? But I don't think I ever really led him on. Not really. Our families have just pitted us together since we were babies."

"Hmm... I don't think that's all."

I glance up to find Sarah staring at me with those large, perceptive hazel eyes.

She murmurs, "Could it be your mind is changing because of a certain broody, dark-haired guy?" She smirks before continuing, "I mean, I can totally see the appeal—mysterious, intense, other side of the tracks, completely different from the way we were brought up."

Twirling the end of my braid, I begin walking toward the library with Sarah sauntering next to me. I'm bursting with so many thoughts and emotions. "It's not that. I know it's easy to think 'Oh hey, Adrian is different, so that makes him cool,' but that really isn't the case. He's like...a complicated symphony. On the first attempt at playing the score, it might seem like random notes strung together...a bit difficult to grasp, but you practice because you're curious about the end result, how it's supposed to sound once you've mastered it. Then, with each time you play it, the sounds blend into something else, something bigger, something more beautiful. Then, before you know it, you're left wondering how many layers you haven't discovered yet, and you keep going back for more."

Silence meets my answer and I turn my head, only to find Sarah staring at me with furrowed brows and concern in her eyes. "Oh...wow. That's something else altogether."

Heat rushes to my face as I realize how dramatic I sounded. But I don't want to take the words back, because I feel them in the depths of my soul, the marrow of my bones. With every interaction with Adrian, I learn something more about him—his selflessness, his concern for the people he loves, the way he hangs out at the beach most nights, all cut up and bruised because of what I now know is probably from his illegal fights at the boxing ring. I suspect he's worried about me being there alone, and it seems like this is typical of him, the way he's silently providing for the people he cares about.

I don't see a poor person. I see someone rich in character.

"I know I don't need to remind you to be careful. Don't let your parents find out how you feel about him. I can't imagine what your mom would do. I don't want to see you get hurt." She links her arm with mine.

"I know. Thanks for looking out for me, Sarah." I give her arm a little squeeze. Mother would blow a gasket if she ever learns of Adrian. He's probably her worst nightmare for me.

"Of course. Ride-or-die, my friend."

A short walk later, we arrive at the library where we part ways. The building is a grand structure rivaling what I imagined majestic historical European libraries would look like, with high arches, marble floors, dark woods, the rooms bathed in the golden light of lamps and sconces. Adrian sits in the back corner, half-hidden by the book stacks for Latin and ancient literature. He has a unique commanding presence which seems to overtake the entire space. A lock of his too-long hair falls over his forehead, hiding his eyes.

The musty smell of aged leather and worn pages lingers in the air. A quiet hum fills the cavernous space as students study or work on their papers. He lifts his head the moment I step into the main hall, a ghost of a smile appearing on his lips. He keeps his eyes trained on me as I make my way toward him.

I traipse quietly across the room before setting my books on the table and take a seat in front of him. After I retrieve my thick, spiral-bound notebook from my bag, I flip to the section on Shakespearean influences in modern literature and inch the notes over to him. His lips curve up in a wry smile and he slides the volume in front of him and peruses my detailed documentation...and fancy doodles.

Dang it. I forgot I doodled all over my notes as well.

Adrian's smile widens as he props his face up with one hand. He flips to another page, his eyes roving up and down the document like a copy machine, seemingly absorbing all the words, committing them to memory. His face turns serious as he reviews the copious notes page by page. Taking this opportunity, my gaze cascades over his profile. The strong Roman nose, light eyes currently glowing amber from the warm lamplight, the sharp jawline, the full lips. The faded bruises and fresh cuts don't take away from the beauty of his silhouette. I glance away before my thoughts trail elsewhere.

Taking out my advanced calculus coursework, I inhale a deep breath and begin completing the problem sets. Ten minutes or so later, I'm interrupted by a scrap of paper being pushed in front of my face.

I'm finding it hard to focus when I'm admiring your sketches of Romeo on the margins. Still denying you are a closet romantic?

My eyes flicker to him, only to find him staring intently at my notes. If it weren't for the soft curve of his lips, I'd never know the note was from him.

"I'll have you know—" I whisper.

"Shh!" a few students sitting at the table next to us hush us, throwing cold glares our way.

Pinching my lips together, I take out a scrap piece of paper and scribble down my response.

I'll have you know there's nothing wrong with being a romantic, not that I am one. And these are free notes out of the goodness of my heart. Take it or leave it.

I shove the slip of paper back in front of him as I complete another set of math problems.

A few moments later comes his response.

I'm kidding. I love your drawings. You captured Romeo and Juliet the way I imagined them in my mind when I read the play a long time ago. Of all the Shakespearean plays, this one is my least favorite. I think it's cowardice the way they ended their lives and left their families behind to deal with the aftermath.

He underlines "cowardice" twice. My heart tightens at the anger I feel from those harsh strokes.

At least they had the courage to love and face the end together. I'd like to think their story ended with them being together in the afterlife. If love can allow someone to feel so much, such that you cannot live without that person. Wouldn't it be something worth experiencing?

My thoughts flicker to the sterile relationship my parents have in comparison. I'd rather be single than have what they have. But if love were to be passionate, like the play or the movies, then maybe...

Shoving the scrap back to him, I tap my pencil on the desk as I wait impatiently for his response. Sensing my stare on him, his gaze meets mine and his lips twitch up in a half smile and he resumes reading.

He doesn't send a response back.

For the rest of the day, my question nags at me and I wonder... perhaps my parents' relationship isn't all there is out there. Maybe, just maybe, some relationships are worth experiencing.

That night, I told Mom I had a study session with Sarah after dinner. But instead of burying our heads in our books as promised, she and I snuck out of her house to drive to the boxing ring near the local community college.

My heart beats against my rib cage as I walk through the metal doors of a nondescript white building next to a seedy liquor store in a run-down part of the city. A strong, musty stench hits us in the face as we step into the structure. Looking around, I notice chipped ceilings, and faded gym equipment which seem to have seen better days. We follow the rowdy cheers to a dark doorway. A singular bright light shines on the elevated boxing ring as hordes of people gather around the ropes, jeering at the two fighters in the ring.

"Baby girls, you look out of place here. Need me to show you the ropes?" An oily voice belonging to an older guy with a beer belly and buzz cut calls out to us, his leering gaze crawling up my skin.

Ignoring him, I quickly pull Sarah with me as we move toward the crowd.

"Are you sure Ryan said it was here?" Sarah asks as she nervously tucks a curl of hair behind her ear, her eyes darting from side to side.

"That's what he told me. He said Adrian fights here a few nights a week."

"I can't believe this. It's illegal. If the school ever finds out, they'll kick him out."

Nodding, I drag her to an open viewing spot next to a group of girls dressed in low-cut shirts showcasing their abundance of curves. They shriek and fan themselves with their hands, apparently fawning over the fighters in the ring.

Sweat beads on the back of my neck as unease creeps up my body. My eyes dart around the dark space, my mind wondering if I made a mistake by coming here. I turn my head toward the ring just as a loud *smack* reverberates in the air and one of the fighters goes down.

That's when I see him.

Adrian, half-naked, his lean, wiry muscles glistening with sweat, his hair dripping and plastered to his face. He's clad in a pair of black shorts, his hands encased in blue gloves as he towers over his opponent.

"Oh shit. Raven is totally on a roll tonight. This is his third fight? He's so hot. I'd totally bone him," one of the girls, a tall blonde in the group, says.

More giggles.

"I hear he's fighting for money because his family needs it. Why don't you pay him? Maybe he'll take you up on it," one of her friends replies. Their gazes are glued to the ring.

An unfamiliar burn rushes through my chest as I realize they're talking about Adrian. They don't know anything about him, about how subjecting himself to this torture is probably a last resort for him. I clench my hands into fists as wetness prickles my eyes.

The referee is counting as the fallen fighter struggles to stand back up. I hold my breath as I stare at Adrian, who has returned to his corner of the ring, his eyes wild, the fire within threatening to scorch everyone in sight. It's as if he's temporarily unleashing the demons inside him. He thumps his gloves together as he waits for the referee to count to ten.

Just as the count reaches nine, the fallen fighter, wearing blue shorts, staggers to his feet, his legs wobbling for purchase until he steadies himself. I clasp my hands over my mouth as I witness the two fighters circle each other, emanating menace; two predators warring over a territory of which only one can be a victor.

Blue Shorts lunges, landing a hard jab on the lower left side of Adrian's chest, the smack is loud and resounding. I viscerally recoil from the sight.

"Adrian!" I shriek as I watch him crumble, the wind literally knocked out of him. Tears blur my vision as I see the tense set of his jaw, his furrowed eyebrow, his body curling into itself in apparent pain. My heart clenches as if I were the one to get hit. I blink my tears away and clench my fists, wanting to run up there and wrap him in my arms and shield him from the beating. Blue Shorts prowls toward him, his hand raised to land another blow.

"Adrian! Watch out," I scream, not caring I'm calling him by name and not his fighting moniker.

Adrian ducks at the last second and his face whips in our direction. Our eyes connect, the split-second feeling like minutes as his shocked blue gaze meets my teary one. His nostrils flare and a vein pulses on his forehead before he turns back to his opponent, who is gearing for another offensive attack.

He darts out of the way, his feet as fast and nimble as a dancer, before he delivers a powerful punch to the upper right side of Blue Short's abdomen. Cheers erupt in the boxing ring as Blue Shorts sways unsteadily for a few seconds before crumbling to the floor like a house of cards, seemingly incapacitated.

The referee counts to ten but Blue Shorts is still on the ground, clutching his left side, apparently in severe pain.

"Oh shit. I-I'd never—" Sarah gasps beside me as my heart threatens to give out in my chest. My lips wobble and moisture gathers in my eyes; tears for Adrian, for the bruises on his body, for his tenacity in standing up again and again after life beats him to a pulp.

"And tonight's champion is our fan favorite, Raven!" The announcer holds Adrian's hand and raises it into the air. Adrian rakes his wet hair, his chest rising and falling in deep pants, his face grim without any semblance of happiness at being the victor. As soon as the announcer drops his hand, Adrian stalks toward us, his fierce eyes pinning me in place.

"Uh oh. Incoming," Sarah whispers as I nod wordlessly.

He leaps over the ropes and, with a few long strides, he stands in front of me, his chest still heaving, sweat dripping down his face in rivulets. My eyes automatically rove down his muscles, each pec and ab defined, down to a sprinkle of hair below his belly button. Heat rises to my face as my hands tremble. A reddish bruise mars his chest, looking painful to the touch, in the area where Blue Shorts hit him a while ago. My pulse beats loudly in my ears.

"What the *fuck* are you doing here?" he growls, his voice low, the fury barely contained.

I drag my gaze back up to his face. "Y-You're hurt."

"I asked... What. Are. You. Doing. Here?"

"I-I... Ryan told me you were fighting here most nights. And you wouldn't t-tell me where you were getting your cuts and bruises, so I had to find out for myself. I had to see..." I bite my bottom lip as fresh tears gather at the corners of my eyes. "Adrian..." I murmur as my trembling fingers touch his wound.

He hisses, but doesn't flinch. He lifts up his bandaged hands and gently swipes the tears off my face, the softness of his touch completely at odds with the coiled intensity in his frame. "I told you not to worry. I'm fine."

I roll my lips together and nod, blinking rapidly, not sure why his injuries are affecting me so deeply.

His gaze softens as he turns to Sarah. "Can you take her home? This place is no place for you girls. It's not safe."

Turning back to me, he murmurs, "I won't be at the beach tonight. Go home and rest. Don't worry about me, okay? I really have everything handled. Believe me."

I nod again, my emotions clogging my throat. I wipe my wet eyes with my arm. Sarah tugs me away toward the double doors. My mind is in a haze as I come to realize I care more about Adrian than I originally thought. The sudden realization floors me and I can't help but glance back, only to find him staring at me with searing passion in his eyes.

That night, I lie in bed thinking about those sky-blue eyes, burning with the flames of anger and anguish, and I fall into a fitful sleep.

The next day, before I head into cheerleading practice, I open my locker and gasp.

"Everything okay?" Sarah asks as she slams her locker shut.

On top of my notebooks sits one long-stem lily, white at the edges, the deepest pink in the center. The sweet scent disseminates from the open locker. My fragrance of choice. My fingers trail softly over the fragile petals. Under the lily is a folded sheet of paper.

Pixie,

This flower reminds me of you. I'm not Shakespeare and I'm not a writer, but if I were to use one word to describe the lily, it would be "alluring." Thank you for your notes in the library yesterday. And to answer your question, I'm beginning to reconsider my stance on *Romeo and Juliet*. Perhaps you are right, some things are worth experiencing.

Please don't come see me at the boxing ring again. I can't bear to witness your tears and I don't want to have to worry about your safety. The bruises and cuts are temporary and superficial. I'd never do anything to put myself in harm's way. Please trust me.

Gratefully yours,

Adrian

I quickly fold the note and tuck it against my fluttering heart. Warmth spreads from the organ to the rest of my body and I feel like I can fly, like somehow I've grown wings.

"Everything's fine. More than fine," I reply to Sarah.

I don't know what possessed me to slip the note and the lily in her locker last week. Ever since she saw me at the fight and I saw her tears for me—which wrecked me more than any punch or blow could—I can't stop thinking about her. I can't stop craving for her smile to replace her tears, her grins to replace her frowns, her laughter to replace her sobs. Somehow, Emily has wormed her way into my mind. She's the spark of light I look forward to in the gilded buildings of Warwick. When I'm with her, it's almost as if I can forget about my family's problems.

She gives me peace by simply being there.

The little moments, precious vignettes of treasured memories, are scraps I collect in my mind—us sitting side by side at the beach gazing at the stars, watching her traipse on the sand looking for more seashells while I try my best to focus on the textbook in front of me, her teasing winks when she passes by me in the hallways at school, the way she tries her best to eke smiles out of me like it's her personal mission, seeing her furrowing her brows when she thinks about her future, her eyes looking lost and confused, when all I want to tell her is, things will be okay, because with a heart as generous as hers, she will dazzle the world with her brightness and make a way for herself in the future.

All I know was when I saw the stargazer lilies in the floral section of the grocery store, I knew I had to get it for her. If I were to hazard a guess, since she wears the scent day in and day out, this is her favorite flower. My chest warms as I imagine her face, a face I've memorized and imprinted in my brain, when she opened the locker that day. Did it bring a smile to her face? Did those dimples show?

So, this began our dance of passing notes at random moments during the day. I unfurl the last few notes I received from her. She'd sporadically slipped them into my locker.

Adrian,

Thank you for the note and the lily. I have so many questions. Why do you call me pixie? How did you get into my locker? How do you know my favorite flower is the lily? To even the scales, you need to tell me a secret no one knows.

I love like the lily. I may have hung it upside down and pressed it into a book to keep it forever. I won't admit it, though.

I feel like I've stepped foot into the nineteenth century with this letter or note writing. But please continue. *smiley face*

Always,

Ems

P.S. I promise you I won't see you fight again. I don't want to distract you at the ring and frankly...it hurts too much. I may have a new wish in my wishing jar for you. I wish you'll have your heart's desire, so you won't have to be at the ring much longer.

P.P.S. Why are you called the Raven in the boxing ring?

My heart hiccups as my fingers trace over her words. *She has a wish for me.* An unfamiliar warmth, something that has been making an appearance more and more these days, fills my insides as I reread her note.

Heaving out a sigh, I glance at the clock on my dresser. Six a.m. I have a little bit of time before I need to wake Millie up for school. I guess there are advantages to not having a text plan on your phone. Now I get to keep these little physical souvenirs of our messages to each other. I pick up another slip of paper.

Adrian,

I remind you of a fairy? Is this something to do with my height? I'll have you know I quite like being short. I can wear all sorts of heels and not have to worry about towering over anyone. You guessed my locker combination? I shouldn't have told you my birthday. Or maybe I should stop using something so obvious for my combination.

I didn't know bird names have so many meanings until you told me. I agree with the Celtics, Raven suits you—battle, war, and victory. I did some researching on my own. Do you know in other cultures, the raven represents good luck, wisdom, and protection? I'd like to wish those things for you as well.

Sharing with me your least favorite food in the world is pickles in sandwiches does *not* count as a secret. Try again.

Always,

Pixie (It's a cute nickname—I'm keeping it)

A loud thump from my parents' bedroom distracts me from the note in my hand. I quickly fold the papers back in half and tuck them into my copy of *Romeo and Juliet* and shove it beneath my pillow on the futon. Despite my reservations and powerful feelings about this play, it's Mom's favorite, and apparently Emily's favorite as well, and so it holds a special place in my heart. I walk to the closed bedroom door and knock.

"Dad? You okay in there?"

A muffled groan sounds in response.

By the time I came home late last night, his door was already closed, so I haven't had a chance to talk to him until now.

Frowning, I open the door to find my dad sprawled on top of the bed, empty beer bottles on the floor and on the nightstand. He shakes and shudders as he mutters unintelligibly under his breath. The smell of alcohol and greasy food reeks and I open the windows, letting in some cold air. He has been resorting to the bottle more and more these days, burying himself under the haze of alcohol instead of facing reality.

He barely notices the cuts and bruises I get from my fights. Or if he does, he chooses not to address them and opts to just believe my lame-ass excuses about getting injured playing sports. Fury laces through me as I think about him, the man who's supposed to protect me and Millie, rendered to a useless heap.

I'll never be like him when I get older.

"Dad, what's going on? Don't you need to get ready for work?"

Despite everything, I still love him and my mind holds fast to the memories of when Mom was healthy and Dad would take us to the beach for a day in the sand, when he'd take me to my first boxing lessons, saying it's good for a man to know how to defend himself, how to be strong in the face of adversity.

How much things have changed.

Grunting, he sits up and stares at me with bloodshot eyes. He swallows audibly before responding, "I got put on administrative leave."

"What?" I sit on the edge of the bed.

"Son, I m-made a mistake, and I think they'll find out."

"What did you do?"

He glances up at me before hanging his head in apparent shame. "I stole from them."

"What!"

"W-We're so tight on funds. I don't make enough as is and with your mom's bills and everything...one day I saw an opportunity at the bank and I took it, and then it happened again and again."

My heart plummets to my stomach. He can't lose his job. What will we do then? Who will pay for Mom's bills? What if he gets caught or gets put into jail?

"How could you do something so *stupid*, Dad? How could you?" I bury my face in my hands, trying not to hyperventilate. "So what now?"

Dad lets out a shaky sigh. "I-I don't know. I just hope the investigation comes back clean somehow. Kingsley is a shark. He—"

Kingsley.

"Who?" The thudding pulse is loud in my ears and I could barely hear myself think.

"Robert Kingsley. He's the chief legal counsel, and he's a shark, not known for his mercy. His wife's family pretty much owns the company. So far, I haven't had to deal with him yet, but I've seen him copied on an email they sent to me. If he's involved, I-I'm afraid I don't have too much time..."

Dad mumbles about his work concerns, his words slurring together, no doubt under the influence of alcohol, but I don't hear him. All I can think about is her. The girl who has bewitched me since the first day of school. The girl who has recently made me start to dream again. The girl who cried for me when she saw my injuries. The girl who gave me one of her precious wishes because she cares about me.

Emily Kingsley.

The slimy feeling of dread coils back into my stomach as I reflect on the first day we met, when I paused at her last name. My mind finally snaps back to an article I read at the library last year about the Kingsley-Lee clan and their influence at TransAmerica. Everything clicks together and I realize my dad's livelihood, our family's livelihood, is now at the mercy of her family.

Because of Dad's desperation. Because of our fucking shitty circumstances. Because life is unfair.

"How much did you steal, Dad?"

Dad pauses, the air between us thickening with the stench of the alcohol on his breath. He reaches for the half-empty bottle on the nightstand and I stop him, my hands gripping his forearm tightly. *No. No more of that.*

"Fifty thousand over the past three months," he whispers. "Most of it went into the rent and the medical debt from the last few rounds of chemo and the hospitalizations."

"What about Grandpa and Grandma? Can we ask them for money? Surely, they'd help. Mom is their daughter—"

"I asked, and they said no!" Dad shouts, his face turning beet red. "They said the day she married me was when she died in their eyes."

Anger coils through me, the heat smoldering into the sharp blades of hatred. The callousness of these rich people, having the resources to help yet choosing not to. Instead, they spend their time pretending to be philanthropic, contributing to this cause or that charity for the sake of photo ops. I've never met my grandparents from Mom's side. I used to want to meet them, but now I don't want to waste my time and energy on them.

Someday, I'll show them. I'll make them regret treating us this way.

"Adrian...I *killed* her when I married her." Tears swim in Dad's eyes as he looks at me. "If I could do everything again...I wouldn't go after the girl who's worlds away from mine. Maybe then...maybe she'd have the best resources, have the best doctors, have the best chance."

A burning sensation pricks my eyes.

The hole keeps getting deeper, and no matter how I try to dig us out of it, the earth seems to collapse beneath us. My fights bring in a few hundred dollars a week, but nowhere near enough to replace Dad's lost income if he loses his job.

"We'll figure things out, Dad," I murmur, still clutching his forearm.

It's all lies.

The tie on my uniform feels like a chokehold, slowly cutting off the oxygen to my lungs.

Adrian,

How was your weekend? Mine was fairly uneventful. We had cheer practice on Saturday. I'm very nervous, to be honest. The double full twist basket toss is still a challenge for me and we'll be debuting the move at the game tonight. There's going to be a big crowd there too. I hope I don't fall flat on my face.

Here's a question for you: why did the chicken cross the basketball court?

Cue suspenseful music

Because the referee called "fowl!"

Get it? Hope this puts a smile on your face. I know I can't help shoulder your burdens at home, but I hope this lightens your heart.

Yours,

Pixie

I clasp the new note I just retrieved from my locker to my chest as a barrage of emotions hit me like a bulldozer. A burst of warmth at the chicken joke, my mind already imaging my pixie grinning mischievously at me, with the dimples on her face. A sinking weight on my chest when I remember how my dad has stolen from her family's company. A nauseating sense of shame. I don't deserve her kindness or her smiles. I'm not worthy of someone like her.

All my life, I've always wanted things I couldn't have.

A large house for my parents. The fancy little sandwiches I see Millie eyeing whenever we pass by the French patisserie at the mall. Good health for my mom, so she'll be free of pain. Strength for my dad, so he can be happy again. For the first time in my life, however inconveniently, I finally want something for myself.

I want her, my pixie.

Somehow, during these past few weeks of late-night strolls at the beach where she has started bringing first-aid supplies to bandage me up after my fights, the study sessions at the library, and the little notes in the locker, Emily has become my pixie, the fairy who brings me happiness, who bestows upon me a spark of light in the darkness I'm constantly surrounded by. My heart brightens, the heaviness in my chest lifting whenever she is in my presence. My lungs fill with fresh air and it's as if I can finally breathe.

She'll never know, though.

Because I can't have her, because we're worlds apart, because a pauper like me can't provide for someone like her. Because I shouldn't drag her down from the pearly gates of heaven to the fiery hell I currently live in. Because the last thing I should do is to follow my dad's footsteps. It'd be irresponsible, especially after I've experienced living in the aftermath of Dad's choice. But I can't help the desperate yearning in the deepest recesses of my soul.

Perhaps I'm a writer, after all.

Swallowing the lump in my throat, I tuck her note away in the pocket of my blazer and walk toward my next class, AP World History.

As I pass by the music room, a haunting melody on the piano stops me in my tracks.

The "Moonlight Sonata."

The sweeping rhythm and emotions of the piece lure me to the entrance of the room. Ducking behind the partially opened door, I recognize the tune after listening to it online the day after Emily told me it's her favorite piece to play during one of our late nights at the beach.

The music swells and crests, the passion in the notes heavy and intense, and I know who I'd find when I peek through the crack at the door.

My pixie plays at the piano, her eyes closed as she moves flawlessly over the keys. Her head sways to the rhythm, her body becoming one with the instrument. Her shiny hair is curled over one shoulder and her lips are tipped up in a small smile, as if thinking about something happy. My feet move forward a few steps, drawn to her since the beginning, but I stop myself.

You're worlds apart, remember?

I grip the doorknob tightly as my chest clenches in pain at the unfairness of everything. If I were a regular boy and she were a regular girl...things would be different. My arm shudders with tension before I drop my hand, forcing myself to walk away.

Someday, I vow to put that smile on her face.

Someday, I'll be worthy of her.

Someday, my circumstances will be different.

And I realize...hope is a dangerous thing indeed.

• • •

I glance at my watch. Seven-thirty p.m. If I leave now, I may still make it in time for her halftime performance and can come back afterward. *You're just going to support a friend, that's all.* Emily has been so worried about the stunt she is to perform tonight. I want to be there to support her from the sidelines, even though I don't care about basketball, and I definitely don't care about anything Ryan is playing in.

"I can't believe you're considering cutting your shift short, dude, and you're missing the fight tonight. This must be some historical moment." Jack sidles up to me as I pack up the few belongings I have. I grab the flashcards from his hands—as much as he complains, he's been helping me with my studies while we toil away at Grocery for Less.

"Shut up. There's just somewhere I need to be."

"I bet that somewhere has to do with a hot cheerleader who has an equally hot friend."

Slipping on my jacket and picking up another long-stem lily I purchased when I got in this evening, I walk to my shift manager, Brandon, with Jack trailing behind me.

"Hey, Brandon, I need to run an urgent errand. Is it okay if I step out for an hour or so? I'll be back afterward to finish my shift." I've adjusted my shift to shorter hours on fight nights, but it's still very early tonight.

Brandon's eyes trail down to the lily I have clenched in my hand and smirks. "If it were Jack over here, I'd say no...but you, Adrian, I'm glad you're getting out there. You sure need it. Take the rest of the night off if you want to. It's pretty quiet tonight."

Jack busts out in laughter as we walk toward the exit of the grocery store. "See? You aren't even fooling Boring Brandon with the whole 'I've gotta run an errand' excuse."

Rolling my eyes, I turn to him, wanting to wipe that smirk off his face. "I'm just supporting my friend, that's all, wiseass. Don't you have work or something?"

Backing away, Jack curls his fingers at me. "Naughty, naughty Adrian. Skipping work for pussy. Don't do anything I wouldn't do."

Shaking my head, I wave him off and get into my car, which thankfully is still running and hasn't caused any issues lately. A short drive later, I arrive at the school gymnasium and walk in just as cheers erupt on the basketball court.

The atmosphere is thrilling and the stands are packed with fellow students and parents, decked out in navy and greens. The squeaking of sneakers on the wooden floor travels across the room, and the smell of buttery popcorn fills the air. The crowd shrieks as the buzzer sounds. It appears Ryan has made a three-point shot just as the second quarter ends.

Walking to the bottom of the stands, I sweep my eyes over the commotion at the court, as players return to their seats and cheerleaders begin their formation on the center of the floor. Up-beat music plays from the speakers, the bass vibrating the wooden floors, and the cheerleaders begin a series of complicated moves and dances more fit for acrobats than high schoolers. The crowds and sounds slowly fade away as my eyes locate the one person I'm searching for. The one person—a vice—who I've allowed to detract me from my job and my responsibility to make money for the family. *Supporting a friend,* I remind myself, ignoring the nagging pinch of guilt.

Emily hollers as she dances to the beat of the music, her hands sliding down the sides of her tits, the perfect handfuls I've imagined caressing time and time again as her hips twitch and shake to each thump. Blood rushes uncomfortably south as I watch her sway her sinful figure to the song, her body completely in tune with the beats. She swings her head around in a circle, her high ponytail whipping through the air as she kicks her leg straight up. My pixie spins in place and as she completes her rotation, her eyes sweep through the crowd and suddenly land on me.

Her beautiful brown eyes widen in apparent surprise and recognition. She gives me a flirty wink and bites on her plump bottom lip before turning back to the crowd. The pounding of my heart eclipses the beats of the song as she suddenly jumps into the air and lands on three cheerleaders supporting her as base. I hold my breath as the anticipation grows and the electricity buzzes in the air. This is the move she was worried about for the last few weeks.

The music quiets for a beat before erupting into a crescendo and they throw her high off the ground. Emily tucks her arms closely by her sides as she flips backward and completes two full twists upside down before landing in the arms of her teammates. I exhale, my heart racing a mile a minute, as if I were right there in the action with her.

The crowd erupts in cheers. "Kingsley! Kingsley! Kingsley!"

After finishing up the rest of their performance, the girls take a breather and Emily breaks into a run toward me with the brightest smile on her face. I see classmates pointing and staring, hear the murmuring in the nearby crowds, but she doesn't appear to notice. Without any hesitation, she leaps into my arms as if she knows I'll catch her, and I stagger back, my hands automatically grasping her small body, my fingers curling around her firm ass on instinct. The sweet scent of lilies fills my nostrils and I hold still, my hands wanting to squeeze, to mold, to feel.

The stares blur into the backdrop as I focus on my pixie in my arms, as if she belongs there all along. She hugs me with all her might and shrieks excitedly in my ear, "Did you see that? I landed it! It was perfect!"

Laughing, I'm swept away by the exhilaration in her voice as I hug her tightly back. "Yes, I did...you were breathtaking." *In so many ways.*

I can feel the moment she realizes she's in my arms in full view of everyone. Her body stills and muscles tense. Her breathing takes on a lighter, quicker rhythm. I hear the faint audible gulp from her dainty throat. My hands reluctantly let her go as she slides off me, every inch inflaming my nerve endings despite the clothing between us. My cock grows hard and I shift in position, trying my best to hide it.

Emily's gaze trails up my body as if she's cataloging my features the way I have with hers before her mocha eyes land on mine. Her soft lips part and the pulse on her neck flutters. Her smooth cheeks pinken. She bites on her plush lip and fuck does my cock harden some more. The air grows thick between us, the tension palpable, and we stand there by the bleachers, staring at each other. My fingers curl into a fist, fighting the temptation to reach out, to pull her flush against me again.

"Ems, it's time for us to go back. The game is about to start again." Sarah's voice pierces through the veil and loud sounds of the gym rush back into my consciousness. Emily visibly flinches, as if she, too, was in the same trance as me.

She glances at Sarah, seemingly dazed, and says, "O-Okay. I'll be there. Give me a minute."

Sarah smiles at me, a knowing glint in her eyes, and trudges back to the rest of her team. I glance back at Emily, whose face is now fully pink, as if embarrassed. Pulling the flower from the pocket of my jacket, a little smashed from the hug, I hand it to her. My heart is in my throat. Somehow, I don't seem to remember anything I thought about earlier—all the reasons why I shouldn't pursue her, why we can't be together. With her standing in front of me, her eyes wide and bright with rioting emotions seeming to mirror mine, nothing else seems to matter.

"I needed to be here." *To support you.* "I couldn't stay away." *Even though I should.*

My breath catches in my throat as I hand her the long-stem lily. "Congratulations on your successful performance," I whisper.

"Thank you." She clasps the flower lovingly in her grip, her lips curving in a small smile, so sweet, so beautiful.

"Emmie! Stop hanging out with the loser!" Ryan the Terror hollers, but I don't spare him a glance.

"I-I have to go back. Adrian, I..."

I nod, suddenly overwhelmed by the feelings overflowing inside me. Lifting my hand in a small wave, I watch her as she hurries back to her team. She glances at me at the last second and graces me with another one of her breathtaking smiles.

And I realize my life will never be the same.

CHAPTER 11

Adrian

The cancer ward is livelier today. Red and pink paper hearts decorate the receptionist's desk and nurses' stations. Shiny, metallic balloons with phrases like "I love you, my Valentine," and "With love, anything is possible," adorn the halls. The sterile scents of cleaning agents and disinfectants still linger in the air, but the bright colors and the exciting hum of energy seem to distract me from noticing the usual chill on the floor.

Valentine's Day is a day celebrating the beauty of love, where hope also seems to be synonymous with romance as well. For the past week, I can't be in a conversation at school without at least one mention of this holiday. Girls whisper to each other while throwing glances at guys in the hallways. Guys appear sheepish when asking out their crushes at lunch. The atmosphere feels somewhat...hopeful. Normally, this holiday to me is just another day of the week—a commercialized holiday, at best. But this year, the annoying kernel of hope has latched itself on to my heart. I'm sure it's all courtesy of a certain dark-haired pixie in my life.

I clutch half a dozen wine-red roses in my hand, careful to avoid the thorns, even though I've shorn most of them at home this morning already. I wish I could buy a dozen roses for Mom, but with money being tight and the holiday prices for flowers, this is all I can afford. Letting out a deep breath, I knock on Mom's door.

"Come in." Her voice sounds weaker, but is still warm.

I push open the door, making sure a wide smile is on my face, the usual mask I wear around her.

"Adrian!" Her thin arms tremble as she grasps the railings on the bed, struggling to sit up. An oxygen breathing tube is across her nostrils.

I hurry to her side and lift her into a sitting position, my heart twisting in pain. There's no denying it. She's on the decline.

"You can't breathe?" I sit down on the chair next to her and clasp her hand in mine, warming her icy fingers.

"Just a little bit this morning. No big deal. It comes and goes." She smiles at me as she gives me a soft squeeze.

I place the roses on the blankets. "Happy Valentine's Day, Mom. Dad and Millie will come by in the evening when I'm at work."

She clasps the flowers in her hands, brings them to her nose for a sniff, her lips tilting up in apparent happiness. She lets out a satisfied sigh and sets the roses to the side.

"Thank you, sweetie. Is everything going well at school? Is your dad doing okay at work? And Millie?"

Smoothing my face into what I hope is a reassuring expression, I reply, "Of course. Things are going well. Millie got an A on her spelling test. You should ask her about it. She's very proud of herself. And Dad is doing fine too. There's nothing to worry about."

She frowns as she stares at my face, notably, the faded bruise on my cheek. I even bought some cheap makeup at the grocery store to cover it up, but it doesn't seem to work.

"Just the guys getting rowdy at sports, Mom. It looks worse than it feels."

Her fingers graze the healing discoloration and I fight to stay still, to not wince from the pain. I tip my lips up in a bright smile. *See? Nothing out of the ordinary. Just boys being boys.*

She closes her eyes, seemingly appeased. Her hand falls back on her blankets. "Your dad must be so busy at the bank right now.

Holidays are always a busy time, especially since this isn't a federal holiday."

I hum in agreement. She'll never know about Dad's situation at work. It'll break her.

Her eyes flutter open and she asks, her voice as gentle as I remember from my childhood, "So, tell me, any special ladies in your life? Today is Valentine's Day, after all."

"You mean, beside yourself and Millie?"

"Oh hush, you sweet talker."

I bite my bottom lip and look down, not knowing how to answer her. There is someone, but nothing will come of it. Nothing can ever come out of it.

But, more often time than not, I want to be selfish and say fuck it.

"What's the look on your face? There's a special girl, isn't there?"

"She…" I chuckle mirthlessly, my eyes on the flowers Mom set aside. "We're worlds apart. Nothing can ever happen. Well, nothing should, but…"

"None of that. Any girl will be lucky to have you, sweetie." Mom tugs at my hand, forcing me to look up at her. "Do you feel this way because she's wealthy?"

"That's part of it."

"Did I tell you how your dad and I got together?" she asks, her eyes unfocused, as if reminiscing about the past.

"Not really, not the entire story."

"Well, I met your dad at a bookstore. I was searching for a travel guide to Spain for my high school graduation trip and your dad, well, he was just flipping through the photos in the books. He told me he'd go there and spend hours in the travel section and imagine himself going to all these exotic locations since he couldn't afford to travel. We were young. I was rich and couldn't comprehend how some people had so little to live on. So, we got to talking about our lives, my travels, his bucket list of locations, and soon half an hour became one hour, then two hours."

She coughs and I quickly hand her a glass of water for her to take a sip. "We'd meet there every week, behind my family's back, of course. I fell in love with his spirit. His family was poor and his parents died when he was in college. It was just him, struggling to make ends meet while finishing school. He'd never let that get to him, you know. Your dad showed me how beautiful dreams could be, how life isn't measured by the number of dollars in your bank account, and how, as long as we have love, we can survive everything."

Except this disease. The dollars in the bank account could've gotten her the best treatments. Perhaps if we had the money in the bank, she wouldn't have skipped so many doctor's appointments because she was busy working two jobs and she would have caught it sooner.

Mom's eyes shift to me, and she lets out a satisfied sigh. "Your grandparents did eventually find out and forbade us from being together. But I knew, deep inside me, that my life was incomplete without this man. That no amount of riches and material comforts could be more important than him. So, we eloped, two young people desperately in love. I didn't get to go to college, but we made it work. And while I'm sad my parents cut me off because of this, I don't regret the decision. We're so happy, Adrian, so very happy. And I have you and Millie, and you both are worth more than anything in the world."

Tears gather my eyes as I listen to Mom and I rapidly blink them away. My thoughts stray back to Dad and what he said before, about how he thought he killed her the moment he married her. If I were in his shoes, would I feel the same?

"Adrian, don't let fear get in the way of love. If this girl is worth it, and I believe she is if she has touched your heart, don't let the what-ifs or dollar signs keep you from experiencing the love I was blessed to have with your dad. Our love blossomed into the love of four people, including yourself and Millie. How miraculous is that?"

"You've never regretted your decision?" I whisper.

"Never! If I got to choose again, I wouldn't change a thing." Her lids droop as she yawns. A small smile appears on her face.

The ache in my chest clashes with the poignant happiness from her story. Her's and Dad's love story is bittersweet at best and I can't help but feel like I'm being dragged on the same tracks, heading toward something that will surely lead to heartbreak. But I'm not sure I can stop it...or that I even want to.

In ten years, will I look back at today and wonder if I should've chosen differently?

"Sleep tight, Mom. I'll be back later this week."

I tuck the blanket over her shoulders and walk out of her room, a heavy weight on my chest.

Warwick is buzzing with excitement today, but I feel like I've swallowed an anvil. The football field is filled with colorful stands rivaling the boardwalks of popular beaches nearby, and frankly, looks like a rainbow has exploded with the pieces scattered all over the grass. Small tents are pitched with large, heart-shaped balloons decorating the entrances. Today is the much-anticipated Valentine's Day carnival and dance. The festivities will begin after school, with the carnival portion kicking into full gear, and will end with the dance in the evening.

From what I've overheard in the last few weeks, the events committee went all out this year. They've hired a mini circus to perform in one of the large tents. There's also a fortuneteller, complete with the expected crystal balls and tarot cards, and a variety of rides rivaling the smaller theme parks in the county. One can't miss the giant Ferris wheel sticking out like an eyesore at the edge of the field. The athletics teams each have their own booth as well. So, I know I can expect the usual "dunk a jock into the water" or water gun shooting contests.

I wasn't even planning to go to the carnival or the dance. After all, everything costs money, and I also have work after school and it's fight night at the boxing ring. But what's causing the unease swirling in my gut isn't any of these activities. What's distracting me as I walk to the locker bay after my last class of the day is the topic I overheard a group of cheerleaders discuss in the halls earlier.

The kissing booth.

They're going to run a fucking kissing booth.

The thought of Emily offering her perfect lips to idiots who are willing to pay for it—and there'll be a line for her kisses I'm sure—has me wanting to hit something or walk up to a certain someone, shake her, and ask her why.

My hands clench into tight fists as I approach my locker. I enter my combination and open the door, finding yet another note inside.

Adrian,

Happy Valentine's Day. I know you'll be working and won't be joining any of the fun activities today...but know this, I'll be missing you. And you may have heard by now, I'll be working at the dreaded kissing booth today...all for a good cause, though. You know, the funds we raise in the booth will go toward lymphoma research? I'll be thinking of that when I work there for my time slot today. I'll wait for you at our spot at the beach tonight. And...stay safe in the ring, Raven.

Thinking of you,

Pixie

The heat coursing through me briefly abates at her words. My pixie. We're both traveling on this invisible line between close friendship and something more, a delicate waltz of push and pull, where I find myself tugging her closer and closer against me with each twirl around the dance floor. Exhaling forcefully, I carefully tuck the letter away in my bag and walk over to her locker. I prepared something for her too.

I enter her locker combination, which she hasn't changed, and open it. A faint scent of lilies wafts through the air, no doubt from the flowers I've placed there once a week in the last few months. Rummaging through my bag, I pull out another long-stem stargazer lily and place it atop her books. The flowers are an extravagance I shouldn't be spending money on, but I can't seem to help it, like most things with my pixie. Somehow, thinking of the bright smile on her face, with the two alluring dimples, has me shelling out the bills for the flowers week after week. Jack's words echo back at me, *"You're so fucked, dude."*

That I am. I've given up denying it.

I pull out a small bag of seashells I've gathered on my own time. Sometimes, I'd go to neighboring beaches to see if the selections were better there. I can't afford a nice steak dinner, flowers, or chocolates...heck I can't even afford to attend the dance tonight, but this... This I can do. Hopefully, these shells will bring her more wishes and dreams because my pixie deserves all the happiness in her future. I place the shells next to the flower and retrieve a piece of paper and a pen from my binder.

Dearest Pixie,

I wonder why you didn't tell me about the kissing booth earlier? I won't tell you how I felt when I heard the news, but...I'm repeating to myself that it's all for a good cause. You deserve everything, the most delicious food, the best presents, but I'm afraid all I can offer you on this holiday is the flower and the seashells. If I can't give you anything else, at least, I hope I can contribute to your hopes and dreams for the future.

Yours,

Adrian

P.S. Knowing you care about my well-being is enough to sustain me in the ring tonight.

P.P.S. And you don't need to ask. I'll always be at the beach. Always.

Slamming the locker shut, I pick up my bag and head to my car. Pick up Millie from school, fix dinner, get ready for work and the fight—the usual checklist of chores and tasks runs through my head. Loud jeering snaps me out of the mental exercise and I find myself standing at the edge of the football field, which is currently overflowing with students celebrating Valentine's Day like it's Mardi Gras. I don't even know how I got here. It's as if my body is acting out the secret pining of my heart. My eyes scan across the bustling space, automatically searching for the kissing booth.

Don't do it, Adrian. Don't go looking for her. It'll only piss you off.

But before I know it, I'm moving through the crowds, weaving through the bright stands, ignoring the screeches, the smells of grilled meats and treats that'll usually tempt any passersby, and suddenly, I see her.

My pixie, with her bright eyes and lush lips, a Siren calling me to her.

Emily pokes her head out of a small booth covered with a red velvet cloth on the sides, except for a small window, no doubt for some semblance of privacy yet letting in some light. A huge sign in bright pink and sparkles says, Kissing Booth: Once in a lifetime chance to kiss a hot cheerleader for $20! Sarah and another cheerleader, Chelsea, I believe, are standing behind the table in front of the booth and collecting the money from a line of horny teenagers, all wanting a piece of the action.

A burning heat travels up my body, singeing my insides as I see a guy, probably a sophomore given his size and appearance, walk up to my pixie with a smug grin. Emily scrunches up her face and forces out an unconvincing smile. She sweeps aside the curtain hanging over the doorway of her little booth and squeezes her eyes shut as she leans forward. Her lips are rolled in and pressed in a firm line. The little punk plants a loud smack on her lips and steps back, raising his hands in victory to his friends standing on the sidelines, hooting and hollering. A red haze fills my vision, devoid of any rational logic. The burn in my chest knocks the air out of my lungs.

The only person she should be kissing is me.

I want to rip these guys into shreds.

I clench my fists, fingernails biting into my palms, as the next guy steps up and grabs her face, pulling her in for another kiss. Emily visibly cringes and wipes her mouth with a tissue afterward.

"Get out of my way, you idiots," a familiar blond jock hollers at the boys in the line. "You want a kiss from a cheerleader? Wait ten minutes. No one else is kissing Emmie on my watch." Ryan trudges toward the front of the line, shooing his classmates away as my heart pounds in agreement.

Finally, something the dipshit and I can agree on.

"What the heck, Ryan? This is all for a good cause. I only have ten minutes left anyway," Emily yells as she steps out of her booth, her hands on her slim waist, which is showcased by the crop top and short skirt of her cheerleading outfit. The outfit has starred in so many of my depraved fantasies.

"What does your mom have to say about you working at a kissing booth?" he asks, his face mottled with anger.

"It's none of your business. Get it in your thick head. You're not my keeper."

"I don't care. They shouldn't be kissing you."

"It's for a good cause, and I'm fine with it."

Ryan presses his lips together, takes out a bill from his wallet, and slaps it on the table. "Fine, you want to be kissed? Kiss me then."

Emily shrinks back as I hurtle forward, wanting to steal her away from the scene. Before she can reply, Ryan hauls her against him and presses his lips on hers.

And I see blood.

My hands clench with a desire to decimate. To throw a right hook on his face.

To tear him off her.

My jaw locks with tension and my heart pounds so loudly in my chest, I can barely hear the sounds around me. I charge toward them as fast as my legs can carry me, desperate to peel her off his person as she dangles in mid-air. Just before I reach them, she lands a solid kick on his shin and Ryan releases her with a loud yelp.

"Get out of here! You've had your kiss." She turns away and takes a new tissue, wiping her lips as she shudders.

"Emmie! I wanted—"

"She said...Get. Out. Of. Here," I growl as I finally reach them, my last strides eating up the remaining distance.

"Adrian?" Emily gasps, as if shocked to see me in front of her.

Ryan steps up to me and shoves me with his beefy hands. "What did you say, loser?"

"Get the *fuck* out of here."

"She'll never love you, you know. You and your piss-ass poor family, who do you think you are? You are nothing but trash beneath our feet, loser. You—"

My fist flies across the air before I can control myself, landing on his cheek in a loud *crack*. The roar of satisfaction pounds through me, my hands barely noticing the pain from the hit. He staggers back, holding his jaw as he snarls at me like a rabid dog.

"You, y-you—"

"You *fucking* piece of shit, I've been wanting to do this for a long time," I pant as I stalk toward him. "You want some more, dipshit? Cuz I've got more where this came from."

Ryan snaps out of his shock and charges toward me with the force of a football defensive lineman. We topple onto the grass, and I curl my arm around his neck in a chokehold. Screams sound in the distance, but I don't notice, my blood boiling in my veins. Ryan struggles against me, his elbows and arms landing random hits on my body, his feet driving into mine. I flinch from the blows but maintain my hold against him. He shouldn't mess with someone who fights for money.

He shouldn't mess with me.

"Adrian, stop! Let him go. Please. I don't want you to get in trouble." More shrieking lands on my eardrums, but I seem to be in a daze. "Adrian! Please." Emily's sweet voice pierces through the veil and I release Ryan. He collapses on the grass next to me, coughing and wheezing.

Panting harshly, I get up and notice Emily first, her hands clutching my arm as she stares at me with tears in her eyes. My pulse thunders in my ears as my fingers trail across her cheeks and wipe off the wetness there. Slowly, I walk back toward Ryan and murmur with barely concealed rage, "Don't you *dare* talk shit about the people I love."

Ryan struggles against his teammates' clutches as they pull him away and the rest of the environment slowly comes into focus. A small crowd has now gathered around us, the whispers and pointing, all white noise I don't give a shit about as my gaze trails back to my pixie.

"I'm sorry for scaring you," I murmur as I prowl toward her, each step feeling like I'm walking toward an inevitability.

I'm tired of staying away, of denying myself.

I'm tired of living for other people.

Emily parts her lips, her eyes widening as I approach her. Her dark hair gleams under the afternoon sun. "W-Why are you here? I thought you had to work?"

Reaching into my pocket, I pull out my wallet and take out a twenty. Placing it in front of a wide-eyed Sarah, I tug Emily to her booth and push her gently inside.

As the velvet curtain drops behind us and we're cloaked in relative darkness with only the small ray of daylight streaming in from the window, I reach out and gently cradle her face, my fingers smoothing over her silky skin.

"I can't leave here without kissing you."

Her eyes widen, her pupils dilating as she gasps. Tangling one hand in her luscious locks, the other still caressing her cheek, I lean in and seal our fates together. My lips graze hers, gently at first as to not scare her even though I want nothing more than to devour her whole. She moans and shifts closer to me, her arms curling around my waist. I nip at the plump bottom lip that has been tormenting me in my dreams, earning myself a whimper. She tastes of strawberries and sunshine laced with dark chocolate. She feels like an angel with a devil's body in my arms.

My cock stiffens and I wrap my fist around her hair, my other hand trailing down her back and tugging her flush against me, her softness against my hardness. My tongue teases the seam of her lips and she whimpers, opening slightly, inviting me in.

That's when I lose it.

I release her hair and hoist her up, her tiny body fitting against mine in all the ways that matter, and I devour her mouth, my tongue sweeping against hers in a war of dominance in which there are no losers. My palms cup her curvy ass, squeezing the tender flesh the way I've wanted to for so long, and she locks her legs firmly around my back. I grind her against me, my hard cock scraping against her clothing-clad pussy as I trail kisses down her neck, seeking the source of the addictive scent of lilies. She lets out another loud moan.

"Shhh... You don't want everyone to hear us and know what we're doing in here, do you?" I nip at her ear as she shudders against me.

"A-Adrian...oh my God..." she stutters, and I claim her lips against mine again and move harder against her. I can come just like this, rutting against her like an animal in heat, all the while standing up with all our clothes between us.

"Yes, say my name again, Pixie," I growl against her ear.

"Adrian..."

I gyrate my hips desperately against her as she rubs against me in a maddening rhythm. My lips claim hers again for another scorching kiss. She tastes like fire and ice and everything in be-tween.

I can't get enough.

Someone coughs in the background, but I barely notice. The coughing sounds louder until I hear Sarah's voice. "You guys, um... Time to get the show on the road, my turn in the kissing booth so uh...wrap up whatever you guys are doing, yeah?"

Emily whimpers in frustration as she releases my bottom lip and she opens her eyes, which are hazy with pleasure. Groaning, I slide her down my body, the friction the most exquisite torture. I want to haul her off to a dark room somewhere and finish what we started. Panting harshly in the dim light, we disentangle from each other. I smooth my hand over her messy locks as she bites her bottom lip. I trail my finger across her face, releasing the lip from her teeth and wiping off the lipstick marks around her mouth. She gasps, her lips appear bee-stung from our kisses, and I almost haul her against me again.

My cock is so hard, I could blow with one stroke down the shaft. I adjust my pants, and her eyes zero in on the motion, her small frame heaving with tension. Slowly, I slip off my jacket and tie it around my waist, a poor attempt at hiding the massive tent in my pants. I step back, my arm sweeping out to open the curtain covering the door. Emily exits the booth in a trance and I follow silently, even though my heart feels like it's going to give out in my chest at any minute.

Sarah pulls Emily aside, whispering something in her ear as Emily flushes the prettiest shade of pink. Her gaze lands on mine again as I slowly back away, my eyes holding her as I'm robbed of speech, but I don't think words are necessary. My fingers clench before tilting up in a half wave, and I walk toward my car with the feeling of her lips against mine, the sweetness of her on my tongue, and the knowledge I'm changed forever.

CHAPTER 13

Emily

"**S**o, spill. Who's putting that look on your face?" Liz Chapman, Jess's best friend, James's older sister, asks as she sits on my bed and waits for me while I get ready for my piano recital at school. She decided to meet earlier at the house to catch up before we head there together. Jess is also on her way from ULA.

"What are you talking about?"

"Don't you deny it. Your eyes had this faraway sheen to them just now, as if you were thinking of something...or someone," she teases as she tucks a curl of her golden-brown hair behind her ear.

Liz is twenty-five and a close family friend. When I was younger, she was more like an older sister to me, but now that I'm finally nearing my twenties, we seem to have more in common.

"You need to get your eyes checked. I'm just thinking about the recital later on," I murmur as I spritz myself with makeup setting spray.

The truth is, my mind was elsewhere and has been far away since a week ago, when Adrian gave me the hottest kiss I've ever experienced. I've replayed that kiss more than once in my mind, and each time, my heart flutters in my chest, heat gathers in my core, and I find myself wanting to relive that moment over and over again. I've dated and fooled around with boys before, but have never gone all the way with any of them because none of them felt "right."

None of them elicit the feelings Adrian easily draws out of me with a simple kiss.

Last week, after I went to the dance with the girls and stayed there for two hours, I feigned a headache, which I suspected Sarah saw straight through, went home to change, and rushed to the beach to see if Adrian was there. He stood in our spot, his hair still damp from his earlier fight at the ring, waiting for me, and wrapped me in his arms as the waves lapped gently on the shores. Everything felt right in his embrace. I felt safe and loved, like everything will be okay in the world as long as he's by my side.

I don't need bouquets of flowers. I don't need presents. I don't need fancy meals.

I only need him.

He could only stay there for half an hour because he had to go home to study for an exam the next day, but it was the most glorious thirty minutes of my life. I bandaged his raw knuckles as best as I could. It's the least I could do for him while he fights to survive. Adrian intertwined his hands with mine as we sat there side by side, my head on his shoulders, and we just breathed and existed.

No worries, no fears, no disguises. Just the two of us.

He gave me another panty-melting kiss before we left the beach and, frankly, I don't think I've recovered from the experience.

Nor do I want to.

"You're doing that thing with your eyes again," Liz snickers, her blue eyes twinkling.

Rolling my eyes, I turn to her. "What about you? Any special someone in your life? How was Valentine's Day?"

Just then, the soft voice of my older sister filters up to the second floor.

"Jess! You're here," Liz exclaims as Jess steps into my room, carrying a small paper bag.

"Liz, I haven't seen you in so long. So glad you could make it!" Jess smiles at our longtime friend before turning to me. "Ems, I got you the *tres leches* cake you loved from the bakery across campus when you visited last time. You'll rock the recital. I'm so excited!" She hands me the bag as she plops down next to Liz on my bed.

"Thanks, sis, I'm actually pretty hungry. I skipped lunch earlier, so I'm going to dig in." I eagerly take out the cake and lick my lips. "You guys want any?"

"No thank you, I'm full," Liz responds.

Jess shakes her head and purses her lips as her eyes are glued to the cake. She's no doubt thinking about her diet or Mother's ridiculous comments about her appearance. She's beautiful, but no matter what I tell her, I can't seem to get through to her. Perhaps it's because she got the brunt of Mother's criticisms, but when it came to me, I just never even tried to measure up to her unrealistic standards.

I scoop one big bite of creamy goodness onto my fork and bring it to my lips, tasting the fluffy frosting first before savoring the rest of the cake. Screw diets. Desserts all the way.

"Before you arrived, I was just asking dear Ems over here who was putting this dreamy look on her face," Liz unhelpfully says just as I stuff my mouth full with cake, unable to defend myself. What a cheater.

Jess's eyes widen. "You have a guy, Ems?"

I shake my head vigorously as I try to swallow the dessert as fast as I can. Damn it, I need water.

"She's saying she doesn't, but I don't believe her."

"If you have someone...and I won't force you to tell me before you're ready, just try your best to keep it from Mother. I don't want you to go through what I went through in high school," Jess comments, her brows pinching together as if she's remembering the many arguments she had with our parents over the boys she was interested in.

Finally, swallowing the last bits of cake, I hold up a finger and take a sip of water before replying, "Hypothetically speaking, if there is *someone* I may be interested in, but he's definitely not any-one Mother would approve of, what would you do?"

The girls look at each other before Jess answers, "Hide it or wait until you move out of here and go to college, where she won't be on your case twenty-four seven. She won't be able to sabotage your relationship then."

College. Will Adrian be going to college? Perhaps we can go to the same school, far away from here? The wings of hope flutter anew as I think of the possibilities of our future.

Knock. Knock.

"Hey, Mother is calling us. It's time to get going, don't want to be late," Steven hollers from the other side of the door.

Jess gives me a side hug before we leave the room. "You can call me anytime if you ever want to chat, okay?"

I nod as we head downstairs. Steven rolls his eyes when he sees us. "Why are girls so slow? And what are you whispering about? *Women*," he mutters the last word under his breath with the tone of a grumpy old man, not a fifteen-year-old.

"Mark my words, Steven, one day, one of these 'slow girls' will be your downfall." I give him a playful shove as we head out the door.

. . .

The auditorium is packed to the brim with people. There are the immaculately dressed high society fashionistas with their equally model-esque looking husbands and kids, turning their noses down at anyone who appears to be less well-off than they are. Then, there is the more "normal" variation, if there's such a thing at Warwick, the families in polo shirts and dresses, with nary a hair out of place. It's like the Palos Verdes Elite Country Club has gathered in this one tiny room.

I glance at the doors from behind the curtains on the stage, wondering if he'll show up. Today is a Saturday, so he is most likely at home helping with Millie or his dad or at the hospital spending time with his mom. Adrian has so many responsibilities, far more than an average guy his age. I didn't want to disrupt his schedule by asking him to come, even though I secretly wish he were here to cheer me on.

Ryan and his equally blond family sit in the second row with my parents. Jess and Liz spy me from afar and give me a quick wave. Steven sits on the side, his face buried in a book. Sarah is with Chelsea and a few girls from our squad in the back. I can see them gesturing excitedly to each other, talking about God knows what. A few minutes later, the emcee walks onto the stage, and the lights dim in the auditorium.

"Welcome, ladies and gentlemen, to the much-anticipated musical recital of our gifted students here at Warwick. As you know, we have one of the best high school musical programs in the country, so I know this will be a treat for everyone. First up, we have our beloved senior and cheer captain, Emily Kingsley, with two pieces, Claude Debussy's *Clair de Lune* and Ludwig van Beethoven's "Piano Sonata No. 14," "Moonlight Sonata." Please welcome Miss Kingsley to the stage."

Applause rings out and I faintly hear Sarah's, "Go get them, girl," as I step onto the floor. The bright stage lights temporarily blind me, and I slowly move toward the grand piano in the center. Anticipation bubbles in my veins as I approach my beloved instrument. Smoothing my hands on my blue velvet flounce dress, I sit down and take a deep breath as the room quiets until the only sound I hear is my own breathing.

My fingers move over the keys as my heart beats to the hopeful melody of *Clair de Lune*. This piece, along with the "Moonlight Sonata," are both favorites of mine, and are both tributes to the beauty of the moonlight. There's a famous quote, which some attribute to Debussy himself and others believe it was Mozart who said, "The music is not in the notes, but in the silence between." I used to think that made no sense, but now I understand. The music I love is just like a person I know, so much unsaid, yet so much lies in his actions, his gazes, his caresses. That's what makes Adrian mesmerizing. That's what makes the music beautiful. My head sways to the melody, my soul floating away at the high notes, falling at the low keys as the room slowly melts away, leaving me alone with my music...and with him.

The time flies by and suddenly, I find myself at the last few chords and I let out the breath I've been holding in toward the end of the score as applause filters in to my ears. Glancing up, I see my family clapping, politely of course, because there's no way they'd do anything as outrageous as cheering out loud. Steven lets out a shrill whistle, earning him a glare from Mother. I grin and wink at my pesky little brother. My eyes involuntarily scan the rest of the room, hoping to see a familiar tuft of brown hair, so dark it's almost the color of the midnight sky. But he isn't here.

Disappointment slices through me as the room settles and I begin my second performance, a piece that'll forever remind me of him, the "Moonlight Sonata." As I strike my first chords, I hear the faint sound of the doors opening. A brief stream of light illuminates the room. My eyes flicker up and I see him.

Adrian, standing at the back, a tall, reassuring presence, so far away, yet I feel his aura intensely. Heat travels through me, my heart pounding to the beats of the music, as if it senses its other half nearby. I can feel the weight of his stare as I continue playing. Soon, I'm transported into the world of dark seas and cold nights, but I'm warm as if he's next to me, curling himself around me, sheltering me from the wind. I glance up again, my lips tilting in a smile as our gazes connect, and I play for him, and only for him.

Turning my face back to the piano, I close my eyes and my fingers waltz with the keys as we twirl and twirl around the notes, the chords, the haunting melodies with him by my side, in a dance that may go nowhere because my family will never approve of him.

But I don't care. I'll fight. I'll wait. And if he'll have me, perhaps this feeling in my heart is what Juliet felt toward her Romeo. Perhaps this is why lovers leap into the unknown, without regard to consequences.

The music reaches a crescendo, a series of complicated chords and scales, as my soul soars with the music, the hope and anticipation for the future laced in my blood, my heart pounding against my rib cage and I finish the sonata in a flourish, my breathing coming out in short pants, as if I ran a mile or leaped into the dark abyss with nothing but a parachute.

Thrilling. Enthralling.

The auditorium erupts in applause as I slowly stand and dip into a curtsy. My eyes find Adrian again and he smiles at me and bites his bottom lip, his hands clapping vigorously, as if he knew I was playing only for him. Butterflies flutter in my chest, taking my breath away as happiness radiates from inside me.

I wait in the backroom with the other musicians, tapping my legs and glancing at the clock, wanting to go back out there to find him. After the recital is finally over, I rush out to the main space, eager to see if Adrian stayed behind.

"Ems! You were brilliant." Liz rushes up to me and envelops me in a warm hug.

"Thank you." My eyes rove the background, searching for him.

She pulls away. "I just wanted to tell you how proud I am of you." She checks her watch and says, "By the way, I need to run an errand and will meet you guys for dinner, okay?"

I nod as she sprints away.

My eyes search for him through the crowds of people gathering around, as photo ops were occurring in front of the stage, and congratulatory messages were being passed around.

Damn it. I can't see him. The torture of being too short.

"Looking for me?" A deep, husky voice, as smooth as the richest chocolate, sounds from behind me.

I turn around and find him staring at me, his sky-blue eyes brimming with warmth, his full lips tipping up in a wide smile, a rarity on his face.

"You came." I let out a breath.

"I wouldn't miss it for the world." He breathes in.

I stand there, grinning like a madwoman, my heart pounding so hard it feels like it may give out at any moment. He reaches out, his large palm cupping my face, and I lean into it, my eyes fluttering closed. A scent of mint wafts through the air as he suddenly pulls me into his arms.

"My pixie is so breathtaking. You're so talented. I don't know what I ever did to deserve you," he whispers against my temple, his breath eliciting shivers in me.

"No. It's the other way around, Adrian. You have so much on your plate, so many things on your shoulders. I don't know what I ever did to earn a place in your life, to be part of the group of people you care about." *And maybe more.*

He eases me apart as he pulls out our signature flowers, three of them today, from a Grocery for Less paper bag he was carrying. He must have been at work before he rushed over. He has been working extra shifts lately. Things must be tough for him at home.

"A special occasion...so, three lilies this time."

I clasp the aromatic flowers in my hand and bring them up to my nose for a sniff. This was my favorite smell before I met Adrian, but now it has become an irreplaceable scent in my life. One that'll forever remind me of him.

"Thank you. You know you don't need to keep giving me flowers. I know things are tight—"

"I want to. A little bit more scrimping on my end is worth it to see the smile on your face." His reply was immediate, as if he didn't even need to think about it.

Inhaling a deep breath, I curl my arms around his neck, pull his head down, and brush my lips against his cheek—we're in public after all, even though I'd want nothing more than to have his lips on mine. And judging from the way his fingers dig into my waist, he's feeling the same way.

"Emily, who is this?"

The warmth cloaking my entire body quickly dissipates at Mother's voice, which is grating with disapproval. A cold front travels across my body as dread seeps in.

We disentangle from each other and face my family and apparently Ryan's family trailing close behind.

Swallowing the lump in my throat, I clasp one hand in front of another to stop my trembles. Thinking back to Jess's words earlier, *"Hide it or wait until you move out of here and go to college."* I don't want Mother to cause any trouble for Adrian, and she has the power to make things uncomfortable for him at school, with her close friendship with the headmaster.

"This is Adrian Callahan. He's my..." I look at him, imploring him to understand my intentions. "Friend."

Adrian furrows his brows, almost imperceptibly. My fingers twitch, wanting to hold his hand in mine.

"Adrian, these are my parents, Audrey and Robert Kingsley."

A muscle tics in his jaw and he flinches, the movement so small and subtle, I wouldn't have noticed if I didn't know him so well. Adrian takes a deep breath and reaches his hand out to my parents. "Mr....and Mrs. Kingsley." His voice is deeper, heavier, with something I can't place.

Something flickers in Father's gaze, gone as quickly as it appears. My father straightens up, his hazel eyes sharp as he stares at Adrian, before he takes his hand in a brief shake. Mother examines Adrian, her eyes traveling from head to toe, no doubt cataloging every aspect that makes him "unsuitable." Her eyes linger on the split lip on his face, then travel to his jacket, which hangs loosely on his frame, down to the faded jeans with a small hole in the pockets, something I hadn't even noticed before until now. She gives him her society shake, her fingers touching the tips of his fingers before turning back to me, clearly considering him as inconsequential.

Anger boils in my veins at their chilly reception. I clench my fists, wanting to give them a piece of my mind, but refrain from doing so, knowing that'll embarrass Adrian. Instead, I clutch both hands around the lilies and twist my face up in a smile, my jaw aching from gritting my teeth together.

"He was just congratulating me on a successful recital."

"Of course it was successful. We'd expect nothing less from you. It'd be an embarrassment if it weren't." Mother's clipped reply causes me to falter for a bit.

Just then, Jess and Steven walk up to us. I relax a smidge, thankful for reinforcements. Turning to Adrian, I say, "This is my older sister, Jess, and my younger brother, Steven." I then face them and add, "This is Adrian." I don't downplay our relationship. Somehow, I don't want to lie to my siblings.

Jess's eyes land on me before breaking into a warm smile. "Nice to meet you, Adrian." Steven waves and his gaze travels to mine, his lips twitching in an attempt not to smile.

Adrian visibly relaxes with the earnest welcome from my siblings. Then Ryan and his family walk up to us.

"Mr. and Mrs. Kingsley, Emmie was so brilliant today. I was completely speechless." Ryan flashes his pearly whites at my parents and Mother warms a smidge. He turns toward me and hands me an enormous bouquet of roses, probably at least two dozen of them. I've never been too fond of roses—I prefer my flowers without thorns, the beauty without the pain.

"Thank you." I gather the bouquet in one hand, the three lilies in the other. The beauty of the three simple flowers far exceeds the dozens of the roses. Adrian shifts uncomfortably as he stands next to me.

"Mr. and Mrs. Kingsley, we're going to dinner now at Montclair's to celebrate Emmie's success, right? I called ahead and made sure they had your favorite Merlot waiting for you." Ryan walks up next to me, shoving Adrian behind me, and attempts to throw his arm around my shoulder. I shrug him off and take a step back toward Adrian, who is so still, one can barely tell he's there, except I can feel the heat and restrained anger emanating from him. Transferring the lilies to the other hand, I reach out behind me and twine my fingers around his, out of sight of my parents.

Adrian's hand tenses...then he slowly slides his fingers along mine, an intimate dance only we are privy to. My breath catches in my throat as my nerves awaken.

"Yes, Ryan, you're so kind. Let's go now, so we won't be late." Mother smiles at Ryan before walking away, not sparing a glance at us. My parents and his family talk quietly amongst themselves as they walk toward the doors.

"I'll be there shortly. You guys go ahead," I tell Jess and Steven, who have stayed behind.

"Okay, nice to meet you, Adrian." Jess smiles at him as he dips his head in acknowledgement. Her eyes meet mine with a question in her gaze before she follows the group.

Steven smirks. "Nice to meet your *friend*, sis." He turns to Adrian and says, "Hope you treat your *friends* well...or else." He then stalks off.

I let out a deep breath before turning to Adrian.

"I'm sorry, if I were to tell my parents what we are, they'd—"

"What are we, Emily?" Adrian stares at our interlinked hands and slowly lets go, his head shaking as if he's disappointed in himself. He's not calling me his pixie anymore.

An arrow pierces through my chest, the pain so excruciating, I could barely breathe. "What do you mean? I'm your pixie."

His blue eyes meet mine, the torment apparent in his gaze. "Are you?" he scoffs and looks down again. "I-I can't give you what you deserve, Emily. And you don't know the entire truth about my family, my dad...never mind."

"I don't need anything from you other than yourself!" I whisper, gripping his arm, the bouquet of flowers falling to the floor. I don't give a shit about them.

Adrian looks around, as if remembering we're in a public place. He slowly peels my hand off his arm. "This is not the time or place. But maybe some relationships are best left unexplored. Leave when everything is at a high, when everything is beautiful. Before it all collapses and the ugliness seeps in."

Nausea roils in my gut as tears prickle my eyes. *Why is he saying these things? Why is he doing this to me?*

I glance away, blinking my eyes rapidly. I won't cry, not in here. Not for him. He won't even try to fight for me. I deserve more.

"Look, I need to go back to work. I just want to support you as your...*friend*," he whispers. His face is contorted with what looks like pain and he turns away, leaving me standing in the auditorium, feeling like I've landed at the bottom of the abyss, only to find out there's nothing but darkness and agony there.

The atmosphere is stifling at Montclair's, a fancy French restaurant with the usual white linen tablecloths, five-star waitstaff, names of dishes most people can't pronounce. Liz and Jess are chatting softly. Ryan is laughing at something Mother is saying, and Mother isn't a humorous person, so I don't even know how he fakes it. Steven is working hard at the specialty breadbasket.

I just want to throw up and cry.

My hands twist the napkin on my lap as my thoughts keep returning to Adrian. Why would he say these things right after he met my family? Everything was fine before. It doesn't make sense. Was he angry I introduced him as a friend? Why wouldn't he let me explain?

"Emily, prom is in a month or so. Have you gotten your dress made yet?"

"Huh?" I look up, finding Mother's shrewd eyes on me.

She sighs before blotting her lips with her napkin. "Prom? You only get one senior prom. Did you make any appointments with the designers to get your dress made?"

"I haven't yet." I couldn't care less about prom at this point. Funny how things change in a matter of months.

"Emily Kingsley," Mother begins. "I thought you already—"

"Now, now, Audrey, I'm sure Emily will look resplendent in anything she wears. Ryan and her are the cutest couple," Ryan's mom chimes in, attempting to diffuse the tension. "Right, Emily?"

I stare at the napkin on my lap, my fingers twisting it into a convoluted mess.

Steven's hand snakes in front of me as he taps on the table imperceptibly. I glance at him, finding his dark-brown gaze staring intently at me. My little brother can be very perceptive sometimes. *You okay?* he mouths, his face devoid of the usual arrogance of a fifteen-year-old.

Taking a deep breath, I set my napkin down and look up, finding everyone's eyes on me. "I'm sorry, everyone. I'm feeling unwell. I think I'm going to go home early." I stand and push my chair back.

Liz places her napkin on the table as well. "Emily, you don't have a car. I'll drive you. Jess, you stay. It's a family dinner, after all. I'm just tagging along."

Jess's eyes meet mine, a small frown on her face. I know she'll grill me later. Mother's lips are pressed in a firm line, displeasure written all over her face.

"Emmie, I can take you," Ryan offers.

I shake my head. "No thank you. You stay and enjoy dinner."

Liz links her arms with mine as she leads me out of the restaurant to her car. The sun has set not long ago, with the darkness chasing away the rosy hues in the evening sky. A moist chill permeates the air, but I barely notice. I just want to go home and curl under the covers of my bed. I don't even want to go to the beach tonight.

The car ride to my house is quiet except for the noises in my head. Liz glances over once or twice, her hand reaching to pat mine in reassurance, but doesn't comment on much. She's always so considerate and kind. I hope I can be like her in the future. Stopping in front of our gates, she finally says, "Ems, I know something is going on. Whatever it is, whenever you feel like you want to talk about it, let me know, okay?"

I let out a ragged breath and give her a sad smile. "Will do. Thank you, Liz. If you talk to Jess later tonight, tell her not to worry, okay? Even though I'm sure she'll chat with me soon."

Liz nods and I wave before walking through the gates and letting myself in the dark, quiet house. It's still too roomy for my comfort. The darkness is overwhelming tonight. A part of me still feels like the scared five-year-old little girl who cried herself to sleep in the closet.

I flick on the lights as I enter each space. Foyer. Living room. Hallway. Stairs. Another hallway. My bedroom. I know it's a waste of electricity, but right now, I don't want to challenge my fears. I just want comfort and the feeling of safety. Plopping down on my chair, I brush my hair as I take in my appearance in the mirror. Pale face, large eyes, small lips. I still look like the Emily Kingsley who returned from winter break, looking forward to prom and graduation. Why do I feel so different inside?

You know why, a voice whispers inside me.

Letting out an exhale, I change out of my dress into my cotton sleep shirt and climb into bed. I turn on the TV, surfing the channels until it lands on a familiar scene, Meg Ryan meeting Tom Hanks on top of the Empire State Building in *Sleepless in Seattle.* The happily-ever-after. My eyes tear up as I recall that night at the beach with Adrian.

Tap. Tap.

I mute my TV and crane my ears to listen.

Nothing.

Just as I was about to press the unmute button, I hear it again.

Tap. Tap. Tap.

My heart thuds loudly in my chest as a chill rushes through my body. Glancing around my room, I notice my softball bat propped up in the corner by my closet. I quickly get out of bed and retrieve the bat, then slowly creep up to the sliding French doors.

Tap. Tap.

My pulse throbs in my ears as I pull the thick curtain aside and peer outside. A smattering of pebbles flies to the window from below the balcony. Huh?

This is a bad idea. Don't go out there. Don't be an idiot. Call the cops, Emily.

Just as I turn around to grab my phone from my desk, I hear his voice.

"Emily! Pixie! Are you there? I see the light in your room. Emily?"

Adrian.

I quickly drop my bat and open the sliding doors. I dash onto the balcony, the cold air greeting me by surprise as I forgot to put a jacket on over my thin sleep shirt.

Leaning over the stone railing, I see him standing there, still clad in the T-shirt and jeans from earlier, his hair in disarray, as if he's spent the last few hours tugging it, his eyes blazing with desperation. His hands are full of pebbles he no doubt gathered from the small garden near the first floor.

"Adrian? What are you doing here? How do you know where I live?" I whisper, glancing around. It appears no one is home yet and the neighbors have not been alerted.

"I can't!" His voice is deep with passion.

"What?"

"I-I tried. I tried walking away, but I can't do it, Pixie. I just can't."

My pulse riots inside me and I'm bewildered at this turn of events. "What do you mean? You hurt me, Adrian. What you said earlier when you tossed me away like I was meaningless." Tears prickle my eyes as I remember those agonizing moments in the auditorium.

"I'm sorry. I didn't mean those words...at the moment, I thought how you'd be so much better off without me and I..." He tugs at his hair again as he starts pacing on the lawn. "I can't give you anything other than myself and I thought it was selfish of me to make you suffer by being with me." Adrian looks up, wetness shining in his eyes. "Please, please give me a chance. I'm so sorry for hurting you."

Swallowing the lump in my throat, the anger fading into hurt, I whisper, "Come up before anyone sees you." I point to the oak tree I use as a climbing device during my regular excursions to the beach at night.

He climbs up with the stealth and the speed of an agile cat, his lean muscles flexing with each movement. A few short moments later, he swings his long legs over the railing and stands in front of me, slightly out of breath.

We stare at each other in silence, our breaths fogging up the tiny space in between us. I stare into his beautiful eyes, dark and glittering under the moonlight. His body is coiled with tension and I shiver, not knowing if it's from the cold or from...him.

His eyes trail down to my body and he sharply inhales. I follow his line of sight and notice my nipples have pebbled up from the chill, saluting against the thin cotton shirt. His breathing grows more ragged as he drags his gaze back to mine, his pupils dilating. A molten heat gathers at my core as the nerves come alive.

Wordlessly, I back away from him and step back into my room. He prowls toward me, his steps silent as he crosses the threshold, closing the doors and the curtains behind him. The room is quiet and dim, except for the faint glow from the television.

"Why would you feel this way...about everything, Adrian? How did you find me?" My heart still beats for him despite everything.

He stalks forward as I tread back, my feet accidentally stepping on the remote, which must have fallen to the ground in my haste to investigate the tapping sound. The room plunges into darkness with no illumination other than the soft glow of moonlight filtering through the curtains.

"I asked Sarah, and she told me where you live and which room is yours." He clenches his hands into fists. "I didn't mean any of it," he rasps, the deep timbre of his voice sending shivers through me.

He steps forward again. I continue backing away.

"For the last few hours, I've tried convincing myself why I'm not worthy of you. Why I should stay away from you. Why you would be better off without me dragging you down with me. My parents are a prime example of what happens when two people who are worlds apart get together. Mom...she couldn't even get the healthcare she needs because we are poor. She gave everything up to be with my dad. And I'm scared of what will happen if you stay with me, and not only because I'm poor and you're rich. That's a big part of it, but...someday, you may find out something that'll make you think differently of my family."

My back hits the wall by my bed as he advances toward me. I dig my fingers against the wallpaper for support.

"What do you mean? Adrian, I like you not because of how much money you have or don't have. I like you because of you, not because of your family or connections. I...I just want you, that's all I want, and you threw my feelings away as if they didn't mean anything..." Tears gather in my eyes, the pain from earlier still fresh.

Adrian steps in front of me until he's but a hairsbreadth away. The faint light illuminates the sharp angle of his nose, a portion of his face, and his eyes, so dark and blazing with intensity. "I should've stood firm. I shouldn't have wavered. I'm sorry. At that moment, I just felt so unworthy and I thought perhaps... Perhaps things would be better if we stopped our relationship at a high before it inevitably collapses."

He lets out a ragged exhale, his voice thickening. "But I *can't*. Please forgive me. I can't stay away from you...and I don't want to. Screw the world. Let's live for us. Let's not think of the future, of what-ifs, and just live in the present. You and me." He touches his forehead against mine. He closes his eyes, his breath ghosting over my face as he whispers, "Please, continue being my pixie."

Tears fall from my eyes and I say the only thing I can say, the only answer to his question. "Yes. I'll always be your pixie. But please..." I touch his lips and he presses a kiss against my finger. "Talk to me if you feel this way in the future. Just...talk to me."

He curls his hands on my face, his thumb brushing off my tears. His eyes open, wetness tipping his lashes. He nods.

"Thank you."

Adrian's lips descend on mine. My heart blossoms as my body relaxes against his, the earlier agony fading and, in its place, a blistering heat. He nips and chases. I grapple and swipe. One of his hands curls around my head and the other travels down my back, sending flutters of pleasure down my body. He tugs me tightly against him as he leans down and devours my lips. I moan with each suction, whimper with each lick. He groans as he teases my mouth apart, his tongue slipping in, tangling with mine in an intimate dance. My body is on fire, and I want to throw myself into the burgeoning flames.

"I can't get enough of you, Pixie. I'll never get enough of you," he whispers, his voice hoarse as our kiss ratchets in intensity. His hand inches up my sleep shirt, his fingers grazing the sensitive skin of my thigh, traveling to my hips, hovering around my waist. Wetness pools between my legs. His hard cock, within the confines of his jeans, presses against me.

I wrap my legs around him as I chase his hardness, just like that day at the kissing booth, except this is much hotter, with less clothing between us, in the darkness of my room. I feel every single sensation as I rub my underwear on the seam of his pants.

Adrian grunts as he palms my ass, squeezing the muscles there. I arch back, baring my neck to him, and he traces his lips down the column of my throat, drawing another whimper from me. His face nuzzles my breasts over my shirt and he sucks in one of my nipples, the nip and abrasiveness of the cotton, creating an erotic sensation I haven't experienced before. I mewl, squirming against him.

He carries me to the bed and lays me on top of it. He slowly crawls over me, settling part of his weight on me as his hands slip inside of my shirt again, reaching my breasts, which feel very sensitive and swollen.

"Have you done this before? Has anyone touched you here?" He plucks at my nipples and I arch back with another moan.

I shake my head. "Guys have tried, but I've always stopped them."

He grunts his approval before trailing his hand to my wet underwear. His fingers trail the lace from the outside, hovering over my clit. "What about here? No one has touched you down here before?"

Moaning, I shake my head as his finger rubs light circles around my clit, not giving enough pressure, a tantalizing preview of what he can do. Slowly, he slides the damp lace to the side and his fingers come in contact with the hardened nub.

"Adrian, please, I need..." I whimper against his fingers as he flicks my clit.

"What do you need, Pixie? Do you need to come? Do you want to come on my hand?"

"Y-Yes...I need you, Adrian." My hips tilt toward his fingers, urging them faster.

He groans, his lips swallowing mine in another ravaging kiss. "What my pixie wants, I'll deliver." He slides one finger inside me, my muscles clenching at the foreign sensation. Then he uses his thumb to circle my clit as his finger curls and moves inside me, the combination a sensation so sharp and intense, I let out a loud cry.

"Shhh...what if your family comes home? You don't want them to hear, right?" He moves his fingers faster against me, his thumb rubbing harder around my clit. Molten heat builds in my core as I thrash underneath him, fighting my desire to get away from the barrage of sensations, or to succumb to them. "Your pussy is so wet and tight. Someday...my cock will be here, taking you hard, so you'll be mine and mine alone." He grunts as if he's climbing the pinnacle with me.

The fire builds between my legs and he pins me down, rendering me immobile as he continues his savage finger fucking. The slurping sound of his finger inside my pussy is loud in the quiet room, accompanying our harsh breathing like an erotic symphony.

"Come, Pixie. Come for me. I want to see you cream my hand." His voice is low and guttural at this point, his words sending me over the edge.

"Adrian!" I shriek and fall off the cliff, the warmth bursting into a thousand sensations. He captures my cries with his mouth. His fingers continue to move inside me as my muscles clench against him.

"Yes, that's it. Give it to me," he whispers against my lips. I tremble against him, my juices leaking out.

As I slowly come down from the best orgasm I've ever experienced, my body lethargic and relaxed, I hear the front door closing in a loud *bang*. Adrian freezes on top of me, his panting harsh against my ear.

Shit, they're home.

He rolls off me and adjusts his pants, which still showcase a very hard cock threatening to break out of his jeans. He leans down and kisses me softly on the lips. "Thank you for forgiving me, my pixie, and for being with me."

I motion to his pants. "I'm sorry you didn't get to... You look so uncomfortable."

"This night is for you, not for me."

Footsteps thud up the staircase and fear creeps through my body. "You have to leave, Adrian. They can't find you here."

He nods as he backs away toward the French doors, his eyes never leaving mine. He opens the door and presses his hand across his heart before disappearing out into the night. My heart races in my chest as throbbing lingers between my thighs, and now I know why Juliet risked everything to be with her Romeo.

I close the door softly behind me, careful to not wake anyone up when I return home from my shift at the grocery store. The gym is closed today, so I'll be headed straight for the beach after I swing by to pick up Emily's jacket. She left it at my place last weekend when we stopped by because she was curious about where I lived. Dad took Millie to meet her friend that day. As much as I want to introduce Emily to my family, I don't want to have to explain to Dad why I'm dating the daughter of the very family he stole from. That conversation won't end well.

Creeping quietly to the living room, I spot her suede jacket in the corner of the sofa, half-hidden by my stack of textbooks. Rolling my shoulders, I wince at the soreness there, all courtesy of my fights in the ring. As much as I was against the illegal fights in the first place, it has become some sort of an outlet for me, akin to cracking open the lid slightly on a pot on the stove to let out some steam before the contents boil over. A few letters are on the coffee table. I glance at them as I was about to pick up the jacket. They're all addressed to me. My heart skips several beats, an electrifying hum of anticipation filters through my body, the muscle aches temporarily forgotten.

My hands shaking, I pick up the three letters and look at the senders. Cornell University. University of Los Angeles. Berkeley. These three nondescript envelopes may hold my future. I not only need to get into college, but I also need financial aid.

My fingers carefully pry open the Cornell letter, my dream school, first. Nausea churns in my gut. It's thin. Surely, that must be a bad sign, right? Taking a deep breath, I take out the letter and unfold it.

Dear Adrian,

Congratulations! The admissions selection committee in the College of Arts and Sciences approved your application for admission to Cornell University...

Tears gather in my eyes as a jolt of elation rushes through me, the potency so strong, so sudden, it's as if lightning has struck. I want to cry; I want to scream; I want to hit something, to hug someone. I want to yell from the rooftops that I, Adrian Callahan, is giving a big middle finger to the world, because things are going to change.

Finally.

Fuck. I got in. I did it.

I quickly scan the rest of the letter, searching for the financial aid and scholarship components and my heart bursts inside my chest at the words "full ride." A strangled sob escapes my throat and I sit down, my hands trembling as I read the letter over and over again. I shake my head in disbelief, half-expecting to wake up from this dream at any moment. My heart beats in joy, kicking up a strong rhythm, a soundtrack to what very well could be the turning point in my life.

Maybe this is the way out for all of us. I can finally see the spark of hope in my future, in my family's future. I can get us out of this shitshow we're in. My muscles coil in tension, this time not from stress or anger, but from the need to share my news with someone. My first thought goes to Emily, but I'll see her soon, and I can tell her in person.

Just as I'm about to check to see if Dad is awake, the joy thrumming in my veins, I hear a low, muffled sound of sobbing emanating from his room. The happiness from moments ago quickly dissipates as if a bucket of ice water has been poured over the fire, and dread snakes inside me. I approach his room, my hand clutching the acceptance letter in a tight grip.

"Dad? Is everything okay?" I push open the door and find him sitting on the edge of the bed, his face buried in his hands as his shoulders tremble.

My breathing slows as I approach him. The slither of unease morphs into a full inferno. I know something is horribly wrong. Sitting next to him, I carefully place my free hand on his lap.

"Dad?"

He stills and exhales loudly. "They fired me."

My heart sinks. We knew this was a definitive possibility, an inevitability. After all, he is guilty of the crime.

"Are they going to call the cops?"

He shakes his head, still unwilling to look at me. "No. Mr. Kingsley actually let me go. He said I had you and Millie to take care of, along with your mom in the hospital. He...was actually sympathetic for once."

I reflect back to the day I met Emily's father at the recital, the way his eyes sharpened in recognition when she introduced us. No wonder. He knew about me all along. He must think we are a joke. A father who steals, a mother who got cast out by her family...a son who is trying to win his daughter over. I hate it when people pity us...but perhaps it's this pity that's saving my dad from going to jail.

Swallowing the gravel in my throat, I take a deep breath. "Well, at least there's that, Dad. At least you won't be in jail. You can find another job." But with his mental state, will anyone even want to hire him? It doesn't matter. We'll get through this. An impulse bounces through me and I want to tell him the good news, something to offset the bad, something to perhaps provide hope for the future. My fingers drum on his lap. "And in a few years, I'll graduate from college and I'll be able to provide—"

"It's the end of the month next week, Adrian. I'm going to lose our health insurance then. What will we do about your mom's medical costs?" he whispers as he looks at me for the first time tonight, his eyes bloodshot, the familiar hopelessness reflecting back at me.

My palms grow sweaty as my pulse picks up. What are we going to do? The pit in my stomach widens and my heart free falls into the darkness, the earlier elation pulverizing into nothing with each passing second. Maybe ambition and drive aren't enough to change our circumstances. Luck and fate have plans all along and we're all just puppets in this sick, twisted show. Maybe we'll never get out of this. The whiplash between hope and disappointment is disorienting and I want to throw up.

And yet you're still dreaming about a future with your pixie, a girl who has everything, who will most likely need to give it all up to be with you because there's no way her family will accept you into their fold. What a selfish bastard you are, Adrian.

But maybe not. Now that I have the acceptance letter, maybe our path will be different than Mom and Dad's story.

Shaking away the thought, I hold on to the last vestiges of hope. "Find a job, Dad. There has to be something out there. Or..."

A thought occurs to me, one that pierces my heart and rips it to shreds. But it is a distinct possibility, especially with Dad being so fragile right now, his employment prospects are probably not hopeful. The pulse thuds in my ears, the stable beat no longer of joy but of sorrow.

I let out a shaky breath and fold up my acceptance letter into a small square, squeezing it in my palm until the edges of the paper digs sharply into the tender flesh, the physical pain nothing compared to the emotional agony. The letter that was a source of hope is now a weapon of dreams, a thief of what-ifs.

"Maybe...maybe I'll quit school. I can try to get a full-time position at Grocery for Less. My boss likes me there and they've been looking to hire full-time for the produce section. That way, they can give me medical benefits. I'll need to check if California allows for that, but I think if I have dependent parents, they may let me. I'll research."

I close my eyes to fight the wetness prickling behind my eyelids. Deep down, I know this is my path.

He shakes his head, his face mottled and red. "Son, you can't quit school. What about your future? Without your high school diploma... What about college?"

"Nothing is more important than my family, than Mom." Moisture coats my vision and I turn away, blinking rapidly.

This is the agony of soaring to heaven and free-falling into the flames of hell. All in a split second. I wish I could plummet to the ground and never wake up.

I can go to college later, I tell myself. But I know, chances of a full-ride scholarship to Cornell are once in a lifetime.

Dad exhales a ragged breath and places his hand on mine, giving it a soft squeeze. "Y-You've been put through too much at such a young age. I failed as a parent too."

I press my lips together, willing my tears not to fall. We were just dealt a bad hand, that's all. I was forced to grow up sooner than others, but that's okay. I'll rise again like a phoenix from the ashes.

Maybe.

At moments like these, I'm not so sure anymore, and I'm exhausted.

"We'll take it a day at a time. We'll figure something out together, Dad. We need to fight for Mom," I murmur, my voice thick and raspy.

Dad nods before wiping his eyes. "Go to sleep, son. Tomorrow is another day for you. You need rest."

Clenching the letter that made me so happy just moments ago but now is part of the farce that is my life, I walk out of his room to the living room and collapse on the sofa.

After staring into the quiet space for a few minutes, I take out my phone and finally call Emily.

"Adrian?" I hear the sound of waves in the background. She's at the beach already.

"Pixie, I-I..." I clear my throat, not wanting her to hear the despair in my voice.

"Is everything okay?"

"I can't go to the beach tonight. Something happened at home. I need time to think."

"Do you need me to come to your place?" Emily's voice is laced with concern. I can picture a small frown on her face.

I shake my head, even though she can't see me. "No... It's really late already. Why don't you go home and sleep? Call me when you get home safely, okay?"

We hang up and I stare at the blank walls in front of me, my chest heavy, my heart exhausted. The damn wetness in my eyes won't let up. *You need to be tough, Adrian. Someone in this family needs to be.* I repeat the mantra over and over to myself. Even though I want more than anything to be the little boy in elementary school again, burying my head against my mom as she wraps me up in a warm embrace.

To be happy again. To have no worries other than what to wear to school the next day.

Some moments later, there's a soft knock at the door.

I stride to the door and look through the peephole, finding Emily standing there, her hair in a ponytail as she fidgets in place. Frowning, I quickly unlock the door and step outside into the dim hallway.

"Emily? Why are you here? Aren't you supposed to go home?"

She twists her fingers as she replies, "I-I'm so worried about you. Something is wrong, isn't it? Is everything okay, Adrian?"

I look at her, my beautiful pixie, who could be warm in her bed, but instead is out here in front of my crappy apartment, worried about someone like me, and tears threaten to break free again.

Closing my eyes, I reply, "My dad lost his job. We'll lose our health insurance at the end of next week. I don't know what we'll do about Mom's medical bills." I don't want to see sympathy or pity in her eyes.

She gasps before she wraps her arms tightly around me. She may be petite, but she gives the warmest hugs. Her comforting scent of lilies surrounds us, cloaking us in a small bubble. "Your dad works at a bank, right? My father works at TransAmerica and they have a huge banking presence. Maybe I can ask him to give your dad a job?"

I clutch her closer to me, burying my face in her hair. "No, don't. We'll figure it out. Please don't bother your parents." Because I can't tell her it was her father who fired my dad because he stole from them. Mr. Kingsley has the reputation of a shark. The fact he isn't pursuing criminal charges is already a miracle. If his precious daughter begs him in order to help me, a son of a criminal...I'm afraid he may end up pressing charges. I can't risk it.

"I want to help. Please let me do something," she murmurs against my chest.

"Just being here is enough. That's all I need. Dignity is all we have left." I exhale, my breathing loud in the quiet of the night. And in this moment, her being here is all that matters.

CHAPTER 16

Adrian

"**A**drian. I have your dad on the line... It seems urgent." Brandon frowns, the concern in his gaze unsettling as he finds me replenishing the lettuce and cabbage in the produce section, something I'll most likely be doing in the future instead of going to Cornell.

"Why didn't he call my cell?" I murmur to myself as I take out my phone from my pocket. Damn, it's dead. I must have forgotten to plug it in last night. Shaking my head, I walk toward the small office in the back. Dad doesn't usually call me, but sometimes he'd like me to pick up some things for him at the store while I'm here.

It's a quiet Wednesday night after the devastating news Dad delivered last week. He'll have medical insurance for two more days and then we'll be cut off. Dad has been job searching, but as I expected, he hasn't had any offers yet. I already told Brandon of my situation and he's assured me the full-time position in the produce department is mine if I want to take it.

Based on some research I did at the library, it also appears I can claim my parents as my dependents. If I start my full-time job by the end of next month, I'll get health insurance for the entire month. Mom will be covered. Things will be as they should—normal. I haven't said yes yet, even though I know I should. Somehow, I can't bring myself to do it, to resign myself to this reality. Closing the door shut behind me, I take a deep breath and walk over to pick up the phone. The fluorescent lights flicker for a moment.

"Dad? Everything okay? My phone died. Do you need me to pick up something?"

Heavy breathing sounds from across the line. A chill seeps into me.

"Dad, what's wrong?"

He lets out a shaky breath. "S-Son, I'm at the hospital. Can you come right away? It's your mom... Things took a turn for the worse. I don't think we have much time left."

The receiver slips out of my fingers and clatters on the wood desk, the sound jarring in the otherwise quiet room. *No...please, I can't take this anymore.* I pray to anything and anyone who'll listen, but as usual, I'm met with silence.

With shaking hands, I pick up the phone again. "I'll be right there."

I don't remember much about the minutes following Dad's call. Everything is a blur. Jack came into the office when he saw me hunched over the desk after I hung up. I briefly remember him wrapping me in a hug when I told him what happened. He gave Brandon a quick update and insisted on driving me to the hospital, saying I was in no condition to drive. The ride to the hospital was quiet except for the noises in my head, the memories flitting through my mind like a slideshow. Mom baking cookies with me after school. Mom cheering in the stands at my first junior boxing match. Mom hugging me after my first heartbreak in junior high when Sandy Henney said no when I asked her out, saying my clothes are too old and I never do anything fun. Mom and me playing hide and seek with little Millie when she was three years old. Family dinners at our small table where laughter filled the air.

Wetness coats my cheeks as I realize the inevitable is about to happen. Despite all my best efforts, I still can't stop bad things from happening. I can't stop the Russian roulette of life from landing with a bullet in the chamber, aligning with the barrel and inflicting the fatal shot.

"Hey…I know I don't have much and I'm a piece of shit half the time, but if you need anything from me, just let me know," Jack murmurs, his voice thick as he parks the car by the curb next to the front entrance of the hospital.

Swiping the tears away with my fingers, I nod. "Thanks, man. Appreciate it."

"Do you want me to come in with you?"

"N-No." I swallow the lump in my throat. "Just go back to work. Thanks for being here for me."

He leans over and wraps me in a hug. "Mrs. Callahan is the best mom ever. I'm so sorry for everything that's happening to your family and I hate I can't do shit. But if you need me, just call me. Anytime, dude." He pats me awkwardly on the back.

I nod again, rubbing my hand over my face, and exit the car.

Be strong, Adrian. Be strong for Dad and Millie. They need you.

I keep repeating this to myself, even though I feel like my engine is running on fumes, and the car may be beyond repair at this point. The automatic doors open and the whiff of antiseptic agents hits me in the face, the smell especially jarring tonight. I tread on those familiar marble floors, my footfalls sounding loud in my ears as I come to realize this is probably the last time I'll be walking these halls. It feels as if my legs have been encased in cement blocks, each step heavy and resounding.

Barbara, the morning charge nurse, intercepts me in front of Mom's room. "I had to take on a night shift this week," she replies, answering my unasked question. Her eyes soften as she reaches out and squeezes me on my shoulder. "I'm so, so sorry, honey."

I flinch and swallow the lump in my throat before pushing open the door.

The beeping sound is loud—a slow, steady beat. There are unfamiliar machines in the room. The florescent lights are bright, illuminating every cold, sterile inch of the space. I feel numb, like this is an out-of-body experience, and it's not really happening to me. It *can't* happen. Millie is on Dad's lap, whimpering against his shoulder, her small frame shuddering as she curls her hands around his neck. Dad's eyes are red and swollen as he glances at me. He shakes his head, ever so slightly. One of his hands is clasping Mom's frail one. I look everywhere but the bed, my last attempt at denial.

"Adrian, sweetie, is that you?" Mom's faint voice finally draws my gaze to her. She looks so pale, so thin, all skin and bones really. Her eyes are sunken in, the dark circles more pronounced than ever. Her face is sallow, lacking the usual glow, as if the life is already leached out of her and she's just hanging on by a thin thread. She reaches for me with her free hand, the very effort seeming to take the last ounce of her energy. The numbness from a moment ago breaks as a deep torrent of grief washes over me, almost knocking the breath out of my lungs. My hands tremble and I bite my bottom lip. I let out a ragged breath.

I curl my hands into tight fists as I walk to her. My eyes burn with unshed tears. "M-Mom." I sit down and hold her hand, which seems especially cold tonight. She is barely lucid, her eyes glazed and unfocused, but she held on...to see me. I flinch as nausea roils up inside me, threatening to relieve myself of dinner from earlier tonight. There is a tightness in my chest, like someone has bound my body in duct tape, and I can't breathe.

"Oh sweetie." She coughs, her thin body shaking with exertion. "Don't be sad. W-We all knew this was coming. Soon, I won't be in pain anymore, and I'll watch over you all and protect you from above."

I lay my head on top of the blankets as she gives me a soft squeeze. My heartbeats are in disarray as I clench her hand, with its faint warmth, but not for much longer. I choke back a sob—I don't want the last image of me in her eyes to be one of me crying. I want her to know how much she is loved.

"I love you, Mom. I'll take care of Dad and Millie always." My voice is thick with emotion. So much to be said, yet not enough time. I don't want her to worry about us. I want her to leave this world at peace, knowing I'll take care of the people she loves the most.

"Sweetie, don't fear love." Her voice is so faint. She tries to lift her hand again, but the exertion seems too much for her. I lean in, putting my ear next to her mouth. She whispers, her voice shaky, almost a light breeze in the night, so soft I can barely hear her. Tears well in my eyes as a stabbing pain hits me in the chest. She smells different now. Her scent has long faded away. A tear slides down my cheek and I squeeze her hand, letting her know I'm listening. "Be brave. I love you, Dad, and Millie so, so much. I don't regret a thing..." Her voice fades away as her eyes flutter shut and she slips out of consciousness.

Dad chokes up in the background as I curl my arms around my mom, standing vigil for her last moments in this world, watching as her breathing weakens and slows, until her body stills, the last breath eking out of her.

Beeeeeeep.

The flatline of the heart rate monitor sounds definitive. Permanent. Just like that, a wonderful soul has been snuffed out of this world. The goodbyes we've been saying internally for the last few months are now final.

I bury my head in the blankets as I fight to stem the sobs. A chill runs through me and my body succumbs to the pain in my heart. More memories of Mom flitter through my mind. Her taking Millie and me to the park for picnics under the sun. Me curling next to her while she reads a bedtime story at night when I was a kid. Memories I haven't thought about in a long time flood me, as if reminding me whom I've lost. As if I need a reminder. I don't know why I'm even doing it at this point, but I still try to hold back my pain when I want nothing more than to cry, to scream, to collapse on the floor. But deep down, I know I need to be strong for Dad and Millie, because there's no one else now. There's only the three of us.

"Please, don't leave me..." Dad curls his hands around Mom's still face, his tears wetting her cheeks. "I-I'm so sorry... If it wasn't for me... Please, I love you..." he chokes out, half sobs, half unintelligible words.

Millie is curled up in a ball on the chair, her eyes squeezed shut, whimpering, "Mommy" over and over again.

The agony slicing through my chest knocks the air out of my lungs and I try to rein in my galloping emotions, trying to dig myself out of the deep well of grief. I grip the blankets tightly as I struggle to breathe. The worries I had hours ago are now no longer, but the relief is nonexistent. It's hollow and filled with pain and agony, like my heart has been pierced with a thousand arrows.

Millie is crying louder as Dad wails against Mom's still body. I stand up, my legs weak, and stagger over to my little sister, pulling her into my arms, whispering how much I love her. How I'll protect her. My mind feels hazy as the sorrow overwhelms every one of my senses, rendering me incapable of experiencing anything else.

The next moments are a blur of still images. Nurses and doctors come in. I briefly remember Barbara pulling Dad off of Mom. I faintly recall hugging Millie and telling her Mom loves her and is now an angel watching over us. I fight to stay strong for my little sister, who is far too young to lose a parent. I remember smoothing my hand over Dad's back as he shudders against me.

Moments later, in what could've been hours or minutes, as time ceases to matter, I remember sitting in the quiet, empty room with Dad, with Millie asleep on my lap, apparently exhausted from crying.

"It's like she knew," Dad murmurs, his voice thick with tears. "She didn't want to burden us with her medical bills. She wouldn't have wanted you to quit school for her. It's like she knew…"

The air feels stale and thick. I can't breathe. I feel like I'm going to suffocate under the torrent of emotions and thoughts. Mom. Family. Mom. My body shakes as an uncontrollable urge to escape pierces through me. I need to get out. I need to see her, see the one person who can let me breathe.

And before I know it, I end up standing on my pixie's balcony.

"**A**drian?"

I hear the familiar tapping against my French doors and quickly open it, finding him standing there, the night breeze ruffling his thin T-shirt. A sharp pain slashes my chest as I take in his expression.

Devastation. Haunted. Alone.

His eyes are bloodshot and hollow, heartbreaking sorrow leaching out of those baby blues. Wetness clings to his thick lashes as he stares at me, his body trembling, his bearing silent. He swallows, his Adam's apple rippling in the corded muscles of his neck.

Adrian collapses on me, his body curling against mine, as he wraps his strong arms tightly around my back. I stagger back, struggling to hold him upright, and I tug him toward my chair. He crumbles on the seat and pulls me to stand between his thighs. My heart kicks in my rib cage, the thuds sounding loud in my ears, and he buries his head against my chest.

"She's gone." His voice is a rough, deep whisper, as faint as the moonlight shining in from the glass doors, partially obscured by dark clouds.

Agony slices through me as I realize his mom passed away. Tears gather in my eyes and I hug him closer to my chest, my palm smoothing the tense muscles of his back. I place my face on top of his head, wanting to wrap him in the cocoon my body can provide. "I'm so sorry, Adrian. I'm so sorry."

A harsh cry emits from him as he shakes against me. His breathing is frantic, and he clutches me tighter to him. He gasps for air, his struggles loud, and he chokes on his apparent grief. His fingers grip my back tightly to the point of pain, but I don't notice it because my heart is bleeding out for him. It's as if his sorrow is choking him from within and he doesn't know how to let go, how to take a breath, how to let himself feel.

"Let it out, Adrian. Don't hold it in. You've been so strong for so long. She wouldn't have wanted that for you."

Guttural sobs wrench from him, each one more devastating than the last, and I hold him in my arms, wishing I could take away any part of his pain. Adrian cries, his sounds rough and muffled, his tears wetting my sleep shirt. The anguish in his wails is a knife to my heart. To see this strong person being reduced to tears—tears he's probably been holding back for too long—annihilates me. He trembles in my arms as he roars with sadness, the haunting sounds echoing in my dark room. Tears trek down my face as I curl myself tighter against his shaking frame, attempting to give him all of my love, all of me, anything to take away even an ounce of his pain.

I stand there as the boy who's making me feel too much finally breaks down in front of me, the castle crumbling down from the harsh elements. I feel helpless as I watch him weep, finally letting himself be vulnerable, letting himself be the little boy who has lost his mom. After what could be thirty minutes or an hour, his frame hangs limply around me and he pants harshly, as if he's still struggling to breathe. His body is heavy in my arms. The emotions have no doubt taken a huge toll on him.

We don't speak because some things don't need to be said.

I just hold him until his breathing evens out. My shirt is soaked with his tears, evidence of the unspeakable pain in his life.

Mrs. Callahan, if you're watching over us, don't worry about Adrian. I'll watch over him...always.

Adrian calms and he finally tilts his head up to look at me. His eyes are swollen, the whites red in the dim light. He cradles my face and brushes his thumb on my cheek, his calloused fingers wiping away the moisture there. His hand shakes and I press my lips against his palm. A piece of me has been bleeding with him this entire time.

"My pixie," he rasps, his voice thick and hoarse, his blue gaze still piercing, unblemished by the tragedies of his life. "What have I done to deserve you?"

I shake my head. "What have I done to deserve you, Adrian? Before I met you, I just lived life, like a clueless teenager, worrying about things that don't matter, but my life has changed for the better with you in it...and now I feel so, so much."

"No, perhaps this was what Mom was talking about..." he whispers as he holds my gaze.

Our breaths fill the tiny space between us as I stroke his soft hair, wishing I could do something to ease his pain. Even though I know nothing can fix the hole in his heart. My mind flutters to my piano and my music, sources of comfort to me when I'm sad. Music has transcended emotions and words and I hope it'll do the same for him.

"Stay here, okay? I'll be back."

He nods and I quickly wipe the tears with my arm as I step away. I wish I could play for him in the open, not under the guise of a recital or in the darkness of the night. Turning off the light, cloaking Adrian in the shadows, I leave a crack open by the door as I stagger toward the music room down the hall.

Sitting down on the bench, my hands hovering over the keys, I think about him, about the boy who just lost the person who loves him unconditionally but still has to be strong for his dad and his sister.

I want to be the shelter from the storm for him.

I want to be the person he can cry, laugh, and scream in front of.

Closing my eyes, I play "Moonlight Sonata," our song, a piece holding so much loneliness, so much pain, yet so beautiful and hopeful at the same time. My body sways to the music as my fingers travel across the keys, having long memorized every chord and every position. The tears which had abated before slip down my face once again as I cry for him, telling him I'm with him through my music.

"The music is not in the notes, but in the silence between."

My words are in what I haven't said, but I know he can feel.

After the piece is finished, my fingers don't stop, and I automatically continue with another song I hope will bring him comfort, Franz Schubert's *Ellens Gesang III,* otherwise known as "Ave Maria," wishing the grace of the music will wrap around him, wishing my love—because I can't find another word to describe the feeling coursing through me—will travel to him through this song. This music is usually brought to life by a soprano, singing the German lyrics that transcend languages. I don't know the words, but I hum to the melody, my voice breaking at the high notes, untrained yet full of emotions and words I couldn't bring myself to say.

I only hope this offers him a little piece of comfort. So he knows he's not alone.

Not anymore.

The last notes of the song slowly fade into silence, with only the sounds of my breathing as accompaniment. Swiping my wet face with my arm, I pad quietly back into my room and shut the door behind me. The faint glow of the moonlight cloaks the room into the shadows I hate. But I don't find myself scared.

Adrian doesn't speak, but I know he's still sitting there. I can feel his presence as if he's standing in front of me. With him here, I'm unafraid of the dark. I walk up to my chair, seeing the dark silhouette there, motionless except for the faint movements as he breathes.

"Thank you, Pixie," he murmurs, his deep voice still thick and raw. "Thank you for being here with me." He understood what I was trying to tell him with my music.

I stand in between his legs and tug his head up toward me, my fingers caressing the planes of his face, the sharp angles of his jaw, now slightly covered with stubble, the faint bump on his nose, another relic of his fights at the ring, the soft eyelids, still a little wet from his tears. His hands curl around my hair, his fingers tangling with the thick strands. I bring my lips to his, softly kissing him, attempting to use my kisses as bandages over his broken heart.

My lips tease his, my tongue licking at the seam, and he opens, letting out a deep groan. Soft nips, teeth clashing, tongues tasting each other, our kiss turns heated. I let out a moan as he tugs my hair in an effort to bring me closer to him, the pain only adding to the erotic torture.

"I want to forget...I want to forget everything," he whispers as we part for air.

"Let me help you forget," I answer as my hands graze the front of his T-shirt, coasting over the hard planes of his lean muscles, and I drop to my knees.

He sucks in a breath as I unbutton his pants and tug down his zipper, the sound loud in the quiet room.

"You don't need to—" Adrian's hands fist harder in my hair.

"I want to. Let me make you feel better." Even though I know this will only bring short-term relief, a temporary salve to a permanent loss.

I tug down his jeans and underwear and his erection pops out, already hard and thick. My mouth goes dry as I wrap my hand around his base, relishing the warmth and the silky skin there. He hisses and leans back, his hands relaxing a smidge before clenching my hair again.

I rub my hand against his long shaft, and it twitches against my ministrations. Squeezing my thighs together as wetness gathers at my core, I press a small kiss at the tip, my tongue darting out to lick the slit and the drop of liquid gathered there.

"Fuck," he rasps as he moves my head in an attempt to direct me.

I've never gone down on a guy before. I hope I'm doing this right.

Opening my mouth, I suck him in, one inch after another, as one hand curls around the base, moving up and down while my other hand cups his balls.

He flinches and arches into my mouth, his cock hitting the back of my throat. His fingers pull hard at my hair, eliciting another tug of pain.

I move up and down, lapping my tongue around him, sucking in as far back as I can, my hands massaging him as he thrusts his hips against me in an erratic rhythm. Wetness seeps through my underwear at the apparent pleasure on his face, and I move faster against him.

"Emily, fuck me. Shit, I-I'm close." He pulls harder on my hair, no doubt wanting to warn me as his hips piston his cock harder in my mouth. The sounds of slurping and gagging fill the air as he bottoms out with each gyration, his body trembling around me.

Ignoring him, I suck even harder, my tongue laving him with each slide and soon his cock jerks against me as warm, salty liquid fills my mouth in thick spurts.

"Fuuuuck," he grunts as he rides out the rest of the crest. I swallow his cum and he slows down his movements, his eyes glazing in a sheen of lust and sadness.

Releasing his cock with a pop, I lick an errant drop of cum at the corner of my lips. His fevered eyes snare on the movement, and he tugs me up and brings my face in for a deep kiss.

"You're my angel." A kiss.

"My pixie." A kiss.

"The light in the darkness." His lips feast on mine as I sit on his lap. His hand trails over my thin sleep shirt and he groans at my puckered nipples. "Let me help you," he murmurs, but I stop him, my hand on his that's currently resting over my fluttering heart.

"No. Tonight is about you. Let me just be here...with you."

He kisses me again, deeper this time, and I taste the salt of his tears.

"My pixie."

His. Always.

They say there are five stages of grief for most people. I must be defective because I seem to have two stages—anger and depression. Lately, anger seems to be emerging as victor. It's been a few weeks since Mom died and I took one of those weeks off to stay home and help with the arrangements. The funeral was beautiful, with Mom's friends and former coworkers all coming to pay tribute. Emily stood by me, helping me take care of Dad and Millie while I handled the people who came to pay their respects. I finally introduced her to my family, saying she's a good friend from school. Dad was too distraught to question it.

Mom's family didn't come. Even after I called and left a voice message on their machine. *How heartless can you be?*

The abrasive heat of anger courses through my veins as I walk toward the library during my lunch period, my hands curled into tight fists. My chest is covered in bruises as I've picked up boxing again, not only for the money, but also for an outlet to the fire that's burning hotter and hotter inside me. It's either that or I get into fights at school and I'm trying my fucking best to hold it together for the last few months, so I can graduate and get out of here.

It's mid-April, and the weather is resplendent, the sun bathing the courtyard in a warm glow, the late-morning dew still clinging to the blades of grass on the lawn, and the temperatures are at a comfortable mid-seventies. Bright-orange poppies bloom on the grounds as birds flit around in the air. Spring is upon us and life is thrusted in front of my face. But I don't notice any of it.

The annoying whispers and stares, reminiscent of the first day at Warwick, repeat themselves.

"Have you heard? His mom died? That's so sad."

"He looks like he hasn't slept in ages."

"Even Ryan doesn't pick on him anymore. I guess we shouldn't kick someone who's already down."

Their pity.

I don't need their damn pity.

I only focus on the anger boiling inside me as I sit down in front of one of the public-use computers at the library. I bring up the browser and type in "Regis Cornwall III," an equally pompous name for such a heartless soul. My grandfather. I can't find anything on my grandmother other than the fact Amelia Waites married Regis Cornwall III in a lavish high society wedding back in the fifties and had only one child, my mother. Someone they cast out of their family as if she were nothing more than trash to be discarded. Someone whose greatest sin was to fall in love with someone poor, someone they deemed unsuitable for their old-money name.

I scroll through photos of my grandfather shaking hands with people as he presents them with the large, fake checks for charitable donations. A muscle tics in my jaw as I read about an interview with him where he explains how his company, Cornwall Holdings, is based on a family-oriented philosophy, and how they're not only a publicly traded real estate company, the usual corporate monsters, but they're a family at heart. Cornwall Holdings is involved in multiple charities, including ones to help families in need. They're lauded as one of the best Fortune 500 companies engaged in philanthropy.

What a bunch of bullshit.

You wouldn't even help your daughter who was dying, who didn't have money for her medical bills. What fucking hypocrites.

I grit my teeth, fury burning its way through my chest, my fingers attacking the keyboard like it's my worst enemy as I scour the web for more information on the grandfather who's only a grand-parent by genetics.

Cornwall fucking Holdings.

Icy resolve temporarily douses the flames inside me. My breathing evens out.

Someday, I'll make them regret everything. Make them regret ignoring my family, forsaking Mom. Make him pay for everything that happened to us because of our shitty circumstances. Not only am I going to get Millie and Dad out of our poor situation, I'm going to bring vengeance on Mom's family, the real culprits behind our tragedies.

My feet bounce on the floor as a nervous energy thrums through me. I clench my fingers after I close out of the browser. The brief flash of icy resolve has hardened into something permanent inside me. I glance around the library, noticing other students staring at me, some of them looking down on me, their snobby noses in the air, others whispering while their eyes dart in my direction.

Screw everyone.

My mind riots against the chaotic emotions and I find myself wanting to go to the one person who makes me feel everything other than anger and sadness. The one person who makes me feel calm. The one person who seems to understand me even if I don't say anything out loud.

My pixie.

Pushing out the chair, the wooden legs dragging across the floor in a loud screech, I stride out of the library toward the building housing the dining hall. I march toward the tall building with gilded windows glinting in the sunlight, as impressive as they appeared on the first day of school, and push open the double doors to enter the main dining area.

Loud chatter fills the room as students gather in groups around the many tables, eating their meals. I scan the sea of navy and green, reeking of money and superficiality, briefly noting their carefree smiles, the loud shrieks and merry laughs, kids with no fucking worries in the world. A flinch of pain hits me in the chest as I suddenly feel robbed. I feel like this carefree experience has been stolen from me, that in another life, I should be one of these kids, excited about my future, worried about things that don't matter. My current situation hasn't changed, and the past has already occurred, but something about Mom's death unleashed this bottomless barrel of anger, which seems to pour out of me every second of the day.

My eyes rove the throngs of people until they land on a table in the far corner and I spot her. My pixie, her brown hair curled in loose waves, cascading over her shoulders, her large eyes animated as she gestures wildly with her hands as she speaks to Sarah, who is throwing her head back in laughter.

I stride to her, ignoring Ryan and his hooligans, the pointed stares and murmurings of other students, and I stand before her, my chest heaving from exertion. Emily's eyes widen in surprise before softening with warmth. Her mouth curves up into a beautiful smile, my two favorite dimples making an appearance.

My heart hiccups and the anger temporarily fades away.

My pixie is magic, grounding me whenever I'm in her presence. A different pulse of energy thrums inside me now.

I walk over to her and grab her hand, tugging her up.

"Adrian?" she whispers, her elegant brows lifting in question.

"Come with me."

She follows me wordlessly, her eyes still comically big, as Sarah and Chelsea laugh in the background. "Go get some, Ems!"

The murmurings follow us as I lead Emily out of the dining hall. We keep walking down the halls, a sense of urgency rushing through me. I can't explain the need I have for her right now. It's like the intensity of the anger earlier brought out this hunger for her to replace the burning flames with another type of scorching heat. Turning down one of the many corridors in the building, I come across an empty classroom.

I open the door and usher Emily into the dark room. The door closes behind us with a *click* and I lock it, the sound of the latch echoing in the space. Looking around, I see a black grand piano in the center of the room, with music stands and chairs on the side. Belatedly, I realize I took her to the music room. I turn around and face Emily, who is staring at me in confusion, her large eyes crinkling at the corners.

"Adrian? Is everything okay?"

"Yes, now that you're here."

Desperation floods me and I haul her against my body, capturing her parted lips with mine, swallowing her gasps as she melts under my kiss. She's so petite and malleable, so I lift her up and carry her to the piano, setting her on top of the keyboard cover—a blasphemy, I'm sure—as I kiss her like she's the air I breathe. I wrap my hand around her silky strands, one of my favorite features of hers, and I tug her head back and trail kisses down the delicate column of her throat, nipping at the pulse points, licking at the sensitive region behind her ear.

Emily squirms against me, her whimpers and mewls inflaming me even more. My rock-hard cock threatens to break open from the confines of my pants. She wraps her thighs around my waist as she thrusts her chest out, her perfect tits, a wonderful handful, taunting me.

My lips travel to the divots of her collarbone as my hands slide down and cup her breasts, feeling her nipples hardening under her thin bra. I unbutton her shirt and peel up the cups of her bra, exposing her tits to the air.

"Fuck me," I rasp as I stare at her pebbled nipples, light brown, puckered up like the eraser tip of a pencil, and just the right size. My tanned hands on her ivory skin are an erotic contrast as I pluck at the nubs, each twist earning a whimper from her, each moan sending pleasure straight to my steel shaft.

"What are you doing to me, Adrian?" she mewls as I suck a nipple in my mouth, my tongue laving the hard peak in quick, light circles.

She writhes against me, her skirt now bunched over her waist as she gyrates against the outline of my cock, moving up and down in a natural rhythm, even though she's never had sex before.

"I-I'm so wet...I ache everywhere," she whispers, her words causing my cock to harden even more.

Squeezing her breasts, I trail my lips down her body before kneeling before her and propping her legs over my shoulders. She leans against the back of the piano, her naked tits arched up in the air, her eyes closed in an erotic vision that's forever embedded in my brain. I bury my nose against the damp lace of her underwear, soaked through with her juices, and she thrashes against me.

"So sensitive, my pixie." I nip her clit through the thin material, and she shrieks before clamping one hand over her mouth to suppress her sounds.

"Yes, baby, keep that hand there, don't let anyone hear you as I eat you out."

Tugging the lace to the side, my lips suck hard on her nub and her thighs clamp down around my head. Lusty moans emit through her mouth as she gyrates against my tongue, which is now circling her clit in a way I know she loves.

"Yes, Adrian, yes, more…" The sounds of the slurping fill the air as I insert two fingers inside her wet pussy, which practically sucks me in to the last knuckle.

"Fuck. Your pussy loves my fingers." I curl them at the right angle, rubbing against a patch of softness there and more wetness seeps onto my fingers. I lap at it, drinking in the extra sweetness as I bask in the scent of her and lilies. "You taste so good. I want to do this all the time."

Emily tenses against me, her thighs threatening to cut off my circulation as I suck harder at her clit and insert yet another finger, moving in and out of her in a quickening rhythm.

She grabs the back of my head and lets out a keening moan. "Adrian!" she shrieks, my name echoing in the room as she trembles around me, her juices squirting out as she falls off the cliff. I lap her tender folds, swallowing everything she has to offer, my tongue savoring her sweetness, and she slowly climbs down from her high, her body turning limp on top of the piano.

Slowly, I stand up and wipe the juices off my face with the back of my hand. I stare at the half-naked goddess, her tits heaving, her eyes wide and pupils dilated, gazing hazily at me as she's sprawled on top of her favorite instrument. My dick twitches and lengthens even more.

Fuck. I don't think I can stop this train of emotions even if I wanted to. Perhaps this is what my parents felt with each other. Perhaps we are doomed from the start, but I don't think I care anymore.

I stroke my cock from the outside of my pants, the muscles in my jaw twitching. God, I want to fuck her. I want to make love to her. I want to do everything with her. I want to be the first to be inside her tight, wet pussy, even if I can't be the last, even if our love story isn't meant to be forever. A flash of pain pierces through my body at the thought of not being her last, but I brush it aside.

Slowly, I hover over her, my heart and my mind giving in to this crazy tension.

Riiiiiiing.

The ten-minute warning bell rings.

Lunchtime will be over soon. Then, the students will be in this classroom for lessons. Shit. I can't believe I almost took her for the first time on top of a fucking piano in the middle of the school day like some animal.

She deserves romance and candlelight and tenderness, not a quick, rough rutting in the middle of the day.

Hastily, I tug her underwear back into place and button her shirt, my fingers clumsy, as she stares at me, her cheeks still pink from exertion. I smooth out her luscious hair and help her down from the piano and she wobbles against me, her legs almost giving up on her.

I can't help a grin at this point. Nothing pleases me more than satisfying her, than putting that dreamy expression on her face.

"What was *that*?" she whispers, her beautiful lips tempting me to kiss her again.

Instead, I kiss her forehead, my eyes closing briefly as I savor the sensation. "I just needed you."

"But you didn't—" She gestures to my pants.

"Getting you off is what I needed."

She blushes again. Even her neck is pink now, and it takes all of my restraint not to finish what I started. Instead, I flip open the fallboard of the piano, revealing the beautiful black and white keys.

I sit down on the bench and pat the spot next to me. "We have ten minutes before class starts. Why don't you teach me the scales?"

Emily smiles at me, the dimples reappearing on her cheeks, as if she's happy I'm trying to learn something so near and dear to her. She places her dainty fingers on the keys and waits until I mimic her position.

"Let's start with a simple C major scale."

The earlier anger and resentment in my veins have faded into the background, replaced with something so heady, so desperate, an emotion resembling...love.

I couldn't get out of prom.

It's funny how this used to be the highlight of my senior year, the cherry on top of the cake, the scoop of creamy vanilla ice cream in a root beer float. It used to be something I looked forward to. But now, knowing Adrian won't be going as he has to work as usual and finances are still tight with his dad unemployed, I'd much rather stay at home and wait until midnight rolls around, when I can join him at our spot on the beach.

But, of course, since I'm on the shortlist for prom queen, if I don't show up, gossip will spread through the halls like wildfire, eventually reaching Mother's ears. I don't want to get Adrian in trouble. I don't want to imagine what she'd do if she discovers us together. People already suspect something is afoot, as he and I interact so much, even though the only time he blatantly held my hands in full view of everyone was when he pulled me from the dining hall a week ago and gave me the most earth-shattering orgasm in the music room. My face heats at the memory, at how my body was at the mercy of his hands, his kisses, his caresses.

My heart—I've given away to him a long time ago.

And so, I'm standing in front of the full-length mirror in my room, staring at my reflection as I admire the intricate beaded lace on the bodice of my cotton-candy-pink prom dress. The layers of soft, sheer tulle billow at the waist and drape to the floor. I look every inch the pixie Adrian claims me to be. The dress ended up being off the rack from a high-end boutique on Rodeo Drive, a fact Mother is still unhappy about, but ended up relenting since the brand is well known amongst her crowd. She's always concerned about appearances, as if outward impressions matter the most. My dark-brown hair is pinned to the sides, the long curls hitting my breasts over the shoulders. My makeup is light, with a simple eyeliner and a mauve lipstick. I turn on my webcam and dial into a group video chat on my laptop.

"Here I am, as promised." I twirl around, the tulle floating in the air like wings.

My heart feels heavy as I fake a smile. I wish Adrian is going to prom with me.

"You're so beautiful!" Jess exclaims as her eyes grow big on the screen.

"I love the dress, Ems. You always have such great taste." Liz grins at the camera.

"If I didn't have finals coming up, I'd totally be home this weekend to help get you ready." Jess's voice drops, as if she's sad she isn't here to support me.

I shake my head. "Don't worry about it, Jess. I'm only going because I'm on the short list for prom court. I probably won't be staying long."

"This doesn't have anything to do with the guy I met at your recital, does it?"

"I'm so bummed I missed him that day. I have a good eye for men. I can pick the good ones from the bad ones," Liz says, her lips in a small pout.

"No, nothing like that. I'm just not feeling it." Jess can't do anything for me, anyway. Why worry her?

"Well, you look amazing, Ems. Try to enjoy a little of prom, okay? In hindsight, now that I'm working and all that, I wish I enjoyed the last few months of high school more. Savor the experience, you know? Because work is well...work." Liz graduated from grad school not long ago and is a new teacher at an elementary school in Pasadena.

Ding-dong.

"Hey, I have to go. I'm getting a ride with Sarah. We've decided to nix dates this year."

"Have fun, sis. Tell us about it next time."

"Enjoy yourself!"

I tilt my lips in what I hope is a bright smile and shut my laptop, wishing my heart didn't feel so lonely right now. There's something wistful about donning a beautiful dress and longing for the guy you love to be next to you.

Steven brushes past me in the hallway as I exit my room. Upon seeing me, he lets out a low wolf whistle. "Looking good, sis."

"Wow. My little brother complimenting me. I thought the day would never come," I deadpan, fighting a grin.

"I'm trying to turn over a new leaf."

I can feel my eyebrow arching up to the middle of my forehead. He grins and snickers.

"Nah...too hard. I think pesky little brother is more my scene."

He dashes away before I can say anything else. Shaking my head, I head downstairs toward the foyer.

Mother stands by the door, chatting with Sarah as I reach them. She examines my appearance—nothing can get past the infamous Audrey Lee Kingsley stare—before dipping her head in a nod.

"I still wish you had a dress made, Emily."

I smooth a wrinkled part of the tulle, no doubt ruffled up when I was twirling earlier. "It's fine, Mother." My cheeks twitch in an effort to maintain my neutral expression.

"We Kingsleys should never settle for fine. We should strive for excellence."

Fighting the urge to roll my eyes, I turn to Sarah, who looks like a certain mermaid princess coming to life, with her gorgeous strawberry-blonde hair curled in voluminous waves and her sea foam green silk gown, which drapes over her generous curves.

"You look stunning, Sarah!"

"Right back at you, Ems."

I remind Mother I'll be home late because I'll be hanging out at Sarah's after the dance. Then, we leave for the Kensington Elite Suites by the pier, where the prom is being held.

"Sorry to use you as an excuse again," I murmur as she drives toward the pier, the quiet hum of the car in the background.

She glances at me. "Meeting Adrian tonight?"

I dip my head in affirmation. "He told me to save room for dinner with him after the dance. I already told him I won't be staying too long, maybe after the prom court announcements are made, since they usually make them an hour or so into the dance."

"You guys are like star-crossed lovers...so romantic." She lets out a deep sigh, her eyes taking on a dreamy expression.

I twist my fingers in my lap. "Maybe one day our circumstances will be different and Mother won't be so against him. If there's one thing I'm definitely looking forward to with graduation, it's getting away from home. Adrian and I are planning to go to Cornell together. I just got my acceptance letter a few weeks ago. We'll be far away and I won't give a crap about her disapproval anymore."

"Soon, Ems. I'm so happy for you."

"What about you?" Sarah has been deciding between NYU or something closer to home.

"NYU. I've decided I want to start my own adventure. Maybe meet a broody man of my own and have a romantic story to tell you someday." She wags her brows at me as she grins.

"You better tell me."

"Ride or die, bestie."

• • •

Prom is a smashing success. The committee didn't skimp on any expenses. Unlike most school dances, the Warwick prom is over-the-top extravagant and even serves dinner, like any high society event we'll likely be expected to attend from here on out. Five-course meals with everything from lobster to foie gras to decadent desserts and non-alcoholic spritzers—it is a high school dance after all, got to draw the line somewhere—to photo booths and even an ice sculpture decoration made an appearance.

The prom court candidates are seated at my table, which means myself, a few other girls, Ryan, and his friends. I poke the salad on my plate, convincing myself to nibble on a cherry tomato, the rich aroma of delicious food doing nothing to whet my appetite. I'm more curious to see what Adrian has up his sleeves later on.

"Not hungry, Emmie?" Ryan asks from next to me.

"No. Not really. Not feeling it, to be honest."

He sets his silverware down and turns toward me. "Um, look. Since we're approaching the end of the school year and all that, I want to be honest with you. I like you. I really do—"

"Ryan, how many times have I—"

He holds up his hand, imploring me to listen. "I get it. I know you don't like me that way and you most likely like the loser. I won't lie and say that doesn't piss me off because I don't see how he can provide for you, how your futures will even align. But I won't argue with you, because I know you can't argue with these things..."

Ryan rakes a hand over his blond hair, gleaming gold under the dim light. "I guess what I'm trying to say is, with the end of the school year approaching...I just want to wish you luck. With him, college, everything. I know you don't think much of me, but I think the world of you, and I just want you to be happy."

I blink a few times, my mouth parted, surprised at this turn of events. Thinking back to our childhood to now, when our families had get-togethers and we'd be inevitably paired together, I guess perhaps I too fell victim to seeing him only as a nuisance, a jock without a brain or a heart—a bad first impression. Perhaps I'm just like all the other people who've treated Adrian poorly because of a few cursory glances at him, turning their noses up at him because of his clothes or his old car.

Perhaps I've been too harsh on Ryan as well.

"T-Thank you, Ryan. This means a lot. Truly," I say sincerely and smile at my classmate, and I guess...friend.

Seemingly satisfied with my response, he doles out another one of his annoying smirks and resumes eating with a gusto I'd expect from basketball players.

"Ladies and gentlemen, hope you are enjoying prom night. Without further ado, I'd like to announce our prom king and queen," the emcee, the head of the prom committee this year, speaks loudly into the microphone.

All of us turn toward the stage as a dramatic drumroll plays from the speakers. This is the moment most of my classmates have been waiting for, what some of them consider as the epitome of the high school experience.

"This year's prom king is...Ryan Van Pelt!"

Cheers and applause fill the room as Ryan stands and waves to his adoring fans before stepping up to the stage to don a metal crown because Warwick won't stoop so low as to use a plastic one instead.

"And this year's prom queen is..." The chatter silences as we await with bated breath. "Emily Kingsley!" Shrieks fill the room as classmates and teammates gather around me in felicitations. Smiling faces surround me as the girls on my squad wrap me in hugs. Muted happiness flitters through me and I thank them for the support, but my mind keeps wandering back to Adrian.

Sarah rushes up to my seat and pulls me up in an embrace. "Congrats, bestie!"

"Thank you."

Smiling, I glance at the room, noting my friends and classmates, feeling bittersweet somehow about the win as it no longer thrills me to the core, and step up to the stage where they place a smaller crown on my head. Ryan takes my hand in his and leads me to the dance floor as a song plays for our first dance, to open up the dance floor for the evening.

"Congrats on the win, Ryan. I wish you well in college and beyond." There's a sense of peace, a sense of finality as I say those words. It's like mending the cracked walls and swiping on a fresh coat of paint before putting the house up for sale, not that I have any experience in that area, but that's what they show on television.

Ryan squeezes my hand, and I glance up at him. "Thank you, and I wish you the same...Emily."

I smile. Emily, not Emmie anymore.

Only a few weeks left before this chapter of my life closes and another one begins.

As soon as the song ends, I dig out my phone from my jewel-studded clutch to call Jack, who is kind enough to come by to pick me up and drive me to the beach. Adrian has been mysterious about his plans and all I know is he's busy preparing something at the moment, so his best friend will act as chauffeur instead.

Twenty minutes later, Jack waltzes up, looking completely out of place in his fitted black T-shirt with some rock band logo on it, a pair of dark-wash jeans, his black hair haphazardly tousled in the effortless, good-looking kind of way. He strides up to the awning Sarah and I are standing under outside the hotel, a confident swagger in his step, as if he's the one who just won prom king. A few girls stare unabashedly at him because, in all honesty, he is objectively hot, and carries himself with self-assuredness seemingly generated from nowhere. Jack winks at them, quirking up a smile, before reaching us.

"Ems, looking gorgeous as expected. No wonder my boy Adrian is a complete goner for you." He flashes a signature grin, his lip ring glinting under the moonlight before he turns to Sarah.

His dark eyes rove over my best friend, as if cataloging all of her features. He lets out a low whistle. "Well damn. Sarah...is it? But I should call you Siren instead because if you called, I'd come any time."

I roll my eyes at his corny pickup line but am unable to stop a smile from appearing on my face because this is so quintessentially Jack. Adrian and I have hung out a few times together with him over the last few months, and I know this harmless flirtation is almost second nature to him.

Sarah doesn't look very impressed. She arches her brow and stares back with a withering glower. "Dude, you've got to work on your pickup lines because they're as lame and as fake as this whole Casanova vibe you're trying to put on."

Jack's eyes darken briefly before he relaxes into an easy smile again—a false bravado. "You'll come around, Siren." He cocks his head in my direction and asks, "Ready to be reunited with your prince?"

My heart picks up in rhythm, the excitement missing in the night finally filtering into my veins at the thought of seeing Adrian again. This is how I wanted to spend my prom night all along. I nod eagerly and bid Sarah goodnight before following Jack to his car.

Living in Los Angeles means enjoying pretty much year-round pleasant weather, even though the highs and lows of our temperatures can fluctuate quite drastically. However, even our cold winters are considered warm in most places in the country. Tonight is no exception. The temperatures are at a balmy seventy degrees, the air dry and devoid of the usual seaside humidity. A small breeze flutters against my dress, carrying the familiar scent of salt with a pinch of woody base notes, as I dip my toes into the sand. I carry my golden heels in one hand while hiking up my tulle skirt with the other, ambling toward our usual spot near the pier lights. The unwieldy heavy crown is in Jack's car. The skies are clear and while the beach is devoid of people, the bright light of the full moon and twinkling stars keeps me company. Anticipation flits inside me as I approach our patch of sand.

But no one is there.

Frowning, I call out, "Adrian? Are you here?"

I glance around the dark beach as a cry of a seagull pierces through the silence. The white foams of the waves wash up on the sand, leaving mementos of the ocean behind. Where is he?

I spot a dim glow of warm light from behind a few large boulders in the distance.

"Pixie, I'm over here!" Adrian's faint voice travels across the breeze and I see the dark shape of his silhouette peeking out from the rocks.

Curious, I stroll toward the distant light, toward him, the sand digging between my toes and embedding into the train of my dress.

As I round the corner of two large boulders towering well above me, I inhale sharply in surprise. A large blue-and-white striped beach blanket lies on top of the sand with clusters of flameless candles at the corners, illuminating the space in an intimate, ethereal glow. Two sets of paper plates, white napkins, and red plastic cups are carefully arranged on top of the blanket. Sprigs of wildflowers adorn the plates as decoration. A small vase with my favorite stargazer lily and baby's breath sits in the middle of the blanket. A large paper bag and a small cooler sit on the side.

A romantic candlelight dinner for two.

It's perfect.

Adrian stands at the side of the small alcove of rocks and sand, his lips quirking in a sexy, boyish grin. He's dressed in a dark-gray dress shirt and black jeans, his hair carefully arranged. In his hand, he holds up another lily. His eyes darken as he takes in my appearance, and he slowly strides toward me. My heart races in my chest at his controlled movements. My tongue darts out and wets my parched lips.

His eyes flare at the movement, the irises darkening in the dim light. "You are beautiful, like a fairytale come to life," he whispers as he stops in front of me.

My breath catches in my throat and I angle my head to look up at him, bathing myself in his intense gaze. "Thank you." I let out a small exhale.

Adrian reaches out and cradles my face in his palm, his thumb rubbing circles on my cheek. My skin feels warm, coming alive under his gentle strokes. Dipping his head down, he breathes in, as if taking in my essence. "Lilies...my favorite smell." He captures my lips with his in the gentlest of kiss, a soft pressure, a hint at what's to come.

My pulse flutters in my neck and he steps back, the harsh angles of his face softening into a smile. He hands me the flower. "Happy prom night, Pixie."

My hands shake as I take the flower and bring it up to my nose to inhale the sweet scent. There are no deejays, no five-course meals, no glitz and glamor like the dance I just came from, but these simple moments have already far exceeded the two hours I spent at prom. Taking my hand in his, he leads me to the blanket, where I carefully sit down, my dress billowing around me. I do feel quite like I've stepped out of one of the fairytales Jess loves to read. Adrian retrieves small plastic boxes from a paper bag and places them in front of us.

"I know this isn't a glamorous date or a gourmet meal...but I picked up the seafood linguine from Italian Factory, without mussels, since I know you don't like them." He opens the lid and carefully serves a generous heaping of pasta onto my plate, which is actually more noodles than seafood, the tart tomato sauce wafting up in the air. "I know it's not the best pasta out there..." he murmurs, referring to the fast-food chain restaurant, as he places a garlic breadstick on my plate. "But I have it on good authority their pasta is decent."

I place my hand on top of his, and he freezes, glancing into my eyes. Biting my lip, I smile at him. "This is perfect. Just exactly what I'm craving. I...love it."

He nods, one side of his lips tilting up in a half smile, a lock of hair falling over his forehead. Reaching out, I brush it off his face and he leans into my palm, closing his eyes and pressing a kiss to the center. My hand falls away as I curl my fingers around his kiss, treasuring it with me always.

Adrian takes out a bottle of wine from the cooler. A sweet dessert wine from the looks of it, and he carefully uncorks it before pouring some into our plastic cups.

"Alcohol, huh?" I tease him. "How did you manage that?"

His lips twist up in a grin, his eyes glinting under the moonlight. "I work in a grocery store... Let's just say these are some *connections* I definitely have."

I giggle as he winks at me. I look around, taking in the large boulders hiding us from the view of the general public, even though there's no one around. But it feels like we're cocooned in our own little slice of paradise, with the vast ocean before us, the waters calm and gentle tonight, the moonlight reflecting on the surface in otherworldly ripples.

If I were to believe in fairytales, I'd say this is pretty close to living in one.

We begin eating quietly, enjoying the simple meal of my favorite pasta, albeit a little overcooked, the tomato sauce a tad overpowering. Candlelight flickers against the blanket, casting shadows on the sand. The quiet is peaceful, not unsettling. A fuzzy warmth gathers in my chest and extends to my extremities. I feel loved, even though the words are unsaid.

The music is in the silence between the notes.

"I may be a closet romantic, but I think you're the true romantic between the two of us," I tease as I finish the pasta on my plate, my stomach satisfied, but more importantly, my heart full.

"How was prom? Am I looking at the newest prom queen?"

"It wasn't the same without you. I missed you," I reply honestly. He turns to me, his gaze gentle. "And yes, you're looking at the newest Warwick prom queen." I give him a wink and a playful smile.

He chuckles softly. "Of course I am. They'd be fools not to choose you for their queen." Standing, he dusts a few grains of sand from his jeans. He bows slightly and extends his hand toward me. "May I have this dance, my pixie queen?"

Butterflies flit and flutter in my stomach as I take his outstretched hand. Adrian grips my fingers, hauling me up, and leads me to the sand. He pulls me flush against him so my face rests against his heart. I close my eyes and breathe him in, his smell of mint and musk, and listen to the thudding of his strong heartbeat, his warrior heart still beating after all the tragedies and unfairness he has experienced in his short life so far. We sway gently to the soft rhythms of lapping waves and the occasional coos of flying birds—nature's sonata.

"Someday," he begins, his voice raspy against my ear. "Someday, I'll take you dancing in public...where we won't have to hide from others. Where we don't have to care about what other people think and feel, because we can finally live for ourselves."

I tilt my head up and gaze into his glittering eyes, the pupils bleeding into the irises like waves overtaking grains of sand on the shores. He continues, "Someday, I'll make something of myself and you'll never want for anything. You won't ever have to be ashamed of being with me."

Placing my finger on his parted lips, I hush him. "None of that. I'm not ashamed of you, of us. In a few months, we'll start our lives together at Cornell...away from my family, away from gossip. We'll be free."

Somewhere along the way, my wishes and dreams began to include him in them. I picture him sitting in the front row as I play music at Carnegie Hall. It's his lips I imagine kissing at the stroke of midnight on top of the Empire State Building.

He smiles, dipping down and touching his lips to mine. "We'll be free," he echoes as he kisses me, his lips ghosting over mine in the gentlest of lover's caresses.

We've stopped swaying and his hands travel to the back of my neck and grip the tender skin in a careful hold. Adrian leans farther down, curling his tall frame against mine, his lips picking up in pressure, in urgency, as he sucks the essence out of me, his teeth nipping, his tongue swiping. Shards of heat flow through my body straight to my core as I clutch his back, my fingers kneading the tense muscles there.

He groans and I press up against him, arching into his embrace. I moan as his lips suckle my neck, the deep suction sending fissures of heat through my entire body. My breasts feel swollen, my nipples sensitive, and wetness gathers between my legs. My body aches for him as tethered lust breaks free from its confines within.

"Adrian..." I whimper. He nuzzles the cleavage in the sweetheart neckline of my dress.

"Yes, Pixie?" he rasps against the sensitive flesh, his tongue lapping the gap between my breasts. His fingers trail behind me and he tugs down the zipper slowly, giving me time to stop him.

I let out a shaky exhale as the top of the dress falls to my waist, exposing my breasts to the cool night air. My nipples are so hard, so achy. They crave to be touched. I rub my legs together as the pressure in my core grows, and I slide my hand to his firm ass. His steel erection behind the crotch of his jeans digs into my belly.

"I need you," I whisper. He drops to his knees, his mouth trailing kisses over my clavicles and breasts before sucking in one erect bud. His tongue lightly flicks at the tip, a tease, just the way I like it. My legs nearly give out as I let out a lusty moan.

"Fuck me, you're so beautiful." His hand kneads my breast as he turns his attention to the other nipple. With each tug of the tender point, my pussy grows wetter and the ache stronger. His other hand tugs down the rest of my dress over my hips and the gown falls to a heap on the sand, leaving me clad only in a lace thong. He groans at the sight of me, practically naked under the moonlight. "You're breathtaking."

He trails kisses over my belly, his tongue swirling over my belly button, and he eases my legs apart before moving in for the kill. His lips suckle my clit over the thin scrap of material and I cry out, nearly collapsing on the sand.

"Fuck, you're so wet. You smell so good. I'm craving a taste." His long fingers drag the sodden thong down my legs as his tongue touches my hardened nub.

"Oh God, oh fuck..." I whimper as he laps against me, each flick of his masterful tongue bringing me closer and closer to the edge. His palms grip my ass cheeks, separating them slightly as his fingers slide down, teasing the puckered hole in the back before trailing to my pussy. He nudges two fingers in my wet channel and sucks to a hard rhythm, his slurps loud in the night.

"This is the tastiest pussy on earth...and it's mine," he growls, the vibrations adding an erotic pressure to the sensitive folds.

My legs shake and fire climbs between my legs. I wobble against his face and he curls his fingers inside, touching that sensitive place. More wetness drips down my thighs as I teeter on the edge of explosive bliss.

"Adrian, I'm going to..." I writhe against his face, my legs shaking as he doubles down. "Come!" I let out a keening cry and I shake against him, my hands gripping his hair as he hisses against me. He suckles my folds and licks me up like I'm the best meal he's ever had in his life, and my inner muscles pulse while I slowly come down from the high.

"Shit, that's sexy." He licks his lips and slowly gets back up. My eyes catalog his features, the tousled hair, slightly too long, his intense eyes, pupils blown, his beautiful lips, parted. He breathes heavily, a muscle ticcing in his sharp jaw. He swallows, his corded muscles rippling in his throat as he picks me up as if I weigh nothing, and lays me on the blanket.

He hovers above me, fully clothed while I'm as naked as the day I was born, and he covers my small frame with his big one, the juxtaposition erotic in the best way. His weight feels reassuring on top of me. His thick, hard cock digs into my stomach as he holds himself still, as if waiting for permission.

For us to cross that last line.

I nod, answering the question in his gaze, before pulling his head toward me, taking his lips in a scorching kiss. Our tongues duel with each other, teeth clashing, my moans blending with his groans. He moves his hips against me, his clothing-clad dick rubbing against my wet pussy at just the right angle. The heat renews between my legs and I place my hands between us, quickly unbuttoning his shirt with mad desperation. He shrugs it off, his movements sharp and urgent, his lean muscles flexing under the moonlight.

Tracing the hard planes of his chest, the small divots of his abs, I graze the dull bruises over his body, kissing each and every one. He hisses and I glance up at him, his eyes squeezed tightly in apparent pleasure, not in pain.

"Fuck," he utters, completely lost under the sensations of my hands on his body as I continue to trail kisses over his pecs, his nipples, his neck. I stare at his face, his eyes closed in rapture as his body flinches against my caress.

I unzip his fly and tug down his underwear and pants. His erection pops free, so long, thick, and hard, the vein pulsing underneath his shaft. He kicks his pants out of the way and he leans into my touch, my hands wrapping around him in a tight squeeze.

"Fuck, that's it, Pixie. Squeeze it harder. It doesn't hurt...oh fuck." He gasps as I grip him tighter, moving my hand up and down his sensitive shaft. My other hand slips between my legs to pluck my swollen nub, my body wanting something I haven't experienced before, my core aching for him.

"I can't hold it much longer and damn if our first time will be me coming before you."

He brushes my hand aside and widens my legs. His eyes turn molten as he takes in my pussy, dripping wet for him. He reaches into his pants pocket and takes out a condom. Tearing the foil package with his teeth, he rolls the rubber over his hard cock. I bite my lip as I take in this erotic sight, this guy who is barely holding on to his sanity with his want for me.

Adrian leans over me, his hand gripping his large cock, and teases the warm tip over my pussy, trailing from the folds to my clit. He rubs his cock against it in small circles until I'm thrashing under him, needing release.

Hovering over me, he looks into my eyes, lust glazing over his face. "You sure?"

"Adrian, I want you to be my first." *And my last, and everything in between.*

Something akin to fire flashes in his eyes as he leans down and crashes our lips together in a fiery kiss. When we break apart, he murmurs against my mouth, "Sorry, Pixie. This will hurt, but I'll make it all better."

He pushes in slowly, inch by inch. "You're so fucking tight. Your pussy is sucking me in so well. Shit." He pauses as my muscles tighten up even further. He glances up at me and his hand slides up my breast, twisting my sensitive nipple. I gasp and arch my back, the pleasure shooting straight to my core. He plunges in, joining us body and soul.

Tears spring into my eyes at the harsh flash of pain. I feel so full...so full of him, so full of love. Adrian breathes raggedly against me, his shoulders shaking as if it's taking every ounce of energy in him to hold back and let me adjust to his length and girth. His hand leaves my breast and trails down to my clit, where he begins a slow rhythm, squeezing and flicking the nub until sparks gather between my legs again, the soreness slowly dissipating, replaced with something headier.

Moaning, I move my hips against him, needing something more. He groans and begins thrusting against me, his movements slow at first. The combination between his fingers rubbing my clit and the new sensations from his cock hitting sensitive regions inside me has me thrashing against him.

"I need more, Adrian. Please..." I wail against his ear and he grunts, his thrusts picking up in speed until all I could hear are the sounds of skin slapping against skin.

He pants in my ear and suckles my neck. I curl my fingers around his back, my legs locked over his hips as our bodies come together again and again, each thrust leaving behind a piece of him with me and taking a piece of me to him. The sparks climb in the area where we're connected.

"I can't hold on...Pixie, come. Come around my cock," he grounds out as my legs start trembling and I explode into a thousand pieces with his name on my lips.

My channel throbs against his shaft as he pistons harder against me, his grunts loud in the air. He shakes and finally lets out a strangled groan and follows me into the heavens. Slowing down his thrusts, he collapses on top of me, his body heaving from exertion. I can feel him still pulsing inside me, my pussy fluttering in response.

The sounds of our heavy breathing fill the air and he rolls off me, careful not to squash me with his weight. Adrian disposes of his condom and takes out a tissue packet from his pants. Gently parting my legs, he dabs the sensitive skin of my pussy as he lets out a growl of satisfaction. I stare at him as he looks at the tissue in his hand, stained with a small spot of blood.

I'm no longer a virgin. I've given myself to him and don't regret it. It feels fated, the rightness burrowing deep into my bones.

Slowly, he curls my body against his, his arms wrapping me in a warm embrace. He places a soft kiss on my hair and whispers, "I love you, my pixie."

Tears gather in my eyes because I feel the very same way. I look up at him to find love shining through his beautiful blue eyes and I reply with the only answer I ever had.

"I love you too, Adrian."

Perhaps this is what great love stories are all about...finding this true connection with someone else, taking their hand, and leaping into the unknown together.

CHAPTER 21

Emily

I creep into the foyer like a thief in the night. My heart is giddy and I feel like I've sprouted wings and I can fly. After our first time, we laid there as he held me in his arms, and we gazed at the stars. We tried counting them, but there were far too many—they looked like a diamond commercial, precious gems scattered across a dark backdrop.

The darkness didn't scare me. Not with him by my side.

We talked about our dreams for the future, what we're going to do when we get to Cornell. He wants to study business management—to make something of himself, to be better than his dad, so no one will ever look down on him or his family again. I told him no matter what he does, I'm sure he'll be successful because he has the drive and the intelligence. He just never had the opportunity before, but now with college around the corner, things will change for him, for the better.

I feel it in the depths of my soul.

I told him the number of stars in the skies is the number of hopes and dreams we can pursue together, and I'll be there every step of the way.

Smiling at the happy memories, I hike up my dress, which is covered in sand and will need to be properly and thoroughly cleaned, and I tiptoe across the cool marble floors toward the living room and the stairs.

Suddenly, jarring bright lights illuminate the room and I gasp, spinning around, finding Mother standing next to the light switch, anger brimming in her eyes.

"Emily Kingsley, where did you go?"

A different type of flutters filter through me now as nausea percolates in my gut. Swallowing hard, I take a deep breath before answering, "P-Prom, Mother. You know that."

"Yes, I know you went to prom. Where did you go afterward?"

"Sarah's place—I told you that earlier already." I hope my voice isn't shaking like the way my legs are under my dress.

Her eyes flash in restrained fury as she stalks toward me, her petite frame, something I inherited, doing nothing to diminish the menacing aura radiating from her.

She stops in front of me and takes in my appearance, no doubt noticing my mussed hair, melted makeup, my swollen lips and flushed face, and the sand on my dress. "I went to Sarah's place earlier and her mom said you weren't there."

"I...I..."

"Don't lie to me. You were with that boy, weren't you?"

"W-What boy?" I bite my lip and tuck a loose curl of hair around my ear, my hands trembling.

"The poor boy from your recital. The delinquent." She paces in front of me, and a chill seeps through my insides.

Dread.

"Adrian Callahan, right? You know, I had someone look into him and his family." She stops in front of me and lets out a deep breath. "Not only is he and his family poor and completely unsuitable for you...for our family...do you know his dad is a criminal?"

My heart is in my throat as I still. "What?"

"His dad worked at TransAmerica until he was fired for embezzlement. He stole fifty thousand dollars from us in the course of three months. Normally, he'd not only lose his job but would also go to jail, but do you know your father took pity on him? Because your father knew he had two kids to support. So, instead of throwing him in jail, he just fired him."

Blood rushes into my ears, the pulse loud and unsettling as I drop to the floor, taking in this unexpected information. "W-What?" *This is why he didn't want me to ask Father to get him a job. He must have known.*

"We let his dad go out of the goodness of our hearts and this is how he repays us? His son frolicking around with our daughter?"

"No! We weren't 'frolicking' or whatever you want to call it. Mother, I love him. I love Adrian—"

"Silence!" she screeches, her voice echoing in the living room. Her eyes dart around and she lowers her voice. "I don't want to wake up your father or your brother. We are the Kingsleys and you aren't allowed to date anyone that far beneath us. You aren't allowed to date a son of a criminal, and that's final."

Heat rises up my face and I clench my hands into tight fists. Locking my jaw, I straighten up, glaring at my mother, who is normally insufferable, but is now unbearable. "No. I love him and I'll be with him, whether you like it or not. I'm eighteen, Mother. I don't need your permission anymore."

Turning around, I stalk toward the stairs, fury flowing through my veins.

"Do you want his father to go to jail? Do you want him to be kicked out of school?"

Her words stop me in my tracks as my heart splinters, the cracks forming into fissures.

"We didn't notify the authorities about his father's embezzlement, but we have all the evidence. He's as guilty as the day is long. I also know the boy is fighting for money in an underground boxing ring, which is illegal. Like father, like son."

She sighs, anguish lacing her voice. "I don't want to do this, Emily. Someday you'll understand. Someone like Adrian can't provide for you. I'm sure you know about his parents. They're a perfect example of what happens when two people from completely different worlds get together. It's beautiful at the highs...the illicit love and side glances, but the illusion and dreams will ultimately fall apart because our lives are too different. You are my precious daughter and I want the best for you, even if you can't see it now."

Tears prickle in my eyes at the unfairness of it all. At her prejudice toward him. At her ridiculous notions of society. At her complete disregard for my feelings.

"So, you're threatening to send his father to the cops and get him expelled from school if I stay with him?" I turn around and look at Mother, my vision blurry with tears. "Graduation is around the corner. He's going to go to Cornell. Don't do this to him. Things will be different. Give us a chance, Mother. *Please.*"

She shakes her head, apparently resolute in her stance. "We can't have a son of a criminal in the family, who by all means reeks of utter desperation, just like his father. I'm sorry, Emily. Adrian isn't suitable for you. His family isn't suited for our family. Someday, you'll realize I'm right." She sighs and adds, "Don't force my hand. Imagine if his father goes to jail, who's going to take care of his little sister? Do you think his father will last in jail? If Warwick finds out about the illegal fighting and expels him, and it doesn't matter if you're only a month away from graduation because they *will* expel him before then, do you think Adrian will be able to go to college then?" She pauses, staring at me, before adding, "One more thing. You aren't allowed to go to Cornell. Don't think you can get around this, young lady."

The tears fall down my face in earnest. Angry, sad, and desperate tears. Every word out of her mouth a stab at my heart, leaching out the hopes I had for our future just moments ago, turning this night from a beautiful dream into a horrifying nightmare.

Adrian loves his family—he'd do anything for them, including giving up his own happiness, his own future. He's loyal to a fault and also has a streak of pride. I don't want him to make a choice between me and his family. I don't want him to lose his chance at Cornell. Either way, he'll blame himself, adding to the heavy weight on his shoulders. He's already had to endure so much. He doesn't need this on top of everything he has suffered. He can survive without me. He'll have a bright future, be able to do everything he wishes to do, and finally get everything he deserves.

Maybe this is what love is about—sacrifice. So the person you love wouldn't need to make an impossible choice. So he won't have to live with the guilt afterward.

I know what I have to do.

This time, I'll be his boulder, sheltering him from the storm.

My soul splinters, the agony so excruciating, it practically robs me of my breath.

Turning my back toward Mother, I head up the stairs, each step heavy, my heart breaking into irreparable pieces. The pain in my chest is immensurable, irreversible, as my tears free fall down my face. My feet thump against the stairs, the hammering of the nails in a coffin, and I lock the pieces of my heart away forever.

"I...I hate you, Mother."

. . .

I close my eyes and feel the whipping winds against my face, the icy coldness like lashes on my skin, perhaps a punishment for what I'm about to do. The beach is deserted as usual tonight but dark clouds loom in the sky, a sign a storm may be on the horizon. The stars are hiding, the moonlight barely penetrating the fog. The waves roar with anger, crashing on the sand in a frenzy, obliterating everything in its path. I shiver, despite bundling myself in my thick puffer jacket.

"Emily? The weather is bad today. Why did you want to meet here tonight?" the familiar deep voice asks from behind me. It's been a week since we made love for the first time, a week for me to collect memories of stolen kisses in the hallways, lilies in my locker accompanied with the sweetest notes making my heart sing, heated passion culminating in orgasmic bliss in my bedroom when he climbs up my balcony at night. I've dragged on the inevitable as long as I can, but Mother's patience is wearing thin. I'm afraid she may do something drastic if I don't act soon.

Adrian comes up behind me, wrapping his arms around my chest, his imposing frame sheltering me from the elements. Mint and musk filter to my nose and I inhale a ragged breath, committing the scent to memory.

"I found a place near Cornell with reasonable rent. I think you'll like it. I can show it to you tomorrow at school," he murmurs, his breath warm against my ear. I can feel the excitement thrumming through his voice.

I lean back briefly, allowing myself to enjoy his embrace one last time, to feel his warmth wrapped around my body, to let myself feel safe in the darkness. My eyes prickle with tears as I gather my courage to do the one thing that'll hurt me the most.

Clenching my hands into fists, I smooth my expression into one of coldness, as if the love we've experienced before has been bled out of me, rendering me dry. I tug his arms off my body and step away. Slowly, I turn around and meet the beautiful blue of his gaze.

"Pixie? Is everything okay?" He's frowning now and starts to step forward.

I hold out my hand. "Stop right there."

"W-What's going on?"

"I have something to tell you." The high winds let out a keening wail.

Adrian stills, his shoulders tense, as if he somehow senses the heartbreak I'm about to inflict upon him.

I clench my jaw and stare at his chest, unable to look into his eyes.

"I'm going to Stanford."

The thudding pulse in my ears eclipses the thundering waves and howling winds. The seconds pass by as we both stand there, me fighting the impulse to throw myself at him.

"What? I thought we were both going to be at Cornell together like we discussed...we were going to pursue those dreams of yours and we won't need to hide anymore."

I shake my head and let out a shuddering exhale. "No...I-I just didn't know how to tell you...but I never had plans to go to Cornell."

He mutters under his breath, his brows furrowing in disbelief. "Where does this leave us?"

"Well...I think someday you'll find someone...someone better for you."

"What are you saying? Are you breaking up with me?"

My first impulse is to say no, to tell him everything I've said so far is a lie. But instead, I take a deep breath for courage and say the four words I've been dreading all night. "It's over between us."

"Why?" His deep voice is rough and barely above a whisper.

I focus on the frayed neckline of his gray T-shirt and reply, "You are a good person, Adrian...but I just don't see any future between us."

"What the *fuck* are you talking about?" He steps forward and places his hands on my arms, squeezing gently. "Look at me, Emily. Look into my eyes and tell me what's going on."

Swallowing the gravel in my throat, I allow my eyes to slowly travel up to his gaze, finding his impassionate blues staring at me, imploring me to tell him what I said was all lies.

I fling his hands off me and step back. "Adrian, you and I were always worlds apart. You were the bad boy from the opposite side of the tracks. You were something new, something mysterious. You were interesting." I grit my teeth as lies continue to pour out of me. "And now the school year is ending and we need to face reality. College is around the corner and I can't enter the best phase of my life with a casual high school fling."

Adrian staggers back, his chest physically flinching as if I'm throwing hits at him in the ring. He lets out a shuddering breath and shakes his head. "No. I refuse to believe what you're saying. This is not you, Pixie. Something else is going on. Is someone forcing you to say these things? Tell me, Emily."

I force out a hollow laugh. "No one is forcing me to say anything, Adrian. I'm just being realistic. What did you think was going to happen? That I'd stay with you through college and beyond?"

He bends down, his hands on his thighs, and stares at the sand, his head still shaking in disbelief. "What we went through... that can't be just fun and games to you. That's not you, Emily. I refuse to believe it. You gave me your first time. You held me in your arms when Mom passed. This can't be 'just a casual fling' to you."

"I never intended to enter college being a virgin," I whisper. "And you were so sweet, so I thought...better you than someone else."

"So, I was just someone convenient for you? That's it? Why didn't you just break up with me earlier, before things got serious?"

I swallow the lump in my throat, my nose burning. "You were going through so much! I didn't want to add on to the wounds. I felt *sorry* for you!"

Adrian staggers back, as if I plunged a knife in his chest. His eyes widen and his lips part in a gasp. "So, you were with me because you...*pitied* me?"

I step back a few more steps, widening the distance, driving the dagger deeper into his chest. I knew that would hurt him the most, because of his pride, because of his hatred for people feeling sorry for him.

"Is it because I'm poor?" he whispers, his voice laced with agony.

"We just come from such different backgrounds." I twist the dagger into the wound, the pain I feel acutely in my chest. "I'm a Kingsley. My family has status, money, connections." I bite my lip and continue, "There's no future for us. I'm accustomed to my lifestyle. The man next to me will have the right pedigree. You are a wonderful person and someday you'll find yourself the right girl..." The words dig into my chest and rob me of my breath. "And you'll be happy with her. It's just...that girl isn't me."

"I thought you were different." He slowly uncoils himself as he faces me again, this time with scorching hatred in his eyes. I force myself to stand still, to not flinch under his withering stare. "I thought you saw past the superficial...the first impressions..." He staggers back and shakes his head again, contempt overflowing in his eyes. "You're just like everyone else, like all the *fucking snobs* at this school, who think they're better than everyone because of shit that doesn't matter."

I bite the inside of my cheek and blink my eyes rapidly; the wind helping to dry the wetness on the surface.

"I gave you my heart, Emily, and you pulverized it and discarded it like it was nothing. I *loved* you," he roars, the anguish in his voice tearing me apart from the inside out.

I grit my teeth before answering. "Well, I guess...we shouldn't give away our hearts too easily." Taking a deep breath, I look into his heartbroken eyes one last time and whisper, "I'm sorry, Adrian."

With that, I spin around and stride away, the wind whipping my face, but I no longer feel the burn. I force myself to keep going, to keep walking, far away from the heartbroken boy standing at our spot behind me. I don't look back, because I know if I do, I may not have the willpower to stop myself from running back to him, falling to my knees, and begging for forgiveness.

The tears I've been holding back this entire time finally slide down my face as my chest spasms in pain, so much pain I don't know if I'll ever be able to breathe again. My heart twists inside of my rib cage, beating wildly, frantically, until I no longer feel this deep-seated agony, until I'm numb to it.

And I realize love has no place in my life...not when it hurts like this.

Not now, not ever.

"**A**drian? Will we like our new home?" Millie asks as she stands next to me, looking at the movers walking in and out of our front door, carrying boxes to the truck outside.

"I think so," I reply, cuddling her close to my side.

I stare at the paper boxes stacked neatly along the walls of our empty apartment, a place full of memories, both happy ones and sad ones. Today is graduation day, the long-awaited day has arrived and I'm finally free of Warwick, free of the past, and...free of her. My chest still spasms in pain, the tears long run dry at the thought of her, the girl who has left an indelible imprint on my soul. The past six months have singed my insides, scarring over my heart. Everyone is no doubt at the ceremony at school, enjoying the pomp and circumstance, hope most likely cloaking the air like the pollen in spring.

I don't believe in hope anymore. Or wishes. Or dreams.

They were thoroughly shattered when Emily ripped my heart out and tossed it to the wolves. Our story is not a great Shakespearean romance like *Romeo and Juliet,* it is more akin to the play, *Julius Caesar,* when Brutus plunges the fatal blow into his friend Caesar. The beginnings of hatred simmer inside my soul, a poison without an antidote. Perhaps there is a fine line between love and hate.

After the night at the beach, she mysteriously "fell ill" and stayed home for the last two weeks of the school year. With her family's status and social standing, the school looked the other way. Dad announced he finally found a job all the way in New York, near Cornell, so he and Millie can be close to me because family is all we have left.

I want to run away, far away from here, and moving across the country sounds like the solution to me, but a dimming ember still wants to see her one last time, to ask her if everything she said that night was real, if she really didn't feel the love we had, if she really didn't see past the superficial impressions and circumstances.

But I don't. Dignity is the only thing I have left.

And I vow to myself I'll never be in a position so vulnerable again.

One day, I'll show them all—my grandparents, the Kingsleys, everyone who has stomped on us when we were at our lowest— they'll see the error in their ways, they'll come to regret treating us this way, and they'll never look down on us again. And love? Love is poison and clouds the senses, muddles the mind.

That useless emotion has no place in my life.

. . .

Emily

He wasn't there.

My eyes search for him in the stands and in the chairs on the lawn as the graduation ceremony concludes, hoping to catch a glimpse of the striking boy with dark hair and sky-blue eyes to store away one last memory of him before our lives diverge.

"I can't believe you decided to go to Stanford instead, Ems." Sarah adjusts the navy cap on her head and loops her arm around mine.

"It felt like a better choice, given everything that happened…" I murmur, looking down at the freshly cut grass at our feet. Mother called in a few favors to get Stanford to accept me after I declined their initial acceptance letter. Sarah is the only person I confided in regarding Adrian and even then, I didn't tell her the whole story. I just told her we decided to part ways to pursue other things in life, and if she sensed anything otherwise, she didn't press me, and for that, I'm grateful.

"Do you regret it?"

I don't need to ask what, or in this case, who, she is referring to. Shaking my head, I reply, "No." And it's true, if I had to do everything over again, I'd still make the same choices. I'd still protect him because no one else was looking out for him.

The bloody wound in my heart is still leaking, partially scabbed over, and I doubt it'll ever fully heal. Tears prickle my eyes again and I look away, not wanting Sarah to worry about me. Blinking rapidly, I take in a few deep breaths, smelling the faint scent of wildflowers with base notes of wood and grass.

I gather my wits and turn to her. "Let's go find our families."

Sarah smiles at me, her perceptive hazel eyes brimming with concern, and we head back to our families to continue the celebrations.

A few weeks later, my nineteenth birthday rolls around. My bags are packed and my flight to San Francisco will be in a few hours. I'll be moving up there early to get situated and, frankly, to escape this suffocating house. I sit in front of my piano in the music room, my hands touching the delicate keys. The weight in my chest hasn't lifted and the tears still appear in the darkest hours of the night. I want to play music, to exorcise the demons inside me, but as I caress those beautiful black and white keys, I realize the music is gone from my soul, smothered in my heart. Slowly, I close the fallboard, shutting away the memories of the most beautiful, yet excruciating, time of my life so far.

The loss of the music is acute, but not as agonizing as the pain I felt on that fateful night at the beach.

Adrian. I miss him so, so much.

But I can't bring myself to regret him, even though our love ended in tragedy and pain.

At least one of my dreams came true. I've figured out what I want to study in college. I want to be in public relations, to help deserving people remake their image, so their first impressions don't become their last impressions, so I can help them turn their narratives into something else.

My mind flitters to something Adrian said the day of my piano recital. "Maybe some relationships are best left unexplored. Leave when everything is at a high, when everything is beautiful. Before it all collapses and the ugliness seeps in."

Perhaps he was right all along.

And I hope someday in the future our paths will cross again, and I can see him happy, successful, achieving everything he wanted for himself and his family. I wish all of his dreams will come true. Perhaps then, we'll be able to gaze upon each other with fondness in our eyes.

INTERLUDE—THE REUNION—ELEVEN YEARS LATER

CHAPTER 23

Emily

"**B**efore I forget, James, my best man here has offered to buy everyone drinks tonight. So, let's raise our glasses to James!" Parker Wellington, Liz's fiancé, soon-to-be husband, architect extraordinaire, announces to the crowded room at their rehearsal dinner at Kensington Hotel in downtown LA. The happy couple will tie the knot tomorrow at the hotel on Valentine's Day. His golden-brown hair gleams under the spotlight, lips tilting up in his signature dimple-showing smile as he gives everyone a wink.

The crowd roars with laughter and I shake my head in amusement. I watch him mutter something to James Chapman, Jess's husband, with a sly grin on his face. No doubt there's a joke in there somewhere. James rolls his eyes, a ghost of a smile on his lips, before taking a sip of his drink until a small, chubby hand grabs at his face. Baby Violet's adorable little hand touches her father's nose and the normally broody and sardonic man turns into a pile of mush in a matter of seconds. My heart hiccups as I take in my sister with her husband and my niece in front of me, the very picture of romantic bliss and familial love, and the deepest wound in my heart unravels a tiny bit, seeping out a slither of blood, a dash of ache.

I wish I could have what they have.

But alas, relationships and marriage are not in my cards.

My mind flits back to a faded memory of a boy who once made me feel everything, who made me want to take his hand and leap into the unknown. The dull ache is still there when I think of him, and I wonder where he is now. If he's finally happy. If he has a beautiful wife and adorable children in tow.

If he still thinks about me.

"Any plans after the wedding tomorrow, Ems?" Melanie Chan, Liz's colleague, a fellow kindergarten teacher and a recently indoctrinated girlfriend in our girl gang asks me as we dig into the dinner in front of us.

I cut into my medium-rare rib eye with vengeance as I think about my plans for Sunday. "Ugh. Don't remind me. I have a buttload of files to review in order to play catch up at work. I still don't know why they withheld the client's name from me for so long. I understand the whole 'reclusive billionaire' thing, but if I'm going to be their lead consultant, isn't it better if they bring me into the fold at the beginning?" I stab a piece of meat and pop it into my mouth, barely noticing the savory flavors as my mind runs through the work tasks waiting for me at home.

"Oooh, is this for your PR project with Adrian Scott and his company? When does it kick off again?"

"In September, approximately. I don't have the exact timeline yet, but everyone is excited about this mysterious man who never shows his face to the press to 'debut' his presentation to the media with us. Rumors are flying about why he wants to do that after literally being in the shadows for so long." I let out a deep sigh and grimace. "Nothing about this job is usual. I'm used to dealing with politicians, celebrities, companies that may have had a scandal or two and want to clean up their image. This is all so strange and they didn't give me a lot of time to prepare. I know it's still half a year away, but a lot of the media schedules are packed months in advance. It's like planning a wedding. You want to do it early. So now, I'm digging through the archives trying to learn anything and everything about him and Scott Enterprises. And from what I could find, he's a difficult man to work with and is pretty much known as 'The Shark' to everyone who has come across him in New York City. Just my rotten luck."

Melanie nods in commiseration and takes a sip of water. "Sounds very stressful. But you're a badass, so if anyone can do it, it'll be you." She then smiles, her eyes warm, and pats me on the shoulder. "If you're going to be buried in work for the foreseeable future, I think we better party it up tomorrow. Enjoy ourselves— one last hurrah."

"Hear, hear!" I grin and pick up my flute of champagne, clinking it with hers before taking a sip, the bubbles sliding down my parched throat. "I do have some good news, though."

"Oh yeah?"

"My best friend from high school, Sarah, is moving to LA from New York for a few months to work on a charity project for her family. She's the sweetest. You girls will like her."

Melanie grins, her dark-brown eyes twinkling. "Can't wait to meet her. Is she single or taken? Because I need more single ladies to bond with."

Laughing, I arch my brows at her. Melanie is experiencing a long dry spell. She's quite bitter at all the couples in love around her. I can't say I blame her. "Well, girlfriend, you'll always have me...and yes, Sarah is single."

"Yes!" She pumps her fists up in the air, her long signature ponytail whipping behind her. "We can go clubbing and partying together."

Grinning, I resume the lavish dinner celebrating the beautiful love story of my best, and only, sister-in-law, Liz, and her wonderful fiancé, Parker. They've been through so much and I'm so thrilled to be part of their happily-ever-after.

The rehearsal dinner concludes with more laughter and tears of joy, and soon, folks begin filtering out the doors to head back home or back to their hotel rooms to retire for the night before a hectic day of wedding festivities tomorrow.

"Hey, Ems. Can you ask Liz if we've tipped the vendors for tonight? I'd do it myself, but Violet is having a little breakdown right now." Jess cradles my adorable niece in her arms as she rocks her from side to side. Violet's skin is flushed, and she's wailing loudly on her mother's chest. James is packing up the diaper bag with the speed of an experienced father who has been doing this for far longer than the few months since Violet was born.

"Sure thing. She and Parker just left. I think they're still out in the lobby. Let me go ask her."

Grabbing my silver calfskin purse, I hurry toward the small group of people currently gathered in front of the elevators. I spot the familiar silhouettes of Liz and Parker, both striking with their dazzling golden-brown hair, as Parker chuckles and converses with a tall man in front of him, his back blocking my view.

More words are exchanged and Liz reaches out and gives the imposing stranger a big hug, her heels tiptoeing up to reach his shoulders. The man curls himself down and pats Liz on the back, his dark hair glinting almost black in the dim lights. He slowly straightens up and his lips tilt up in a gentle smile.

Ba-dum. Ba-dum. Ba-dum.

My heart stutters and stops as shock electrifies my system when I see the face of a person who haunts me in my dreams. Someone I never thought I'd see again, but secretly wished one day our paths would cross and there'd be no more heartbreaking agony when our gazes met.

The mesmerizing sky-blue eyes, so piercing and intelligent.

The brown hair so dark it's the color of the midnight skies.

Adrian Callahan.

He looks different now, his tall frame even more striking and imposing than a decade ago. He's wearing a black, pinstripe, three-piece suit that's draped over his body like a second skin, a crisp, white shirt with a navy tie fashioned in a complicated knot. He looks to be more muscular and filled out, the familiar coiled tension still radiating from him. His face is even more chiseled than in high school, the sharp jawline more pronounced, more masculine. Short, carefully maintained scruff decorates his jaw, highlighting the divot of his cleft chin. The high cheekbones and aristocratic nose are even more prominent in the dim lighting. His hair is meticulously coiffed in a tousled hairstyle and his eyes, my favorite feature of his, are still intense, with a touch of warmth as he speaks to Liz.

My heart restarts, pounding against my rib cage, leaping into my throat, and I gasp, my hand clasping over my mouth as I stare at the boy I once loved, who is all man now. Unbiddenly, I whisper, "Adrian?"

Adrian's startling gaze lifts up, finding mine. His eyes widen imperceptibly as he stares at me, recognition dawning in the blue pools. He swallows, his Adam's apple bobbing in his muscular neck, and his hands slowly clench into fists.

Time slows to a crawl as we stare at each other with only a few feet of distance but over a decade of memories separating us.

I don't notice much except for him.

Not the sound of the blood rushing in my ears, the heaviness of my breathing.

Not the murmuring of partygoers around me.

It's as if I'm ensnared by his magnetic gaze, my body shocked into place.

Liz turns around, her sapphire eyes alighting with laughter but quickly dimming in concern as she scans my face. "You know Adrian Scott?"

I flinch, my pulse roaring in my ears, unsure if I've heard her correctly. "What?" My brows scrunch up as I shake my head in disbelief. "This is Adrian Callahan."

My eyes return to Adrian, whose expression is inscrutable, the blue of his eyes darkening as he pins me with his glare. His hands are still clenched, his leg moving to take a step toward me, as if on impulse, but he stops himself at the very last second. A muscle tics in his jaw and he swallows again, his lips pressing into a firm line.

His blue eyes turn cold, the chill emanating from his gaze sending shivers through my body. He replies succinctly, "I go by Adrian Scott now."

My chest constricts in pain, the sudden twisting sensation robbing me of my breath.

He still hates me.

Ding. The elevator doors slide open. The sound akin to the clash of a gong in a quiet room, shakes me to the core.

Stepping back, he dips his head toward the happy couple. "Liz and Parker, congratulations again. May you both have a lifetime of love and happiness." With those words, he turns around and steps into the open elevator, the doors closing on his tensed face.

Ba-dum. Ba-dum. Ba-dum.

My heart is racing and my hands turn into ice. Hurt and elation war with each other, slashing my insides as I struggle to even out my breath.

"Are you okay, Ems?" Liz asks, a small frown marring her face. I'm still rooted to the floor, unable to move, unable to speak, unable to comprehend what had just happened.

Slowly, I shake my head, my mind in a haze, my heart still pounding as if I've run a marathon. The ache resurfaces, stronger than ever, and the scab opens in my damaged heart. I fight myself from reaching up and rubbing the throbbing in my chest. "I'm fine. Sorry about that. Ha. Blast from the past." My hands tremble as I twist my lips in what I hope to be a convincing smile.

Lies. It's all lies. I'm not fine. Far from it.

And I have a feeling my life is about to be turned upside down again.

ACT TWO——THE HARSHEST HOPE

I stare at the man in front of me, barely refraining from curling my lips up in derision. Sweat drips down his ruddy cheeks, his breathing shallow, his thick fingers gripping the pen tight enough his knuckles are showing white. The anger simmering in my veins is tightly leashed and I notice him swallow, his nostrils flaring.

Almost there.

Fucking sign the damn paper.

"What are you waiting for? This is a once-in-a-lifetime opportunity," I murmur, my voice steady as a thrill of satisfaction whips through me at his flinch.

"You snake," he seethes, his face mottled with anger. I lean back in the leather chair in my office. They come and see me now, even if it means they'll be on the chopping block.

Adrian Scott never gives without getting something back.

I stay silent, a ghost of a smile twisting on my face, and I tap my fingers on the redwood desk.

Tap. Tap. Tap. Tap.

Marvin Granish's face pales even further. Beads of sweat form on his upper lip. His breathing picks up in speed.

Almost there.

Just one last push.

"We wouldn't want your daughter to find out you're fucking her best friend on the side, would we?"

The blood drains out of his face, and his shoulders slump, a sure sign of defeat. He presses the tip of the pen onto the contract, digging his signature into the paper before slapping the instrument loudly on the table.

"You asshole."

Smirking, I stand and place my palms on the desk. "Pleasure doing business with you. Don't let the door hit you on your way out."

Pressing a button on my phone, I instruct, "Kim, Mr. Granish is done here. Please escort him out."

Moments later, my secretary opens the glass doors of my office and Granish stomps toward the exit, not before lashing out, "One day, someone will fuck you over, Scott."

Ignoring him, I stroll over to the floor-to-ceiling windows of my office on the top floor of a high rise on Lake Avenue in Pasadena, north of downtown LA. The victory feels hollow, nothing but a morsel to feed the ravaging beast inside me, the anger or ambition never fully satiated. I slide my hands in my trouser pockets and look down at the world at my feet. My company owns half the free land in this city and we're in the process of purchasing more as I build my empire on the West Coast. Companies are migrating away from Silicon Valley and Santa Monica due to staggering rent and limited options, and Pasadena is a viable solution, being close enough to the heart of LA yet relatively undiscovered by large corporations. As I stand forty stories above the ground, staring down at the tiny cars on the street, crawling to the beat of the traffic, I feel empty, numb to the victory just now.

Granish holds twenty percent of the stock for Cornwall Holdings, my grandfather's company, and that twenty percent is now mine. Unfortunately for this old-money geezer, he had a fondness for women outside of his wife, with his latest illicit affair being his precious daughter's best friend, fresh out of college at twenty-three years old.

The disgusting pig, much like most of his peers.

The insults Granish hurled at me before he left don't faze me. I've heard worse in my climb up the ranks. Jack once told me he overheard his patrons at The Orchid commenting about the cold-hearted bastard, The Shark, who kills and decimates without remorse. He is currently living his best life, working as an entertainment manager at The Orchid, the pinnacle establishment of the world-renowned Fleur Entertainment in New York City.

You can't show mercy when you're the outsider who's climbed into the ranks of the incestuous circle of old money and powerful families. These people don't respect you if you're weak, something I unfortunately have firsthand experience with from my younger years.

A fairy with long, dark hair, large eyes, and a heart-shaped face materializes in my mind. Emily Kingsley. I knew there'd be a good chance she would be at Parker and Liz's rehearsal dinner half a year ago. It was a step I needed to take as part of the plan, but nothing could've prepared me for facing her for the first time in over ten years. A huge part of me wishes I could look at her in disdain, my emotions long deceased, but unfortunately, life doesn't work that way.

The organ serving only to pump blood through my body unfortunately kicked into a deep rhythm when my eyes met her mocha-colored ones, still framed with the lushest lashes I've ever seen. Her hair is shorter now, just past her shoulders in a blunt hairstyle, the silky strands gleaming in the warmest of chocolates and caramels. Her face is slimmer, and her lips are still as enticing, ruby-red, plump, a softness begging to be kissed, touched. Her petite figure has filled out, her curves more rounded, fitting into her purple dress like a glove, her toned legs still lean and smooth. She has an air of sophistication and maturity, an innate sense of seductiveness I'm apparently still not immune to.

And frankly, that fucking pisses me off.

However, it's her eyes that are the most unforgettable, the most haunting. The flinch of pain I saw in them when our gazes connected is an image seared into my brain. The pain I felt so viscerally, gutting my insides, a flash of agony; something I haven't felt in a long time in my emotionless soul.

The burning embers of anger unfurl into a dark flame, sizzling my chest as I clench my hands and stare at the people walking on the sidewalks, worker ants toiling about the day. Everything is going according to plan, but somehow, instead of elation or excitement, I feel a slither of dread, a coiling of unease. Gritting my teeth, I pound on the glass in frustration as a soft knock at my door jolts me from my thoughts.

Kim steps in, professional as always, and says, "Mr. Scott, I have Mr. Wellington on line two. Do you have time to speak to him now?"

"Transfer it to my cell, but tell him to give me five minutes. Please have Pierre get the car ready for me."

She nods and shuts the door as I stride to my chair and shrug back into my navy bespoke Italian suit jacket. No more frayed clothing for me. Those days are long gone.

A few minutes later, I sit in the comfortable leather seats of my town car while my trusted driver for the last five years chauffeurs me to a small Spanish restaurant by the Redondo Pier. My cell phone rings, the shrill sound disrupting the quiet hum in the car.

"Parker, sorry to keep you waiting. I was just getting out of the office and on my way to meet Millie for dinner." I cross my legs and glance out the window, watching the cars blur into streaks of red, blue, and gray on the 110 freeway.

"Don't worry about it. I wanted to let you know the drawings for the rest of your campus are almost complete. You're really going to turn Pasadena into a mini Silicon Valley, aren't you?" the gravelly voice of my long-time friend and mentor from my days at Cornell sound over the phone. His architectural and interior design firm is helping design my large-scale campus in Southern California, a rival to some of the high-tech space up north.

"More than that. It won't only be for tech companies. There's interest from financial and entertainment industries as well." My gaze trails to the darkening skies outside, glowing in a watercolor of purples and pinks, with a flock of birds flying overhead, soaring freely in the skies. I envy them, nary a worry, weightless and untethered, while I still feel like I'm chained down by a bottomless pit of ambition, a thirst to prove myself to the world that is never quenched, despite me standing within the upper echelons of society now.

"Of course, I'd expect nothing less from you. Did I tell you how proud I am of what you've accomplished? I still remember the serious, heartbroken kid from the mentorship program. I had a feeling even back then you were going to achieve something great, but you exceeded my expectations."

My chest warms as my soul roars with pride, my lips tilting into a grin at his accolades. Parker jumped in the deep end in one of the darkest times of my life when I arrived at Cornell, all the way across the country, my heart carved wide open by the girl I loved, fresh after losing Mom, and pulled me out of the proverbial swirling waters. My grades were slipping, my mind so overwhelmed with grief and anger, and Parker stepped in as my guide in a new mentorship program. He was a grad school student at the time and said I reminded him a little of himself when he was younger, because he too came from humble beginnings and also lost a parent to cancer. He reached out and rescued me from the depths of hell of my mind and helped me re-channel my energies into my studies, into my ambition.

"You had a huge part in it. I'll never forget it."

"How was the deal? You were in final negotiations today, right?"

"It went as expected. If the old man isn't going to sell to me, then I'll get the shares some other way."

"Cornwall is still not budging, huh?"

I scoff as the flames of anger spark again. My grandfather. The true cold-blooded asshole between the two of us. Oh, how the world is fooled.

"No. He's not selling. He's saying my image doesn't fit the family-oriented culture of his company. But one day he will." And someday, I'll do what I do best—take my enemy's most-beloved possession and tear it apart piece by piece, selling them to the wolves, leaving me as the sole victor in the arrangement.

Parker hums noncommittally as if he's distracted. "Hey, I have to go. Liz is calling."

"Say hi to her for me."

The irony of my longtime friend being the brother-in-law of the woman I once would've given my life to isn't lost on me.

Someday, they'll all be sorry. The vows I made to myself a decade ago echo in my mind.

That someday is now.

. . .

"You look stressed," Millie comments as she sits across from me at a private corner booth at Sombra, a small tapas restaurant at the edge of the pier, boasting unparalleled views of the Pacific Ocean around us. We just finished a filling meal consisting of an assortment of tapas, from the aromatic *Gambas al Ajillo,* a savory garlic shrimp dish, to *Pimientos de Padrón,* a fried blistered peppers dish with a spicy kick.

The server materializes next to our table and places a piping-hot ramekin of *Crema Catalana,* a close cousin to the French crème brûlée, and a slice of *Tarta de Queso,* the Basque cheesecake, in front of us. My sister has a sweet tooth, and nothing makes me happier than watching her eyes light up as she digs into these dishes she was deprived of as a kid.

As expected, Millie licks her lips, automatically reaching out for the custard dish, and glances at me in question.

Shaking my head, I motion for her to dig in and she scoops a large spoonful to her mouth. She closes her eyes and moans in delight. "This is too good, Adrian. You're missing out."

Chuckling softly, I say, "Take it to go if you don't finish it. We can always come back later on when you're craving these desserts again." She'll never want for anything anymore. That's the one thing I'm sure of. That's the one promise I made in high school I'm delivering on now.

She grins, flashing her bright smile, and the warmth burrows deeper into my chest. My younger sister has blossomed from the morose little kid who lost her mom to a confident, beautiful nineteen-year-old. She is currently at ULA for a one-year exchange program from NYU. I prefer it this way. I can keep an eye on her and make sure she doesn't fall for any idiots at school.

"Don't think you can distract me. Is everything okay?"

"Things are fine, Millie. You don't need to worry about me."

She cocks her eyebrow as she swallows another bite of dessert. "You've always worried about me and Dad. I'd say it's fair game."

I smirk. "Well...don't. Your big brother has the world by its balls and work is just busy, as always."

She pats her belly after finishing the custard dessert and groans in satisfaction. Shaking my head, I signal the waiter, who comes hurrying over.

"Wrap this up and please bring me the check." I motion to the untouched cheesecake.

"Is school going well?"

Millie nods, her long brown hair swaying with the movement. "The semester just started not long ago, and I'm pretty busy. Do you know one of my professors is a guest lecturer from New York? He's pretty big over there...you may know him."

"Oh really? Who is it?"

"Ryland Anderson." Her face flushes pink, but it may just be the candlelight playing tricks on my eyes.

I settle the bill and hand her a paper bag with the cheesecake as we head toward the doors. "I know of him. He's part of the prominent Anderson Family. They own half of New York City, including Fleur Entertainment, which..." I glance at her and raise my brow, "I'm sure you've frequented their clubs."

She shoves my arm gently. "It's part of the college experience. Clubbing and dancing, you boring old man."

Laughing at her impishness, I wrap my arm around her shoulder, giving it a soft squeeze. The night air is cool and dry as we stand by the curb outside of the restaurant. "Drive safe. Don't stay up too late and text me when you get back to your apartment."

Pierre pulls up next to us and opens the door. Millie glances at me with curiosity in her light-blue eyes. "What about you?"

"I'm going to make a stop somewhere before I head back. Good night, Millie."

She wraps me in a hug, a light, fruity scent emanating in the air. I stay behind to watch her get into her car and drive away before I slide into the leather seats of the town car.

"Pierre, Palos Verdes Beach, please."

"Got it, sir."

I lean back in my seat and close my eyes as the car hums to life, the scent of expensive leather and crisp cleaning agents lingering in the small space. My fingers trail the smooth surface of the handrest as my mind flickers back to Mom, who never got to see me succeed.

Mom, if you're up there looking down at us. I hope you're happy. I hope you're at peace.

I slip into a light rest, the Rolodex in my mind fluttering to the little boy in front of the elementary school with the hole in his T-shirt and the older boy who felt completely out of place at a school with gilded buildings and gold-tipped fences.

A short drive later, a knock on my window wakes me up from my trip down memory lane. Pierre opens the door quietly. "We are here, sir."

I swallow the lump in my throat as my pulse picks up in speed. Exiting the car, my senses overload with a myriad of sensations as buried memories force their way into the forefront.

The salty breeze, the moist air, the scent of brine forever reminding me of this beach. The temperatures are mild, albeit a bit cold this fall evening. This place which holds so many memories for me. Beautiful ones. Painful ones. My heart stutters and restarts and I inhale a ragged breath, desperate to take in more of the salted air I've missed in the past decade, for no beaches in New York could ever compare, could ever touch me in the deepest recesses of my heart, than this one.

The beach where I experienced a life-altering love, two souls melding together. Or so I thought at the time.

The beach where I suffered the most tortuous heartbreak.

The place where hopes and dreams were once resurrected.

The beach where those same things were snuffed out of me.

The place where I decided fate only lies in my hands and there is no greater power out there looking after me.

I amble on the soft sand, not caring the grains are probably ruining my expensive leather shoes. I can always have my secretary buy me a new pair. A shiny object a few feet in front of me catches my eye. Crouching down, I pick it up, a perfect scallop shell, pink in appearance, smooth at the ridges, a rarity based on the knowledge I've gleaned on seashells throughout the years.

I've turned something important to her into something motivating for me. Instead of wishes and dreams, each shell I collect represents one more target for me to pursue...a larger house, a nicer car, another acquisition. Things I control. Picking up the shell, I slide it into the pocket of my trousers before standing up.

The waves are calm tonight, softly lapping against the coastline in a quiet rhythm, a perfect offset to my thundering thoughts. The area is devoid of people just like all those years ago. It's the first time I've stepped foot onto this beach since I moved back to LA. Somehow, I never felt ready to walk along these shores, to see if anything has changed, if my feelings are different. But tonight, things feel different. Perhaps it's because I know I'll see her soon once again. Perhaps I want to test myself, to determine if I can brave these shores unscathed knowing Emily will be a fixture in my life in the near future and I need to steel myself to prepare for her presence.

The feelings of love and warmth perhaps have long drained away from my soul, like the waves stealing pieces of kelp and wildlife in its hasty retreat into the vast, dark ocean.

But the ache is still there. It has apparently lain dormant all these years.

My eyes flutter closed as I approach our spot. The spot belonging to a lonely boy and his pixie as a flash of pain suddenly splinters my chest, the throbbing so intense, my legs tremble. I slowly sit down in the area that once brought me happiness and stare out into the dark waters, the waves glistening, tipped in threads of silver, illuminated only by the bright moonlight. A crescent moon tonight.

There's something about the past that seems to haunt you the moment you least expect it. A unique smell. A familiar sound. A special place can trigger memories and emotions that have been tightly tethered down and stored deep away from the surface. A simple match can light the greatest fire.

I inhale and exhale forcefully, willing my body to calm, willing my mind to settle. Adrian Callahan may have been weak and poor, but Adrian Scott is strong and rich. This fleeting pain in my chest is just a scar which has broken open, an old wound acting up when the storm is raging outside.

It won't stop me.

Gritting my teeth, the muscles in my jaw ache as I tamp down the torrent of emotions I've bottled up inside...perhaps for the past eleven years.

I'm back.

And no one can hurt me any longer.

CHAPTER 25

Emily

Mother: Your father misses you. When will you be coming home for dinner? I'll have the chef prepare your favorite sweet and sour pork.

I stare at the text from Mother, not knowing how to respond. Ever since high school, our relationship is tenuous at best, but has been steadily improving since Jess stood up to her a few years ago when Mother was trying to matchmake her with "suitable partners." I think, perhaps she finally realizes the birds have flown the coop and if she wants to have any relationship with us, she needs to start treating us as adults.

Mother: I also made the bone broth which you liked last time. Your father is coughing a lot more these days. He works too hard. I want to get him to retire. Maybe you can talk some sense into him. He's too intent on leaving TransAmerica with a powerful legacy.

While I never forgave her for what she did to Adrian and me all those years ago, I can tell she loves me, even if her actions are misguided. She believes by bestowing her words of criticism as a gift upon us, she'll improve us and better set us up for the future. And now, in classic Asian parent fashion, she's making sure my favorite food is on the table, a roundabout way of telling me she loves and cares about me.

Because nothing can be as straightforward as saying those words out loud.

"Emily, *mon cheri*, over here." Antoine Moreau, the executive chef at the popular, trendy restaurant, Le Cirque, waves at me from a secluded corner of the restaurant. The immense number of exotic flowers and green foliage decorating the walls and partitions within the establishment never ceases to amaze me. It's as if I've traveled thousands of miles away from Los Angeles and stepped into the middle of a rainforest, minus the humidity and mosquitoes. Soft chatter and occasional laughter pierce the intimate atmosphere of the restaurant. All the tables are packed to the brim—a normal occurrence.

Grinning, I slip my phone into my purse and amble toward my friend, whom I once dated for a few months a couple of years ago, but in a rare outcome, our friendship has survived our breakup as we were far better suited as friends than lovers.

"Bonjour, my friend. How have you been doing?" I smooth out the wrinkles on my white linen, cut-out sundress before sliding into a chair at the table across from him.

"Can't complain. Business is still booming, as you can see. All thanks to you."

I worked on the opening of Le Cirque, from organizing a media team to hype up the restaurant on social media and blogs—which in the culinary hotspot that is LA is no easy task since new venues opening are everyday occurrences—to assisting with the sharp uniform designs for the chefs and waitstaff because image is considered paramount in the entertainment capital of the world. The late nights and long hours paid off, and Le Cirque usually has a wait list of at least a few months.

"I'm just stopping by to pick up your famous desserts and to say hi to you before I head to Liz's place for a girls' night."

"I figured that was the case when your order came through earlier. Please say hi to them for me. I haven't seen Jess and James for a while." He drums his long fingers on the table as his gaze takes on a faraway look. It's as if he's running through an invisible task list in his mind. "Things are going well for the most part. I'm working on opening a new location in Marina Del Rey. Folks over there don't tend to venture so far east due to the heavy traffic, but there's a very hip crowd on the West Side. I think we'll do well there."

I take a sip of the iced latte he prepared before my arrival, the creaminess of the milk with the extra-strong espresso is just what I need after tossing and turning in my bed last night, dreading what I'm about to face tomorrow, or better yet, whom. "Sounds like a smart plan. If you need help, you know how to reach me." I grin and he flashes a brief smile, his toothpaste-commercial-ready teeth making an appearance.

"So, anything new with you these days? Any new men in your life?"

An image of a man with dark hair, chiseled jaw, and light-blue eyes materializes in my mind and my heart hiccups. I quickly shutter the thought and shake my head. "No, taking a break."

"Still on your three-month plan?"

The girls used to make fun of me, saying I date a man for three months, then dump him at the high of the relationship. An old adage from the only man I've ever let close to me flits to the forefront of my consciousness. *Maybe some relationships are best left unexplored. Leave when everything is at a high, when everything is beautiful. Before it all collapses and the ugliness seeps in.* The void in my chest, something I usually mask by filling my social calendar with meetings and activities, resurfaces, the emptiness causing a pinch in my stomach. Adrian was wise beyond his years and his words are something I've subscribed to all this time. In the deepest corners of my heart, I don't want to fall in love again.

Because the pain of the aftermath was too terrible, the devastation of the free fall from the heavens was too traumatizing, too heartbreaking, I don't believe I've ever truly recovered from it.

Jess has always considered herself to be the worrywart of the family, the anxious soul, but little does she know, perhaps I'm the true coward between the two of us because I don't even want to take the leap anymore. It's safer and more comfortable to stand on solid ground, even though I remember the weightless exhilaration of the jump, the freedom of the flight, and the energy thrumming through my veins.

But the withdrawal when it's all taken away from you—something I'm not interested in ever experiencing again.

"You know me, date them, have fun, then..." I wink before wagging my brows, my lips tilting up into a smirk.

He rolls his eyes in exasperation and completes my thought, "Dump them before things get rough." Antoine shakes his head, a frown marring his classically handsome face.

"Emily, I know we had our fun a few years back, and you told me you weren't looking for something serious and I believed you then. But you know I care about you as a friend, and now, after knowing you for so long, I sense there's something more behind the sentiment. You're a sweet person and capable of so much love, and don't think I haven't seen those longing glances you throw out when you see other lovey-dovey couples when you think no one is paying attention. I hope one day you can find the right person, settle down, and not flounder from relationship to relationship. That must be lonely."

My heart hitches as heat spreads to my face. His words hit too close to home. I force my lips into a smile. "Just because you have Jolene doesn't mean you need to matchmake everyone under the sun, Antoine." Jolene is his fiancée, and those two are blissfully, disgustingly in love. I guess my acting skills weren't enough to hide the occasional loneliness leaking out.

"It's one thing if you're truly happy being the awesome powerhouse woman you are, but it's another thing if it's something you want but are somehow afraid to pursue because of whatever reason."

I take a large sip of coffee, the icy drink doing nothing to settle my rattled nerves and the flush I'm sure is on my face. I shrug, stirring the straw around in the glass, listening to the ice cubes clinking against each other.

A waiter comes by our table with a large paper bag, no doubt filled with the pastries I ordered for my contribution to the girls' night. Relieved at the interruption, I pull out my wallet to pay for them, but Antoine waves off the staff with a nod before turning to me.

"How many times do I have to tell you, friends don't let friends pay for food at the restaurant said friend helped launch?" He winks, flashing another bright smile, his charm effortless in a way that seems to be innate with the French.

Gathering my belongings, I stand then wrap him in a firm hug. "*Merci beaucoup, mon ami.* Thanks for looking out for me. See you next time."

He chuckles and waves me off. "Your accent is still terrible."

"You appreciate me for trying. You know you do." I laugh, my voice sounding forced and hollow in my ears.

A short drive later—a stroke of luck, really, because it's rare for there to be no traffic in LA—I arrive at Liz and Parker's majestic, two-story contemporary home. With its sleek lines and sloping roofs, carefully manicured gardens and terraces, this home has been featured in multiple architectural and interior design magazines, which isn't a surprise given Parker's occupation. Heck, even the man himself has been featured in articles and websites, coined as one of the hottest and most eligible bachelors in architecture. Of course, with him being happily married to Liz now, the bachelor nickname is no more, but that doesn't stop us from making fun of him occasionally.

The door swings open before I get a chance to ring the doorbell and I spot a blur of a miniature human with warm-blonde hair barreling into me, wrapping her arms around my waist.

"Auntie Emily!" Lucy shrieks with excitement.

Laughing, I crouch down and give her a proper hug. "Lucy, you pipsqueak! You scared me for a bit there."

Parker's daughter is six years old now, or almost seven, as she likes to remind me, a proud second grader at the school Liz teaches at. Her mother passed when she was two years old, and there was definitely drama when Liz, her kindergarten teacher, nannied for Parker during the summer a few years ago, which resulted in the couple realizing their love for each other and overcoming some pretty tough obstacles.

"Mommy, Auntie Jess, Auntie Sarah, and Auntie Melanie are in the backyard. Daddy is at work."

"Lucy! What did I tell you about opening the door without letting me know?" Liz runs up to us, slightly out of breath, as she frowns at a contrite Lucy.

"But I saw Auntie Emily at the window. She isn't a stranger." Lucy pouts her cute little lips, her blue eyes wide and pleading. Darn little kids for being so adorable and brandishing those skills to the best of their abilities.

Liz sighs and blows a thick lock of golden-brown hair that has escaped her bun. She presses her lips together in an effort not to laugh before shooing Lucy back inside. "Next time, still tell me, okay?"

"Okay!" Lucy scurries away, her quick footfalls echoing down the halls.

Liz turns to me and smiles brightly, her sapphire eyes twinkling before suddenly sharpening, staring at the paper bag I have in my hand. "Is *that* what I think it is?" she whispers in awe, her eyes growing as big as saucers.

Chuckling, I wrap her in a tight hug before pulling away. "Of course. Antoine's pastries. Not going to show up empty-handed, and I know you're bananas for his eclairs."

"I love you." She fawns over the bag and cuddles it to her chest.

"What's not to love?" I wink, sauntering past her into a spacious living room, which used to be minimalistic and embellished in neutral grays, whites, and blacks, but now has pops of bright color splashed throughout. Lavender and blue pillows decorate the sizeable sectional sofa, colorful art prints on the walls, all courtesy of Liz, I'm sure.

As I step into the backyard oasis, my favorite girls in the world greet me with hugs and kisses. They are my lifeline. They always say I'm the life of the party, but little do they know the so-called life is recharged solely by these precious interactions. Sarah, with her thick, strawberry-blonde hair shining under the afternoon sun, sits on a padded sofa next to Jess, who has her sleek black hair tied up in a low bun. Melanie is sitting across from them, sipping a cocktail of some sort, a pink glow already on her pale skin.

Liz pours me an orange-red drink, the color of the early hours of the sunset, and I arch my brow in question.

"Sangria. Homemade recipe."

Taking a sip, I relish the cool, sweet liquid washing down my throat. "This is so delicious. Liz, you're so good at cooking, and apparently...bartending. Parker is lucky to have you."

"Oh, shut up." She shoves me playfully before taking a seat in her favorite egg-shaped recliner.

I plop down next to Melanie and nurse my drink, needing all the liquid courage I can get to face tomorrow. And the days after.

"What's the look on your face?" Jess asks, her perceptive hazel eyes trained on me. She may be the quiet one of our group, but nothing ever escapes her eyes.

Letting out a deep exhale, I explain, "Tomorrow is the first day of my gig with Scott Enterprises, and I'm not looking forward to it."

"Something tells me this is more than Adrian Scott being known as an asshole. You didn't tell us the last time we asked, so I've been digging through my memory because something about him just nags at me...and I think I've made the connection." Jess stares at me, her elegant brows furrowing pensively.

The heat flooding my cheeks has nothing to do with the alcohol. Even the Asian glow, the pinkening of the skin a lot of folks with Asian genes experience when imbibing alcoholic drinks, doesn't show up this fast. "W-What do you mean?"

"I saw him a few times these past few months when James, Parker, and he would hang out at our place, and every time I see him, I get the faintest sense I've met him before." She takes a sip of her drink and I hold my breath, hoping she doesn't remember, hoping she doesn't bring up the past. "I couldn't place it until I was looking through old photos the other day. Wasn't there an Adrian in your life a long time ago when you were a senior in high school? That's him, right? I remember thinking there was something about him...and I thought perhaps the two of you were dating, but you told me it wasn't the case. Is that the same Adrian?"

"Oh! I remember the recital. You're right, Jess. I didn't get to meet him because I had to run an errand, but I faintly recall his name coming up later on," Liz chimes in.

I glance up, my gaze automatically snagging to Sarah, who has her lips pressed in a firm line as her amber eyes meet mine in sympathy. She nods imperceptibly, as if telling me she has my back. She's the only one out of the girls' group who knows the most about my past relationship with Adrian.

Letting out a ragged breath, I glance at the drink in my hand, staring at the condensation on the outside of my glass as I fight to keep my face nonchalant, to shutter my eyes so they won't ask any more questions. Once I feel I have my wits about me, I reply, "Yes. It's the same Adrian. That's why I was shocked to see him at your rehearsal dinner going by a different last name."

"It makes so much sense now, why you were so surprised that night," Liz muses. "I wonder why he changed his last name." It's a question that has been percolating in my mind as well.

"Ems, I always had a gut feeling back then but then you didn't really mention him, so I thought if there was anything, perhaps it wasn't serious, but seeing your face now..." Jess trails off, her eyes still cataloging my expressions. I curse myself for not hiding my thoughts well enough. "Was it serious?"

I twist my lips into a grin and force out a halfhearted laugh. "Fine. You got me there. We were together for a little bit in high school and it didn't end well. And...I don't want to talk about it. But yes, I'm definitely dreading work tomorrow. Things may get awkward." To be in such close proximity to him, but for him to look at me with hatred in his eyes... I don't know how I can bear it. Nausea rolls around in my stomach and suddenly, I'm not so thirsty anymore. I carefully place my glass on the table, fighting the trembling in my hand.

Jess reaches out and stills my hand with hers. "Ems, are you okay?" she asks softly as a lump forms in my throat.

My nose burns and wetness prickles my eyes. The old wound in my heart has been acting up and with each passing day since the rehearsal dinner, my thoughts have been filled with more and more memories. It's as if my mind can't shut off and is replaying every single moment I've had with him. The joyous ones, the devastating ones... Every snippet I've kept under lock and key in my broken heart.

Blinking rapidly, I dole out a watery smile. "I-I'm fine."

"Oh sweetie." Jess gets up and wraps me in her arms. She smooths her hand on my back in reassuring circles as I fight to control my chaotic emotions. "I'm here if you ever want to tell me about it," she whispers in my ear.

Nodding rapidly, I disentangle from her before smiling at the rest of the gang. "Working with your ex-boyfriend can do a number to your feelings, sorry about the drama, girls."

Melanie refills my drink. "Another reason for more alcohol, Ems. Men suck." She rolls her eyes. "They really do. Do you know I got an unsolicited dick pic the other day from *InstaConnect*?" She pats my lap as she switches the topic to her miserable love life and the lack of quality candidates on the popular dating app.

Sarah walks over and sits next to me. "You sure you're okay there, Ems?" She gives me a gentle shove. The rest of the girls have moved onto the topic of nightmarish first date stories.

"You know how it was, Sarah," I whisper, the lump in my throat growing in size. "He hates me still, you know." My eyes burn as the ache returns to my chest when I remember the freezing chill in his stare. *What did you expect, Emily? You broke his heart.*

"You never did tell me the details, but I got a sense it ended horribly." She lets out a languid sigh. "Do you think you can ask your boss to put you on another project instead? I mean, you work at one of the most world-renowned PR firms. There has to be other top talent there who can service him and his company."

I rub my face, my eyes suddenly feeling very heavy and tired. "I've tried. Kristi wouldn't budge, no matter how many times I asked her. She said I have to be the one taking on the project and if I do it well, then maybe I can make director and pick my projects for next year, including the nonprofit ones I've been angling toward for so long."

When I picked my path to pursue public relations in college, I was hoping I'd get to work with nonprofits or with people who've been dealt a difficult hand in life and want some magical PR make-over, such as good press junkets, social media stories, even physical makeovers or etiquette training to get them to overcome branding issues. It's my dream to help these deserving individuals conquer the unfair biases formed based on whatever less-than-ideal first impressions they've made in the world. But naturally, these jobs are usually not the top-paying engagements at the firm and man-agement has been opposed to one of their best consultants working on low-profit-margin projects. Until recently, because I'm up for promotion to a director position and if I get it, I'll finally be able to pick some projects that interest me, projects that got me into this career in the first place. They're dangling the carrot in front of me as leverage.

"You have a team, right? Maybe some of your associates can directly deal with him instead of you?" Sarah muses, her eyes thoughtful.

"Maybe. We'll see."

"Hey, Ems. Lucy wants to go to the beach next week and play in the sand. The girls are coming for a day of relaxing under the sun. Do you want to come this time?" Liz asks.

The beach. A place I've avoided since him. Even after all these years, I can't bring myself to visit beaches voluntarily. It was a place that used to bring me peace and joy, but now only brings me melancholy. It's another reason I don't commit to long-term relationships. I'm not built to escape unscathed. With Adrian, I lost not only him but also my love for the beach and my affinity for the piano. I've mourned the losses, but I don't think I'll ever truly get over it.

I shake my head and answer with my usual excuse, "You guys have fun. I'll be working as usual. Hollywood never sleeps, you know." Winking, I pick up my drink and swallow a large gulp of the fruity spice, waiting for the warm buzz to kick in.

You're a badass woman, Emily Kingsley. So many people see *their exes. If they can do it, you can kick ass at it.* I mutter the mantras under my breath as I stand in front of the conference room doors in the ultra-sleek, modern Los Angeles offices of Taylor Henrickson, the world-renowned public relations firm I've devoted almost eight years of my life to. A ball has formed in my throat, my mouth parched, as I work up my courage to push through the matte-glass barriers and step inside and face him.

The man who has shown up in my thoughts almost daily since the rehearsal dinner half a year ago.

Inhaling a ragged breath, I plaster a practiced smile on my face, something I've done at countless PR events in the past, but this time it feels more forced, more restrained. Pushing open the double doors, I stride in, channeling my inner girl boss.

"Emily, good morning! This is an exciting day for us, the beginning of a wonderful relationship between Taylor Henrickson and Scott Enterprises." Kristi Thorne, the managing partner of the office, stands up and greets me with exuberance, her light-blonde blunt bob haircut shining almost white this morning under the cool florescent lights.

My eyes delay the inevitable, skating over the imposing man who has risen to a standing position from his seat on the other side of the long, white lacquered table, and focus on my big boss. My thundering heartbeats reverberate in my ear and I could swear I smell a faint scent of mint and expensive cologne.

"Kristi. I hope you had a great weekend." I smile even wider, my teeth showing, hoping my face doesn't betray the chaos happening inside me.

Kristi nods as she smooths her manicured hands down her fire-engine-red sheath dress. Damn it, I wish I had gone with red as well instead of the black pantsuit I have on. Maybe then I'd be emanating a badass aura. She turns her head to the man across from her and says, "Mr. Scott, may I present to you our top consultant, Emily Kingsley. She'll be your point of contact for our arrangement." She glances at me, cocking her head toward Adrian. "Emily, this is Adrian Scott. It's an absolute honor he has chosen our firm for his media debut."

Swallowing the lump in my throat, I let out a slow exhale and meet his startling blue gaze for the first time in seven and a half months. My pulse quickens, the nerves in my body coming alive in his presence, as if the years haven't come between us. My heart leaps to my throat, warring with my mind in an urge to be closer to the person who once was my entire world and an impulse to escape the stifling room, the animosity in his eyes.

I stare into the stormy pools of blue, a chilly intensity radiating from them. My gaze skates over his masculine face, his dark hair carefully tousled, the strong jawline covered by the slightest bit of scruff. His muscular body is encased in a crisp white shirt, a maroon tie, and an expertly tailored navy pinstripe suit. Adrian's body is coiled in tension, radiating strength and power. Unlike the proud boy from high school, his head held defiantly high in the face of gossip and murmurings, the man in front of me is quietly assured, someone who owns the boardroom without saying a single word, a person comfortable amongst the predators in the business realm, a king ruling them all.

I smile brightly despite the tension in my neck, the crick in my muscles. I saunter up to the table and extend my hand toward him. "Mr. Scott, it's a pleasure to meet you. I'm looking forward to working with you and making sure your needs are met." My eyes plead with him, *Please don't acknowledge we've met before. I don't want to be subjected to questions later.*

The light-blue flames in his eyes flare slightly at the word *needs* and I internally cringe. It sounded better in my head. He leans forward slightly, his movements measured, and he takes my hand in his for the first time in over a decade. His eyes darken as he stares at me. A jolt of awareness, sizzling in intensity, slithers through me at the point of contact and he takes in a quick gasp of air, barely noticeable to anyone unless you know him well. It's as if every atom in my body has awakened from a deep slumber and all the sensations are tenfold and magnified. His rough fingers radiate warmth as he squeezes gently, his thumb circling my skin briefly before letting go.

"Ms. Kingsley. Looking forward to working together." His deep voice travels across the table like a soft caress, and I fight the urge to shiver. He sounds different now, the familiar voice deepening with age, with a slight raspy undertone, more potent and dangerous than before.

My hand tingles, my mind unsettled, and we take a seat, Kristi and I on one side, Adrian on the other. He leans back in his chair, his posture a statement of leashed power, the epitome of an alpha male very comfortable with himself in any environment. I stare at his tie instead of his face.

"Emily, can you walk Mr. Scott through the high-level plan we've discussed previously?"

I nod as I press a few buttons on the conference room tablet, loading up the presentation on the large flat screen in the front of the room. Staring at the monitor, I recite the words I've practiced many times before, grateful my voice is steady and self-assured.

"In our planning process, we've outlined the goals of your media and image rehabilitation campaign, as you've discussed with Kristi in the past." I glance at him, finding his searing gaze pinned on me, his face inscrutable. My eyes dart away and I continue, "The overarching goal is to deliver an impressive media debut for you and to craft an image and persona of someone who is amiable and has the family-oriented qualities that'll align to the interests of Cornwall Holdings, which are known for their family-first philosophy."

My pulse settles into a calming beat as I fall into the rhythm of my presentation. Work is something I'm familiar with, something I enjoy and excel at. "We've combed the existing media archives to take inventory of your overall image as of today. Because you've always shied away from the spotlight and have refused interviews and images of yourself to be published, the major media outlets have resorted to educated guesses and extrapolation on your personality. You're the only individual who has graced *Time, People, and Forbes* magazines 'person of the year' without showing your face. Your billion-dollar net worth is well known. You're branded as 'The Shark' and there's a saying, 'when The Shark comes, everyone swims away.' From the few comments leaked by individuals not under your numerous nondisclosure agreements, your reputation is known to be cutthroat, merciless, and since you're reclusive, there haven't been any rebuttals to offset the first impression established for you."

I peek at him, hoping I haven't offended him. His only response is a small dip of his head, his long fingers tapping gently on the table, and his searing gaze on mine, still unwavering. His face is a mask of indifference, as if I'm debriefing him on weather forecasts. Two fingers lift off the lacquered surface and curl slightly, an indication for me to continue.

Swallowing hard, I move on to the next section of the research. "Your romantic relationships are not public due to the gag orders you have your partners sign. But there is a reputation of you being a playboy, of treating women as disposable. How much of that is a fact, the media doesn't care about. This makes for a good story and that's what's floating around online."

My pulse hums in a rickety rhythm again as my mind flits back to the articles and gossip rags my team has compiled in our in-depth research on him. He has been rumored to be with super-models, actresses, heiresses and the like, supposedly depraved in the bedroom, and dates and discards them like articles of clothing. He does not get emotionally involved and is known to be cold, even to his romantic partners. These are rumors, of course, but my heart clenches at the loyal boy I knew back in the day, becoming this person I barely know.

"We need to establish a baseline in order to measure the progress of our campaign," Kristi adds. "We understand most of this information is false rumors, so we hope we haven't offended you in any way."

"Not at all. I'm aware of this. That's why I hired your firm." His voice is controlled, his words succinct, his face still betraying nothing, not even a flicker of acknowledgement or rebuttal of the veracity of the rumors. The ache in my chest resurfaces as I realize perhaps the rumors are true, and somehow, the pain deepens at the thought of him moving from woman to woman, even though I have no right to feel this way.

"Our usual image rehab and media campaigns generally involve a wardrobe rehaul, which you obviously don't need." He's too damn well dressed for his own good. My eyes dart back to him, finding his full lips tilt in a ghost of a smile, as if he's aware of the thoughts swimming in my mind. "The media debut will be the simple part. We've scheduled media appearances, interviews, and red-carpet events for you to attend, where you'll be photographed and you can dictate the narrative and give the press what they really want from you, your face and your story. We'll coach you through some talking points and behavioral items when the time comes."

I take a deep breath. This next part will be a hard sell. Wings flutter in my stomach as nausea seeps through my veins. "As for the playboy reputation, whether warranted or not, we will arrange for someone to date you for a duration of one year to show to the world you're settling down, which, of course, aligns to the family-oriented philosophy Cornwall is seeking. Nondisclosure agreements will be signed." Heat rushes to my face at the idea of arranging fake dates for Adrian for the foreseeable future. I brace myself for his fury and protests.

But they never come.

"Fine. Sounds reasonable." His tapping stops. "Where will you find the woman?"

My eyes whip up to his and I frown at the placidity there, as if I just asked him if he wants coffee or tea.

Remembering his question, I reply, "We have recently partnered with Fleur Entertainment, which I'm sure you're aware of. Their full range of entertainment services also includes companionship and escort services...legal ones, of course. They're known for their discretion to high-net-worth individuals. We'll set agreed-upon boundaries with this individual and schedule dates and public outings to encourage the narrative. Before we select the candidates for your consideration, I'll need to know if you have any preferences for her physical attributes." Nausea churns higher inside me and I'm glad I didn't have a large breakfast this morning. Logically, this is all part of the job, but emotionally I'm having a difficult time reconciling how I'm setting up dates for the only man I've ever loved.

And perhaps still... I give myself a mental slap on the face and snap myself out of this inner ridiculousness.

"Blonde. Green or blue eyes. Tall. Curvaceous." *Everything I'm not.* Each phrase an ice pick to the scab in my heart, opening a fresh stream of blood. Heat stings my eyelids at the unfairness of it all, and I blink, forcing myself to breathe through the pain.

I clench my hands into fists and freeze the neutral expression on my face as he scrutinizes me, his eyes the color of a burgeoning storm, as if picking apart every movement and reaction. His nostrils flare and he sinks farther back into his chair, placing one ankle on top of his knee, an image of relaxed nonchalance. Slowly, I exhale as the moment passes.

Nodding, I sit back down, my face heated despite my efforts. I twist my lips up into a bright smile.

"How does the high-level plan sound to you, Mr. Scott?" Kristi asks as she leans forward, clasping her hands on the table.

Tap. Tap. Tap.

Adrian resumes his drumming on the surface again as he cocks his head to the side. He dips his head in a curt nod. "Sounds fine. Contact my secretary to set up future meetings."

"Of course. I promise you, we have this well in hand. We'll be in touch."

Kristi stands and I follow suit, eager to escape this room, desperate to get away from him and his penetrating gaze. Adrian remains seated, his fingers still tapping the soft rhythm on the table.

"I'd like to speak to Ms. Kingsley in private," he murmurs, his low voice calm, with a thread of dominance, as if daring anyone to disagree.

My heart kicks against my rib cage, and I'm ensnared by his gaze again. Tearing my eyes away, I glance at Kristi, finding her furrowing her brows briefly before smoothing her face back into a calm façade. "Of course. Thank you for coming in, Mr. Scott." Throwing a glance my way, she glides out of the room. I have no doubt I'll be called into her office later on for a debrief.

The door closes with a soft *click*. Silence fills the conference room as I stare at his fingers, still rhythmically tapping. My heart leaps and free falls, completely out of rhythm.

"Emily..." he whispers, his gravelly voice reminding me of memories long buried away. My chest clenches at my name on his lips, my eyes suddenly burning as the past and present collide. *Not now. Fuck these hormones.* "I figure you and I should talk before this arrangement continues. It's been a long time..."

Swallowing the glass shards in my throat, I blink a few times, thankful the burning sensation has briefly abated. "Yes, it has." I slowly drag my eyes up to his, finding his steely blues inscrutable. "You've done well for yourself," I murmur, the wound in my chest aching with both elation and pain. I was right all those years ago. I knew he would make something of himself and he would rise like a phoenix from the ashes with the right opportunities.

I made the right decision. A painful one, but the right one nonetheless.

The victory feels hollow somehow.

And in the midst of the ache and rioting emotions inside me, I'm still proud of him. So proud of the boy who used to be on the outskirts of society to not only survive, but to successfully fight his way all the way up to the top.

Adrian's eyes turn cold and a muscle twitches in his cheek. A chill befalls us. "No more pity for me, huh?"

I flinch, remembering how he accused me of being with him because of pity, of toying with his emotions and callously discarding him on our last night at the beach. Letting out a ragged exhale, I straighten my shoulders and calmy reply, "No. I'm proud of you."

His irises darken even more and he swallows, as if taken aback by my response. "We aren't going to have a problem here, right?" He points his fingers between the two of us.

"No. Because I'm a professional."

"Good. Just making sure."

Wiping my clammy hands on my pants, I walk toward the door but stop and turned around. "Why did you change your last name, Adrian?"

He stares at me, his gaze shuttered and unreadable. "I needed a fresh start. One that didn't include the pitiful kid from back then."

Silence befalls us as we stare at each other, the tension thickening with each passing second. I let out a soft exhale and break eye contact.

"Looking forward to working with you, Mr. Scott."

Spinning around, I stride toward the door, only pausing when I hear his response, so soft I wonder if I've imagined it. "Likewise... *finally.*"

My legs tremble the moment I'm outside of the room, my heart racing, threatening to give out at any second. I heave out a deep exhale. Clasping my hand over my chest, I slowly walk back to my office. My cell phone dings—an incoming text. I glance down at the screen.

Sarah: How was the meeting? How are you holding up?

My mouth runs dry as I type out another lie.

Emily: It went fine. I'll live.

How am I going to survive this project unscathed?

"That's all you got, Scott?" Parker taunts, his feet dancing around the boxing ring with practiced ease, his glove-clad hands shielding his mouth. Sweat soaks through his golden-brown hair. "So, how did your meeting go with my sister-in-law?" I guess it counts, with Emily being Jess's sister, and Jess married to James, and James being Liz's brother.

"You fucker." I fake a lead uppercut, followed by a rear hook, landing across his jaw in a satisfying *smack*. "You talk too much."

"Shit. No face, dumbass," Parker mutters before resuming his fighting stance. "So, it didn't go well?" He launches into a combination punch and one of them skims my side, taking the breath out of my lungs, the pain barely registering as my mind wanders back to the conference room, when she waltzed in, her chocolate gaze fiery and determined, the sleek pantsuit draping over her tight, sexy body. The alluring woman is still heating my veins, much to my dismay.

Oh, the meeting went well, all right. All to the fucking plan, but instead of me feeling excited, I feel like shit. Her haunted eyes surface in my mind, the way she flinched imperceptibly when I mentioned my preferences for my fake date. Like I was the one who wounded her all those years ago instead of the other way around.

I throw out a few powerful jabs as he tries to dart to the side, a move I predicted a mile away, and I pivot, surprising him with a lead uppercut, the punch landing in his abdomen, and he attempts to block me with his hands. I switch between a combination of harsh jabs and swift hooks, pinning him to the corner, where he has absolutely nowhere to go. Just how I like my opponents to be.

"She's the one who got away, isn't she? The one who made you all depressed and shit when I met you," Parker huffs out, his lips curled up in a smug snarl. He flinches as I land more punches on him, the building fury bleeding into my veins. He coughs as I continue my assault, the loud smacks reverberating in the private boxing ring of Dominick's, a gentlemen's club for the rich and famous in downtown LA, another Fleur establishment on the West Coast.

"Damn. You're on a roll today. I'm not going to act as your punching bag." Parker taps my arm as he uses his free hand to block my flying punches, the fire seeping from my pores.

Blood roars in my ears and it takes a few seconds for me to recognize his submission. Gritting my teeth, I step back, spitting out my mouth guard and yanking off my gloves in the process before tossing them on the floor. I rake my fingers through my hair and grab a towel to wipe my face dry. After I uncap a water bottle, I chug down half of its contents in a few large gulps, but the cold water does little to tamp down the burning anger inside.

Collapsing in the chair in my corner of the ring, I pour the rest of the bottle on my hair, attempting to short-circuit my system into straying back to the present, and leaving the memories where they belong—in the past.

Parker approaches me and squats down. "Hey, man, you okay there?"

"I'm fine."

"You don't look fine. You look like shit, like I stole from your grandma or something."

I snort and shake my head. "Just thinking about work."

"Bullshit. Ever since you've been back—and I still haven't heard a reasonable explanation why you dropped off the face of the earth after college, by the way—you've been a workaholic, which I have a feeling is your constant state. This is different. And my gut tells me it's Emily."

I grip the empty bottle tightly in my hand, the bottle crinkling under my abuse. Tossing it to the ground, I reply, "I send emails sometimes. And you're overthinking."

"Emails," he scoffs. "What the fuck were you doing, anyway?"

"Building my empire. It took some time." And a lot of shady deals, blood, and sweat.

"Tell me, is she the girl who got away?" Parker's green eyes peer up at mine and I fight the urge to look away. Don't ever shy away from an opponent's gaze, whether in the ring or in the boardroom, the principle is still the same. Realization dawns on his face as he picks up on something in my expression.

"Shit," he breathes. "She is, isn't she? I knew there was something off when she called you Callahan at my wedding rehearsal. It didn't register until recently and I realized that was your old last name before you changed it."

I stay silent and grab another bottle of water at my feet and uncap the top. Taking a few slow sips of the cooling liquid, I buy myself some time.

"I don't know what your plans are, but you're known as 'The Shark' for a good reason, I'm sure." His eyes turn serious and he clutches my free arm in a death grip, his fingers digging into the muscle in warning. "Don't hurt her. She's like a sister to me and a kind, generous soul. I don't care what happened between the two of you in the past, but I won't stand by and watch you hurt her."

Capping the bottle, I slowly set it back on the ground and turn my gaze to his. "And if I do, what are you going to do about it?" My voice is barely above a whisper, but he heard it loud and clear.

A vein pulses in Parker's forehead and his startling green eyes blaze with intensity. "You don't want to find out."

Our gaze connects for a few seconds as we size each other up. I'm no longer the poor, heartbroken boy when I met him in the mentorship program. And Parker...well, he's powerful and successful in his own right, and I'd expect nothing less from him, someone

I've long admired, even from afar, when I disappeared from society after I graduated from Cornell.

"She'll be fine." *For now.*

Holding my gaze for one more second, he narrows his eyes before letting go of my arm, stepping away, seemingly satisfied with whatever he saw in my expression. "You coming for drinks with the guys, right?"

I nod as we climb out of the ring and head toward the locker rooms for a shower, then upstairs to meet up with Parker's friends, a few I've met before.

Half an hour later, five of us sit on luxurious black leather sofas facing a glass fireplace in a private room on the third floor of Dominick's. This club is decorated in dark woods and warm lights, leather and upholstered seating in the general lounge area and in the private rooms. Floor-to-ceiling grid windows are adorned with thick, neutral curtains, towering bookshelves filled with volumes no one probably reads, and multilevel lighting from wrought-iron, old-school gas lamp sconces to stained glass floor lamps, making it seem like we've stepped back in time to the regency era. A faint smell of cigars and amber linger in the air, the scent of opulence and success.

"You know James, and I believe you've met Charles from your days in New York City," Parker begins, motioning to his best friend and Emily's brother-in-law, the Chief Data Scientist at a prominent investment firm, and a blond man with light-blue eyes and an aristocratic air, a person I've come across once or twice when my firm dealt with his family's Bank of Columbia back East. "And this is Steven Kingsley, the youngest of the Kingsley siblings. He's the head of the investments department and one of the partners at Pietra Capital." I glance at the quiet, brooding man sitting next to James, his brown gaze unflinching as he takes me in, his lips tilting up in a small smile.

"I remember you," Steven says, and he takes a sip of whiskey from his tumbler, looking very comfortable with the surroundings. Typical Kingsley behavior. My insides rankle at his last name even though my net worth far exceeds the Kingsley family now, except for Steven—I don't know much about him. Steven's ankle crosses over his knee and he unbuttons one button from his dove-gray suit jacket.

My mind flashes back to a scrawny kid at Emily's recital, the one who gave me the lightly veiled warning about hoping I treat my friends well. He's definitely all grown up, imposing and self-assured, as one must be if he's risen to the top of the ranks at what I presume to be around twenty-seven, twenty-eight years old.

"You've grown up." I smirk. "Wouldn't have recognized you on the street. I don't think I've had dealings with Pietra Capital yet."

"If you're ever interested, you know where to find me." His eyes continue to bore into mine, as if he's trying to figure out the inner workings of my mind.

A few seconds pass while we stare each other down, like two lions fighting for power in a pride. He arches his brow at me with muted amusement, his brown eyes unblinking.

"Well, now that we've got that out of the way and the peacocks are showing off their feathers, let's cut to the chase," James says as he turns his sapphire eyes to me. "I'm sure Parker has shared our concerns about you working with Emily. Jess mentioned briefly the history of the two of you, even though she doesn't know all the details. Whatever it is, all I know is your relationship ended badly and Emily is visibly distressed with finding out the Adrian Scott, her client, is actually the Adrian with another last name from her high school. All of us treat Emily like family, so, shark or not, we don't give a fuck. If you hurt her, you'll answer to us."

She's distressed? Anger sizzles through my body, the heady burn I relish because it has been my fuel all these years. She was the one who wielded the dagger back then and now she's playing the victim card?

My eyes sweep across the room, taking in the men staring at me, all nodding at James's words. However I may feel about Emily, she is one lucky woman to have these men, most of whom I respect, go to bat for her.

Swirling the contents of my tumbler, I murmur, "You guys have nothing to fear from me." The number-one rule in my rule-book is to strike when no one is expecting and right now, everyone's guards are up.

"Whew, well, now that we got that out of the way, welcome to the official 'Asshole Friends Group,'" Charles quips, his eyes glinting in laughter.

I cock my brow at the nickname.

"Trust me, I felt the same way when they brought me in. We have this chat group going and fuck am I glad I'm not the newest member anymore because these guys are brutal to newbies."

James and Parker snicker in the background, clearly enjoying themselves.

"It's a rite of passage," Steven adds.

"So, Adrian. I have a burning question for you. Jess said your last name used to be Callahan. Why do you go by Scott now?" James asks as he leans forward in his chair, his forearms resting on his knees.

"Callahan represented a tough part of my life. I changed my name to start over in college."

"And your family is okay with that?" He lifts a brow in skepticism.

"My dad didn't know until well after I graduated. He's since come to terms with it." After I explained to him this was the only way to get back at my grandfather, who would recognize the Callahan last name from a mile away.

He hums noncommittally, as if deep in thought.

"How's baby Violet?" Parker asks James, whose eyes light up and soften at the mention of his daughter.

"She's great, finally sleeping through the night and is acing tummy time." It's disconcerting to see this brooding man transform into a lighthearted, warm soul in a matter of seconds.

A long time ago, I thought marriage and kids may be in my future. Perhaps in another life, I'd look like James, with the love shining in his gaze. But there are some things I've found even money can't buy. Getting married and starting a family are things I'm no longer interested in. A nagging ache pinches me in the chest, and I quickly brush it aside. It's a phantom ache, not reality.

"The girls are doing a beach thing this weekend. Do you guys want to get together to watch the game at my place?" Parker asks the group.

"They're all going to the beach?" Steven's brows hike up, his tone incredulous. "Even Emily?"

My heart skips a beat at her name, something I curse myself for.

"No. Emily said she has to work. I don't know if it's true or not."

"She doesn't like the beach. According to her, the sand is disgusting and the waves are too loud." Steven snickers, as if making fun of his older sister.

A curl of unease snakes its way inside me. The Emily I knew loved the beach. It's the place where she found her hopes and dreams, the place where she collected seashells for her wishes. It's the place where she felt free. What happened?

"How long are you and Steven in town for this time?" Parker rolls out the muscles in his neck and directs his question at Charles and the youngest Kingsley.

"I'm flying back next Wednesday and this fucker is leaving on Friday." Steven points to his friend, his tone light and obviously in jest.

"So, are we on for the Lakers game at my place on Saturday, then? Lakers against the Celtics. Bets?"

The guys murmur their agreement as they hurl out insults regarding the teams and the players.

"No card carrying Angeleno will bet against the Lakers, man," James mutters. "Even though I think the season is going to shit, but out of loyalty and *not* from the data, I'll bet on the Lakers winning."

Parker takes out his cell phone and types in a few notes as I stare at them in amusement. "Charles?"

"New Englander here. Put me down for Celtics."

Steven shakes his head. "All of you with your misguided loyalty. I don't care if I'm from LA, but the numbers don't lie. Celtics for me."

Parker nods. "I'm with James on this one. LA pride over here." He types a few more notes on his phone, his fingers flying over the screen.

"You, Adrian? You in?" Steven asks, his deep voice friendlier than before.

I'm not used to having many friends other than Jack, who's stuck with me through thick and thin, and to some extent Parker, whom I'll always be grateful to for his mentorship. I've climbed my way up the ranks by leveraging secrets, and wielding decisions with cutthroat precision and no emotional entanglements. The unfamiliar warmth spreading through my chest makes me want to squirm in my seat.

"Sure. Count me in. Celtics for me." I never go into anything to lose, even if it's a bet amongst friends. Emotions and loyalty can go hang themselves. The only loyalty I have is to my family, Dad and Millie.

"Stakes?" Charles inquires, and he tosses the remaining contents of his drink down his throat and adjusts the navy tie around his neck.

"Ten grand each to the winners, and the winners also get to pick the destination of our next group trip this winter. Losers get to foot the bill." Parker slides his phone back into his pocket.

"I want to go sledding with the huskies and also stay in an igloo in Alaska," Charles comments, his mouth splitting into a wide grin as if he knew the group's response beforehand.

"Hell no. Out of all the places in the world, Vaughn, you want to go to fucking Alaska to freeze your balls off in the middle of winter?" Parker gapes at him, apparently bewildered.

"Put on your big boy pants, man. Not every vacation is about sleeping on soft mattresses and taking hot showers. Go and see the world. Be adventurous."

"I see the world plenty."

"I mean, just think about it. It'll be cold and Liz will be freezing and who'll she turn to for heat and comfort?"

"Hm. You may have a point there." Parker quirks his lips, a dimple making an appearance, his eyes taking on a wicked glint.

The guys chuckle as the ice in my heart melts a smidge.

The rest of the evening passes by in a haze of delicious food, lighthearted heckling and banter, ending with Parker and James going home to their families and Charles and Steven returning to their hotel to do some work and get on a few late-night, international conference calls.

I step into my penthouse apartment, the entire top floor of a high rise owned by the real estate branch of my company. My body is physically tired but my mind is awake, as it usually is these days.

"Welcome home, Mr. Scott," Anna, my middle-aged housekeeper, greets me, taking the wool coat I've shrugged off and draped over my arm.

"Thank you, Anna. You may go home. Enjoy the rest of your evening."

She nods, her gray eyes filling with warmth and crinkling at the corners. She pats me on the shoulder as she retreats to the coat closet. Of all my employees, Anna has been with me for the longest. I hired her after I made my first million, a few years post getting my MBA at Harvard, after a series of lucrative investments. In some ways, she is almost like a surrogate mother, looking after my needs when I forget about them, making sure my clothes are laundered, I have food in the refrigerator when I return home in the middle of the night having skipped dinner. She always nags me about settling down and finding someone to be my partner in life. She wants to see cute little kids running around, as she said a while back. The pinch in my chest returns as I stare at her retreating form. *Mom would've been around her age if she were still alive. She never got to enjoy all of these things I have now.*

The simmering heat rises to the forefront and I remember the days of barely scraping by, the moments when I thought we'd be evicted because rental payments went toward Mom's medical bills. My mind snags on the moment when Dad told me how he begged my grandparents for money to pay the staggering hospital bills but they said no. An image of Emily telling me she pities me after I've declared my love to her over and over again flutters to the forefront. I clench my aching jaw and lead seeps into my chest, weighing me down. This is why I've worked so hard, with blood, sweat, and tears to get to where I am now.

The past is bitter, but revenge will be sweet.

I amble toward the spacious living room, a statement of modern simplicity with tall ceilings and white walls, monochromatic furniture of blacks and grays, the floors made from flawless Calcatta marble, imported directly from Italy, costing at least a grand per square foot. My footsteps echo in the cavernous space, the room so quiet I can actually hear my breathing. My eyes trail to the built-in bookshelves in the living room, filled with photography books and novels I've lost myself in, and land on a large, sphere-shaped glass jar, filled to the brim with different colored seashells I've amassed over the years, with the pink scallop shell from the other night lying on top.

Tearing my gaze from the jar of memories or ambitions, I stare out the window, taking in the balls of illumination outside, the city lighting up like the milky way. I realize I have everything the nineteen-year-old in me ever wanted. But my life is meaningless. The abyss inside my chest is infinite, and no money, acquisitions, or deals seem to make a dent in the void. The success is tasteless on my tongue, the fire burning in my veins driving me forward as I set the world ablaze around me with no aim or reason.

Tugging my tie loose around my neck, I take in a huge breath, the air sustaining my life but not filling my soul. I walk down the quiet hallway, open the first door to the right, and flick on the light. A singular spotlight shines on a black grand piano, the craftsmanship of the instrument flawless, the tune crisp and clear.

I flip open the fallboard and gaze at the keys. The flames burning in my heart travel to my fingers and I close my eyes, playing the one song which has bought me both anguish and company in the darkness of the night when the loneliness creeps in, when I feel its vicious lash on my skin the hardest.

My fingers traipse over the keys, the chords succinct, the somber notes heartbreaking, the classic melody haunting. The rhythm and music fill my lungs, temporarily finding a place in the void inside me, and I lose myself in the melody.

The first song I ever learned.

Beethoven's "Piano Sonata No. 14," "Moonlight Sonata."

The sound of the car door shutting behind me alerts me to the presence of another person. It's an early fall morning, but the city is already awake as Angelenos start their workday. Glancing back, I see Adrian climbing out of his town car, his shiny dress shoes stepping onto the pavement. Then the rest of him catches my attention. His striking figure is clad in a gray suit, two-piece today, pale-blue dress shirt—the color of his eyes—and a navy striped tie. The clothes drape over his body like a lover's caress, highlighting his strong and powerful musculature. His hair is immaculately arranged as always, his eyes shielded by dark aviators. The scruff on his jaw is carefully trimmed and the divot in his chin begs me to kiss it. My body mentally flinches at the image as a curl of heat gathers in my gut. Memories of the boy who taught me the meaning of love flash to the forefront and a sharp pain scythes my chest. Adrian Callahan, the person who would look at me with love in his gaze, is long gone.

Adrian Scott is all man now, radiating a presence that captures attention.

He stalks toward me, sliding off his sunglasses and slipping them inside his jacket pocket in a smooth motion. He pins me with his startling blue gaze, the color of the Arctic in the blue glow of the morning light. No ounce of warmth or love can be seen in his eyes. I find myself unable to move as I watch this powerful man strutting toward me with sizzling intensity and tightly coiled tension in his muscles. His full lips are flattened in a firm line, but as he approaches me, he tilts up one corner—a half grin—and my heart, the irresponsible organ which can't seem to behave logically, skips a beat.

"Ms. Kingsley," he murmurs, his voice raspy, ghosting over my skin.

"Mr. Scott."

Silence befalls us as we face each other at the entrance to the Taylor Henrickson building. Cars whiz by in the background, the familiar cacophony of the occasional honk of impatient drivers, engines of city buses starting and stopping by the curb, but the sounds are muted, as if we're encased in a bubble where there's only the two of us.

"I've looked over the candidates you sent over and don't like any of them. Please send me more to review."

Anger unfurls inside my chest, and I narrow my eyes. I sent him the dossiers of ten beautiful women from the archives of Fleur. All of them meet the physical requirements he mentioned last time—blonde hair no doubt from the bottle, pouty lips capable of seducing the coldest of men, abundant breasts even I can't help but take a few moments to admire, and legs rivaling the best supermodels. My heart ached the entire time I was selecting these women and imaging all sorts of sordid entanglements the one he chose would no doubt have with Adrian. The contract doesn't include sex, only companionship in public, but seriously, who wouldn't want to have sex with him? Anyone with a pair of functioning eyes would jump him for free. These women are cream of the crop. What more could he want?

I let out a sigh and will my pulse to calm. "What are they lacking, Mr. Scott?"

"Half of them are too fake. I like my women with natural curves. The other half of them look too frail, as if they only eat salad for meals."

"What?" I stare at him incredulously, having given up trying to maintain a professional face with his insanity.

"I'm paying your firm a hefty sum. Go figure it out."

"Okay, the plastic surgery piece should be easy to take care of. But too frail? Come on, Adrian. They're just supposed to look good on your arm. They aren't here for an endurance test."

His eyes flare at his name, and I curse myself for not biting my tongue. Calling him Mr. Scott allows me to maintain a bit more distance between the two of us, which I desperately need for my mental health.

Adrian prowls closer, his steps measured, and I find myself stepping back until I'm pressed against the glass wall of the building. Slowly, he raises his hand and places it next to my head, effectively caging me in on one side. The scent of mint and musk is overwhelming and my breathing picks up in pace.

He leans in, his voice ghosting over the whorl of my ear, and says, "Come on, *Emily*. You don't think I'll have a fake girlfriend in name only and not enjoy her other charms, right?"

The blood rushes in my ears as my eyes dart from his baby blues, now darkening at the edges, the familiar silver threads more pronounced, to his beautiful lips. My mouth dries as images of the alpha male tangling in the sheets with a beautiful woman assault my senses and the burn of anger and the ache of heartbreak slowly morph into a blistering heat in my core. My tongue slips out to wet my parched lips.

His gaze snags on the movement, his eyes flaring ever so slightly. He leans in, completely taking over my personal space. "I like my woman to be able to take a good, hard *fucking...*" His head bends even closer as he whispers against my ear, "All night long."

My body trembles and my nipples pebble under my bra at his crude words. It's as if I can't control my reactions around him. *I wonder how he fucks now.* I swallow the lump in my throat and my breathing becomes gasps, the small sounds seeming to inflame him even further. Heat rises in my face and I squeeze my legs together in an attempt to stop the climbing ache between them.

"You're disgusting," I seethe, my hands landing on his chest, his very hard and muscular chest, and I shove him. He doesn't budge an inch.

Adrian chuckles, his voice taking on a rough tinge. He rasps, "And if I were to put my hand between your legs, would that pussy of yours be wet?"

My mouth falls open in shock. "Y-You..."

"I'm good enough for you now that I'm as rich as Croesus, huh? Before, you fucked me in pity...now, you're wet because of my money."

My hand lifts to slap him across the face, but he catches my wrist, his grip firm and unwavering. "I like my women feisty. But too bad you no longer do it for me."

His words cut through me, daggers to my heart, and I recoil, physically unable to stop my flinch. My eyes burn and prickle as hurt takes precedence over all other emotions swirling inside me. "Back up, Mr. Scott. I won't take this bullshit from you, client or not."

Adrian's eyes narrow, his thick brows furrowing for a split second, and his face smooths into a placid expression, as if the last few minutes of exchange didn't happen. He steps back, taking away his warmth, and I gulp in a few deep breaths, suddenly able to breathe.

Biting my bottom lip, I curl my hands into tight fists and draw myself up to stand taller, though he still towers over me, even in my three-inch heels. "I'll see what I can find on the women. But I won't tolerate any disrespect from you, Mr. Scott. If you'd like to change your consultants, Taylor Henrickson would be happy to oblige."

I spin around and push open the doors, not sticking around to witness his reaction.

My heart slams against my rib cage as I let out a shuddering exhale.

What happened to the sweet, loyal boy from a long time ago?

• • •

Ding.

The chime from my phone draws my attention as I finish a project plan in my office. I type the last few sentences and click save because the last thing I want is to accidentally close out of the document and lose hours of work, which unfortunately, I've done before. Picking up my phone, I glance at the text and frown.

Sarah: Ems! Did you see the news yet?

Emily: What news?

Sarah: OMG. Go to *Gossip Times*. You're plastered on the front page!

Liz: And you were saying there's nothing going on between you two?

What? I quickly open a new browser and navigate to the biggest gossip website in the country and clap my hand over my lips as I see what's front and center in bright colors on the homepage.

"Reclusive Billionaire Adrian Scott Finally Shows Face in Lovers' Quarrel."

A photo of my encounter with Adrian in front of the office building is attached, the image blown out and clear, thanks to the telephoto lens of the paparazzi who somehow caught us without us knowing. The camera is fond of Adrian, the photo illuminating every sharp angle, the fiery intensity in his impassioned eyes, a faint flush in his neck, the clench of his jaw as he stared down at me, his hand pressing against the glass wall next to my face. I looked up at him, my lips parted, my skin pink.

It looks like we are one second away from making out.

Shit. Shit, shit, shit. This derails the entire plan and doesn't bode well for his playboy image, which is most likely true.

My phone dings with two more texts.

Jess: Are you okay?

Steven: Do I need to beat the asshole up?

Panic rushes through me and a sudden wave of heat travels to my face. I'm a modern, independent woman and couldn't care less about being called out for having a boyfriend or two. But what am I going to do with this campaign?

I stand up in my office and pace in front of the desk, thankful my door is closed and I don't need to face anyone right now. My dreams of picking my own clients are on the line, not to mention the hot water the firm will be in if we lose a client as rich as Adrian Scott. I gnaw on my bottom lip, not noticing the pain, my mind racing through multiple solutions, nothing seeming to stick.

Riiiiiing.

The shrillness of the office phone shocks me in position as the thumping in my chest accelerates. Scurrying over to my desk, I answer the call.

"This is Emily." I'm thankful I still sound remotely calm.

"Please come to my office," Kristi's sharp voice commands.

"Now?"

"Yes." With a *click*, she hangs up.

Shit to the nth degree.

Heaving in a deep breath, I exhale forcefully, attempting to calm my racing heart. I'm good in a crisis and this is what makes me kickass at my job. Fuck this shit, I'll figure something out because I'm a badass. A few calming breaths later, I open the door and stride out of my office like I own the place and nothing could faze me.

I sense the weight of my colleagues' stares and hear their muffled whispers as I traipse over to Kristi's corner office. Tilting my head higher, I square my shoulders back and embrace the chaos. Because nothing will strike me down. I won't let it.

Knocking on the frosted glass of her door, I wait for her response.

"Come in."

I inhale a ragged breath before swinging open the door and stepping in.

Kristi's office matches the décor of the rest of the floor. It's a sea of white, minimalistic furnishings with pops of ruby-red accents. The shades are drawn up, and the room is bathed in natural sunlight and the windows boast beautiful, panoramic views of downtown LA. A faint scent of lavender lingers in the air, courtesy of an essential oil diffuser shaped like a modern art sculpture on one of her avant-garde bookshelves, which appears to be straight out of a contemporary art museum.

"Emily, have a seat," Kristi instructs from her throne, a long, uncluttered lacquered desk, with only a white computer monitor, a flat keyboard, and a few articles of stationary artfully arranged in acrylic shelves.

Swallowing the pins and needles in my throat, I fight to keep a serene smile on my face, as if the world isn't gossiping about me with a certain billionaire, and I take a seat in one of the leather chairs on the other side of the desk.

She's direct and to the point. "I'm sure you've seen *Gossip Times*." It's not even a question. If it wasn't because I was so in the zone with my work and temporarily muted my phone's automatic notifications from the site—because it's easy to get sidetracked with the frequent pinging of breaking news—I would've found out firsthand too, before my family and friends caught wind of it. Being on top of the news is one of the primary requirements of working in PR.

I nod. "Kristi, I can explain. Mr. Scott and I had a brief disagreement—"

She holds out her hand. "You and I both know the truth doesn't matter in the news cycle. We create the news...spin the so-called truths."

Biting my bottom lip, I dip my head in response. The public doesn't want to know the truth. They only want what's salacious and juicy and a hot, reclusive billionaire who's never been photographed before, caught in an apparent "lovers' quarrel" is the stuff of dreams for the gossip rags.

"We need to do damage control."

I agree and lean forward in my seat. "I have a few ideas. Perhaps we could move up the interview we set with LBC and he can discuss the professional disagreement we had outside the building. I think that'll endear him to the masses...even billionaires get into arguments—"

Kristi shakes her head, her blonde hair swishing from the movement. "No. I want the interview to be focused on him telling his story, not as damage control. The public always tears apologies apart, anyway. I have something better in mind." She lifts her eyes to mine and I freeze, recognizing the look on her face.

Dread slithers inside me, the nausea rising to my throat. Sweat beads on the back of my neck. *Please don't tell me she's thinking what I'm thinking. Please—*

"Mr. Scott needs a girlfriend for his image revamp, anyway. Why not you?"

My mouth drops open as I gape at her in shock.

I let out an incredulous chuckle, my stomach plummeting to the ground. Heat rises to my face and I shake my head. Vehemently. "Kristi, you can't be serious. You heard him. The physical attributes he's looking for are the polar opposite of me. I'm running his campaign. This is a complete conflict of interest." I gnaw on my lip with savagery I'm sure I'll regret later. "What about the firm's reputation—"

Kristi taps on the table in front of me, drawing my attention back to her. She arches her brow at my rambling. "It's fake dating, Emily, not real dating. He doesn't need to actually be physically attracted to you. He just needs to pretend."

I freeze as dread glides up my torso and coils around my lungs, restricting my airway.

She continues, "It'll be the perfect love story the public will gobble up. Reclusive billionaire meets a beautiful, smart woman with a wonderful background." She gives me a pointed stare. "True love couldn't be stopped and he falls head over heels for her. They had a minor disagreement because he works too hard and has been neglecting her and he's so very sorry about it."

My mouth runs dry and I stare at her, stupefied and speechless. I blink a few times as I absorb her words.

Kristi smiles the way a predator bares its teeth before going in for the kill. Her eyes are sharp and laser-focused on my face. "And Taylor Henrickson won't step in the way of a true love story because as much as the money is vital to us, our client and our employees' well-being are even more important. Therefore, in the interest of professionalism, we have assigned another consultant to lead the project."

My hand travels to my face, the heat long faded into a bone-deep chill. Dread is too little of a word to describe the rioting feelings inside me right now, a discordance including anger, fear, disappointment, worry, and hopelessness. She's planned the entire story already. I can see the press releases floating in her mind.

"Kristi, I'm not sure I'm comfortable with this."

"Emily, do you want to make director or not?" She stares at me, a new steeliness in her gaze. There's a reason she's the managing partner of one of the biggest offices of our firm.

My eyes dart around the room, searching for something, searching for nothing. I can feel the searing heat from her eyes, threatening to laser me on the spot. My gaze returns to her. "Yes, of course I do."

"If you do this job well and keep Mr. Scott happy, the promotion is yours."

I feel as if someone has bound me tightly in a rope, pinning my arms by my side, dragging me to God knows where, and I have no choice but to follow. I could always complain to HR or be a whistleblower, but that'll only blacklist me in the industry. And for what? Pretending to be chummy with a billionaire in public for a few dates? Most women would line up for the opportunity.

"B-But...maybe Mr. Scott won't be on board with the plan. H-He did mention his affinity for tall, curvaceous blondes..." I protest, my voice feeble even to my ears.

"Well, we'll just have to see, won't we?"

Kristi picks up the receiver on her phone and presses a button. "Candice, can you connect me to Adrian Scott and tell him it's urgent?"

She taps her manicured fingers on the table, the clacking sound grating to my ears as she stares at the view outside her windows. "Mr. Scott, this is Kristi Thorne. I have Emily Kingsley here with me. Let me put you on speaker." She clicks a button and turns her attention back to me.

"I'm assuming this is regarding the front page of *Gossip Times?*" The deep timbre of his voice takes over the entire room. His powerful presence can be felt over a simple phone call. "How much am I paying you for *this?*" Anger drips from his voice.

Kristi's gaze flickers up to me, her calm eyes unfazed. "I understand your disappointment, but this is an opportunity for us."

"Explain."

Kristi describes her logic to him as I sit in the seat, my back ramrod straight. My hands are sweaty and I wipe them on my dress. Adrian hasn't said anything other than an occasional "go on," to prove he's listening.

"I think this will actually serve your campaign well," Kristi concludes, folding her hands in front of her as we await the verdict.

A few seconds of silence follows, the lack of sound feeling resounding for whatever reason. My breathing quickens and I twist the fabric of my emerald sheath dress.

"Fine."

One word to change the course of the next year of my life. My heart leaps in my chest as a heaviness sits on top of my lungs. My body, like my mind, can't make sense of the situation, can't figure out how my life got flipped upside down in a matter of hours. My emotions can't settle between the nonsensical joy of being the woman Adrian will have on his arm and the burning anger at being forced into this position after a ridiculous argument with a man who resembles nothing like the boy I fell in love with all those years ago.

"I'll contact your secretary to set up a meeting to discuss the details," Kristi says, a small smile on her lips as she sweeps in, and in her opinion, saves the day. She disconnects the call and glances back at me, her perceptive gaze scanning my expression, missing nothing.

"Any questions?"

I twist my face up into a bright smile. "None."

My insides are warped in a chaotic mess.

Shit.

CHAPTER 29

Adrian

I sit on the white leather sofa in Kristi's office and her assistant brings me a cup of coffee. Drinking a sip of the warm liquid, an expensive blend from the richness of the taste, I smile internally at this turn of events. What I'd give to be in the office when Kristi suggested Emily be my fake girlfriend. Was her pale skin flushed red? Were those brown eyes molten with anger?

Things are going according to plan. Another domino set in place for the grand finale, when I'll be the one to push the first piece over, sit back, and watch the rest of them collapse in front of me. The love is no longer there, but the anger is scathing hot. I'll take the pity and the callousness bestowed upon me and return it tenfold. This time, I won't be the one walking away heartbroken.

The door suddenly opens and Emily struts in, her posture straight, her muscles stiff as if she's a gladiator stepping onto the field. Her brown hair is sleek and sways with each step. She's wearing a red, long-sleeve sheath dress, the fabric clinging to her petite body, highlighting her tempting curves and showcasing her toned legs. On her feet are tall heels, at least three inches from the looks of it. My thoughts automatically turn lurid, imagining wrapping those lean legs around my waist, her sexy heels digging into my back as I pump into her until she screams and pulses around me. The heat, which I normally associate with anger, turns sultry, and my cock twitches in anticipation. I cross my legs, set down the coffee on the table in front of me, and lean back into the sofa, watching this tiny Amazon stalk toward me. Emily's chocolate eyes are steely and determined, her lips pressing into a firm line.

She's *magnificent,* the fire radiating from her, captivating anyone in her presence.

Including me.

You don't have to like someone to admire their qualities.

Emily takes a seat in front of me and crosses her legs at the ankles, every inch the pompous Kingsley of old-money fame.

"Mr. Scott."

I curve my lips up into a half grin, my face giving nothing away. She's using my last name as a shield, as if anything will erase the past. "Ms. Kingsley." I don't miss her quick perusal as her gaze cascades over my body, no doubt appreciating my physical attributes, which I know females love. Her eyes flicker away and return to my face. A soft flush creeps up her cheeks, as if she's embarrassed at being caught ogling just now.

The door swings open again and Kristi sweeps in, as quick as the breeze. She's efficient in her movements, a quality I appreciate.

"Mr. Scott and Emily, sorry for being a few minutes late. I had a conference call with London that went long."

She takes a seat in the tufted chair next to Emily's and lays out a few documents for our review. "Mr. Scott, I know your time is precious, so I'll dispense with the pleasantries. As we briefly discussed on the phone the other day, we're fast tracking your fake-dating because of the article on *Gossip Times,* which, by the way, has over five million likes and is still trending in internet searches. I believe both of you have experienced more run-ins with paparazzi in the last few days."

Kristi pauses and glances at Emily, who is nodding. My brows furrow as I wonder how many assholes are bothering her. I have a team of security personnel who have been dispatching these annoying gossipmongers with ease. But Emily, she has no one, unless her family provided some for her, which, if she's anything like the firecracker I knew in the past, I bet she'd refuse. I grit my teeth at the pinch of guilt in my chest and shove it away. This is what she signed up for.

"I'm happy to provide security if needed."

Emily looks up, her eyes wide, as if she's surprised I would offer.

Kristi replies, "I think that would be wise. But in the meantime, in order to start cultivating your image as a family-oriented man, given the recent developments, Emily will act as your fake girlfriend for a period of one year, after which you'll part ways amicably." She glances at us, seeing no complaints, and continues, "In order to make sure there are no misunderstandings or confusion, we'll draft an agreement between the two of you to lay out the terms of the arrangement. Please read them over."

"I'm familiar with the terms, as I drafted the agreement." Emily picks up the paper in front of her and places it on her lap.

My eyes scan the document, noting the following provisions:

This agreement ("Agreement" or "Contract") establishes a faux-romantic relationship (the "Arrangement") between the following parties: Adrian C. Scott ("Boyfriend") and Emily S. Kingsley ("Girlfriend"), employed by Taylor Henrickson LLP, collectively known as the ("Couple") and will be effective for 365 days after the first media appearance of the couple.

Section A: Rules of the Arrangement

The couple will follow the provisions outlined below. Any party violating any of the below provisions will render this agreement null and void. Taylor Henrickson will be indemnified in any damages resulting from any violations of the provisions.

1. The couple will be seen on dates in public at least once a month.
2. The couple will attend at least two high-profile events (i.e., movie premieres, award ceremonies, etc.) during the course of the arrangement.

3. The couple will travel by plane on a long-distance trip meant to appear as a vacation at least once during the course of the arrangement.
4. The couple will appear to be physically affectionate in public. This may include the following behaviors:
    a. Handholding
    b. Hugs
    c. Kisses on the cheek or back of the hands
    d. Caresses on the face or arms
    e. Arm around waist or shoulders
5. The following behaviors are prohibited:
    a. Kisses on other areas of the body
    b. Boyfriend touching girlfriend's torso in any manner other than 4(e) above
    c. Sexual intercourse

"And one more thing. During the duration of this arrangement, we will remain exclusive to each other. That's the only way this is going to work and be believable." Emily stares defiantly at me, as if daring me to disagree.

I glance at her, fighting the urge to smile before I scan the rest of the document. There's more standard contractual terms and legalese of little importance. I reread the document, dragging out the silence, the blood in my veins sizzling with anticipation at shredding this contract into pieces—my specialty.

The silence is loud in the room as the minutes pass by. I can hear Emily shuffling in her seat, her breathing picking up in speed. She clears her throat. More shuffling and squeaking of the leather chair.

Finally deciding enough time has transpired, I look up and widen my legs, leaning slightly forward—a demonstration of dominance. Kristi sits comfortably in her chair, her face placid as she stares at me, her eyes revealing nothing—a worthy opponent.

Emily, on the other hand, is one step away from shaking like a leaf. Her fingers twist on her lap as she bites on her plump bottom lip. Her breathing is shallow, her pupils dilated—a sure sign of attraction or anxiety, and my bet would be on the latter.

"No."

"What do you mean, no?" Emily shoots up, her voice pitchy, and she glares at me. "These are all very reasonable provisions."

"You want the public to believe we have a relationship consisting of handholding and superficial caresses and kisses? Who are you fooling, your blind great-grandmother?"

"I'm not going to have you maul me in public to further your campaign—"

"No one is saying anything about making out. But kisses on the mouth are on the table or we have no agreement."

Her eyes drop to my lips as her tongue darts out, as if she's imagining my lips on hers. The sultry heat ratches up in my veins.

"Fine. One kiss per outing."

"Ten."

She stares at me incredulously. "Why on earth would we need to kiss ten times in public on one date? This is not a porn shoot." My cock stiffens to half-mast at her mention of adult entertainment and I could imagine acting in some of those lurid scenes with her. Her eyes widen at whatever she notices on my face and she hastily adds, "Three. That's it. No more. Even that's pushing it."

"Five. Final offer."

If looks could kill. Emily gives the barest of nods.

I glance at the document again. "I don't think we can do 5(c) without 5(b). Why mention it at all?"

Her pale skin turns pink, a shade I've always liked on her before because it made her look cute, but now, I just enjoy seeing her flustered. "B-Because I want to make sure it's spelled out. This is a fake relationship."

"Who said you need to be in a real relationship in order to have sex?"

"You, Adri—I mean, Mr. Scott, I *respectfully* disagree." She pins me with another freezing glare. "And even if I were to agree to casual sex, the person would not be you. The clause remains."

"Fine, then I want to add a clause that either party can change their mind at any time."

"I won't change my mind." She crosses her arms across her chest, her body language defiant.

"Never say never, *Pixie.*"

Emily gasps, her cheeks reddening at my usage of her old nickname. She's apparently rendered speechless.

I smirk inwardly and turn toward Kristi, who's watching us in amusement, a faint smile on her lips. "See to it the clause is added."

"One last thing. No to the exclusivity clause," I state before leaning back in my chair. This is all too easy. My eyes find Emily's again, her earlier flush morphing into apparent mottled anger.

Emily stands up, her hands clenched, and she paces in front of her chair. "Mr. Scott, I will not abide having the press reporting my 'boyfriend' is cheating on me."

"I have iron-clad nondisclosure agreements I make my partners sign. That's a nonissue."

"No!"

I arch my brow at her vehement response, as if daring her to continue her tirade. "I have needs, like a normal man. If you aren't going to satisfy them, I need to go elsewhere."

Emily slides her hand across her face as she turns away from me, the movement drawing attention to her curvy ass hugged by the body-clinging material. I swallow, my eyes glued to her curves. I wonder how tight her body is now.

She whirls back. "I don't care what you do for your 'needs,' this is nonnegotiable."

We stare at each other as she holds my gaze admirably. If anything, she tilts up her chin in defiance and flattens her lips. Most grown men would have withered under my glare and acquiesced. I couldn't help but be impressed.

"Fine. I'm sure you'll abide by the same provision."

"Of course I would, unlike someone," she curls her upper lip in apparent disdain, "I have self-control. And I suggested this for a reason."

I turn back to Kristi, whose smile widens as if she's watching the most riveting soap opera.

"So, it seems we are in agreement?" she asks. "I'll have the changes to both of you within the hour."

"It would appear so." I drum the handrest on the sofa, my body on fire, but I don't show it. I lay my coat across my lap, hiding my stiff cock, which is inconveniently aroused from this heated debate. A physical reaction—nothing more.

Kristi turns to Emily, who doles out a stiff nod as she stands still, her arms now hanging loosely by her sides as if in defeat. Her beautiful eyes, capable of such warmth and coldness, are ablaze, barely masking her hatred.

My lips twitch up in a smile. Her frown deepens.

I'll enjoy slowly ripping down her defenses one by one and making her fall for me.

Then I'll leave her.

Just like she did to me all those years ago.

I slowly stand and extend my hand out to her. Her lips part on an exhale and her eyes dart to Kristi, then to me, before she clasps her small hand in mine, a slight tremble in the motion.

Squeezing her flesh softly, I circle my thumb, lightly caressing the skin, a motion I know she reacts to, and a small gasp escapes her lips and goosebumps prickle on her arm.

"*Pleasure* doing business with you." I let go of her and she quickly covers one hand with the other, her fingers wiping the skin as if trying to scrub my touch off her, a poor attempt at hiding the feelings I elicited in her just now.

Another domino slides into place. The game is on.

Mother: Why did I have to learn about Adrian Scott from Ryan's mom? When will you bring him home to meet us?

I scoff and respond. Of course, she's happy I'm "dating" a billionaire.

Emily: We are dating and it's new.

I can't tell her about our "arrangement" because of the thick nondisclosure agreement I signed. I'm lucky Adrian even relented to letting me discuss some particulars with my girls, a small grace or else I'd go crazy.

Mother: I'd like to meet him. I never thought I'd say this, but for once, you're finally choosing someone who is worthy of a Kingsley alliance. Maybe I don't need to ask you to consider Ryan now. By the way, he just took over his family's business and is doing very well for himself. His mom says he asks about you sometimes.

A tiger can't change its stripes, no matter how hard she tries. At least, it doesn't appear she recognized him as the Adrian from my past. One less thing for her to nag about. I rub my temples, hoping she is done with her inquisition.

A few moments later though, another text comes through.

Mother: I know we've had our differences, Emily. And I understand you and your siblings are adults now, but my concern is out of a desire to ensure your well-being. I've always wanted you to meet someone who can stand by your side and be a worthy partner. Don't make your father worry about you. You know his health is not so good these days.

Silencing my phone, I bite the inside of my cheek, annoyed at having to deal with her and this situation I have with the maddening man in front of me.

"Why so serious, my love? If anyone's watching, they'd think I kidnapped you and forced you to sit down for coffee," Adrian says, his voice dripping with sarcasm as he stares at me, his eyes cool and indifferent, completely at odds with the words out of his mouth.

I flinch internally at the endearment, so fake and disgusting I lose most of my appetite. We're sitting at a small table at Le Cirque, home court advantage for me, for our double-whammy of a first public appearance. The midday sunshine is bright, but the weather is comfortable and thankfully not sweltering. The skies are clear and today is, by all means, a beautiful day in LA, but I couldn't care less. The man before me is souring my appreciation of my environment.

On the docket today is a brief coffee date here, then volunteering for the dinner segment at New Beginnings, the homeless shelter Parker and his firm helped design a few years back. The purpose is not only to "out" our relationship, but also to show the public The Shark is capable of human kindness.

"I don't know why you agreed to this if you're going to be an asshole the entire time," I mutter under my breath.

"I hope this isn't how you treat your other clients, because it's completely unprofessional."

I manage campaigns, not play fake girlfriend on my other projects, my mind retorts. My nostrils flare and I twist my lips into a saccharine smile. "Of course not, *babe.* I'm a professional." My smile slips off my face like a pancake sliding off the griddle. Heat crawls up my body and I unzip my light jacket, revealing a heather-gray tank top with the top two buttons opened.

Adrian's gaze trails from my face to my neck and lower, as if he's undressing me in public. My face heats as I inhale a slow gulp of oxygen, trying to calm the rollercoaster of emotions within me. He takes a sip of water, his muscular neck rippling as he swallows, his eyes meeting mine once again. I might be mistaken, but it looks like the blues in his irises are darker and more brilliant than before.

He's wearing dressy casual today, a dark-gray Henley shirt clinging to every divot of his body and a pair of dark-wash jeans. He obviously spends time in the gym and those muscles are showcased beautifully today.

"Finding my appearance satisfactory to your expensive tastes?" I arch my brow.

"Not my usual taste but..." he returns my arch with a lift of a brow, "you'll do."

My teeth gnash together and I plaster a fake smile on my face, gritting out, "You're making it very hard for me to pretend right now."

"Aren't you a professional? Can't hack it?"

Yes, I goddamn am. Something about this man drives me insane and sets me off my rhythm. I straighten up my body and lean forward. Two can play this ridiculous game. I reach out and trail my fingers over his hand on top of the table, traveling to his forearm, the strong appendage flexing in tension. Tilting my head to the side, I expose my neck and bite my plump bottom lip, painted in fire-engine red today because I need to channel my inner vixen. His blue eyes smolder as his pupils dilate slightly, his gaze trained on my lips. Slowly, I release my lip and twist my smile into the fakest society smile I've been trained to do by Mother since I could walk.

"Babe...I've *missed* you. How was your day?" My fingers slide over his forearm, gently tracing the sexy vein running amidst the muscles and caressing the fine dusting of hair there. My heart kicks wildly in my chest and my mouth runs dry, but I persist.

Adrian's face is expressionless, and he's eerily still, other than the lifting of his chest as he breathes, a quality I recognize from the old Adrian of the past. My heart pinches and I stare at this debonair enigma in front of me, wondering if the boy I knew is gone for good—the loyal, passionate, and broody boy who had a heart of gold. I swallow the ball in my throat as my nose burns, temporarily assaulted by memories of the past, something this stranger in front of me most likely doesn't remember. My smile falters and I glance away, afraid he's going to see something in my gaze. My fingers start sliding off his arm.

He grabs on to my hand at the last second, his large palm warming my chilled one. "What were you thinking just now?" he asks, his voice raspier than before. A muscle tics in his jaw, the only sign the last few minutes impacted him somehow.

I wet my dried lips before turning my eyes back on him. Smiling brightly, a joy I don't feel within, I reply, "Nothing. Just enjoying our date."

"Always so good at pretending. I see nothing has changed." He leans back, the flames gone in his eyes, the blues turning frigid again.

Clenching my hands under the table, I bite my inner cheek. Part of me wants to grab him by his shoulders and shake him, tell him every word out of my mouth the last night at the beach was a lie, that I did this for him and this is why he was able to graduate and go to college and is now sitting in front of me with the moniker "reclusive billionaire."

But I don't, because the Adrian Scott in front of me isn't Adrian Callahan. The Shark won't believe me, nor care, and in the rare chance the Adrian Callahan I know is still buried deep in the depths of his dark soul, he would be devastated and perhaps filled with guilt. And apparently, I have a masochistic streak in me, because I still can't bring myself to hurt him. I'd rather his eyes be cold, his shoulders strong, his bearing tall, than to see those eyes dim in anguish or his frame to shudder with sadness. I also don't want him to retaliate on my parents, as misguided as they were. I still love them. And something tells me The Shark won't be so forgiving if he finds out the entire truth.

You're thinking too much, Emily. Adrian Callahan may feel all those emotions. This man before you won't feel a thing. As the core tenant of my industry states, the truth doesn't matter. He wouldn't care.

Adrian suddenly straightens, his eyes sharpening as he stares at something behind me.

Or in this case, someone.

"Emily, I can't go about my day without saying hi to you," a low-baritone voice declares and I turn around and find Antoine striding over with his casual ease radiating self-assuredness, his golden hair glinting in the sunshine. He winks, his hazel eyes crinkling at the corners.

My heart warms and I turn around and stand up to greet my friend in a tight hug. I've been told by my friends I give the best hugs, something I take immense pride in. Nothing can put someone at ease or make their day feel better than a decent hug. He curls his arms around my back and squeezes.

"My name sounds fancier in French. I love it." I grin.

"Everything is better the French way, and I love your koala hugs, Emily." My heart squeezes at the nickname he doles out— friends say I give koala hugs, not bear hugs, because of my petite stature. He releases me and smiles, his eyes never leaving my face.

"I'm Adrian Scott, her boyfriend. And you are?" Adrian growls with barely concealed menace, interrupting my conversation with Antoine. A dark presence radiates from beside me as Adrian somehow materializes next to my chair, his arm extended. Warmth slides up my face and my heart hiccups at the word *boyfriend* from his lips.

Antoine glances at the man next to me, his eyebrow lifting in recognition. He clasps his hand in Adrian's and an awkward silence befalls us. Antoine's eyes narrow as Adrian glowers at him, the men engaging in some sort of silent communication. My gaze falls to their clasped hands, their knuckles white. Antoine's gaze hardens before releasing his hand, ending the handshake. "I'm Emily's friend. And I've seen you from the news."

Antoine's eyes trail over to mine, warming up immediately. "I didn't believe it when I saw the photos circulating around. I was going to check on you to see if you're okay." His brows furrow in concern.

"She's fine." A clipped reply.

Antoine ignores him and I definitely admire my friend in a new way. Not many people can survive Adrian's withering glares, which will probably fry any living thing in its trajectory, but Antoine is standing tall, apparently nonplussed about it.

I place my hand on his shoulder and squeeze. "Things are fine. They're going well." I smile, hoping it'll reassure him.

Antoine softens and pats his hand on top of mine. My arm falls away as he turns his attention to Adrian. He says, a lethal quality in his voice I haven't heard of before, "Treat her well, or else."

Adrian stiffens beside me, the tension in the air so thick and palpable I can almost taste it. "Or what?"

"Okaaay," I interject, because this "first date" is disastrous so far and the last thing I need is another photo and story about two men fighting over me. I pin Adrian with a hard glare before twisting my face in a smile. My cheeks are going to hurt from all this fakeness today. "Thank you, Antoine, for fitting us in at your restaurant today. I know you're fully booked, but opened up a table just for me. Things are going perfect." I want to puke at the ridiculousness of the current situation.

"*Mon ami*, let me know if you ever need anything." Antoine glances at the brooding man next to me and whispers, "Anything at all, including rescuing you from the bastard next to you." He leans down, kissing my cheek in the French way of greeting, and saunters away, a languid ease in his bearing.

I motion Adrian to sit his ass back down as he scowls at the retreating backside of Antoine, a rare display of emotion from his usual unflappable exterior. Sliding back into my chair, I take a sip of coffee, which could be tasteless for all I care. My shoulders ache with tension and stress, and a nagging flinch of pain pierces my head.

"We have an exclusivity clause, remember?" The deep tinge of Adrian's voice is laced with fury as he stares at me, a vein pulsing on his forehead.

"Antoine is a friend. I'm not violating any provisions of our contract," I whisper, my eyes darting around, scanning the surrounding area for paparazzi or hidden microphones.

Adrian scoffs, then takes a sip of his beverage, his lips curling in a sneer. "Bullshit."

I shake my head and fight the urge to roll my eyes. "You sound jealous."

"No, I'm protecting my investments. I won't be a laughing-stock in this deal."

"That's rich coming from you, since you were the one who didn't want the exclusivity clause in the first place. So what, you can get some while I need to be a nun?"

His eyes flash in anger, the frigid blue now the color of the hottest flame in the Bunsen burner. "You aren't fucking him."

I arch my brow and sit back, watching this tightly coiled man slowly unravel in front of me.

"I'll destroy him if he lays his hands on you."

"Your investment," I reiterate, more for myself than for him. My heart flutters at the possessiveness in his voice, and adrenaline courses through my veins.

"Don't test me, Emily."

"Or what?" I lean closer to him on the table, watching the flush creep up his face and a muscle tics in his jaw.

"You don't want to find out. I'm known as The Shark for a reason."

I curl a lock of hair around my finger as an unusual energy thrums inside me. Perhaps I have sadistic qualities as well, because watching this man squirm thrills me. "Even if I do *fuck*..." I whisper, watching his eyes darken, "you won't ever find out."

Our breaths linger in the space between us as we're held immobile by this invisible showdown. The rest of him is a statement of coiled anger, a viper getting ready to launch at an unsuspecting victim. A scent of mint and musk mixes with lilies, but I barely notice. My breathing is coming in sharp gasps, as if I ran a marathon and the man in front of me is a tall glass of water.

Adrian's eyes drift to my lips and I can't help but flick my tongue out, wetting the surface, taunting him, and watching his blues darken some more, the color so brilliant, it's almost blinding to my eyes. The ambient chatter in the restaurant falls away to a quiet hum, the background blurring, and we stare at each other, enclosed in a myriad of heated emotions, the burning hatred heady and deadly.

"I'll buy out this restaurant and close it down with a quick phone call," he growls, his voice quiet and simmering with intensity.

I roll my eyes and lean back. This is getting out of hand and part of it is my fault. "I told you, Antoine is my friend, and he has no interest in me."

"Any warm-blooded man who looks at you like that wants to get in your pants."

Throwing my hands in the air, I whisper shout, "Oh my God, stop being ridiculous! Antoine has *already* gotten into my pants, okay? He's my ex, and he has a fiancée now. No clause is or will be violated."

His hand clenches the paper napkin into a ball, his knuckles turning stark white. *Shit, that was the wrong thing to say.* Adrian snaps his neck in an audible crack, and his eyes narrow at my statement.

Riiiiing.

The shrill ringtone of his cell phone interrupts this strange dance between us and he answers, "Scott." Pushing his chair out, the metal dragging on the gravel of the floor in a loud screech, earning a few curious stares our way, he stalks off as he dictates to the poor soul on the other line.

Groaning, I bury my face in my hands.

This is a disaster of epic levels.

Kristi: Emily, what's going on? If you can't do this, let me know. We can't lose Adrian Scott as a client.

I groan as I stare at the stern text from the big boss, watching my hopes and dreams go up in flames. A link with the title "Kingsley Princess ID'ed as Mysterious Girlfriend of Billionaire Adrian Scott," this time from the popular video news channel, *CelebTV,* is attached, and plastered on the thumbnail is an unflattering shot of me throwing my hands in the air with an angry Adrian sitting across from me when I told him Antoine was my ex-boyfriend.

Shit.

I have been unprofessional and an amateur, something that hasn't happened to me since the early days of my career when I was a green college graduate. I know I'm not an actress and this is a bit unusual but I'm goddamn good at my job, which includes handling any crazy curveballs thrown my way. I'm surprised Mother hasn't called and chewed off my ear yet, but I'm betting it's only a matter of time before that happens.

Adrian sits next to me in his helicopter as we travel the short distance from Burbank to downtown LA, which, in rush hour traffic, usually takes forty minutes to an hour, but instead, the trip has shortened to fifteen minutes. *Time is money,* he said when I stared incredulously at him when we were standing on the helipad on top of one of his buildings earlier, watching the atrocity to the environment land for such a short flight.

"What are you groaning about?" His voice comes through the headset and I glance at him, finding him scrolling his phone determinedly, his thumbs moving across the device as he no doubt is terrorizing someone via email.

I forward him the video, a short clip recorded by another patron at the restaurant, capturing the last minute of our conversation earlier, when he was visibly angry and stormed away to take his phone call. Of course, the public didn't record the moments when I was trailing my fingers up the corded muscles of his forearm or when his gaze was snagged to my lips when I played the role of a vixen.

A low chuckle sounds from the headset, the deep timbre of his voice no less lethal over the microphone. "And *you're* their top consultant?"

I bite my lip to keep from responding because the pilot is in front of us. The Adrian I knew in the past didn't speak much, but whenever he opened his mouth, his words were insightful and thought-provoking. This Adrian is still provoking all right, more like violence-provoking. *Putting out fires, I've done this many times before.* I type out a text to Kristi.

> **Emily:** Ironing out some wrinkles. We're going to the shelter now. You won't be disappointed.

Then I type something to the maddening man beside me.

> **Emily:** I was told you wanted this campaign to improve your image in order to acquire the controlling interest of Cornwall Holdings from the largest shareholder of the company. A relationship can't be sustained only by me. If this is something you want, and are paying us a good sum of money for, I need you to put aside your personal feelings, whatever they may be, and commit to the agreement.

I sense the moment the text comes through. Adrian stills, his thumbs no longer moving as he stares at the screen. His neck ripples as he swallows and his glacial eyes find mine. I return his stare with an arched brow. He knows I'm right. If he intends to sabotage this campaign, I'd rather resign than damage my reputation in the process. His eyes rove over my face, as if searching for something, and I fight the impulse to move, to fidget. Never show your fear to a predator or an alpha asshole. In my dealings with rich, pompous men in the past, they tend to overlook me due to my size, my gender, and my mixed heritage. That is, until I find their pain points and exploit them to my advantage.

In my opinion, Cornwall Holdings may be the Achilles heel for Adrian, the man who has spent the last decade shrouded in mystery, not even allowing a single photograph of him to be published, who is now suddenly doing a one eighty all for the sake of this acquisition—it must be important to him for reasons unbeknownst to me.

He inclines his head, the barest acknowledgement of my sentiment, but I'll take it. Soon, we land on a helipad on top of an office building a few blocks from City Hall in downtown LA. Whipping wind assaults my senses as the doors open. Adrian leaps out of the helicopter and buttons his casual dress jacket in a smooth motion. His hair is windswept and in disarray, but instead of looking messy, he appears to be self-assured, every inch of the rich CEO, despite his casual wear. He reaches out to me, his palm extended, and waits for me to alight from the aircraft.

I stare into his beautiful eyes, currently serene as a tranquil lake, and my mind can't help but think...in another life, this would be my soulmate, whisking me off to paradise, every ounce of him seeping with chivalry as he helps me off the helicopter with love in his eyes.

In another life...

Swallowing the needles in my throat, I curve my lips into a smile and place my hand in his as my body involuntarily reacts to this brief touch, a sizzling intensity that takes my breath away. His fingers tighten against mine as the pulse in his neck becomes more noticeable and I find purchase on solid ground.

"Mr. Scott, Ms. Kingsley, if you need my services tonight, please let me know. The exit is that way," the pilot says, the helmet cradled in his arms.

Adrian nods as he laces his fingers with mine, the movement bringing memories of scorching kisses on the beach, dancing in the moonlight. The past catches up to me, ever so inopportune, and my eyes burn as the lump in my throat solidifies again. I roll my lips inward as I fight to regain my composure and not let this simple act of pretense touch my heart. While the heat of his palm is the same, the callouses on his fingers still scraping my skin in just the right way, everything has changed.

And it's too late.

Blinking my eyes rapidly, I walk quietly alongside him as we reach the elevators. As the doors close, I move to disentangle my fingers from his, but he holds on tighter. I glance up at him, finding his perceptive eyes pinned on my face, his brows pinching at whatever he sees there.

"Commit to the arrangement, remember?" he murmurs, his voice soft and deceptively gentle.

Right. The arrangement.

I nod and parse out a shaky smile. His frown deepens as his free hand reaches toward my face, his thumb lightly swiping my cheeks, and I realize it's too late. Apparently, an errant tear has made an appearance.

"Why are you crying?" he whispers as he steps closer to me, crowding me to the handrail.

I stare at his beautiful face, now in an expression of the concern I recognize from years ago, and I choke out a breath, unable to respond, unable to comprehend the avalanche of sadness and wistfulness tearing my soul and overpowering my heart.

"I-I just...I—"

Ding.

The elevator doors slide open and cameras flash in our faces. The reporters we've arranged to be part of this excursion are early and apparently want photos of us walking across the street to the shelter. His glittering eyes are still trained on mine as if the crowd of paparazzi isn't there, as if nothing else is more important than finding out what made me so sad. His hand grips mine tightly, his fingers caressing the tender skin in maddening circles again, this time in reassurance, I'm sure of it.

Twisting my lips into a wide smile, I curl my other arm around him and lean against his body, playing the role of the adoring girlfriend, the role I want to have in this other life in my imagination, and I tug him along as we step out of the elevator and stroll across the street to the homeless shelter.

"Look over here, Ms. Kingsley and Mr. Scott!"

"What a beautiful couple."

Small crowds of passersby have gathered at the street corners, attracted by the commotion of the flashing lights and cameras. People whip out their phones, no doubt taking videos of us or streaming footage somewhere. I keep my gaze on his, temporarily swept away by the moments of soul-shattering intensity probably only felt by me. Adrian's eyes never stray from mine, the chill in them replaced with a sudden warmth, a shade of tenderness that may be fabricated, but I don't care.

And I play a game of pretend.

My mind travels back in time to the lonely boy by the ocean, who is alone no more, because he has his pixie by his side once again.

• • •

"Thank you for allowing us to do this. This evening has been an absolute pleasure." I give Bob, the chef at New Beginnings, a burly man with a sleeve of tattoos and a white mustache, a warm hug as the night comes to a close after a few hours at the shelter serving hot meals to the less fortunate. The media has long gone home, with the press having a field day with numerous photos of the two of us, which I'm sure are already circulating the news outlets if the constant buzzing of my phone in my pocket is any indication.

"Any friend of Parker's is also our friend." Bob gives me a hearty slap on the back, almost knocking the wind out of my lungs, before stepping back. "And since you're Parker's in-law, that makes you practically family."

Parker utilized shelter services as a child, after he and his mom were evicted from their home shortly after his dad passed away and it was here where he met Bob, who took him under his wing. Ultimately, it all came full circle as the boy who had nothing ended up being somebody who was hired to head up a county-wide redesign project of its shelters, a massive undertaking which earned him many accolades, and hopefully some closure.

"Technically in-law once removed...if that's even a thing?" I laugh and give him a wink.

"In all seriousness though, thanks for reaching out. We can use some spotlight from the media on the homeless situation here. We need a lot of funding to maintain these shelters and our battered women shelters as well. Hopefully, with the media's interest in the two of you, this will help shine some light on our plight."

I hum in agreement as we stand at the entrance of the contemporary building, constructed with reclaimed timber and decorated in soothing shades of green and tan, colors found in nature. My gaze trails to the kitchens, where I see Adrian strolling out the doors with a grin on his face as he laughs at something a worker is saying while carrying platters of food to a long table to finish setting up dinner for the shelter's employees and volunteers. His penetrating voice is hypnotizing, especially when it sounds like this, free of its usual restraint and shackles. He wipes the sweat on his forehead with the sleeve of his shirt as his eyes meet mine. My lips automatically quirk into a grin and he winks at me, the simple movement sending a jolt of electricity to my heart. He mouths, *I'll be there in a few minutes. Almost done,* and strides away.

My pulse flutters in my veins as the moments of the evening come barreling back in flashes—the gentle caresses on my waist as he passes by me when he delivers fresh food from the kitchens to the serving station where I was scooping piping-hot beef stew to folks in need, the graze of his lips on my temple during my break as he hands me a bottle of water. My heart collects these scraps of moments and stores them inside the invisible jar of seashells within me, the shells I no longer collect because I don't go to the beach anymore, but nonetheless have been imprinted in my soul.

The rational side of me warns it's all fake, everything is for show, for the cameras and the campaign, but my heart doesn't care. After a decade of existing solely as the organ pumping blood throughout my body, keeping me alive, it leaps at the thought of becoming something more, of feeling all the emotions that make it soar.

"He's an interesting one, isn't he?" Bob's rough voice reminds me he's still standing there as we watch Adrian traipse back and forth, carrying more platters, bowls, utensils, and cups to the table.

"Adrian?" I murmur, staring once again at his retreating back. "Yeah, he is."

"Tell him thank you for us."

"You don't need to thank us, really. This is a publicity campaign and also helps the shelters—it's a fair trade."

"No." Bob pauses, his voice suddenly deep and thick, as if overcome with emotions. I crinkle my brows and turn to him, finding a wet sheen glossing his warm eyes.

"Bob?"

"He wired us twenty million dollars."

I gasp, my hand flying to my throat. "What?"

Bob nods as he wipes his eyes with his beefy arm. "We were tight on funds and with everything becoming more and more expensive these days, we were working out a plan to take out some loans and to cut certain expenditures. I briefly mentioned it to him the last time you were here for our preparation meeting, not thinking much of it, and this morning, the director notified me twenty million dollars has hit our bank from Scott Enterprises."

At my bewilderment, he nods and continues, "I didn't believe it either. So I asked him earlier, and he shrugged and simply said, 'Money is easy to make, but second chances aren't easy to come by' and he's glad to help our cause. Then he just walked away like his money didn't change our lives. I've never met anyone like him before. I was expecting a pompous billionaire who'd waltz in, thinking he was better than everyone in this room but..."

"He's not… He's acting like he's one of us," I finish for him, my voice choking up as I realize maybe, just maybe, the Adrian Callahan I know is still buried under the thousand-dollar suits and cutting remarks. Of course he'd understand how important money is for the poor, how the pennies to him now can turn around the lives of the people less fortunate…much like the position his family was in all those years ago.

Adrian strides over, an easy smile on his face, something I haven't seen outside of the last few hours, and his arm automatically curls around my waist. "Thank you for accommodating us, Bob," he murmurs.

Bob shakes his head and guffaws, apparently having regained his composure. "The pleasure is all mine, son. Please come back at any time. Are you sure we can't interest you in dinner with us?"

Adrian shakes his head. "A pile of work is waiting for me at home. Thanks for the invite."

Nodding to both of us, Bob struts away, heading to the table where the rest of the staff and volunteers have congregated.

Adrian links his fingers with mine, the motion so natural and fluid, I almost believe our relationship is real, and we step out the doors into the cool breeze of the night.

Pierre suddenly materializes in front of us and opens the door of the town car.

I arch my brows at Adrian. "What, no helicopter ride home?"

Chuckling softly, his voice husky, he replies, "No. There's no traffic at this hour and I live fifteen minutes away."

Sliding into the plush leather seats, I wait for him as he murmurs something to Pierre before taking a seat beside me. "I'll drop you off first. Where do you live, Emily?"

"The Mirabelle on Fifth and Olympic."

His eyes widen a smidge before he instructs Pierre. As the car hums to life, Adrian clicks a button, closing the partition between the driver and passengers' side of the vehicle.

"That was a good thing you did there…your donation."

Adrian glances at me in surprise, his eyebrow arched. He hands me a bottle of water before uncapping his and taking a sip. "It's nothing."

"You, of all people, know it's not 'nothing,' Adrian."

His jaw flexes and he stares ahead, silent. My cell phone buzzes in my pocket again. Sighing, I check my notifications, wondering how the public reacted to this outing.

Kristi: Glad to see you're back in the game, Emily. Keep up the good work.

She includes the link of a recent article from *Gossip Times*. "Lovebirds Have Reconciled and are Spotted at Homeless Shelter Volunteering." A candid photo of Adrian gently tucking a curl behind my ear as I smile at him is plastered front and center. My heart squeezes, remembering the exact moment when a lock of my hair fell in front of my face as I was unpackaging a fresh platter of food and his fingers swooped in and brushed the errant strands away.

"I take it Kristi is pleased with tonight?" he murmurs, his voice flat. My head whips toward him, finding his eyes pinned to his phone, his thumbs swiping on the device once again. His gaze flickers to me at my silence, the warmth from the blues dissipating into the usual frigidness.

Ice crystals form around my heart as the curtains fall. The play is finished to a standing ovation and I'm not feeling victorious. Instead, there's a heavy sense of loss as I'm once again reminded everything is all for pretense.

Glancing out the window, I notice the car slowing as we approach my downtown high-rise, where I have a small studio apartment. "Yes, good job today, Adrian."

Pierre opens my door and I step out. The cool breeze, which seemed comforting before, now seems biting. Squaring my shoulders, I turn around to say goodbye, only to notice Adrian standing behind me, his expression inscrutable.

"Why are you following me?" I ask.

"I live here."

"What? Since when?" A slither of unease settles inside me.

"Since I came back to LA."

"I haven't seen you around before." I cross my arms and narrow my eyes at him.

He mirrors my stance and says, his voice dripping with caustic sarcasm, "There are fifty floors in this building. Do you expect to meet every single one of its occupants?" He sidesteps me and strides toward the doors. "You coming?"

We stand in front of the elevator bay where he swipes a key and presses the light to the exclusive elevator straight for the penthouse—of course he'd be living on the top floor, while I wait for the elevator for the commoners to arrive. Silence befalls us, except for the footfalls of the security guard patrolling in the lobby.

My fingers twitch and I play with the buttons on my coat as the lighted numbers slowly count down from the thirtieth floor.

The security guard whistles.

I hear myself letting out a ragged breath.

Footfalls, this time sounding closer to me.

I glance up, finding Adrian standing before me, his eyes alight with an unidentified emotion. He tilts his head up to the security cameras in the corner and leans in slowly.

"W-What are you doing?" I gasp as my muscles lock in tension.

His hand reaches up and cradles my face, his thumb caressing the skin, which a moment ago was cold but is now burning hot. He tilts my face up and murmurs, barely an inch between our lips, "I didn't claim a single kiss tonight and the public is still watching."

Right. The cameras.

My eyes flutter shut as his soft lips gently touch mine in the briefest of caresses, sending a jolt of awareness inside me as butterflies take flight in my gut and I shiver from the gentle gesture, completely at odds with the tension radiating from his body. He deepens the kiss, his lips tenderly sucking my bottom lip in before his teeth snag on it, the sudden sharp bite sending a shock of pleasure mixed with pain to my system, and my eyes snap open.

Adrian pulls back, his tongue darts out and briefly laves the bite mark in a move so sensual, so erotic, it sends bolts of heat to my core. His thumb trails over his wet lips before he slides it into his mouth, as if to taste the essence I left behind. His eyes smolder in a flash of heat as my heart kicks in my rib cage and wetness seeps into my panties. I swallow and part my mouth, unable to breathe, and I feel lightheaded.

Ding.

His elevator arrives, and he steps in, his gait measured and precise. The fiery expression on his face has disappeared, leaving the cold billionaire in its place, as if the last few minutes were figments of my imagination. "Good night, Ms. Kingsley."

The butterfly wings beat inside my chest and my fingers trail to my swollen lips, the faint ache still there, and I wonder if our story did end all those years ago, or if...

If things have only begun.

Adrian

"Here is your table, Mr. Scott. Would you like some champagne or other refreshments?" an attendant dressed in the finest livery asks us as we sit at our private table at the Hollywood Bowl for a special evening performance from Enrique Sandros, piano prodigy from Spain, an event sold out well in advance. The infamous arched auditorium is lit up with blue lights tonight, a striking contrast to its stark white exterior, and blends seamlessly into the backdrop of darkening skies and glittering stars.

I glance at Emily, who is taking in the stage in front of us with anticipation. "Yes, champagne and water for now," I answer, "and you can serve dinner when the food is ready." The attendant nods and strides away.

"This area isn't usually used for dining, Adrian. The boxed seats are farther back." Emily's eyes widen in apparent wonder as her gaze is trained on the black grand piano, rumored to be one of the rare Steinway & Sons Fibonacci pianos even money can't buy. Her nimble fingers drum across the table as she's seemingly mesmerized by the instrument a mere few feet away from us. I don't think she's torn her eyes from the stage since we've been seated.

She's clad in a dark-red silky dress held up by the thinnest spaghetti straps. The material clings to her every curve and wraps over her porcelain skin in a lover's caress. Hints of cleavage peek out at the modest neckline, an enticement of what's beneath. A pair of pearl earrings adorn her delicate ears. She radiates an effortlessly sultry presence, the years bringing on an innate sensuality, something that wasn't there when we were younger.

I can't keep my eyes off her, despite my best intentions.

"I called up the director, and they were happy to accommodate once I promised them a sizeable donation to their endowment."

We're seated in the Pool Circle, an area between the raised stage and the garden boxed seats behind us. Normally, rows of chairs are arranged in this small space for folks who can afford to pay to be as close to the music as possible without being physically on stage. I rented the entire space for the night and the area is cleared except for our table, dressed up in a white linen tablecloth and small candle votives, giving the space a romantic glow. My bodyguards blend in with the background and the rich and famous loiter in the garden boxes, with the general public being farther back.

Emily's gaze flicks to mine, her plump lips parting with shock. "How much did you donate?"

"Ten million."

"What? For a dinner?"

I shrug. It's nothing to my overall net worth. The irony isn't lost on me how chump change to me today would've changed my life in the past. I'm here to wine and dine my fake girlfriend, to give her the best date ever, and to convince everyone I'm settling down. You can't put a price tag on that.

Keep telling yourself that.

At my silence, she shakes her head and sits back in her chair, her mocha eyes glimmering with unreadable emotions. Her gaze finally roves across the table, as if taking it in for the first time, and she gasps, clasping her hand over her mouth in apparent surprise.

Along with the sparking crystal candle votives, the table is decorated with a variety of lilies, from the Easter lily, its petals soft and white as snow, to the Royal lily with its purple-tinged backs. The starlet of the arrangements is a large bouquet of stargazer lilies artfully arranged in a low, circular vase, punctuated with clusters of pale pink and white hydrangeas. The sweet scent permeates the air, mingling with the cool evening breeze.

My chest clenches at her parted lips, the wonderment in her eyes. How the young me would've died to put this expression on her face, to surround her with the flowers she loves instead of only being able to afford to give her the one lonely stem each week. I wonder...does she still like them today? Is she happy with this arrangement? Does she remember?

You're only doing this for show. Keep your eyes on the prize.

I grit my teeth. Sentiment has no place in my life now. Only revenge.

Emily stares at me, her gaze taking on a shiny sheen as she swallows and swipes her enticing tongue out to wet her lips. "The lilies..." She exhales, her petite frame trembling slightly.

"Came with the venue." I clench my jaw and watch her eyes shutter, the hope within snuffing out. A spark of guilt worms its way inside me, but I smother its embers.

"Sir and ma'am, here are your champagne and water." The attendant returns, pouring the sparkling liquid into our flute glasses, and placing a bottle of distilled water on the table. A server steps up from behind him with plates of aromatic food. "For the lady, *Frutti di Mare* without mussels as requested. The seafood is sourced fresh from local fishermen and the spaghetti is handmade by our executive chef. Our house made *Arrabiata* red sauce is made from imported sweet San Marzano tomatoes and offset by a light kick from the garlic and chili peppers." He places the beautifully plated spaghetti in front of her and Emily's eyes dip down to look at her food, a lock of silky hair escaping the loose bun, blocking my view of her eyes. The attendant places the squid ink pasta with succulent shrimp and scallops in front of me, bows, and struts away.

"My favorite..." Emily whispers. "You still remember..." Her head is still bowed low as she grips the tablecloth in front of her. Her small frame shakes as she stares at the pasta, still unwilling to look up.

My hands clench on my lap, my fingernails digging into my palms. My fingers itch to trail over her shuddering frame in comfort, to tell her I understand. Memories I've buried deep inside me float to the surface—the candlelight dinner we had on the beach the night she gave me her first time. The pasta was chewy and overcooked; the seafood was almost nonexistent, but we were so happy. I was so happy.

The warmth spreading in my chest is halted by a torrent of bitterness, the poison seeping in, polluting the atmosphere. We finally have the meal I wanted to give her all those years ago, but the sentiments are ruined, the façade shattered, and now the expertly cooked pasta is tasteless on my tongue.

I silently ingest the perfect meal as I keep my eyes trained on her, unable to look away, unable to comfort her.

Unable to hate her.

My heart, a dormant organ all these years, sputters to life, the ache inside returning with a vengeance and my nose burns as I take in a ragged breath, struggling to hold on to the impenetrable armor I've built over the years.

That's the thing with memories. They may be from moments in the past and no longer relevant to the present, but it doesn't make them any less lethal, any less painful. And they often sneak up on you when you least expect it.

Emily finally tips her face back up and locks her beautiful eyes with mine, and what I see in her gaze threatens to take my breath away. In the first unsheltered moment since we began this farce of my own making, her chocolate eyes, still framed with the thickest lashes, are filled with warmth and something my soul has craved all these years, but I don't dare name. The wet sheen is more obvious now, the dew tipping her lashes, and she rolls her lush lips inward, as if she's struggling to contain her emotions.

"It's all for show."

She flinches, her lips trembling, before the vulnerability on her face is wiped away and replaced with a guarded veneer. Smiling widely, a fake smile she doles out to the public, she replies, "Of course. I'd expect nothing less."

Her stance is rigid, the earlier softness gone, and I find myself wanting to drag it back, even though this is for the best. Unbiddenly, I reach over and clasp her hand in mine, reveling in the sharp inhale from her luscious lips—lips that have been taunting me all evening, lips which have reminded me of our brief but scorching kiss the other night at the lobby. Gently brushing my fingers over the back of her hand, I lift it up and press the lightest of kisses on her smooth skin, enjoying the slight tremor from her, the pink flush spreading from the soft expanse of her chest to her delicate neck, making me want to chase the swipe of color and watch her melt under me.

"Eat, before your food gets cold," I murmur as I reluctantly let go of her hand.

She nods, a small smile gracing her lips and we quietly enjoy the expertly prepared meal before us, the richness of the pasta finally registering on my tongue.

Soon, the lights dim and the spotlights on stage brighten. The musicians settle in place and tune their instruments as anticipation fills the air. Minutes later, Enrique Sandros, a striking man not older than mid-thirties, strides on stage, confidence in his bearing, his tuxedo sharp on his figure. He dips into a curt bow and applause sounds from the venue as he takes a seat in front of the piano.

Emily freezes, her body angled toward the stage as if she couldn't get close enough. She intakes a sharp breath as the first chords sound, an infamous piece of Hungarian composer, Franz Liszt, titled *Liebestraum No. 3,* befittingly translated as "Love Dream." It's a beautiful song considered by many to be difficult to play, mainly from the dexterity needed to reach the keys, but Liszt is known to have larger hands, so this piece may be less challenging for him than the average pianist. Her food long forgotten, Emily breathes in with each high, breathes out with each low, her body swaying to the melody and a wistfulness creeps into her eyes as she stares lovingly at the stage.

She's lost in the music and I'm lost in her.

For a moment, I forget about my plans for revenge. I forget about her hurtful words all those years ago. I forget about her pity. I forget the simmering hatred in my veins.

In this moment, I pretend. A small reprieve. I forget about the game of dominos I'm setting up.

I pretend I'm just a regular man, taking the girl I love on a date she so deserves, watching her eyes light up and her lips part in wonder.

The auditorium erupts in applause as Sandros moves on to another piece, this time with the magnificent orchestra in accompaniment. Emily hasn't moved a muscle, her luscious lips still parted in apparent awe as she watches the musicians become one with their instruments, much like how I used to watch her play all those years ago in the music room or at her recital. The crowd may be staring at Sandros, the brightest spotlight on him, but no one can tear my gaze away from Emily, the girl, now woman, who was once my pixie, once the brightest spot in my dark life, the person who still, to this day, illuminates from within, the North Star amongst the flames in the nighttime sky.

Minutes or hours could've passed by, but it all blends together. The waitstaff quietly clears our table and Emily shivers, the goosebumps prickling her skin from the music or the evening chill. I take off my suit jacket and place it on her unsuspecting shoulders. Unable to resist, I lean in and press a kiss on her hair, relishing the soft scent of lilies from her body, the familiar smell mixed with a fragrance that is uniquely hers. She inhales a sharp breath and shivers once again. This time I don't believe it's from the temperature. I sit back, my heart aflutter as a long-buried warmth crawls back up my chest, heating me from within.

Sandros has moved on to his final piece of the evening, the haunting melody which connects us is crisp and reverberates in the air, the beautiful chords and aching notes of Beethoven's "Moonlight Sonata." Emily closes her eyes and sits rigidly in her chair, her teeth snagging on her plump bottom lip as if she's struggling to contain a storm within her. The notes pierce my soul and my chest clenches, an old wound slicing wide open.

The music reaches a crescendo; the audience awaits with bated breath, and I struggle to let oxygen into my lungs as my eyes are pinned to the woman next to me, listening to our song, the beautiful melody, one of both elation and sorrow, very much like our story. As the piece wraps to completion and the audience erupts into a standing ovation, a tear slides down Emily's cheek as she claps.

A sharp pain pierces the organ I thought was long dead and my eyes burn with unspeakable thoughts, unsaid emotions.

"The music is not in the notes, but in the silence between."

I read this quote a while back and it resonates in the depths of my frigid soul as an ember of fire threatens to reignite.

The auditorium fades into the background, the applause dulling to a quiet thrum in my ears, and all I can see is the beautiful woman in red sitting next to me, her cheeks shiny with tears, her eyes squeezed shut, the loneliness radiating from her so heartbreaking, even my damaged psyche can feel it. In this moment, the burning anger abates as another emotion, a tsunami, eclipses everything else in existence, and the only thing I want is to see a smile shine on her face once again.

Lacing her fingers in mine, I give them a quick tug, pulling her toward me. I clasp my free hand at the nape of her neck and seal my lips with hers, swallowing her gasp of surprise. This time, my kiss is not gentle. My lips move over hers with desperation, savoring the sweetness I've never forgotten despite my efforts, tasting the saltiness of her tears, relishing the heated passion that perhaps never died between us. She whimpers, her sound driving me wild as I curl my other hand around her waist, tugging her onto my lap and I surround myself with her scent, her essence, her energy.

My tongue teases the seam of her lips and she opens willingly and I sweep in, invading her senses, obliterating mine in the process. Our teeth clash, her fingers tightening around my neck, her nails digging into my muscles as we part for air. Her fevered eyes meet mine before I dive back in for another taste, already drunk on our kiss. My dick throbs under my dress pants and she gyrates her tiny body on top of mine, her warm core moving against my erection with expert precision.

"Oh Adrian," she moans as I bite her bottom lip, tugging on the tender flesh. Her breathy voice sends blood straight to my cock, hardening it even more.

My tongue swipes out and licks the spot, earning myself another whimper. "What do you want, Emily?" I rasp between kisses as she throws her head back to bare the fluttering pulse on her slender neck for me to rake with my teeth.

She makes small sounds from the back of her throat and unravels in front of me, dragging me into the flames with her and my fingers ache to rip off her dress right here and now, slide into her tight, wet heat, and fuck her senseless in front of everyone.

Pop. Pop. Pop.

The thundering sound of fireworks jolts us apart as the sky is emblazoned with a cornucopia of colors and a wave of murmurs and awe-filled gasps surround the large space. Panting heavily, I stare at the vixen on my lap, her hair now in waves across her shoulders, having unraveled from her bun, her tempting lips swollen as if bee-stung, her cheeks—no longer wet with tears—are searing pink, her eyes wide in apparent lust and shock.

"Adrian," she breathes out, her voice sweet and airy, a sound I thought I would only hear again in my dreams.

My heart thunders in my rib cage, the sound eclipsing the booming of the fireworks, and my skin feels hot to the touch, my nerves awakening as if I've been asleep this entire time. The crowd cheers at a barrage of what no doubt is a spectacular display of firepower, but I pay no heed, for nothing could be as breathtaking as the woman before me.

A bright flash shines in my eyes, not from the fireworks, but from a camera of a paparazzo who has somehow entered the vicinity in the distraction of the grand finale of the evening. A brief scuffle occurs, and my bodyguards intercept him without issue, but the interruption is enough to drag me back into reality, back into the world of money and power, where winners are respected and losers are pitied, where true love doesn't exist, and emotions are a liability, where people only love you if you're rich and powerful, and being poor and having a heart of gold is bullshit you feed to your kids.

The heady fire inside me extinguishes immediately as the familiar chill sweeps back in. My muscles tense and I slide her off my lap, not before whispering in her ear, "How is my commitment to our 'arrangement,' Ms. Kingsley?"

She flinches and stiffens, hurt flashing in her eyes, but not before plastering a fake smile on her face for the cameras. "Perfect. An Oscar-winning performance, Mr. Scott."

A sharp pain carves through me.

Anger and hatred—that's what this is.

Somehow, the victory seems bitter and hollow, the revenge not tasting sweet.

"There are days when I'm very jealous of your job, Ems," Liz whispers as I sit on my couch and await my carriage—aka Adrian's town car—to be readied to sweep us off to the Kensington Hotel for the red carpet premiere of the newest remake of *Romeo and Juliet* titled *Star-Crossed Lovers* featuring heartthrob Travis Bollinger of the infamous Bollinger brothers, and sweetheart starlet Reina Evans. Considering we live in the same building, Adrian will call me downstairs when the car is ready instead of coming to my door and picking me up like any normal date.

Because this isn't a real date, Emily. Remember that.

Ever since the night at the Hollywood Bowl, I feel the tides have shifted slightly between us. The scorching kiss during the fireworks finale, which I can still taste when I lie in my bed at night, awakens my senses, and makes all the intimacies I've experienced with past flings pale in comparison. Kissing Adrian is like touching a live wire, and despite knowing it's dangerous, I can't help but go back for more.

However, despite my feelings, he has been more reserved lately. He has tamped down on his kisses, avoiding them altogether, or brushing superficial ones over my temple or my hair. The arctic chill in his eyes is still there, but there are moments I catch him looking my way with a heated glance, or he'll link my fingers to his even when there aren't cameras around. He'll tell me everything is for show, that this is all for his campaign, but somehow, those words seem more insincere than before.

Or perhaps it's wishful thinking.

"You're only seeing the glamorous side of my job, which, by the way, this is unusual since I'm usually behind the scenes and not actually on the red carpet." I fiddle with my dress as I put my phone on speaker. The girls insisted I tell them all about the planned festivities for today.

"But Travis Bollinger!" Her voice lowers even more. "He's so dang hot. If I weren't with Parker…"

"Don't think I didn't hear that, baby," Parker's gravelly voice drawls in the background.

"Someone's in trouble," Sarah singsongs, barely containing a snort. "I call dibs on him. I'm single, after all."

"You guys can have Travis. I want Rhett. Those tattoos. The piercing eyes." Melanie sounds wistful, as if she's imagining her future with the youngest of the brothers, the bad boy of the trio.

I snicker, imaging Sarah's gaze dancing in laughter and Melanie making moony eyes at the brothers if she actually meets them.

"How are you feeling about 'this' so far?" Jess's concerned voice sounds over the receiver, worried about my mental well-being, as always.

Standing, I take a deep breath before striding to the full-length mirror by the door. I look at my appearance, admiring my hair, artfully arranged into a French twist with loose curls draping over my face, skimming the tops of my collarbones. My champagne-colored silk dress, simple in design, but daring with the thin spaghetti straps, the dangerously low back cut of the gown exposing most of my skin, but not to a point of gaudiness. The neckline is subtly draped and accentuates my breasts. The dress elongates my figure, making it seem like I'm taller than my five-foot-one, and even includes a thigh-high slit on one side. I opt for a dramatic cat-eye and lash extensions, but keep my lips simple—a neutral nude color with a thin coat of gloss.

Remembering Jess's question, I reply, "It's going. I won't lie and say it's easy but I'm trying to compartmentalize and to remind myself none of this is real."

"Do you want it to be?" My sister's soft voice carries through the phone.

That's the one question I can't bring myself to answer.

The one question that can lead to a road of pain.

Exhaling an anguished breath, I let out a hollow laugh, hoping it sounds sincere over the phone. "Of course not. Who are you looking at? I don't do long-term relationships, remember?"

"Riiight. Hmmm..." Liz chimes in, sounding a bit unconvinced. "I'm beginning to wonder about that. Call it a gut feeling—"

"Ems, do send us some candids from the red carpet, okay?" Sarah interrupts, and I want to hug her for it, because I know she's doing this to steer the conversation away from my relationship with Adrian, something even I don't understand at the current moment.

"Of course. If you're lucky, maybe I'll have the Bollinger brothers do a quick video with me where they say hi to you guys."

Melanie shrieks, "Oh my God, please. That'll make my day... no scratch that...make my year!"

My cell buzzes with an incoming text.

Adrian: The car is ready. Please come down.

"Hey, girls, I have to go. My carriage is here."

Disconnecting the call, I glance at my appearance one more time, give myself a mental pat on the back for cleaning up so nicely, grab my velvet clutch, and leave my apartment. A short elevator ride later, during which I try not to fidget from nervousness, I exit the building, only to find Adrian standing next to a black stretch limo. No town car this time.

Even though I've seen him multiple times in various mouth-watering outfits, nothing can prepare me for the sight of Adrian in a form-fitting tuxedo, which accentuates his well-built musculature and highlights his impressive height. His hair is immaculately styled, shorter on the sides and longer on top, side swept in a debonair vibe. His startling blue eyes trail over my body as I stride toward him and his lips part on an exhale before pressing into a firm line. His jaw is freshly shaven, every sharp angle illuminated by the waning sunlight.

My breathing grows shallow and my pulse kicks up, my body much more aware of him now than when I was younger and inexperienced. I can feel myself heat up and an aching want forms between my legs, making me want to clench my thighs together. His eyes darken as I approach him, as if he's aware of the thoughts crossing my mind.

"Emily, you look beautiful tonight," he murmurs as he opens the door for me.

At least he isn't calling me by my last name today.

"Thank you. So do you." I can't help but slide my palm across his chest, before reaching up and pressing a soft kiss on the corner of his jaw, where his scent of mint and musk is the strongest. I see him swallow, his muscles clenching, before I pull back and enter the luxurious vehicle.

Adrian raps on the partition and the limo hums to life, driving the short distance between our building and the Kensington Hotel. He takes a seat far across from me, as if he can't bear to sit next to me as he has in the past.

The silence is thick and unease festers inside me. He stares out the window, the muted sunlight hitting his profile at all the right angles, illuminating someone who is rich in material possessions, from the expensive watch on his wrist to what no doubt is a suit costing at least four-to-five digits, to the well-crafted shoes on his feet. However, the light also unveils the stark loneliness in his clear blue eyes, the tense set of muscles in his jaw, and someone who isn't truly happy.

"What are you staring at?" His eyes are still trained outside.

My hands fiddle with my garment, absentmindedly smoothing over the silky fabric. "I'm just thinking about how you did it... everything you said you wanted to do when we were kids."

He scoffs and crosses one leg over the other. "Not yet."

"What more do you want?"

Adrian stays silent, but a vein pulses on his forehead. The tension ratches up.

"Are you happy, Adrian?" I whisper, desperate to know if my sacrifice all those years ago yielded any joy for him after he recovered from the pain.

"It's a useless emotion."

"But now, you're on top of the world. You can provide your dad and Millie everything they desire. Isn't that what you wanted?"

"Why are we talking about this, Emily? Is this your way of backtracking what you said in the past? Because I'll let you know..." he turns his face toward me, his eyes hardening in frost, his voice low and lacing with bitterness, "*nothing* you say will make me forget what you did in the past. *Nothing*. So, save your breath."

I swallow the lump in my throat as my chest absorbs the verbal blows from him. "B-But what if I had a good reason—"

He laughs, the sound hollow and grating. "You have a reason *now?* After I've become one of the richest men in the world? How *fucking* convenient, Emily." Adrian leans forward, his nostrils flaring as he utters, "If that's the case, then that makes you a liar. And I fucking *despise* liars, so save your excuses and your reasons. They don't mean anything to me. *You* don't mean anything to me."

I flinch and my eyes burn at the onset of tears. His words are sharper and more lethal than any bullet. A visceral pain lands in my chest, and I'm suddenly unable to breathe. My lips tremble and I glance away, unable to stare at the hatred in his eyes and listen to the venom in his voice.

My heart clenches in agony and I blink rapidly, willing the tears not to fall. I won't break down in front of Adrian Scott. Clenching my fists tightly, I take in a few shuddering breaths to stem the bleeding in my heart. It's as if his words tore open the scab, and the pain I've leashed away all these years comes pouring out, the hemorrhage tenfold.

I feel his sharp gaze on mine as I stare out the window this time. His words seep through my defenses and weaken the armor I've been wearing all these years. I can't let him get to me. As we approach the hotel, our limo coasts to a stop and we wait for our turn to alight at the red carpet. Closing my eyes, I imagine stuffing the heaviness into a small box to be hidden away and instead focus on the nonprofit projects I want to land after this tortuous year with Adrian ends.

A few moments later, the limo pulls to a stop right next to the red carpet. Hordes of people are pointing and screaming at the celebrities who have walked before us, the sounds muted through the thick windows. Groups of photographers, dressed in black, like clusters of crows, descend upon the rich and famous, the flashes from their cameras like shooting stars in the sky.

I take a deep breath. "Ready, Mr. Scott?" Glancing at him, I perform my best rendition of a doting girlfriend, my lips curving into a fake smile, which shields my bleeding heart.

Adrian's steely gaze is on my face, his muscles locking in tension. His hands are fisted on his lap. At my expression, his lips flatten before he exhales. "Always, Ms. Kingsley," he answers, rearranging his façade into one of indifference. His hands slowly relax, his frame loosening, and he curls one corner of his mouth up into a cold grin, his appearance deceptive, a predator lulling prey into a false sense of security.

The door opens and the booming sounds of the crowd invade the quiet space as lights flash inside the dim interior. Adrian steps out and straightens up, every inch The Shark and the billionaire, before he leans down and extends his hand toward me.

"Emily?" He smiles, but the expression doesn't reach his eyes, which remain as frigid as ever.

I place my hand in his, a frisson of awareness pulsing through me at the point of contact, and slide out of the car, my head tilting up at him as my mind travels back in time to our first dance with the moonlight as our company, where he also took my hand in his. Pain-laced warmth infuses me and I smile at my memory of Adrian Callahan, the boy with the heart of gold, because I can't face the Adrian Scott of today. His eyes flicker in confusion before darkening into a brilliant hue, as if he, too, is having trouble navigating these rough waters.

"Mr. Scott, Ms. Kingsley, please look over here," reporters shout at us from all directions as Adrian leads me down the red carpet, his arm curled tightly around my waist.

"Will we be hearing wedding bells in your future?" another reporter asks as we pose for photos.

Adrian answers, "If it happens, you'll be the first to know." He flashes an award-winning smile and I swear I hear a few females gasp in the background. He then turns toward me with warmth in his eyes I know is fake, and says, "If anyone were to make me consider it, it'd be this woman right here." He leans in and presses a barely there kiss on top of my head.

My heart soars even though I know the words are fake and heat travels up my face. I close my eyes to control the chaos inside me before fluttering them open and reaching up to press my lips to his jawline. He freezes, albeit briefly, before he resumes tugging me along the carpet to the next set of photographers.

"Is this beautiful woman the incomparable Emily Kingsley?" a low drawl, a voice I definitely recognize, calls out a few feet away from us.

I turn toward the sound of what could easily be three of the hottest men of the evening, aside from the brooding billionaire next to me. The trio, with their imposing heights, chocolate-brown hair, and eyes as green as the rainforest, are the Bollinger brothers.

"Travis, long time no see." I grin, waving at the eldest of the cinematic heartthrobs. They were my former clients, but you'd never find me admitting this to the girls. "A fantastic event tonight. I sense a golden statuette with your name on it in the future."

I begin to step forward, only to find Adrian's arm tightening around my waist, his fingers digging into the soft flesh. Frowning, I glance at him and find his expression hardening, displeasure swimming in his eyes. He lets go and I walk toward the eldest of the brothers.

Travis dips down and wraps me in a friendly hug. "Thank you. I had a great experience filming this movie." He chuckles and purses his lips. "I never thought I'd hear Emily Kingsley settle down, and I didn't believe it until I saw it with my eyes."

Laughing, I shove playfully at him and reply, "You can too, if you want to."

"Nope. No, thank you. Why deprive the public of this?" He sweeps his hands up and down his body, his handsome face grinning with mischief.

"Emily, we missed you around here." A deeper voice, one belonging to the youngest, Rhett, joins our camaraderie. His grin is more subdued, but no less lethal.

"You, sir, clean up very nicely." He's clad in a form-fitting tux, his sleeve of tattoos hidden away except for one peeking through on the back of his hand.

"All thanks to you."

The middle brother, Jared, the moodiest of the trio, saunters up to us, his eyes scanning over my face as if he's trying to figure something out. He frowns. "You sure you're doing okay, Ems? Need us to rough up somebody?" His emerald gaze travels to the man behind me, who has been lasering me with the weight of his stare.

Jared is too damn perceptive for his own good.

He leans forward, and murmurs in my ear, "I don't like the way he's looking at you, Ems. Just say the word, and we'll be your backup."

Before I have a chance to formulate an answer, I hear pounding footsteps, and a commanding presence materializes himself next to me. I smell the tension radiating off his warm body. Suddenly, Adrian slips his arm around my waist and tugs me flush against him, his hand straying low to cup the top of my ass before he leans down and slams his lips on mine.

Electricity flows through me as my senses come alive. He sucks my bottom lip in, the sensation akin to touching a live wire. His teeth graze the plump flesh and I nearly moan aloud. Clutching the lapels of his tux, I arch back as he bends me over, his strong frame easily enveloping me, his lips chasing mine in a kiss that is ravaging, angry, heated, and everything in between. It's as if we can't get close enough, as if our bodies are making up for the distance between us these last eleven years. Unable to stifle a whimper, I part my lips as his tongue sweeps in, tangling with mine in a sensual dance. I feel his hard erection pressing against my stomach and my core weeps with arousal as he kneads the top of my ass.

This is a claiming. The male lion marking his territory.

A thrill of elation sweeps through me, even though the nagging voice in the back of my head tells me this is not real.

A wolf whistle penetrates the fog of desire and I freeze, remembering where we are. *Shit.* "You're touching my ass," I hiss as we break apart for air, my chest heaving, and I stare into his lust-filled eyes.

His hard chest shudders against me and he exhales against my lips, a masculine smugness on his face. "Screw the provision."

"You—"

He clutches me tighter against him and a new shard of heat shoots to my core. "You're *breathtaking*." The blues of his eyes are smoldering as the grin slips off his face.

My heart flips and flops at the sudden intensity in his words as the worlds of fake and reality collide in front of me and I can't tell which is which anymore. My hand trembles and I reach out to touch his face. His eyes briefly flutter shut as he leans against my palm. The world falls away and the only person who exists is the man before me. A searing ache pierces my chest at this intimacy, something I've only dreamed about in the middle of the night with the face in the shadows always belonging to him, the person my soul has never forgotten. Wetness prickles my eyes and my breath catches in my throat.

I may have been the one who left him all those years ago, but he's the one who really never left the confines of my heart.

"Aaand maybe I'm mistaken," Jared murmurs behind me and the crowds around us slowly come into focus, the screeching and chattering finally piercing the veil.

My heart tremors in agreement, my soul standing at the edge of the cliff once again, working up the courage to leap off the threshold, but my brain pulls me back, tethering me to solid ground.

What is the difference between illusion and reality? If the illusion feels so good, can I stay in it forever?

I lost control.

And damn if that doesn't piss me off.

I pride myself on having a tight leash on my emotions, for not wearing my thoughts on my face for all to see. It's something that has aided me in my rise to the top of the world. It's the reason why everyone runs away from The Shark.

But somehow, this pocket-sized woman can easily plow through and obliterate the thick armor I've painstakingly constructed over the years with the ease of a missile. I've tried to stay away from her, to maintain distance ever since the night at the Hollywood Bowl, when the kiss became too real and intoxicating for my taste. The kiss that has stayed in my mind front and center ever since, the image I think about each night as I fuck my hand to a frenzy, coming with her name on my lips, hating myself afterward for being so weak, for still being so captivated by her...even if it's in the privacy of my thoughts.

I've made sure to call her by her last name when no one is around, to remind her everything is a farce. I've tried to avoid the scorching kisses I desperately crave. But time and time again, she'd attempt to break through the barriers, with her soft smiles and warm glances, her lilting laughter and teasing grins. I'd react with anger and coldness, feelings that are familiar to me. My heart leaps and soars, however inconveniently, while my mind reminds me of the words she said to me that fateful night on the beach, the ones that tore me apart from the inside out, and the banked fire inside me reignites.

"But what if I had a good reason—" My thoughts stray back to what she said in the limo earlier, but I quickly shut it down. The world wasn't kind to me and bestowed upon me and my family no graces when we were poor, with Emily being the one to wield the final blow. Why should I give people a chance when none was given to me? What kind of idiot makes the same mistake multiple times and expects a different outcome? And so, I hardened my heart, smashed my empathy, even when a devastating hurt flashed in her beautiful bright eyes.

But apparently, life has once again proven to me things are definitely *not* in my control when the fucking Bollinger brothers smiled at Emily like she was theirs to take.

Fuck, maybe she has been with them before. From what I've heard, Emily dates around and doesn't settle down.

The ugly bitterness of jealousy invades my senses and I see red, especially when the third of the trio leaned down and whispered in her ear, an intimate embrace for all to see. And so, I strode up like a caveman and claimed her, kissed the living fuck out of her, reveling in how she melts in my arms, her moans and her sighs, her breathy whimpers, and how she tightly clutches me against her. I was one second away from dragging her down the red carpet and hauling her back into the limo, tearing that silky number off her luscious body, and showing her how Adrian Scott fucks now. But now, as she stares at me, wide-eyed with swollen lips, I wonder if I'm the person who has been claimed instead.

"Come on, Emily, let's head inside," I murmur, my voice rough as I wrap my arm around her tiny waist, her body curling against mine as if it belonged there all along.

She nods, her eyes unfocused, and we head toward the doors. Suddenly, she jolts up, and exclaims, "Oh!"

Disentangling from me, she hurries back to the annoying trio, who is looking at us with shit-eating grins.

"I promised my girlfriends to take a video with you guys!" She pulls out her phone from her clutch, her voice excited, as if she were the one receiving something from her idols. "Oh, better yet. Why don't we call them?"

The brothers shrug in the affirmative and Emily, the enthusiasm practically rolling off of her in waves, hits a few buttons on her phone and suddenly I hear loud screeching coming through the line as I stare at my pixie in bemusement. *My pixie?* Shit.

"I-I'm your biggest fan, Travis...I'm single. Oh shit, I can't believe I said that." I think that's Sarah.

"I love you, Ems. Oh my God, I don't think I'll be able to sleep tonight. Rhett, you're, you're..." Melanie, if I recall correctly.

Jared chuckles and says, "What, no love for me?"

More screaming and after a few moments, Emily hurries after me, her eyes bright with laughter as she slinks her arm around my waist. "I'm so going to milk this in the future. Muahaha. They're going to owe me so many favors," she whispers gleefully.

This spark in her, the one that's been missing since I saw her at Parker and Liz's rehearsal, is like pouring gasoline on a fire and my heart clenches and free falls, the blood rushing in my ears, and I can't do anything except stare at the pixie standing beside me, still wonderfully animated as she was all those years ago, but with an air of maturity and grace so alluring and intoxicating at the same time.

The production company secured us seats near the front of the makeshift theater and the room darkens and quiets as the movie plays. The story of the star-crossed lovers, who shouldn't have fallen in love but did so anyway, even though it ended in tragedy for them, but brought peace to their families. When I was younger, I hated this story with a passion, despite this being Mom's favorite play from Shakespeare. I didn't understand how Romeo and Juliet could be so irresponsible and reckless.

But now, as I sit in the darkness with the girl who stole my heart eleven years ago when she had no right to, when we were worlds apart, who is now this intoxicating woman, someone I still can't walk away from despite knowing she never loved me the same way, a thought occurs to me. I wonder if the beauty of the story rests in the inevitability of love. Somehow, despite differences in family backgrounds, impressions and intentions, the heart wants what it wants and this emotion, transcending all rational thought, is what makes this play so beautiful and romantic. And perhaps this is why Mom risked it all to be with Dad and passed away with no regrets.

Emily shifts in her seat and I glance at her, finding her eyes pinned to the screen where Romeo is kissing his Juliet, their souls reuniting in death, a reimagined ending to the play. A searing emotion, one I still don't want to name, pierces through me, and I can't help but clutch my chest. As if sensing me watching her, Emily turns to me, her gaze shiny with tears and she swallows, as if overcome with the same emotion coursing through my veins.

Shakily, I lift her hand from the handrest to my lips, and place a soft kiss on the delicate skin, my eyes burning as I close them to avoid her seeing what must be showing clearly in my gaze. I inhale the sweet scent of lilies and wonder if revenge can ever give me as much satisfaction as having this woman by my side.

CHAPTER 35

Adrian

“The answer is still no, Scott,” a raspy voice, deceptively weak for a snake, murmurs across the line. I grip my phone tightly, wanting to strangle the man on the other side of the conversation.

My grandfather. Regis Cornwall III.

“I double my offer.”

This gives him some pause. The greedy bastard.

“Why do you want my shares so badly? You have a large enough real estate presence.”

I grit my teeth and take a deep breath. With the inflated ego of this man, using a carrot as opposed to going directly with a stick should have better results, but I’ve been dancing this waltz with him for the better part of the year and I’m frankly getting sick of it.

“One can never be big enough. You should know that. Your company is number two in the industry after mine.”

Laughter sounding more like wheezing comes across the line. Maybe the old geezer can do us all a favor and keel over. Maybe then I can get the person who inherits his shares—forty-five percent of the company—to sell to me. Then, I’ll finally be holding over fifty percent of the shares, the controlling interest of my grandfather’s beloved possession and can destroy it piece by piece, annihilating his precious legacy.

Something he thought was more important than Mom and our family.

"Spoken like a true shark. I wish I had a grandson like you. Someone who understands how to stay at the top of the business world."

Anger threatens to boil over and I take a big gulp of the whiskey the flight attendant placed in front of me a few minutes ago, the burn temporarily distracting me just enough from lashing out over the phone and letting the coldhearted bastard know I *am* his grandson.

"Since we understand each other, why don't you do us all a favor and sell me your shares? Take the sum of money, spend the rest of your days traveling the world or drinking martinis by the beach."

My grandfather chuckles as if he finds this conversation amusing. "No. I've gone with my gut for most of my life and it hasn't led me astray. And something tells me...you won't be leading my creation to brighter paths. My company is known to be the most family-oriented of all real estate companies. Our interests from large-scale nonprofit projects and third-world developments to equal-opportunity housing in prime locations. Scott Enterprises and you, frankly, have the exact opposite image. While it seems like you are coming around and perhaps finally settling down, I don't think a merger will be in the best interest for Cornwall. So, while I like you, son, I don't think I want to sell to you...at least, not yet."

"You know that's illogical. The profit margins I bring to the table are staggering. You can only win in this trade." I toss back the rest of the contents of my tumbler.

"You can't put a price to reputation, Scott. I don't want my legacy to be selling out a well-beloved company to a cold-blooded shark."

I stare outside the window, the dark skies at this altitude akin to staring into the void. Quashing the burn in my chest, I reply, "You'll change your mind. You'll see." I disconnect the call to the grating chuckles of the person I hate the most in the world.

I continue gazing at the blackness on the other side of the glass as we head toward New York City for our required vacation outing in the contract, which happens to coincide with the holidays, the annual ball for the rich and famous at The Orchid, and the Asshole Friends Group gathering—Charles didn't get his Alaskan trip after all. The rest of them are arriving over the next few days except for Liz and Parker, who will join us after they spend their Christmas with Parker's parents. We'll fit in some obligatory public outings, but I'll mostly be buried in meetings and a few business trips to other cities as well. The world doesn't shut off because of a few holidays in December.

After some time of quiet contemplation, I'm distracted by a *thump* from behind me. Turning around, I see Emily stumbling in, her hair in disarray, with a sleep eye mask perched on top of her head. She rubs her eyes as she yawns, then staggers into the main lounge area of my private jet. Her cozy, oversized sweatshirt stretches up with the motion, revealing more of her slender legs.

"Thanks for letting me use the bedroom. Had the worst headache last night and couldn't sleep. You were talking rather loud just then. Everything okay?" she murmurs as she plops into the seat next to me. Her eye mask, a flimsy piece of cloth inscribed with an equally ridiculous nonsensical string of letters "STFUAT-TDLAGG," is partially affixed to her hair, as if she forgot to remove it completely. She stretches her arms as the cobwebs still linger in her eyes and the mask slides farther up her head, pushing her hair up into something resembling a nest. My lips twitch at her appearance and she stares at me quizzically.

"Why are you looking at me like that?" She quirks her brow, her plump lips pursed in apparent confusion.

The anger from moments ago fades into a prickle of amusement. I motion to her hair. "Your mask."

Her eyes widen comically big and she snatches the offending scrap of fabric from her head before stuffing it next to the handrest and smoothing out her hair.

"What does it mean?"

"Hmm?" A flush creeps up her face and she blinks as if she doesn't know what I'm talking about.

Reaching out, I snatch the silky mask from her seat as she tries, but completely fails, at stopping me. I read the letters once more, hoping it'll somehow make sense if I stare at them long enough. "STFUATTDLAGG."

"Give it *back,* Adrian." She lunges over as she tries to snag it from me.

I raise the eye mask high into the air—there are advantages of towering over a foot taller than this pocket-sized vixen—and she struggles, climbing over the handrest to place one knee between my legs, the other sandwiching my thigh. She attempts to grab it from my hand, failing, and only reaching my forearm.

"Give. It. Back," she grunts, determination in her voice.

Chuckling, I hold it up even higher and watch as she flails helplessly against me, her body now practically straddling my lap. "The first four letters, I can guess. Tell me what the rest means and why you're so desperate to get it back."

"It's an internet slang and a gag gift and it makes me laugh. It also means *none of your business,*" she huffs as she presses harder against my chest, her tits perilously close to my face. I sharply inhale as blood rushes south to my stiffening dick.

My muscles lock in tension and my body catches up to the close proximity, her heaving tits swaying gently as she moves her little frame against me, the seductive scent of lilies wafting to my nose. My mouth dries and I clench my fingers, which are apparently clamped over the back of one of her luscious thighs, my thumb skimming the soft skin against her sleep shorts. My heart pounds wildly in my chest and I use every ounce of energy to keep from closing the few inches in front of me and suckling her clothing-clad breasts.

Emily glances down at me, her lips parting in confusion, and awareness dawns in her beautiful eyes, which are darkening into the richest chocolate with flecks of gold in the irises. She pants, the motion bringing her tits even closer to my face, and I grip her thigh harder, kneading the soft flesh there.

I'm rewarded with a breathy moan as her plump lips part in an O. I can feel and smell the arousal seeping through her pores.

"If you want it back, tell me what it says," I growl as the tension thickens between us.

"I..." she whispers, her body frozen on top of mine. She swallows, the sound audible, and a pulse flutters in her slender neck, beckoning me to taste, to suck, to kiss.

"Tell me," I rasp, my voice husky to my ears.

"Shut the fuck up and take that dick like a good girl." She bites on her lip, the enticing pink flush spreading from her neck to her face.

My cock hardens to the point of bursting in a matter of milliseconds as my brain registers her words. I imagine issuing the command to her and watching her drop to her knees and choke on my swollen dick until I come down her throat.

And she's going to swallow every last drop.

"What?" I growl, my hand sliding up to her waist and tugging her flush against me. She whimpers and tumbles toward me, her hands bracing on my shoulders.

"The a-acronym. You were asking..." Her voice is a breathy whisper, the beginnings of a moan.

"Mr. Scott, we are approaching the airport. Hope you had a pleasant flight." The pilot's voice comes across the speakers as I've instructed no one to enter the lounge area during my call with Cornwall.

Emily jumps at the interruption and moves to scramble off me but I clutch her hips tightly, rendering her immobile.

"Tell me..." I lean in, my breath ghosting over her ear. "Are you wet right now?"

She gasps and shoves my chest, practically leaping off my lap as she vaults across the handrest with the practiced agility of a gymnast.

"I'm going to change into my jeans." She whirls around and speeds toward the bedroom with the desperation of someone escaping a burning building.

Smoldering heat zings through my body as the predator in me wants to fly out of my seat and hunt her down to have my way with her, but I force myself to relax. I let out a shuddering exhale, anticipation and excitement seeping into my veins, a heady, intoxicating combination, and I savor the feeling, the earlier anger completely forgotten.

. . .

"Jeffrey will be at your beck and call, Mr. Scott and Ms. Kingsley. Please let us know if you need anything. Thank you for choosing to stay at The Kensington." The manager of the luxury, five-star hotel on Fifth Avenue motions to the portly man with graying hair next to him and they both nod to us before softly closing the door to the Presidential Suite. My fingers dig gently into Emily's slim waist before I reluctantly let go of her, the charade being over now that our audience has departed the room.

She drapes her navy wool coat over the large, velvet blue sectional before traipsing to the floor-to-ceiling windows, her eyes wide as she admires the rest of the suite, with the usual amenities one would expect from something going for upward of seventy grand a night, especially during the in-demand holiday season. There are hardwood floors overlaid with a cream-and-tan carpet, crystal floor lamps and pendant lights, a modern fireplace suspended midair in a clear, glass column. The adjacent dining room and open-concept kitchen features a twenty-seat glass table next to windows boasting views of Central Park, top-of-the-line stainless steel appliances, and the usual marble countertops and island. There's also a second level with a personal gym, steam room, multiple bedrooms and offices, which I'm sure are all equally standard in luxury.

However, everything in this room pales compared to the woman in front of me, dressed in a simple blue sweater and boot-cut jeans, her hair in a sleek ponytail.

"The views are beautiful up here," she murmurs as she peers out the wall of windows, no doubt staring at the wide expanse of snow-covered greenery and glittering lights of cars passing by, the city coming alive in the evening. The energy of New York City is unique and even bad weather can't dull its charms.

"You get used to it if you live here long enough." Despite this being my headquarters for a decade or so, New York has never truly felt like my home.

The city is exciting. The women are beautiful. The cuisines are mouthwatering. I made my climb to success here and carved out a future for myself where no one can look down upon me or my family again.

But everything is muted, an array of neutrals and grays, fueled only by the anger in my veins.

Because this city was missing someone.

I was missing someone.

"I can't believe you're staying here now." The words are unsaid, but I know what she means. The Adrian Callahan in the past isn't fit to step foot into the hotel, let alone stay in its most expensive accommodations.

"I would've taken you to my apartment, but this is more convenient."

My chest constricts and my eyes track her movements as she walks around the room, her fingers trailing over the tufted armchairs next to the windows. Despite my intentions, Emily has wormed herself back into my heart. When she turns around and doles out one of her mischievous, wide smiles, my mind short-circuits, unable to remember why revenge was so important to me.

Don't give anyone second chances, Adrian. Nobody gave you one back then.

Destroy your enemies before they hurt you.

Don't let yourself be vulnerable again.

The logic seems flawed when my heart pumps enthusiastically as Emily stares at me with her warm chocolate eyes, her ruby-red lips now softening into a sweet smile. "I'm so proud of you, Adrian. Your mom would be too."

My hands clench and I swallow the lump forming in my throat. A piercing ache scythes through me and I look away, the muscles in my jaw flexing in tension.

"Adrian?" The person I was missing all along steps toward me, her voice uncertain.

"How I wish you would've said these words that night instead of what you told me then."

She intakes a sharp breath, her eyes widening as unidentified emotions flit over her face, the slideshow too quick for me to decipher. Her lips tremble.

"Adrian, please. Can we drop this? Can you trust me if I tell you I had my reasons?"

I scoff, shaking my head. "Does it matter what the reasons are? Even if I could understand your rationale, it's too late. The damage is done."

I spin around and stalk toward the stairs, my hands clenched into fists—anything to prevent me from turning back and pulling her into my arms. Before climbing the first step, I murmur, "I have back-to-back meetings the next few days, so I won't be around. I'm sure you can take care of yourself. Good night, Ms. Kingsley."

Distance. I need distance away from her, away from this maddening world where the blacks and whites are blurring into a sea of grays and I find myself drifting in the wrong direction, sailing uncharted waters once again.

I don't wait for her response before I continue on, my legs carrying me away from the person who may be my undoing.

• • •

For the next few days, I bury myself in work, conference calls, and meetings with partners. I spend most of my days onsite at the New York offices, leaving the penthouse early in the morning after fitting in a quick workout with the punching bag at the well-equipped gym, and coming back late at night after dinners or drinks with prospects. It's interesting how people will make time for you, even rearrange their holiday vacation plans, when you're rich and powerful. People cater to me now instead of the other way around. They beg me to give them opportunities. I don't need to depend on anyone any longer.

If you told the nineteen-year-old me this would be my future at thirty, this would've been the stuff of dreams, what I'd imagine happiness would feel like. Instead, the void inside me has only grown with each additional zero to my bank account, and the money, the thing I used to despise yet crave, is now meaningless.

As Christmas Eve rolls around, my favorite distraction, pouring more of myself into my business, is no longer working, not when a certain five-foot-one pixie is fluttering about the space mere doors away from mine. My thoughts keep straying back to her, wondering what she's doing, if she's happy, the way her face lights up when she sees me. *Of course she smiles at you now that you're successful.* Gritting my teeth, I shove my thoughts away, my heart pounding in agreement. My grasp on resentment is slippery, precarious at best. I pace around the office in the penthouse, a large space with black bookshelves, a similarly toned desk, white seating, and my cell phone rings.

"Hi, Millie, Merry Christmas."

"Merry Christmas to you too. So, we're meeting at Dad's place tonight? Is she coming?"

"Yes."

Millie vaguely remembers Emily and definitely knows the Kingsley last name. As much as I want to leave Emily here by herself while I gather with my family, I couldn't bring myself to.

"You know, Dad and I don't mind... He told me what happened all those years ago. He understands why he got fired. He doesn't hold a grudge against her. I hope you aren't still mad at her because of it." She believes I broke up with Emily because I found out her father fired our dad. I never corrected her.

"Don't worry about it."

We say our goodbyes, and I disconnect the call. I give up all pretenses of working and open the door of the office, finding a small present wrapped in red-and-gold metallic paper with a small card affixed to the top. Frowning, I reach down and pick it up, reading the note first.

Adrian,

Tomorrow is Christmas, which means it's your birthday. Happy Birthday. I know you probably have everything you can possibly want now, so hopefully, you won't find this gift silly.

If you still have any unfulfilled dreams, I hope they all come true.

Always,

Emily

A thickness forms in my throat as I carefully unwrap the small package. Inside the red leather box is a tie clip with delicate carvings of scallop seashells. My breath catches in my throat as my fingers trace every delicate ridge of the shells.

She still has wishes for me.

An ache forms in my chest, and my nostrils flare from a sudden rush of prickling heat behind my eyes. I bite my cheek as I stare at the best present anyone could ever give me. In moments like this, all the moments of doubt and anger fade into the background, and I wonder what I'm doing, why I'm still fighting when I want nothing more than to hold her in my arms.

After a few minutes of reining in my galloping emotions, I walk downstairs and stride to the living room, where a fire roars in the modern fireplace. I find Emily curled up in an armchair, flipping through a magazine. She has a thick maroon blanket on her lap, her brows furrowed at something she's reading.

My breath catches in my throat as I take in the woman I've tried to avoid for the past few days. The daylight casts a soft glow on her, illuminating the caramels buried deep within the chocolate strands of her hair, her porcelain skin, a light dusting of freckles like the stars have kissed her, leaving their imprints behind. Her smooth shoulder peeks through the wide neckline of her red sweater. Her face is free of makeup and her fingers absentmindedly trail the delicate skin on her neck as she flips the page. Flurries of white snow outside the windows provide a dazzling backdrop—a minx in a winter wonderland.

The pulse thrums in my veins at the sight of her there, the rightness of it all, and the void closes a bit as a ray of light shines through. Brushing the thoughts aside as my mind clamors to remind me of my plans, I take a few seconds to enjoy the first moment of peaceful tranquility since we've arrived here.

I'm standing on a perilous sheet of ice in a vast ocean, a limbo, one movement away from tipping over and drowning in the harsh depths, yet I'm mesmerized by the view.

An exquisite, tortuous pain.

As if sensing my stare, Emily glances up, her eyes brightening, then dimming when she sees me standing there. She straightens up before quirking her lips into a wide smile, her gaze taking on a decidedly determined glint.

"Merry Christmas Eve!" she exclaims before winking at me, as if I haven't tried my best to ignore her these past few days.

The heaviness of guilt weighs on my chest and I amble toward her. "Merry Christmas Eve, Emily." I hold up the red box and clear my throat. "Thank you for your present."

Her eyes widen at my usage of her name again. She smiles and says softly, "You're welcome." We stare at each other, seemingly speechless, yet our gazes hold volumes of unsaid sentiments.

She lets out a soft sigh before quirking up her lips in a teasing grin. "Are you going to be a workaholic scrooge today, Adrian? Terrorizing your partners and employees the day before Christmas?"

My lips twitch in a smile. "No, even workaholics need to take a break."

"So, what are our plans, then?"

"What makes you so sure my plans include you?"

She arches her brow. "With your reputation, my guess is you probably have more enemies than you do friends. If you aren't going home, which, are you?" At my silence, she continues, "Well, if you aren't visiting family, then you only have me."

"And Jack, you remember him, right?"

"He's here?"

I nod. "He works at The Orchid...and I'm planning to visit my family today."

Emily physically deflates as she slouches back into her seat, the large chair dwarfing her petite size. "Oh." She shrugs and pouts. I stare at her, willing my face not to move a muscle, as disappointment creeps into her angelic features. "I guess, maybe I'll call up Steven and see what he's doing. But he's probably working because he's a workaholic like you."

She lets out another dramatic sigh before turning her attention back to her reading material, her lips flattening into a thin line.

Biting my cheek, I chuckle as she glances up at me with a questioning gaze.

"Don't terrorize your brother. You're going with me to meet my family. They've been pestering me about you since reading about us in the press."

"You didn't tell them this is all for show?"

A fleeting pinch lands on my chest at her reference to the arrangement I've forgotten about since walking down the flight of stairs. Shaking my head, I reply, "No. The fewer people who know about it, the better. They think we're dating for real."

Emily nods, her mouth in a comical O. She scrambles off the chair, the neck of her sweater twisting more to the side with the movement, baring more of her tempting shoulder and a hint of cleavage. I swallow as heat travels to my gut.

"Where are we going? What's the dress code?" She hops one legged toward the stairs. "Shit, my foot fell asleep," she mutters under her breath, and the beginnings of lust fade into amusement.

"Just going to Dad's place. What you're wearing is fine."

"Okay! Give me ten." She whirls back, a mischievous grin on her face, and says, "If I'm going to meet the family, I need to glam myself up." Flashing a wink, she runs up the stairs, the excitement leaching out of her.

A sliver of thought, one which has been repeatedly sneaking up on me in the quiet moments, is back once more.

If you let things go, Adrian, you can have this. The past doesn't matter anymore. Don't you want this?

The smile falls off my face and my heart constricts in reply.

CHAPTER 36

Emily

"**M**erry Christmas! Well, almost Christmas anyway. Millie, you look so grown up!" I smile brightly, despite the fluttering nerves whipping up a storm in my gut as I step into the foyer of Adrian's dad's modest apartment. *This is not really meet the family, Emily. It's all pretend.* Somehow, the reminder does little to calm my nervousness.

Millie Callahan, who, by my mental calculations, is probably around nineteen now, walks up to me and wraps me in her arms. "Welcome, Emily. I've always wondered what happened to you after you guys broke up. And my brother has never brought any girls home other than you. I guess I have my answer why."

My heart stutters and restarts. He's never brought anyone home before me?

Don't read too much into it. I pinch my wrist discreetly, as if to remind myself not to overthink. I pull back and stare into her pale-blue eyes, the same shade as her brother's, finding nothing but warmth reflecting back at me. Perhaps he never told her why we broke up all those years ago.

Even I can't forgive myself for saying those hurtful words, although I still don't regret my actions.

Mr. Callahan, a thin man with salt-and-pepper hair, steps up and extends his hand. I grasp it in mine in a tentative shake, not knowing how he'll respond.

"Welcome, Emily. It's so good to see you again after all these years, and call me Tom."

I let out a small exhale, thankful there's no venom in his voice. Biting my lip, I hand him a paper bag. "Sorry, Adrian sprung this on me last minute, so I didn't get a chance to buy presents, but I swung by Estrelle Bakery and was able to get one of their famous banana puddings. Hope you both enjoy it."

"How did you swing that?" Millie exclaims, her tongue dipping out and licking her lips before she snatches the bag away from her dad, earning a few chuckles from him and Adrian. "I hear you need to get in line three hours before they open to snag one of these."

I wink. "Let's just say I have friends in high places."

She wags her brows at me, an impish grin on her face. She glances at Adrian, who's staring at his sister with such warmth in his gaze. "I like her. I remember liking her then and I definitely like her now. Let's keep her."

Adrian shakes his head, his eyes glinting in laughter. "You're sold based on the fact she got you dessert? We need to work on your expectations."

"It's Estrelle's banana pudding. It's not *just* a dessert—what blasphemy!" She gasps in mock horror.

"Come on, kids, let's eat so I can actually try some of this famous dessert." Tom leads us through a cozy living room, the walls filled with photos of Adrian and Millie over the years, along with older pictures of his wife, to a small dining nook by the kitchen. Part of me is surprised Adrian didn't buy his dad a bigger place with the money he has now.

Tom catches my eye as I glance around the apartment, which feels distinctly like a home—very comfortable and a place containing happy memories. "Adrian always insists I move into the city, but I like it here in suburbia in my little apartment. It's where Millie grew up and where we got our fresh start. Luxury living was never really for me." He answers the unasked question in my eyes.

Smiling sheepishly, I reply, "I love it here. Definitely feels like a place your heart can be tethered to."

"So, how are your parents doing?" Tom asks and I look at him, finding no animosity in his eyes.

"They're doing fine. Father is still working hard. We've been trying to get him to retire."

Tom nods as we take a seat at the table. "Your father is a sharp man. I'm sure the work is enjoyable for him." He glances up and smiles. "So, have your parents met Adrian yet?"

"N-Not yet. Mother has been pestering me nonstop since she's eager to meet him." I bite my lip and steal a glance at the imposing man next to me.

Adrian scoffs, the sound barely noticeable. "Of course, she wants to meet me now," he mutters.

Millie unwraps a few platters of food—spaghetti and meatballs, seafood linguini, triple-cheese lasagna, a simple garden salad, and garlic bread sticks. I let out a sigh of relief, thankful for the distraction.

"This is from Luigi's, the place around the corner next to the bodega you probably passed by. Adrian and I used to go there a lot when we first moved here, especially when he was back from Cornell. It's the ultimate comfort food," Millie explains as she hands out the utensils to each of us.

"Seafood pasta without mussels, your favorite, dear bro." She scoops the pasta to a plate and hands it to Adrian.

My gaze darts to his, only to find him staring at the plate, his jaw clenching before he spears spaghetti onto his fork in concentration. He murmurs, as if he could hear the whirring thoughts in my mind, "You aren't the only one who's allowed to like seafood pasta."

I swallow the ball of acid in my throat, the ache forming in my chest once more, before I turn back to the table and attempt a grin at Millie, who is staring at us with slightly narrowed eyes.

"So, Millie, you have been at ULA for one year. How do you like it there?"

"It's great! A nice change in scenery from the cold winters here."

"I can imagine. My sister went there. She says the professors and the classes are great. Do you like yours?"

Millie pauses, her fork suspended midair. Her eyes dart to Adrian, then back at me. A light flush creeps up her face. "T-They're fine. I love my classes there." Clearing her throat, she straightens up and furrows her brows. "Where did you go to college, Emily?"

My gaze darts to Adrian again, the tension from his body radiating to me in pulses as he focuses on the food in front of him. "Stanford."

"Why did you go there? I'm sure you were accepted to many places."

I look at Millie, finding the blues in her eyes hardening, a perceptive glint in them. Perhaps I'm not out of the woods yet and the interrogation is still in progress.

My breathing is shaky as I clutch a glass of water, latching on to the coolness for comfort. Adrian is still not looking at me. His fingers grip his fork tightly, white-knuckled, as the silence drags on. Millie arches her brow at me, not appearing to be uncomfortable with this awkward tension. Perhaps The Shark has taught his sister well.

I take a sip of water before replying, "Stanford wasn't my first choice, but life had other plans for me. But I think things turned out the way they ought to...even though the choice was a painful one to make."

"If it was so painful, why did you do it? Why go to a college your heart's not into in the first place?" Adrian says, his startling gaze snagging on mine.

"If you know going to your dream college will hurt or bankrupt the people you love, would you still go?"

"How would you know that? Stanford is an equally pricey college. How would you know your original college couldn't have given you the experiences you wanted without all the imagined problems?"

"I-I—"

"And if financial concerns are your main issue, wouldn't it be better to talk it over with your loved ones and see if there are alternative solutions? Or maybe you could transfer there later. Why would you just give up? And what financial concerns—you're a Kingsley!"

The ache grows in my chest and the impulse to blurt out why I didn't go to Cornell is strong. I bite my tongue. I can't do it in front of his family.

Adrian takes a few large gulps of water before slamming his glass down. "Or is it because your allegedly top school isn't as shiny and rich as Stanford? So, everything you're saying is really all BS because ultimately you chose your college based on other ridiculous considerations?"

He throws down his napkin and stalks off, his frame pulsing with anger.

The burning sensation returns to my eyes again and I blink rapidly, staring at the plate of food before me, my appetite long gone.

"Hey... Sorry for asking the question." Millie reaches out and pats my hand.

I glance at her and dole out a watery smile. "Right. It's all in the past, anyway. Doesn't matter, right? Ultimately, we ended up where we're supposed to be."

She tucks a curl of brown hair behind her ear and smiles, a dimple appearing on one cheek. "I don't think he ever forgot you. Give him time."

Tom clears his throat and pours more water into my half-empty cup. "Emily, I know I wasn't there for you two in the past. Watching his mom go through everything..." He coughs, his eyes misty. "But I remember enough to be worried about him following my footsteps...going after a girl with such different backgrounds. Ultimately, I know he chose to leap, and when you two broke up, I had a feeling something else broke inside him. Now, all he does is work and make money like a machine. That's not what his mom would've wanted for him."

He stares at me, his expression intense, reminding me of his son. "Whatever you two are going through, please give him time. You may not know this, but I've seen more emotions and smiles from him during our video calls these last few months than I've seen in a long time."

I bite my bottom lip before nodding. "T-Thanks for letting me know."

A few minutes later, Adrian trudges back to the dining table, droplets clinging to his forehead, as if he washed his face. His eyes are placid once again, the fire from moments ago disappearing without a trace.

"Apologies. Dad and Millie, sorry we can't join you for Christmas tomorrow. Emily's family and friends are arriving, and we have a holiday ball to attend."

I sneak a glance at him, finding his lips tipped up in a smile which doesn't reach his eyes, the only sign the conversation from a few minutes ago affected him somehow.

"It's fine, son. Every day is Christmas when you spend it with your family." Tom winks at me and we chuckle, the tension slowly dissipating.

The rest of the dinner passes by uneventfully as Millie nags her father about his diet and exercise program, and I learned Tom had a heart attack awhile back around the time of Liz and Parker's rehearsal dinner. Apparently, that was why Adrian couldn't stay to attend their wedding the next day. I see Tom rubbing his wedding band every so often and my heart pinches. Romance isn't in my cards, but I couldn't help but wonder what it feels like to have a man love you so much even death cannot come between the two of you. The meal wraps up with a surprise birthday cake Millie bought from a bakery nearby and we all sing happy birthday to Adrian, who shifts in his seat, a flush on his face, looking uncomfortable from the attention.

The car ride back into the city is silent and my mind reels with the information I've learned tonight. Somehow, despite the cool exterior, the carefully crafted nonchalance, the man beside me is still hurting and has tamped down his emotions so much, the only ones visible are the occasional flashes of anger and jaded cynicism.

Suddenly, I notice the dark ocean out the window as Adrian navigates his luxury sedan onto a bridge. "Where are we going? This isn't the way back to the hotel, I don't think?"

"I want to take you somewhere I used to go when I lived here."

Some minutes later, I find myself walking along the darkened pathways of Brighton Beach. The skies are murky, a gray haze cloaking the darkness, obscuring the stars. A few pedestrians walk around at the late hour. The colorful umbrellas and booths have been shuttered up, long closed for the day. A smell of burned popcorn and hotdogs lingers in the air. The lights in the surrounding buildings are turned off, much like the rest of the beach. A few loose sheets of newspaper blow across the ground by the wind and a few pigeons peck on leftover crumbs on the ground.

It looks like a ghost town, which was once teeming with life. I burrow myself deeper inside my thick coat, the haunting loneliness seeping in. But with him walking beside me, I still feel safe in the darkness. This, apparently, hasn't changed, despite our years apart.

"Why did you bring me here?"

"We don't have beaches like the ones in LA. I sometimes come here late at night to clear my mind."

We walk along the path as a breeze of salty brine floats to my nose—the familiar, yet distinct scent of the Atlantic. The waves crash on the sand in the distance and my heart flutters, the rhythm picking up, answering the call of nature's music, a symphony I haven't heard in many years yet still remember clearly in my mind.

Adrian's warmth permeates the chilly air as we amble quietly on the path, his hand swaying mere inches from mine. My fingers tremble as our hands graze each other in passing, my heart galloping in my chest.

He doesn't take my hand in his and I clench my fingers to stop myself from reaching over, even though my body wants nothing more than to curl against his and bury myself in his warmth and the feeling of safety.

I swallow as I press down the emotions threatening to over-flow.

The heartache. The memories. The present.

A lone seagull squawks as it flies overhead, the cries penetrating the silence.

It sounds lonely. Like me. I let out a ragged exhale.

"Tell me, Emily. Why have you stopped going to the beach?"

"H-How did you know about that?"

The scent of the breeze now carries his mint and musk, cloaking me with pieces of him, even though our bodies aren't touching.

He stares at the dark waters, his face turned away from me. Wordlessly, he reaches out, his long fingers finally snagging mine before slowly intertwining our digits together, sparks alighting from the simple contact. The ache in my chest simmers in low heat from the simple touch. "Tell me."

At this moment, I know he's asking me to tell him the truth beyond my reasons for not going to the beach.

"The beach became too painful. It no longer became the place where my heart could find freedom, where wishes and dreams seem remotely plausible."

He pauses, his hand still linked to mine, and he turns and faces me, the hazy moonlight behind him hiding most of his features in shadows except for the intense glint of his eyes.

"Why would it be painful for you?"

"Adrian, I have a question for you first. Do you believe in revenge?"

"Yes. Without a doubt."

"What if someone you care about tells you to drop your revenge. Would you do it for them?"

"No. No one gets away with hurting me or my family without repercussions. I don't care what their reasons are."

Deep down, I knew this would be his answer and as much as I want to tell him the truth, I realize I can't. At least, not yet. Unless I'm willing to risk him coming after my parents with everything he has. My mind flutters to Father, who has had health issues in the last year or so, to Mother, who, despite her tiger-mom personality, has mellowed out a bit since Jess stood up to her a few years back. Maybe one day, if and when Adrian lets go of his desires for revenge, I'll be able to tell him the truth without fearing the repercussions.

And I realize I may be a noble idiot, once giving up my happiness for the man before me, and now perhaps forsaking a chance to explain myself, because ultimately, despite my rebellious nature and my arguments with my parents, I don't want to become the reason for their downfall in the last third of their lives.

In Mother's twisted mind, I know she loves us in her own misguided way. My father, even though he's not one for overt affection, supported us in the background, providing us with his stoic love in the only way he knows how. I know TransAmerica is his legacy, something he is proud of, one of the reasons why he's still overworking himself even when his health is on the rocks. If Adrian reacts the way I think he would, he'd shred the legacy without any qualms or remorse.

There are so many moments I want my parents to suffer the pain I've experienced, but I don't wish the fury of The Shark upon them. What type of person would I be if I were okay with my happiness being built upon the pain of the people who are important to me? My decision isn't due to the desire to be an obedient daughter, but is more for the sake of my conscience. The past has already occurred. Nothing I say or do now will change it. Why not keep the collateral damage to a minimum?

"Why?" His eyes are darkening with each passing second as he narrows his gaze at me. "Why, Emily?"

I turn away from his unflinching stare. Slowly, I let go of his fingers, the simple movement taking more willpower than I have to spare, and shreds my heart as the hurt seeps in once more. Our distance widens, the cold breeze chilling me from within. "The beach reminded me of a past when I was innocent and naïve. And it was painful. Why don't we let the past stay in the past?"

Gnashing my teeth, I walk ahead, leaving the lonely man behind me.

The beats of my heart ebb and flow to the roaring sounds of the waves, eclipsing the throbbing pain in my chest.

CHAPTER 37

Adrian

The annual holiday ball at The Orchid, crowning jewel of Fleur Entertainment, is a high-society event rivaling the Met Gala. The attendance rates are usually close to one hundred percent due to the exclusivity of the invitations to only high-net-worth individuals around the world. It's one of the few high-profile events you can't buy yourself into.

The Orchid spans more than fifty floors in a modern, sleek building of silver frames and paneled glass next to the Kensington Hotel in Manhattan. There is a private entrance from the hotel to the entertainment central for the rich and famous and the establishment is cloaked in an air of mystery, as no photos are ever allowed to be published and the press and general public aren't usually permitted inside except for rare circumstances like the annual holiday ball.

One reason for its popularity is due to the unrivaled privacy its members can experience once they're inside those thick double doors. No one has to worry about the press or bad publicity and they could enjoy pretty much everything in their heart's desire, from Michelin-starred restaurants, gentlemen's clubs, nightclubs, spas, and whiskey bars to overnight rooms and even legal companionship. Fleur offers services for members needing escorts to events or just someone to talk to who is legally bound to keep conversations private, and anything "extra" is not part of the job, but that doesn't stop its members or the ladies or gentlemen from the escort/companionship services from partaking in more activities of a lustful nature. It straddles the legality of the system, but with powerful judges and politicians as part of its exclusive clientele list, The Orchid and Fleur Entertainment have reigned supreme in New York City.

Before my media outing, I never said yes to the annual holiday event. But this year, the ball is the perfect place for me to be present, to be seen, like the haute *ton* from the Regency era of England.

It's a perfect place for me to show the world The Shark is settling down.

With Emily by my side.

I stand next to the bar as I watch Emily flit off with Jess and Sarah to the powder room shortly after we arrived at the grand ballroom on the first floor. The large space is decorated like a scene from a winter fairy tale with deep reds, golds, and silvers. The ceiling is draped in luxurious red fabric, punctuated with multiple crystal chandeliers, scattering light off each other like the stars in the skies. Towering Christmas trees, decorated in glitz and glamor, are spaced throughout the room. The walls glow with golden back lights and intricate ice sculptures with dry ice decorating the tables where endless trays of hors d'oeuvres and refreshments are located.

Security is tight, with guards blending in with the general crowd, indistinguishable other than their earpieces and piercing gazes. Only a select few press photographers can be seen mingling, with brief camera flashes alerting us to their presence. They're to be seen and not heard. Any usual antics of the paparazzi will result in their immediate removal from the premises.

"Finally deigning to show your face to the world, ol' mighty one?" a low drawl murmurs behind me.

I grin before I turn around. I'd recognize that voice from anywhere. "You jackass. You on duty tonight?"

Jack shrugs, a lock of his black hair falling over his forehead. He's clad in a tux like the rest of us, seemingly at ease as he leans his elbow against the oak bar top, his charming façade never failing to catch the attention of a lady or two in the room. He lifts two fingers and signals the bartender. "Kevin, two of our best bourbons."

"I'm the entertainment manager...which is a name for Jack of all trades around here, no pun intended. So of course, I need to be on site during one of our biggest nights catering to jackasses such as yourself and making sure you guys don't kill each other." He takes a sip from one of the glasses Kevin has placed in front of us just now.

"Merry Christmas, my friend." I clink my glass with his. Jack, despite his casual and devil-may-care attitude, is one of the most loyal people I know. I can't count how many times he's bailed me out of fistfights or drunken brawls in my low days when I first moved to the city. "How's the family?"

"They're on some cruise in Australia. Lucky them." He smirks as he no doubt is thinking about his parents, whom he has sent off on holiday vacations in the last few years, something he used to joke about in high school but can finally afford because The Orchid pays him really well.

Lilting laughter carries across the room as Emily and the girls walk toward us, this time with James by their side. My mouth dries when I stare at the woman who haunts me during my waking hours, her tight, lithe body clad in a shimmery one-shoulder silver gown with a long cut out in the chest area, revealing a hint of two creamy swells, the dress molding over her firm ass and toned legs. She sashays over to us, oblivious to the appreciative stares from men in the room. The other girls are all wearing rich colors, from Jess's red gown to Sarah's blue, but my eyes are only drawn to Emily with her bright aura.

"Shit. No wonder you're fucked. I'm beginning to wonder if the acting has become all too real for you," Jack murmurs as he takes in my expression. I scoff before sipping my drink.

"The bathroom is like a hall of mirrors. I feel like I'm in some fancy European palace," James mutters as he wraps an arm around

Jess's waist. Jess snickers at the disgruntled expression on her husband's face and curls herself closer to him.

"I kind of like it," Jack quips.

"Why?" A deep gravel voice, belonging to Charles, joins us.

"Imagine how hot it would be if you know..."

Sarah rolls her eyes with barely contained disdain before arching her brow. "Is this appropriate? Aren't you supposed to be a professional and represent this establishment?"

"Come on, Siren, lighten up. Aren't you tired of being a buzzkill? Have a little bit of fun."

"Hold on, you two have kept in touch?" Emily asks, her voice filled with the same incredulity I feel.

"I've seen him around." Sarah flattens her lips in a thin line.

"Always the ice maiden."

"How can I be a Siren and an ice maiden at the same time, Jack?"

"You guys are causing a scene," Steven chimes in from behind us before standing next to me, shaking his head in amusement. "You know, we're on the top of the food chain and are capable of thinking with our brains up here and not just the ones down there." He taps on his temple for emphasis. "But apparently, neither brain is being used tonight. Nice to see you again, Jack."

"You know Jack too, Steven?" Emily asks.

Steven shrugs. "Everyone knows him if you're a member here, which I am."

"And to think I could've been in Alaska with Mother Nature instead of standing here watching you guys fling words at each other." Charles lets out a big sigh.

"It was a vote. The public wants civilization over freezing half to death," James grunts before tilting his lips up in a smirk.

"Emily Kingsley, as I live and breathe," a deep voice, grating when we were young and even more so as an adult, says from behind us.

Slowly, I turn around and find myself staring at the shiny, platinum-blond hair of the bane of my existence from my months at Warwick, Ryan Van Pelt, and another striking man with brown hair standing next to him. Time has been kind to Ryan, unlike some other rich assholes I've run into over the course of the years. The smugness from his youth has faded into a thread of maturity. He stands there gazing at Emily with warmth in his eyes and, like all those years ago, I find myself wanting to smash the expression off of his face. Clenching my jaw, I force myself to remain still as Emily greets him with an exuberant hug.

"Ryan! Of course you'd be here. How are you? I haven't seen you in...three years?"

"I'm sure your mother has probably given you updates about my life as mine has about yours." He chuckles, his white teeth gleaming in the dim light. "But things are going well. How are you doing, Emily? I've seen your name a few times in the newspapers but..." his voice is soft as he murmurs to her, completely ignoring the rest of us. The man still carries a torch for her, even after all these years. It's obvious to anyone with a pair of functioning eyes. Or at least, probably obvious to everyone except her.

Ryan's eyes finally land on me, as if realizing I've been standing next to Emily all along. A burst of pride slithers through my veins as I gently clasp Emily's hand in mine, something I'd always wanted to do in front of him all those years ago. His gaze hardens as he takes me in, and I stand still, unflinching under his perusal, my lips tilting up in a ghost of a smile.

"So it's true," he says, deflating a little. "After all these years, you still chose him."

I curl my arm around Emily's waist, tugging her flush against me, reveling in the heat of her body, the way she melts under my attentions, just like all those years ago, but this time, we don't have to hide anymore.

"It's been years, Ryan. Glad to see you're doing well for yourself," I murmur, as my fingers trail across the sensitive skin of her waist, revealed in a cutout on her dress, eliciting a small but noticeable gasp from her.

A muscle tics in his jaw as he stares at my pixie once again before turning his attention to me. He smooths his expression into a cold, professional demeanor and twists his lips in one of the social smiles I see from plenty of people who want a piece of me now that I'm rich and powerful. He extends his hand and says, "My accomplishments are nothing compared to yours. Let bygones be bygones, Adrian. I hope someday we can partner together."

The rush of satisfaction from his praises never comes. The recognition is hollow. Unfulfilling. Instead, I smirk and clasp his hand in mine, giving it a brief, but hard squeeze before letting go, relishing in the brief wince from him. I bet the jock from the past never thought one day he'd be asking to be in my good graces.

"Who's your friend, Ryan?" Emily asks, eager to diffuse the strange tension.

The silent but imposing shadow next to Ryan steps forward and introduces himself. "Ryland Anderson, nice to meet you."

At his name, I take a pause, thinking back to the conversation I had with Millie months ago when she mentioned him as her professor, when her cheeks glowed pink in the candlelight. Narrowing my eyes, my senses alert to the presence of another alpha male, and I scrutinize the man before me. I see someone who is distinguished, comfortable with the power and status of being the second-eldest child of the prominent Anderson family. His face is a study of Greek sculptures at museums, all sharpness and masculinity, yet the coldness in his slate-colored eyes rivals the chill usually in mine. His lips tilt up in a half grin as he clasps Emily's hand in his before turning to me.

"Adrian Scott. I've heard many things about you, but it's nice to put a face to a name."

I clasp my hand in his and squeeze tightly as an inkling of unease flickers through me. Something tells me our paths will cross again in the future. "Likewise. It's a pleasure."

The musicians strike up a classical melody, the beginnings of a waltz, and couples gather onto the spacious dance floor. The ballroom has a full orchestra, something I would've thought ridiculous and excessive all those years ago but am now unfazed because when one acquires so much wealth, more than they could ever spend, there is no such thing as excess anymore. The lights in the room dim as the dancing begins.

"Parker would love this," Jess murmurs.

"You aren't thinking about his dance moves, are you? We can't have that. Come on, let me wipe those memories away from your beautiful brain." James tugs her onto the dance floor as she giggles behind him.

I arch my brow at the exchange and Charles explains, "James is salty about anyone who has had brief romantic linkage with his wife, myself included. Parker went on one date with her when she was single and he's known for his dancing abilities."

"When the entire time, James didn't realize Jess was also falling for him," Emily murmurs, her eyes dimming in wistfulness. Her gaze trains on her sister, swaying to the music with James.

After we went back to the hotel last night, Emily and I quietly retreated to our separate rooms as years of memories and pain separate us far better than the mere concrete walls could. I tossed and turned, unable to shake away the haunted look in her eyes when she asked me about revenge, the brief flash of pain when I responded to her question, and the nagging disquiet in my gut when she all but begged me to let the past stay in the past. I knew it would only take the slightest effort from my end for her defenses to crumble, for her to fall back into my embrace, to let me back into her heart.

Even if I could rationally separate the past from the present, my emotions apparently couldn't make the distinction, with anger ebbing and flowing, warring with my want for her, my desire to claim her for myself once and for all, to forget about my plans to break her heart. For once in my life, I'm uncertain about my next steps, and I feel lost at sea.

My eyes stay on Emily, who is watching the couples spin around the dance floor as her body sways to the music, and I swear I can see her wings unfurl, wanting to take flight.

I swallow, making up my mind to be selfish to my desires tonight. My memory flashes back to an oath I made a long time ago in the darkness of the night.

"Someday, I'll take you dancing in public...where we won't have to hide from others...where we don't have to care about what

other people think and feel, because we can finally live for our-
selves."

Extending my hand toward her, I ask, "May I have this dance, Emily?"

Her lips part as she stares into my eyes, and I fight my desire to retreat into anger or any other emotion as I stand vulnerable at the edge of the dance floor, something I don't ever allow myself to do. Wordlessly, she slides her delicate hand in mine, the touch sending a zing of electricity through my body, jolting my senses. A breath catches in my throat.

I guide her hands into position as we join the twirling dancers. Swinging her into a series of turns and dips to the swells and lulls of the music, I fly with her. I pull her tightly against me and her body melds with mine. Our bodies move in sync, even though we've never danced these steps together before. Even though the last time and the only time we ever danced together we were two high schoolers awkwardly swaying in the moonlight with sand beneath our feet and the music of the waves as accompaniment. Her eyes alight with fire and she laughs softly, the sweet sound more beautiful than any instrument. Everything feels right with the world, the puzzle pieces finally sliding into place. I clutch her warm hand tighter, not wanting this feeling to escape.

"You may give Parker a run for his money," she murmurs. I pull her close against me once more, her breathing ghosting over my neck as I bend to listen to her words.

Her light scent of lilies invades my nose and I pull back and stare into her beautiful eyes, trailing to her parted lips, the plumpness coated in dark red, drawing me in like forbidden fruit. My lips part on an exhale and I'm held prisoner by her smile, her laughter, the impish quirk on her mouth, which slowly fades as she takes in my expression. Her breathing quickens as my arms tighten around her and I swallow, unable to contain the fire in my veins, the heated blood traveling south and also flooding my heart.

"Pixie," I whisper and watch her eyes widen. She wets her lips, a sheen gathering in her eyes. A sharp pain slices through me at the anguish reflecting back at me from those gold-tinged, mocha-brown pools. Unable to withstand a second more of this tension, of the conversation we've been carrying with our bodies around the dance floor, our torsos touching, our limbs grazing each other, I curl my hand around her neck, dip down, and claim her lips with mine.

We stand in the middle of the dance floor as couples swing and twirl around us, the fluttering colors of jeweled tones and black and white blending into a haze. I only notice the softness of her lips, the sweetness of her taste. I kiss her the only way I know how, with my entire body and soul bleeding into the touch, my tongue tangling with hers as I nip and suck, immersing myself in her essence.

My blood burns hot and my skin feels feverish as my cock stiffens. My pixie clings to me as I bend her body under mine, my lips chasing hers in a mad frenzy, my free hand traveling down her smooth back and resting at the top of her curvy ass. I squeeze the firm flesh and she lets out a throaty moan, inflaming my senses, incinerating all remaining rational thought. Clutching the lapels of my tux, she presses herself more fully against me, her curves and swells melting against my hard planes of muscles. My cock digs into her stomach, needing friction, and I groan under my breath. I want to cart her off to one of the private rooms here and ravish her until the past is overwritten by a haze of pleasure.

A brief flash blinds us, dragging us out of the emotionally charged dream, and we jolt apart, my heart galloping, my chest panting for air. My head whips around in search of the offender only to find a photographer slinking away after taking a photograph of us which will no doubt grace the gossip rags tonight. Emily curls her hand around mine, her fingers trembling, and I face her again, finding bewilderment, lust, shock, anything and everything scrimmaging in her eyes until one emotion remains, one I recognize from all those years ago, the heated fervor of her love.

She loves me.

I don't need her to tell me. I don't need the words when I can see it as clear as day in her eyes.

I have won.

But instead of coldly plotting my next move, sliding the next domino in place, the offending organ in my chest constricts then free falls, dragging my soul behind it as it careens toward the cliff, ready to take another leap into the void, hoping this time what we find at the bottom will be something different. My soul yearns to be filled with her instead of with anger and revenge, but the trauma of the past haunts me still, rendering me unable to jump into the madness once more.

My brain hangs on to solid ground with a flimsy rope, a last resistance.

What will I do with this love? Do I take the leap or do I crush it beneath my feet as I had imagined before when the anger boils over?

My pixie smiles at me, so brightly it's piercing, shredding down the rope to the thinnest string. My heart pounds against my rib cage, torn between trying to escape and clamoring to be closer to the woman in front of me.

She whispers, "You took me dancing in front of everyone, just like you said you would before. You haven't forgotten." Her eyes are shiny as she stares at me as if I hold her entire world in my hands. I let out a ragged breath, reminding myself to breathe, all the while feeling like I'm suffocating under the weight of her eyes, the desire shining in there.

One I want to reciprocate.

"How could I forget anything between the two of us?"

CHAPTER 38

Emily

Christmas changed us.

Perhaps it illuminated something I've always known deep inside me, but refused to admit. When I waltzed with him around the ballroom, my body whirling with his in the most synchronized of ways, my soul unfurled its wings and took flight, soaring high with each turn, free-falling with each dip, yet knowing he'd be there to catch me, to tug me back to his side once again. The way he kissed me in the middle of the dance floor, not caring we were in full view of everyone, the way our lips communicated what we haven't told each other, the feelings we've leashed tightly inside us for so long, I refuse to believe this is all for a performance to the public.

It's too real. Too raw. Too consuming.

The raven and his pixie. Together as we should've been all along.

After the transcendent dance and scorching kiss, Adrian retreated once more, but this time, it's not anger I sense rolling off his frame, it's an invisible weight, two magnets drawn to each other, but something inside him is turning his away, to fight nature, to fight our deepest desires. When we went back to the hotel last night, we headed upstairs, the atmosphere quiet but charged with tension.

As we stood in front of my room, I wished him a happy birthday once more, and he sealed his lips with mine, a light, fluttering kiss and I felt tethered emotions holding him back. When he pulled away, I was out of breath, feeling far too exposed from a brief kiss than with the other men I had been with in the past, who all became nameless and faceless in my memory. We stared at each other, only a few inches separated us, and I could see his chest move up and down with each breath, his throat rippling as he swallowed. I let out a shaky exhale, rendered immobile by the charged tension in the air. His sky-blue eyes were dark at the edges, his pupils blown, the muscles on his neck and shoulders bunched in tension, as if it'd take only the slightest encouragement from me for him to snap, for us to take that final leap once more, this time as adults.

But I knew he was grappling with something in his tense frame, the shadows in his eyes, and while I wanted more than anything to be with him again, I didn't want this to be an impulse, a moment of weakness for him. If we leaped into the flames together only for him to regret it the next morning, my damaged heart wouldn't survive it. And so, I backed away, each step laborious, and I shut myself in my room, secretly hoping he'd make the decision and would crawl in next to me in the middle of the night and tell me he didn't forget me all these years apart, and perhaps, his heart was always reserved for me.

Riiiiing.

A glance at the caller ID on my phone tells me it's Mother. I let out a sigh, wondering what she has to say this time around. I can only ignore her for so long before she'll come find me herself.

"Hope you had a good Christmas with Father and your friends yesterday."

"Emily, we were disappointed the three of you couldn't join us this time around, but your father and I understand you all have lives of your own now. So, don't tell us we haven't given you some space. Baby Violet was so well-behaved, very much like the Kingsley she is." My parents are watching their only grandchild, so James and Jess could have a little bit of alone time. I bite my tongue to avoid mentioning Violet is technically a Chapman, not a Kingsley, and thank God for that. Mother already hired a nanny for the week and is no doubt making some woman's life very miserable right now.

I let out an inward sigh. Leave it to Mother to guilt trip me on something I shouldn't be worried about as an adult, anyway.

"I saw the photos with you and Adrian yesterday. It looks like the relationship is getting serious. Emily, why haven't you brought him home to meet us yet? I want to show him why an alliance with our family will be strategic for him as well."

"Mother, we talked about this—"

"I know. You keep telling me this isn't my business anymore, and you might not agree or see this, but I care about you. And someone like him has many options out there. If you like him and he's with you, we need to lock him down as soon as possible. There are plenty of women out there who are waiting for an opportunity to take him away from you."

I rub my temple with my finger as the doorbell to the suite rings. "Mother, I need to go. The girls are here." Pausing for a moment, I add, "Please tell Father not to work so hard. We all worry about him."

Getting up from my favorite armchair in the suite, I roll out my stiff neck muscles and walk to the door. Peeking through the peephole, I grin. Sure enough, my favorite girls in the world are here.

"Merry belated Christmas, Ems!" Liz wraps me in a warm hug, her vanilla scent wafting through the air. "This is such a treat! Spending the holidays in the Big Apple."

"Too bad Melanie couldn't make it this time around," I murmur, muffled against her shoulder.

"Yeah, she has holiday plans with her family."

Sarah waltzes in with a tray of coffee from the shop downstairs, her long locks breezing behind her. "I'm so glad we're all staying at the same hotel. I don't want to brave the weather outside. This is one part I don't miss about the city."

"You must think we're silly, flying over here for the holidays and happily freezing our butts off while folks from around here go to warmer climates instead," Jess comments as she carries a bag of pastries from Estrelle's inside.

The girls gather in the spacious living room and we marvel at the sea of white outside the windows. It's as if we're trapped in our own snow globe. The fireplace is burning brightly and housekeeping delivered a few more fleece blankets for us to share—all the ingredients for a good girls' day.

"What are the boys doing?" I ask before sipping my piping-hot latte.

"I think they went to Charles's place to watch some sporting event. It's been nice having some adult-only time," Jess says, even though her hazel eyes turn wistful, no doubt thinking about the baby she left at home.

"Mother called just now. It seems like they're having a good time with Violet."

Jess nods. "Trust me, I was so nervous leaving her behind, but I think it's good for them, having a little bit of bright energy in their lives. I haven't seen Father smile and melt as much as he does when he holds her in his arms."

"So, they've been more agreeable these days?" Sarah asks.

I nod. "It may be hard to believe, but I think they're finally starting to mellow out with older age." Arching my brow, I grin. "And Jess here put them in their place a few years back and paved the path for the rest of us." Jess flushes as she tucks her hair behind her ear.

"Adrian isn't here today?" Liz looks around for the enigmatic man.

"He went on a business trip to Boston. I no longer think Steven is the biggest workaholic of the group. I think Adrian has him beat."

"Wow. The Shark never sleeps, I guess." She shakes her head before turning to Sarah, who's curled up on the sofa, her legs tucked underneath her. "Sarah, what are your plans after LA? The charity project you were working on for your family is wrapping up, right?"

Sarah sighs. "To be honest, I don't know. I've been doing odds and ends for my family since I graduated, but I really want to go out there and try something different. See if I can make it on my own like you girls." Like most Warwick students, Sarah hails from an affluent family and after she received her degree in marketing from NYU, she stayed out east to help oversee some advertising campaigns for her family's interests on the eastern seaboard. But I get a sense it's difficult for her to work with her family.

She sits up and shrugs. "I'll figure it out, eventually. Ems knows me the best. I just go with the flow." She winks and the sparkle returns to her tawny eyes. "What about you, Ems? How are things going with you and Adrian?"

"Things did appear awfully cozy last night," Jess quips.

"My jaw dropped when the photo of you two kissing in the middle of the dance floor showed up on the front page of *Gossip Times*!" Liz exclaims, her blue eyes wide in surprise. "Ems, you can't tell me that's all for show. I mean, you're the one who believes in 'vibes' and 'gut feelings,' but let me tell you, my radar was going off the charts when I saw the article. And from the comments on the page, it would seem like the rest of America is completely sold on the two of you. There are even bets going on as to when he'll propose."

The heaviness which faded away for the past ten minutes slowly creeps back into my chest. I swallow, not knowing how much to tell them, yet wanting to talk through the convoluted feelings Adrian elicits inside me.

Glancing down at my socks, I murmur, "To be honest, I don't know what's going on between us."

The excitement visibly cools and I feel the heavy weight of their stares as they wait for me to continue.

I play around with a loose string, my fingers jittery, and my feet bounce on the floor. "I feel pathetic. You know me, I don't do relationships because they get too complicated, but now, I'm not sure what I feel anymore. I'm not sure what's real or fake anymore."

"I've always wondered…" Jess murmurs, her voice soft, which means the next words out of her mouth will no doubt be sensitive. "You claim you don't want relationships because of our parents, but having seen the two of you these last few months, I think your beliefs stem from your experience with him back when you were in high school. Is that right? Things were a lot more serious back then than you let on, Ems?"

My nose prickles as my eyes burn. The lump in my throat hardens and grows. I tug harder on the loose string. "We were going to go to Cornell together and start our future away from LA," I whisper, the ache in my heart splintering me from the inside. The wound which never truly healed is festering. It's as if the dam finally breaks under the immense weight of the emotions I've been carrying inside me all along. "I *loved* him."

Liz freezes, her hands fluttering to her mouth, as Sarah scoots over and curls her arm around my shoulder. She gives me a soft squeeze, a sign of support. "It's okay, Ems. Let it out. You've been holding on to everything for so long."

Tears slide down my face as I relive the most painful night of my past, and I finally tell them the secrets I've kept under lock and key for all these years. My sobs echo in the room as if the pain was inflicted yesterday. Jess slips me a tissue and I pour my heart out, amazed at how much anguish was trapped inside me and how lonely I was all these years, especially after watching my best girls fall in love and move on with their lives while I felt trapped, frozen in time as the world passed by. The loneliness was suffocating, keeping me up in the middle of the night as I tossed and turned in the spacious, cold bed.

"P-Please don't tell the guys. I don't want it to get back to Adrian. Not yet anyway. Someday, I'll tell him, but not now." My hands tremble as I bring a glass of water to my lips, the cool liquid wetting my parched throat after what felt like a cathartic release of tension inside me.

At least now, someone knows what I'm going through.

I'm no longer alone.

Sarah rubs my shoulders in comforting circles. "I'm not surprised, Ems. I probably knew the most out of everyone here, but I always thought you sparkled when you were with him and that somehow dulled when we went to college."

"I can't believe *them*." Jess shoots up from her seat and paces the room. "It's all my fault. If only I had been at home more often, maybe I could've seen something and talked to our parents about this." She throws her hands in the air in frustration. "This is *so* typical of them."

Shaking my head, I say, "You couldn't have done anything. Mother back then wouldn't have listened," I scoff. "Mother doesn't even recognize him now. She's more than happy to have him as a son-in-law. But I don't really care about that. They can no longer dictate who I should or shouldn't see, and their opinion doesn't matter to me anymore."

Liz purses her lips before asking, "So, are you planning to be with him, Ems?"

"I don't know what he wants. There are moments when I think I see glimpses of the Adrian I knew in the past, the man who loves me and would give anything to be with me. But then, it usually is a whiplash, and he'll withdraw or be cold again, as if reminding me or himself that none of this is real. He's so angry still, even more so than we were back then."

I twist the tissue in my hand. "I don't know how he feels and I think I don't want to ask because my heart..." I thump my chest in a futile attempt to assuage the ache there before clenching the material of my sweater. "Can't take another heartbreak. This is where I become the hypocrite, girls, because I always tell you guys to take life by the balls, but when it comes to me, I just want to stay cocooned in my sphere of safety and not risk getting hurt again... because I don't think I ever healed from last time. Sometimes, I guess, it's easier to give other people advice than to actually follow it yourself."

"And so, you continue to play pretend," Liz murmurs, as if finally understanding where I'm coming from.

"And I play pretend...until one day, when the play draws to a close, perhaps I'll finally find the answers I'm looking for."

• • •

The next few days passed by as I caught up on some work during the few days of quiet between Christmas and New Years. Kristi has been impressed about my "performance" thus far, and a few projects I'm overseeing appear to be progressing well, based on the reports I received from my teams. After the girls' day, I felt better, more energized, even though that night was very draining for me. Perhaps the past has been weighing me down and it was good to finally share some of my burdens with the people I trust the most. Even though we didn't come to any conclusions or find any paths forward, at least I'm no longer alone. And I know, regardless of whatever happens in the future, I'm strong enough to survive it.

Adrian and I would text periodically, random messages checking in on each other. Even though the messages aren't particularly meaningful, I find my pulse racing when the chime of a text pings through. Each little message from him feels like his way of telling me I'm still on his mind. And each reply from me I hope is also sending him the very same sentiment.

Ding.

I hastily grab my phone from the bedstand.

Adrian: I'm sick of the East Coast weather. Not sure why I didn't move back to LA sooner.

My lips twist up in a grin before I respond, swiping my fingers over my phone.

Emily: You're only complaining because I'm not there to make things exciting for you. *smiley face*

Adrian: Oh yeah? How are you going to spice things up?

Emily: That's for me to know and you to find out.

My pulse kicks into high gear at the flirtatious tone in the texts.

Emily: It's New Year's Eve. Are you still planning to stop by to join us for dinner before you fly out to Chicago? Hashimoto's. It's going to be the best sushi you've ever tasted outside of Japan.

I wait for a few minutes but no response. His original plans were to wrap up what he was doing in Boston and fly back down to join the gang for dinner at renowned Chef Hashimoto's eponymous restaurant two blocks away before hopping on his jet to fly out to Chicago for another series of meetings. The restaurant has a waitlist for at least half a year out and is one of the season's hardest tables to snag, which again, thanks to my connections through work, I was able to secure a private room a few weeks ago.

Disappointed, I set my phone aside and turn on the TV, scrolling aimlessly through some reruns of holiday movies. Hours fly by as the harsh light of day, illuminating New York in a sea of white, fades into the darkness of night, the city lights sparkling against a hazy backdrop, despite the winter storm outside.

Clad in a pair of black jeans, a simple navy turtleneck, and a thick gray coat, I brave the harsh elements with my friends and finally take a seat in the private room of the trendy sushi restaurant. The rooms are separated by opaque panels of glass, and walls painted pitch black. Pendant lights are interspersed throughout the space, akin to the glow of the stars in the nighttime sky. Jazz music filters through the speakers and the place is vibrant and thrums with excitement of partygoers on the last night of the year, where once again, hopes, dreams, and wishes come to the forefront as people anticipate a fresh start in the upcoming year, letting the pain of the past remain behind them.

Steven rambles on about the source of the fish at the restaurant—he's the unofficial food critic amongst our group of friends—while the guys pepper him with questions. The girls chat amongst themselves, and I think I hear something about a polar bear expedition that was met with a rumble of protest from everyone at the table. My fingers swipe the lock screen on my phone as I check it for the thousandth time tonight.

"Still nothing?" Sarah murmurs as she pats her lips with a napkin.

I shake my head. Adrian hasn't texted me since earlier in the day. Most likely, he wouldn't be able to make it with his packed traveling schedule and the winter storms in the area. Disappointment scythes through me as I reflect how I ended up here, pining for the one man I shouldn't want, the one person capable of obliterating the remnants of my heart. Somewhere along the lines of hatred and love, of pretense and reality, I've lost myself once more. The foolish kernel of hope that has long been buried deep inside me sprouts, as if it has lain dormant all this time, and now my aching heart is begging for the life-giving water once again.

"Ems! What are your New Year's resolutions?"

I glance up, finding Liz's twinkling eyes on me.

Grinning, I lean forward on the table, dragging myself back into the conversation, because Emily Kingsley won't mope over a man, and reply, "Finally making director at the firm and maybe..." I sneak out a sly grin. "Seeing the polar bears in Alaska?"

The guys roar with mock disapproval as Charles salutes me with a cup of sake, humor glinting in his crystal-blue eyes. I laugh, the sound lightening the heaviness in my chest as I focus my attention on the dinner before me with the people I care most about in the world.

Soon, I stand amongst a small crowd of patrons gathering in the waiting area of the restaurant, waiting for the rest of the group while they slip on their coats or visit the bathroom after a wonderful dinner of the freshest fish one could find outside of Japan. The food was delicious, each plate of sushi and sashimi exquisitely plated like pieces of artwork at a museum, and everything was so expertly prepared. The soups were mouthwatering, the fish melted in your mouth, and the dessert, a matcha Japanese-style cheesecake, was perfectly light and fluffy, the flawless punctuation to a wonderful meal. It was by all means a successful dinner, but the ache in my heart remains in the background, my soul registering its missing half.

It's all pretend, Emily. Leave when everything is at a high, when everything is beautiful. His words seep back into my thoughts and I tell myself, perhaps this is for the best. The pretense of the fairytale sweeps me off my feet, the memories capable of lasting me through more decades ahead of me. And I'm okay with that.

I must be.

I let out a sigh before twisting my lips back into a bright smile, so they won't suspect I'm anything but excited for the rest of the festivities tonight. My life is more than having a man. My life is full with people I love, a career I'm excited about, and that should be enough.

But deep inside me, I crave the presence of a brooding man with wicked smiles, penetrating eyes, and a heart so worthy of love, despite it being buried deep inside the rubble of his chest.

Just then, I feel goosebumps pebble on the back of my neck and I become distinctly aware of someone's laser focus on me. Mint and musk waft through the air and I inhale a large gulp, the familiar scent feeding my starving, lovesick heart. My breathing picks up in pace as I bite my bottom lip, the anticipation lacing my blood.

He's here.

"Waiting for me?" his gravelly voice rasps in my ear as I feel his heated presence behind me. My heart cartwheels and my insides flutter. "I was buried in meetings today and my flight was delayed due to the weather."

Linking his long fingers with mine, the touch sending a frisson of awareness through me, he whirls me around and pins me with his bright gaze. His eyes are fevered, his hair slightly disheveled and layered with a light dusting of snow. He pants, slightly out of breath, as if he ran a long distance to get here. Seconds pass between us as I fall victim to his perusal and the crowds around me blur into the background, the jazz music eclipsed by blood pumping in my ears. His calm eyes latch on my lips before dragging back up to mine, a low flame in its place.

"Come. I want to show you something."

He drags me out the door and takes off running. The snowflakes pelt our faces, a flurry of white cascading from the skies like confetti at a party. The air is brisk and my fingers are turning into ice as we dash down the streets, but I don't care. My body is warm and filled with something I don't dare name.

My soul is soaring and I let out a laugh, the sound earning a teasing grin as he turns his head to look at me while he whisks me down the streets of Manhattan, weaving in and out of crowds of people braving the elements to celebrate the dawn of a new year. I'm sure we look like lunatics sprinting on the sidewalk like it's the best thing to ever happen to us. His hand firmly links to mine, his touch reassuring, as he navigates the sea of white and gray toward a mysterious destination I couldn't care less about. My eyes are pinned firmly on his figure, barely noticing the buildings and land-marks we're running past.

I would follow him anywhere, anytime.

After what could've been five minutes or so, for time ceases to matter when I'm in his presence, he pulls me through the doors of a building and nods to a few security guards there before push-ing me into an open elevator. Our panting sounds fill the air as we retreat to separate corners in the small space. Adrian's hair is sod-den, with clumps of snow clinging to the strands. His nose is red from the chilly weather outside. His clothes, a simple black sweater with dress pants and a thick coat, are soaked, the wetness from the elements seeping through the layers. I'm sure I'm faring no better. But it's his eyes that take my breath away.

The pale-blue pools are ablaze with the hottest fire, the flecks in his irises iridescent, his pupils slowly encroaching the flames as he stares at me, his mouth parted as if he's still reeling from the sprint moments ago. I grip the handrail tightly, frozen under his perusal, and I swallow, my nerves fluttering alive, the soaked sweater suddenly chafing my skin and my body heats up.

The tension in the elevator ratches up with each passing sec-ond, each brief *ding* indicating the passage of the floors as it trans-ports us to a mysterious destination. The air feels thick, and he prowls toward me, standing mere steps before me, his own hands curled around the handlebars, his muscles coiling in restraint as if he's one second away from pouncing on me. My breasts feel heavy, the nipples pebbling both under the wetness of the clothes and also the heat of his stare, and I shift on my feet, my thighs squeezing together in a poor effort to relieve the ache building there. His eyes snare on the motion as his nostrils flare.

Ding.

The elevator doors slide open, the soft sound slicing through the atmosphere with the sharpness of a knife, and he strides over and links his hand with mine once more before tugging me alongside him.

"The weather derailed my plans so I don't have much time…" he begins as he glances at his watch and mutters, "two minutes to go."

My feet move automatically as I stare at his handsome face, each sharp plane and curve so heartbreakingly beautiful, so uniquely him. I don't pay attention to my surroundings as I drink in the gaze of him, Adrian Callahan, not Adrian Scott, I'm positive, because I'm not sure when I'll see this side of him again, before he inevitably retreats into his cold, hard shell.

He pushes open another set of double doors and we're met with a gust of blistering wind. I shiver as I glance at my surroundings, finally noticing where we are. My heart free falls and a gasp escapes my lips.

The colorful, bright lights. The distinctive spire and curved railings.

We're standing on the outdoor observation deck of the Empire State Building. The place is completely devoid of people save for a security guard standing by the doors, who dips his head at me when my gaze lands on him.

"H-How?" I whisper, turning my face back to the maddening man before me.

Adrian steps closer, his hands trembling as he cradles my face in his. His thumbs trail my chilled skin in tenderness and his motions elicit a heat shooting straight into my heart. He tilts my face up and leans down, mere inches separating us, in the privacy in this space, with no paparazzi, no agenda, just the two of us.

"I rented it a week ago…because my heart can't stand my pixie losing her dreams and wishes and the selfish man inside me wants to be the one to give them to you…to put this expression on your face once again," he murmurs, his voice hoarse and tinged with emotions before he snakes one arm around my waist and tugs me flush against him.

My heart clamors against my rib cage, threatening to give out as he gently lays his forehead against mine, his breaths caressing my lips. My eyes flutter shut as my soul swells and leaps, breaking into a desperate run once more toward the cliff, no longer caring about what I may find in the darkness below.

Pop. Crackle. Pop.

The thundering sounds and bright flashes of fireworks blaze in the background, bathing us in a sea of technicolor, cutting through the swirl of white around us. Cheers and music erupt on the streets far below. Molten heat liquifies my veins and he whispers, "Happy New Year, Pixie."

Adrian closes the remaining space between us and seals his lips with mine. His mouth plunders in a savage possession, the fire igniting between us, far more violent and passionate than the bursts of lights in the skies. His teeth nip my lips in a frenzy as his hands slide down my back and cup my ass. My body comes alive and melts against him, the clothing between us our enemies, blocking us from coming together body and soul. I claw his back, my fingers finding purchase on his coat, and he groans as if he understands my blatant need for him. His tongue sneaks out and swipes the seam of my lips, then his teeth gnaw on the plump flesh, earning a hiss of pleasure-filled pain from me as he slides in, our mouths dueling with each other, all the while the world celebrates the dawn of a new beginning around us.

I free fall, my soul leaping without an ounce of fear, without a speck of worry, my arms open as I spiral from the skies with nothing but the wings of hope and the gusts of love to keep me afloat.

Tears prickle my eyes at the rightness of it all, the moment obliterating all common sense, annihilating all thoughts of the past or the future, of reality or pretense, of revenge or forgiveness. The aching hole in my heart and the missing half of my soul have finally found their missing pieces in him as his kisses turn feverish and possessive, as if he, too, couldn't get close enough to me.

A distant whirring of machinery creeps closer at each second and we break apart for air. This time, our panting has nothing to do with the sprinting from earlier. His eyes are impassioned, blazing with unspoken emotions, and a vein pulses on his forehead. His hands find my face again, tenderly caressing my eyelids, my nose, testing the texture of my swollen lips, as if memorizing me by touch.

My vision blurs and I stare at my Romeo, feeling still very much like his Juliet, despite all the years and heartache between us. The whirring sound grows louder and I spot a helicopter flying close to us, landing on top of the helipad at the building next door, the blades slowly grinding to a halt.

Adrian's cell phone blares to life, but he pays no attention. His thumb swipes the moisture gathering below my lashes and he whispers, his voice hoarse, "I don't need wishes, hopes, or dreams for me...but I wish the world for you. Because you're worth all the glittering stars in the sky, all the beautiful shells on the beach, and all the love of everything good in the world."

He swallows, his Adam's apple bobbing in his corded throat, his eyes still ablaze as he murmurs, "I'm damaged and flawed, a streak of black paint across your beautiful canvas, but this...this dream...this I can give you."

"Adrian," I whisper, my lips trembling at what he's not saying, because his actions far outweigh his words.

"That's my ride to the airport." He gestures to the helicopter on top of the next building. "But I couldn't start my new year without you by my side."

The gale sends a fresh flurry of snow around us, cloaking us in our own private snow globe. He slowly lifts my hand in his, bringing it up for a searing kiss. "A car is waiting for you downstairs to take you to wherever you wish to go." He slowly backs away, his heart in his eyes. "Happy New Year, Emily."

I stand in place, my feet rooted to the floor, my heart still plummeting from the free fall, not having reached the bottom to find what waits for me there. My eyes are pinned to his retreating figure as he dashes off to catch his flight for the next leg of his trip. My pulse reverberates in my ears, the bright flashes of fireworks littering the sky in a kaleidoscope of colors, and I realize one thing.

He has given me back my dreams. One by one.

Despite everything that has transpired between us, Romeo has still been thinking about his Juliet all of these years.

And he has not forgotten.

Nor have I.

. . .

Adrian

Leaving her standing on the deck, an angel cloaked in a dusting of snow, is one of the hardest things I've ever had to do. Ever since Christmas, every beat of my heart and every thought in my mind is filled with her. That evening when we went back to the hotel after the ball, I thought by putting distance between us once again, things would settle down, but the joke is on me.

I can no longer fight what I feel for her more than I can fight destiny.

Whirling on the dance floor at The Orchid with my pixie in my arms was perhaps one of the few times in recent years where I felt at home. At peace. These memories plagued me during my entire trip in Boston, where my company was negotiating an important deal with a few banks there. Other than the brief respite offered during active discussions, my thoughts trailed back to Emily, her beautiful smile, how soft she was in my embrace, her melodious voice, how she's still so spirited and kindhearted, as if the years between us haven't jaded her.

My heart pounds wildly in my chest as I exit the building and cross the street to another high-rise to take the elevator to the roof where my helicopter waits to whisk me off to the private airfield nearby for the next leg of my business trip. I thought I wanted to hurt her, to take revenge on how she devastated me in the past, but if the last few days of aching want have taught me anything, the need to have her by my side seems to trump all other impulses. Perhaps my hatred for her all these years was a way for me to keep her in my heart.

Perhaps, I've never truly let her go.

And perhaps, it's time to realize that I may never be able to let her go, because my heart reawakens by her side, because my life becomes colorful once again with her next to me.

My thoughts blur together as I let out a deep exhale, my soul already feeling empty the more steps I put in between us. When my business trip concludes, I will show her how I feel, and if anyone in the world has anything negative to say, well...

Screw them.

My fingers ache to play the piano again. After over a decade of slumber, it's as if the musical soul inside me awakens, unlocked by the dreams Adrian fulfilled during the holidays. I want to pour myself into the music, express my emotions with the notes and chords. The musician finds her muse once more. I sit in my quiet apartment, watching the raindrops pelt against the windows, the skies outside cloaked in thick clouds of gray. It appears the winter storms have followed us from New York when we came back two days ago.

My thoughts trail to him, the man who has never truly left my heart, and I wonder what he is doing right now, how he is faring in Chicago. Does he think about our kiss and the words we've exchanged, ladened with meaning, like I have?

After the earth-shattering intensity of our midnight kiss, Adrian disappears once more, but this time, I know he'll be back. I saw it in his gaze when he walked toward the elevator doors; I felt it in his touch, his arms curled tightly around my waist, the possessiveness in his lips, the inferno in his eyes. If he felt even a fraction of what coursed through me that night, he'd need to reflect on what this means for us, just as I have been doing for the last two days.

The roar of thunder shakes the windows, followed by a blinding flash of lightning. The rain pelts against the glass as the downpour worsens, obscuring the views from my tenth-floor apartment into a blur of darkness with brief splashes of lights. A nagging fear attempts to take root in the eerie silence of the apartment—this couldn't all be an act, right?

Shaking my head at my ridiculousness, I stride to the kitchen and take out my favorite pink mug from the cupboard and put a tea bag inside. I pride myself in going with my gut feelings and everything tells me the scorching kisses from him were too intense, too real for pretense. Underneath the thousand-dollar suits and the chill in his beautiful eyes, the boy I fell in love is still very much in there. As I place my cup under the hot water dispenser, I hear a faint noise.

Buzz. Pop. Buzz.

Another loud rumble, followed by a glaring flash of light, fills the space before the apartment is plunged into utter darkness. My heart pounds against my chest as a bone-chilling fear penetrates my insides. My cup falls from my slippery hands. The crash of the ceramic breaking into pieces echoes in the kitchen, which is unnervingly quiet without the humming of the appliances and the crackle of electricity.

My hands tremble. A blackout. *The lights will turn back on, they always do. Everything is okay.* I repeat the words to myself. After all, one of the reasons I moved into this apartment is because of the backup generator they have for such events. I attempt a slow inhale, followed by a ragged exhale. Sweat beads on the back of my neck and I draw in ragged breaths, the irrational fear of the dark slicing through me. After what could be minutes, the lights still don't turn back on and I can feel myself hyperventilating.

Flashlight. I need a flashlight. My fingers shake as I feel my way around the drawers, searching for anything that'll give me an iota of light in this darkness, anything to curb the rising panic inside me.

Thump.

A sharp pain pierces my feet as I unwittingly stub my toes on the cabinetry. Tears spring into my eyes and I struggle to breathe, unable to calm my rioting pulse. The haunted howl of the wind filters in from the windows and I slowly drop to the floor and curl into a ball, desperate for this current of fear to disappear, to release my throat, to let air back into my lungs. My hands are clammy and I try once more to slow my breathing.

Inhale...one...two...three...

Exhale...one...two...three...four...

I can't breathe.

Nausea churns in my stomach, the chilling terror keeping me captive in the dark, once again rendering me into the five-year-old girl who was trapped in the closet when the power cut out, terrified for her life.

I can do this. God damn it, I'm an adult now. It's just a power outage.

Horror curls its hands around my throat and I can feel myself getting lost in the darkness once more, unable to move, unable to breathe, unable to escape.

Thump. Thump. Thump.

My body flinches at the sudden sound coming from the front door.

Another flash of lighting fills the room and I plug my ears with my fingers as black spots dot my vision.

Thump. Thump. Thump.

"Emily! It's me, Adrian. Are you in there? Open up."

Adrian. My lifeline.

I crawl on my hands and knees toward the door, my body trembling as panic is the only thing I feel, taste, and smell. After what feels like an eternity, I find the door and struggle to rise to a standing position, my legs threatening to give out on me. Grasping the doorknob, I shakily wrench open the door.

Adrian stands there, panting heavily, as if he ran a marathon, his arms resting against the doorframe. A dim emergency light in the hallway flashes, illuminating his mussed hair, a thin sheen of sweat dotting his forehead and upper lip, his fevered eyes roving over my face.

"A-Adri-an... P-Power outage. I'm so st-tupid...I shouldn't be sc-cared." My mouth can barely form the words as he hurls me into his arms, his hand sweeping down my trembling back.

My eyes flutter closed, and my muscles finally relax. Safety. I'm safe. I take in ragged inhales of mint and musk, my airways finally allowing me to breathe, to suck in the much-needed oxygen for my body.

"I know. As soon as the power was cut off, I knew you'd be scared. I came down as fast as I could."

"C-Came down?"

"Forty flights of steps in the dark." His words rumble in his chest as he tightens his arms around me, the safety only he could provide blanketing me in a warm cocoon. I don't care how he knew I was in here. All that matters is he's with me. "I'm here. You're safe."

"Y-You're here..."

"Always."

I lift my face from his damp sweater and trail my hands up his chest, feeling each flex of his muscles, each swallow in his throat before grazing over the rough stubble of his tense jawline, the tall, aristocratic nose, and the high cheekbones, as if verifying he's real. He turns his face into my palm, pressing a soft kiss in the center.

"Always," I echo, my heart racing for another reason, one I knew from the deepest recesses within me, the reason the organ beats all these years.

He rasps, his voice hoarse and thick, "Always, Pixie."

He stares at me, his eyes ablaze with intensity, his chest still lifting and falling in harsh pants. A muscle twitches in his cheek and his nostrils flare.

"Fuck this," he mutters.

Cupping my head in his hand, he bends down and delivers life through his kiss. His lips suck and swipe, and he pushes me inside the apartment, backing me into the wall next to the door. Our lips part for air and crash together in a ravaging dance, every nip of his teeth sending a rush of pleasure through my body, chasing away the fear and panic from earlier. Heat spreads from my chest as I curl my hands around his neck and he hoists me up as if I weigh nothing, his palms gripping my ass and he groans with pleasure.

His large frame fully envelopes my petite one and I realize if he wanted to, he could easily snap me in two, and somehow, the thought sends molten lava down to my core. His mouth swallows mine and I fist his hair, earning a hiss of pleasure from him.

"Fuck me," he grunts, curling a fist around my locks, tugging it as we grapple with each other, our motions frenzied and hurried. "It has always been you. Always." He trails kisses up my neck, his tongue licking every divot, every pulse point. Wetness seeps between my thighs, drenching me as his lips move over mine in desperation, like he needs air to breathe. I moan, my nipples beading into hard points, my body overheating, over sensitized, my nerves on fire.

"I thought I could..." He nips the sensitive area where my neck meets my ear, and I whimper from his onslaught.

"I thought I'd forget..." He swallows my lips once more, his hand angling my face so he can deepen the kiss, as if we can't get close enough.

My pussy clenches with each suction and I pant harshly against him, inhaling him as he devours me whole. He grinds against me, his hard erection hitting my clit at the perfect angle. Sharp pleasure floods my veins. I need more.

"Adrian," I moan, undulating against him, my movements driving him wild as shards of heat build up between my legs. Desperate, I grab his hand and wrap it around my aching breast and let out a mewl.

He grunts, his hand enveloping my soft mound of flesh, his thumb flicking over the cotton-clad nipple. It hardens even more.

"Tell me," he rasps as he gyrates harder against me. "Did you ever think of me all these years?" His hand slides underneath my shirt and my skin sizzles from the contact. He massages my tits as he leans down and captures one tip in his mouth, giving it a hard tug followed by deep suction.

"Oh shit," I whine, arching my back, my breasts heavy and swollen.

"Tell me." He nips the tip before laving it with his tongue and my pussy sparks and throbs. My walls clench with the need for him to fill me.

"Y-Yes."

"Even when you were with others." His words were a growl as he moves on to the other side, rendering me immobile with his weight.

Liquid lava builds in my core and I can feel the wetness dripping down my thighs. I let out a shuttering exhale. "Yes... It has always been you in my mind."

My answer inflames him more, and he throws me over his shoulder like a caveman. He strides into the living room, with nothing but the streaks of lightning aiding his vision. He tosses me on the sofa as we're cloaked in darkness once more.

I hear his labored breaths, the rustling of clothes, and the sound of a zipper. My mind is in a pleasurable haze as my nerves are aflame. Then I feel him on top of me, all hard muscles and hot heat. My hands drag over the well-formed pecs and abs, his muscles thicker and more defined than when he was in high school. He hisses as I claw at his back, desperate for him to be closer, so that one can't tell when he ends and I begin. He drags my shirt off me with the desperation of a starving man in front of a buffet. We tumble in the dark, our movements wild and unrestrained, his hands ripping off the rest of my clothes.

"It's always been you, Pixie. I could never forget you. I could never quit you." He takes my mouth in a possessive kiss again as his hand trails to the scrap of damp material between my legs. With a rough tug, he tears the lace off and slides his fingers into my wet folds. The brief burn followed by the onslaught of his fingers is almost enough to send me over the edge. I moan, arching my hips up, eager to ride his fingers as pressure builds at a rapid speed.

"Drenched. Fucking drenched for me. Tell me, Pixie. Is this all for me? Are you going out of your mind the way you've been driving me to the edge of sanity?"

"Fuck me," I pant as I ride him from below. He slides two more fingers inside me and curls them at the right angle. I let out a keening cry. "Fu-uck, me, please. Adrian. Please, I need you." I thrash my head against the sofa, my pussy clenching around him, the wet sounds of his fingers thrusting in and out of me echoing in the space. My words are no longer coherent and I mumble my pleas. My body and soul crave him and the pleasure only he can give me.

He slides down my body, pinching my tender nipples, and I shriek. Parting my legs, he dives in and feasts on me, his mouth sucking on the lips before his tongue swipes from the puckered rosebud straight up to my clit. I buck against him, my lustful cries filling the room. He grunts with pleasure as he works my clit into a frenzy, his tongue flicking expert circles around the hard nub.

"Shit. You're flooding me with your cum." He slurps and laps like I'm the best thing he's ever tasted.

The pleasure builds inside me, rising to a boiling point, and I grip his hair, urging him to send me off the edge, my thighs clamping his face, my muscles locking in tension.

"I-I'm going to come. Oh my God, I'm going to come so h-hard."

Adrian stills as I dig into his skin, desperate for him to continue.

"No, Pixie. You're going to come when my cock is deep inside you."

He crawls up my body, his movements hurried, trailing kisses over my skin as if he's worshiping me. We're a mess of limbs tangling with each other, grasping, clawing, trying to get closer, to meld ourselves to each other. My pussy is on fire. He thrusts his hard cock against my stomach and I can feel a wet trail of pre-cum as he grunts in my ear. My hand slides down between our bodies and I grasp his thick girth and squeeze before sliding my hand up and down his length. He lets out a hiss, thrusting against my grasp, and I thumb the wet slit on the tip, wishing the lights were on so I could see his fevered eyes.

"Don't move an inch. Keep your arms here." Adrian's voice is rusty, and he grips my arms and flings them over my head, locking them into position.

He spreads my legs wide, and a brief chill lands on my wet pussy. Sizzling anticipation floods me and I can barely breathe. Moments later, I feel the thickness of his tip nudging at the entrance. Moaning, I tilt my hips up, my walls clenching, needing him inside me. The thick head slips in and he groans with pleasure.

"Please, more." I pull him to me as he slides in another hard inch.

He growls and wrenches my hands away and positions them over my head once more. "Don't move or else I'll stop." He teases his tip at the entrance and my body jolts with each thrust.

"Give it to me, Adrian," I cry as he slides the tip out again, my mind going mad from the pleasure.

"Fuck. Condom."

"I'm clean. Fuck me bare." I've never had anyone bare inside me before, but somehow, it feels right with him.

"Me too," he grunts as he slams in, his roar of satisfaction sending me into a tailspin. His long, thick cock is spearing me in half; the pain bleeds into pleasure as he moves against me. His thrusts are hurried, sporadic, as if he can't control his body.

"You're so fucking wet and tight, but fuck, I can't slow down." He hammers inside me in earnest, the slaps of skin against skin reverberating in the room, eclipsing the sound of thunder and the flash of lightning raging around us.

"Look how well you're taking me, your pussy clamping down on me like it's desperate. Fuck." *Slap. Slap. Slap.* "You're strangling my cock."

The fire builds inside me, the pressure intense, and I arch my back under his hard body, my hands struggling to stay in position over my head. With every thrust he bottoms out, his cock hitting my clit at just the precise angle. He slides out all the way to the tip before slamming back inside, invading my body, conquering my mind. The sofa bumps against the wall in a staccato as he pistons inside me in this swirl of madness.

He hoists my legs higher over his shoulders as he enters me at a deeper angle.

"I feel you everywhere," I moan as I give up my struggle to contain my hands. I grab my tits, twisting and plucking at the nipples, the sensations tenfold in the dark.

"Shit. You're clutching my dick like you want to milk it for cum. Is that what you want? My cum flooding your pussy, so your body knows it's mine?"

He rams inside me, each slide sending bolts of electricity to my nerves, his breathing stuttering as the sofa slams harder against the wall in an erotic rhythm.

"I'm going to fuck you until you see stars."

Adrian's hips pick up speed as his cock hits me in the sensitive region deep inside me. My pussy gushes as my muscles clench.

"Until you can barely walk tomorrow without feeling me between your legs."

He drives his dick deep, his hips gyrating in a maddening rhythm, every ridge of his length scraping against my insides like flint stones sparking fire.

"Until you scream with pleasure so you forget all the men before me."

I part my mouth in a silent scream as heat coils between my legs where we are joined and my legs start trembling. My core throbs and sharp bursts of pleasure coalesce into a breaking point. Wetness leaks out of me as he hammers inside me even faster.

"Your pussy is a slut for me. I'm going to fuck you so hard until your body only remembers mine," he rasps and slips one hand between us, his fingers plucking at my clit. I open my mouth in a silent plea, my muscles tensing, my back arching up.

"Come, Pixie. Come for me."

"Adrian!" My legs shake uncontrollably and I detonate as waves of pleasure flood my body, my vision going dark even as the light flickers on briefly before plunging the room into darkness once again. My body thrashes against the sofa as he grips my hips and pistons inside me with the desperation of a dying man who needs oxygen to live.

The pressure builds up once more, my orgasm barely ending before I ride up the crest again and I push against him, a futile attempt to escape the obliterating sensations. He grips my ass tighter, his cock, now thicker and longer than ever, jackhammers inside me, using me like a rag doll, his body completely dominating mine. The speed and friction are too overwhelming and I clutch the edge of the sofa in a death grip.

"I-I can't, it's too much," I scream.

"Yes, you can, Pixie. One more. You can give me one more."

Thrust, thrust, thrust, thrust.

"Yes, baby, your walls are clenching against me once again. Strangle my dick. Let me bathe you with my cum. Pixie, come hard against me, flood me with your juices."

My eyes roll back and I scream, the second orgasm more intense than the first, and it short-circuits my nerves. My mind blanks as I throb and spasm against him, stars filling my vision. My cries of pleasure echo the dark space as his harsh grunts join mine.

With a few more punishing thrusts, he lets out a deep, guttural moan and leaps into the flames with me. I feel each throb of his cock inside me and his cum floods me in spurts, the hot liquid prolonging my orgasm as I twitch helplessly against him.

Adrian collapses on top of me, his weight heavy but not suffocating, and he gyrates his body against mine, his hips riding out the last tremors, drawing out one last moan from me as I lie beneath him, boneless. He captures my lips, the kiss deep and passionate, as if he's desperate to keep any part of me inside any part of him.

He doesn't need to try so hard, for he's already an indelible part of me.

The missing half of my soul.

• • •

Adrian

We lay there in the darkness, the sounds of our breathing joining the wailing winds and whipping rain against the windows. Nature's concerto. A rare peace settles over me, deep-seated calmness in the marrow of my bones. It's almost as if the simmering anger which has kept me company for the last decade retreats, leaving me to wonder if the revenge that drives me to get out of bed each morning is worth it. Emily is curled up on my chest, her small curves fitting against me just right. I swallow the lump in my throat as thoughts flitter through my mind. Thoughts that have solidified since the holidays, since the few days I spent in Chicago missing her so much I almost cut my trip short to fly back sooner. In the past eleven years, I've never put anything above work and my need for revenge.

Until now.

Whatever the future holds, I know one thing for sure—my future will include this intoxicating woman, my pixie, by my side. Whatever plans of revenge I had against her have long slipped away as my desire to keep her tethered next to me far outweighs my anger toward her callousness all those years ago. Perhaps she did have a reason. Perhaps we were too young back then. Perhaps everything is different now because I'm rich and the entire world would accept us together. My heart clenches at the possibility of my status still mattering so much to her, but I brush it aside.

It doesn't matter anymore.

My game of dominoes no longer includes her as a future victim. It just can't. Instead, she'll stand by my side, a part of my team. My soul reverberates with the rightness of it all. That night on top of the Empire State Building, when I saw her face light up with joy, her eyes tearing up when she realized I remembered the dream she shared with me at the beach all those years ago, the ropes binding my heart were suddenly spliced open. I remember walking away from her as she gazed upon me as if I gifted her the moon and the stars and feeling tormented, the last vestiges of reservation finally snapping.

Looking back, it was at that moment, I just knew.

I couldn't imagine spending another decade without her.

Even with all the past pain and present doubts, my life is better with her in it.

I curl my hand around her smooth shoulder as the storm rages outside, a tempest in the middle of winter. She burrows closer to me, her scent of lilies permeating the air. One shapely leg splays across my torso and I feel my cock stiffening once more. The sex before she barreled back into my life was meaningless, a tool to release my anger or tension. But with her, it is transcendent, the marriage of souls. My heartbeats flutter in response and I press a kiss on her hair.

They say all roads lead to Rome. For me, all roads lead to her.

"Adrian?" she murmurs, her fingers drawing circles on my chest.

"Hmm, Pixie?"

"I'm sorry for hurting you all those years ago."

"It doesn't matter anymore. You were right. The past is in the past and all I care about is you are in my future."

She sniffles, apparently overcome by emotion, and I shush her, gathering her into my arms.

"We're never going to be apart again."

"Never," she whispers, her voice resolute.

"You and I...we're destined to be together, like the glittering stars illuminating in the nighttime sky, the planets orbiting around the sun, and I'm done fighting it."

Nothing matters anymore other than having her with me.

Emily slowly crawls on top of me and places a soft kiss on my lips, sealing our promises to each other, vows that were a decade in the making.

Minutes later, her body trembles and I tighten my grip. "What's the matter?"

She shakes as odd sounds emit from her mouth. "You know..." She giggles. "You completely trashed the provisions of the contract."

Growling, I flip her under me. "Screw the contract. Consider it null and void. No more pretense. No more secrets."

The lights turn on, suddenly bathing the room in a bright light. The hum of the electricity flowing through the wiring, the buzz of the appliances turning back on interrupt our thoughts. I stare at the vixen underneath me and take in her appearance—her soft hair in a mess over the cushions, her lips swollen and red, most likely from our savage kissing earlier, red marks on her neck and chest, handprints on her thighs. Her lips part and a surge of possession plows through me as I catalog every single mark I left on her body.

My gaze finds hers again, her eyes twinkling with mischief. She murmurs, "Proud of yourself, Adrian?"

Groaning, I claim her lips again, swallowing the gasp and tasting her sweetness, something I'll never be sick of. A thought occurs to me and I murmur in her ear, "Come on. As much as I don't want to do this, get dressed. I have something to show you."

Minutes later, I usher her into my penthouse, the stark space no longer feeling empty and lonely with her beside me.

"So, this is where Adrian Scott lives," she says as she takes in my spacious living quarters. She trails her fingers over my sofa before she pauses, as if a thought suddenly occurs to her.

Turning around, she asks, "Adrian...why did you change your last name? Tell me the truth this time, not the vague answer you told me before...please."

My pulse ratches up and I stare at her curious eyes. Moments ago, I told her there'll be no more lies between us. And while I meant every word of the sentiment, I realize there are some things I won't be able to completely share with her just yet, but this, this I can give her.

"Cornwall is my grandfather."

Her eyes widen as her brain puts the puzzle pieces together. "And you're trying to buy his company..."

"Yes. To rip it into shreds for what he did to Mom, to all of us."

Her hand flutters to her chest as she realizes the depths of my rage.

"He would never entertain the idea of selling to a Callahan..." I continue.

"And so, you changed your last name," she finishes the sentence for me.

I nod, clutching my hands in fists as she stands there, frozen, as if seeing me for the first time. "Are you scared of me? Someone who'll plot and go to such depths to get revenge?"

Time slows as I wait for her response.

She swallows before shaking her head. "No," she murmurs, walking toward me. "You're just someone whose life has been very unfair. I understand."

Her empathy floors me. Her giving heart consumes me. I grit my teeth and my nostrils flare as she steps up to me and curls her arms around my back, resting her face on my chest.

"I understand," she repeats.

Swallowing the ball in my throat, I tug her hand to mine and intertwine our fingers.

"Come. I want to show you something."

I lead her to the bookshelves in the living room. She glances at me in confusion before scanning the shelves, her gaze finally snagging on the jar of seashells.

"The shells..." she gasps.

"I used to tell myself I collect the shells to amass ambitions, a shell for each goal I want to achieve, to remind myself never to open my heart and be vulnerable again. But I realize, all this time, I collect the shells to be close to you. It was a way of tethering my life with yours, even though you were miles away."

Turning her toward me, I cradle her face and stare into her glittering eyes. "If each shell represents a hope or a wish for you, I want you to have them all. I want to make your dreams come true." My voice is thick as I realize the truth in my words.

A tear slides over her cheek and I carefully brush it away. "Don't cry, Pixie. Your tears are daggers to my heart."

She doles out a watery smile and nods.

"Come with me. I have something to tell you."

I lead her into the music room and turn on the light. Letting go of her hand, I walk toward the piano and pull out the bench before sliding into position. Flipping open the fallboard, I take a deep breath before placing my hands on the keys, and I play. Instead of playing the piece to sooth the ragged edges of my heart, to ease the ache of loneliness within, this time, I play to send my love to her.

The notes of the "Moonlight Sonata" fill the air, and I tell her my sentiments without words. The haunting melody cascades around the room like ribbons twirling in the wind and, for the first time in over ten years, I realize the true meaning of the song, the person I was meant to play for. Glancing over my shoulder as my hands move automatically over the keys, the motions long memorized, I find her staring at me, speechless and in wonder as tears cloud her eyes.

The music is our language, our souls' communion.

"What are you waiting for, Pixie? Come. Let's play our song."

Wordlessly, she traipses over to me, sliding onto the bench. She smiles and my heart soars.

We play together.

As we were meant to all along.

CHAPTER 40

Emily

Wincing, I take a seat in my chair at my office. The ache between my thighs reminds me of the weekend of love and sex I've had with Adrian, where we spent hours worshipping each other's bodies, as if making up for lost time. My thoughts trail back to this morning, his molten eyes on mine as I rode him at the crack of dawn.

"Fuck, Pixie. Ride me hard."

I gyrate my hips on top of his cock before I slide down, my ass grinding against him as his balls slap against me and I fall into a rhythm. Throwing my head back, I close my eyes as shards of pleasure pierce through me and I feel my body is on fire.

"You like this? Do you like it when my pussy is sucking in your cock?" My voice is throaty, laced with lust.

He hardens even more inside me and I moan with pleasure as every ridge of his beautiful cock rubs me exactly the right way. His hand grips my tits, and he slaps the aching mounds, the sound reverberating in the room. I let out a scream, molten heat flooding me afterward.

"Your dirty mouth, shit. My pixie is all grown up." He buries his face in my chest and sucks a hardened tip in and I undulate

faster on him. He slides his fingers where we are joined, and he twists my clit in maddening circles as I almost career off him.

"Come on, take that dick deep inside you. Yell, scream. I don't care. Let the world know who you're a slut for."

"Yes. Yes. Yes," I chant before the sharp pleasure pierces through me and I throw my head back, letting out a keening cry.

Riiiiiing.

The blaring of the phone brings me back to the present and heat crawls up my face, my breathing coming in quick pants, which I suspect has little to do with the jarring sound in the room.

"This is Emily," I answer, my voice slightly raspy.

"Emily. It's Kristi. Can you come to my office in around fifteen minutes? I have a call right now, but would like to chat with you about the Scott project."

"Sure thing."

I disconnect the call and sit back in the chair, my mind in a delirious haze, my soul alive with happiness coursing through my veins. I feel like I can fly. The love pours out of me as I think about him, the man who has learned my music, my instrument, in our years apart. While my soul lost the will to play, his soul took on the gift and carried the burden. And now, we're together again, two halves mending into a beautiful whole, the music more magnificent, more enthralling, more mesmerizing.

Ding.

Sarah: You've been MIA this weekend. Everything okay?

Biting my lip, I reply.

Emily: Everything has been great. Excellent. *Winking face*

Sarah: Hold on. Does this mean you and Adrian are *together*, together?

Emily: *Smiley face*

Sarah: I'm so happy for you guys! You need to tell me about it asap. My project ended so I have nothing to do. I need to live vicariously through your romantic exploits.

I grin at the phone, no doubt looking like an idiot who can't stop smiling. I didn't realize how dull my emotions were in the past, how the happiness I thought I felt was actually lackluster compared to what I'm feeling now. It's as if a raw diamond has been polished and shined, finally illuminating the dazzling sparkle to its full intensity.

My computer dings with a reminder of my meeting with Kristi and I grab my phone and square my shoulders, determined to grab the day by its balls, to show the boss I have everything well under control.

Standing in front of her office, I knock and push open the door, finding my boss sitting on the sofa, her gleaming white-blonde hair shiny and perfect as always. She glances up and waves me to the chair in front of her.

"Sit down, Emily. So, tell me, how are things going with Adrian Scott?"

I smooth my dress before taking a seat before her. "Things are going well, as you can see from the press. The public loves him now, and everyone believes he is smitten and ready to settle down."

Kristi nods, her eyes revealing nothing, and she takes a sip of water. "Good. Good. That's what we want for a client as big as him." She lets out a soft sigh. "I was worried when he suggested the paparazzi thing—"

"What?" My heart plummets as nausea unfurls inside my gut. "What paparazzi thing?"

Kristi falters before recovering. "I thought he'd have told you by now. Never mind, then."

The cogs in my brain shift into place, sliding the pieces of the puzzle into their appropriate slots.

Something has always nagged me, something since the beginning of this project, well before I saw Adrian for the first time in over a decade at Liz and Parker's wedding rehearsal. Leaning forward, I ask, "Kristi, why wouldn't you debrief me on the Scott Enterprises project when he approached us a year and a half ago? I'm usually part of the proposal and pursuit team for our biggest clients."

Her cool eyes flicker to mine and her lips press into a firm line.

"Why did you insist I'm the one to lead the project, even though I asked to be transferred before the arrangement started?"

The vise around my chest tightens, restricting my airflow, but I soldier on.

"Why did you insist I'm the one to date Adrian after the photo leak in front of the office? There were plenty of ways to get out of it. I gave you quite a few suggestions, but you were adamant for it to be me." I take a deep breath. "What paparazzi thing were you referring to?"

Kristi sits back, one arm curling around the sofa as she crosses her legs. Her posture is deceptively relaxed, but I see the hard glint in her eyes. She feels threatened.

My heart sinks and I grip the handrest tightly, my nails digging into the fabric. "Please. Please, just tell me the truth. I deserve to know."

She purses her lips and stares at me, her eyes sweeping over my face, cascading to my fingers, clutching the chair like a floatation device in the middle of the ocean. Letting out a sigh, she nods, coming to a decision.

"Fine. I guess it won't matter for you to know now, since we're so far along in the project and all is going well." Kristi sits up and clasps her hands on her lap. "When Mr. Scott approached our firm for a possible arrangement with us, he had one stipulation. If we didn't follow it, we have no deal." She pauses and I hold my breath. "His stipulation was you. He would only work with you. But he didn't want us to loop you in or tell you anything until the project actually kicked off."

My chest spasms as I let out the breath I was holding. The pit in my stomach grows and threatens to swallow me whole. "So, this was all preplanned?"

She cocks her head to the side, her penetrating eyes holding mine. "I figured you two had history, which was confirmed when I saw how he looked at you during our first group meeting."

"W-What about the fake dating?" I swallow, my heart pounding, threatening to break through the confines of the rib cage.

"He knew about it beforehand and approved of the plan. He insisted that person would be you."

Hands trembling, I curl my hair around my ear. My palms are clammy and my skin feels feverish. "But I thought I entered the equation because of the paparazzi photo..." I whisper, my eyes unfocused. "Which he..."

"Arranged it. He said you wouldn't say yes unless there was a compelling reason. And I agreed with him."

I flinch, my eyes flickering back to hers, finding her gaze sympathetic as the truth catches up to me like a train wreck in slow motion. He sounded so convincing that day on the phone when Kristi called him about the photo. Shaking my head, I mutter to myself, "So, this is all premeditated...every move, every setup." My mind trails back to the conversation we had on Brighton Beach.

"Adrian, I have a question for you first. Do you believe in revenge?"

"Yes. Without a doubt."

"What if someone you care about tells you to drop your revenge? Would you do it for them?"

"No. No one gets away from hurting me or my family without repercussions. I don't care what their reasons are."

Then, the intensity in his eyes when he stood in the middle of his penthouse this weekend flashes before me. His words, which at the time I thought he was referring to his plans for his grandfather's company, but now I realize most likely also included me.

"Are you scared of me? Someone who'll plot and go to such depths to get revenge?"

"No." I shake my head in disbelief, the reality I thought I knew shattering. The cracks in the mirror splinter my freshly closed wounds inside me. "No. No. No."

Ruthless. Cutthroat. Merciless.

Those are all words used to describe him by the press when he was shrouded in secrecy. A riot of emotions rushes through me. The hurt mingling with denial, the anger dancing with shock. I shake my head. This can't all be a setup. There's no way everything I felt, everything that transpired is all part of some elaborate game.

Kristi clears her throat. "Are we going to have a problem?"

My mind is muddled, the words in my head louder than her question being spoken aloud. I swallow the pins and needles in my throat as I try to reorient myself, try to make sense of everything, try to find my sea legs in this sudden storm which is turning the world upside down.

"Emily, do we have a problem? Must I remind you, your promotion to director is on the line with this arrangement."

Slowly, I raise my eyes to hers as the heat of anger fills my veins and travels to the rest of my body. "No," I murmur, before I take a deep breath and reply, the confidence in my voice belying the turmoil and rage I'm feeling inside, "No, we don't have a problem. In fact, I'll finish this arrangement with flying colors and I expect you to honor your promises. I'll keep this between us until the end of the contract and he won't suspect a thing."

Without waiting for her reply, I stand, straightening my back. I let out a deep exhale, and clench, then release my hands before I stride out, facing a future I thought was certain mere hours ago, but now may be up in flames.

I scroll through the report my investment banker sent me, which shows my latest holdings in Cornwall Holdings. In the last few weeks, I've purchased more shares, of which two deals were based on lurid secrets I dug up on the shareholders. When I was younger, I resorted to using my fists to get what I want. But now, I realize a well-placed threat, a strategic suggestion, work just as well. It's curious how far people will go to protect their secrets, to hide their shame, to maintain their outward appearances and impressions.

Pathetic.

I now own forty percent of Cornwall Holdings, making me the second-largest shareholder after my grandfather, who is still clinging on to his forty-five percent for dear life. I got to give it to the old snake. He may not know my true identity, but his instincts are right.

"Call it my gut feeling, Scott. Your offer is tempting and I can see the public whistling a different tune when it comes to you. But I'm still not selling. And that's final," he says, his voice raspy before he dissolves into a coughing fit.

"You know I can purchase your stock in other ways. I'm reaching out in courtesy."

He barks out a laugh. "I have nothing you can use against me, Scott. I've been around the business world for a long time and I know how people like you operate. If you're looking for skeletons in the closet to use against me, there are none."

I curl my lips in derision. "How would the public feel if news came out regarding the beloved founder of a Fortune 500 company purporting itself to be held by a family-first standards cruelly disowned his daughter because she married a poor man?"

My grandfather cackles. "You've been digging through the archives, haven't you? Maybe if you came to me with this threat forty years ago when my company was starting out, there'd be an outcry. But now, we're fully established. I'm retired, and the company is overseen by a strong CEO and a Board of Directors. Little you say or do will affect its performance."

My call with him this morning didn't go well. I know it would be easier to wait for him to just keel over.

But no.

I want him to be alive so he can witness everything in slow motion, when I pick apart his company and toss the scraps for cheap to anyone who cares for a piece. I want to see him bow over in pain as he realizes his legacy is gone, that everything he fought for, the reason he cast my mother out, is all in flames, all worthless. I want to see the anguish in his eyes when the very thing he loves is destroyed right in front of him.

I may have given up on my desire to hurt Emily, but the flames of revenge are still burning hot for my grandfather on behalf of Mom and Dad, little Millie, and the boy who had to shoulder immense burdens and lost too much at a young age.

My nostrils flare as I gnash my teeth together. I crack my knuckles and move on to plan B. It doesn't matter if the old man doesn't bend over. As long as other shareholders are willing to sell to me, and they will, I'll still be able to get controlling interest. My pulse thrums inside my chest as the heady anticipation of the next kill seeps through my pores.

Scrolling down the report, I stare at the name of the next shareholder, who holds twelve percent of the company, and lead settles on my chest. I let out a ragged exhale. *Robert Kingsley of TransAmerica Corporation.*

Emily's father.

I always knew there was a possibility I may need to go to Emily's father to get those shares. I hoped it wouldn't come to that, but apparently, life has left me no other choice. Leaning back in my leather chair, I twirl my fountain pen as my mind formulates a strategy to convince Kingsley to sell me his shares without letting Emily know. Because I don't want her to think I'm with her in order to get something from her parents.

Drumming my fingers on the table, I pick up the phone. "Kim, can you please get Robert Kingsley of TransAmerica on the phone?"

"Yes, sir."

If he's the man he's reputed to be, he'd pick up, because he would be curious about the poor boy he met once at the recital who is now purported to be dating his daughter and is also one of the richest men in the world.

My phone rings and I put it on speaker.

"I've been wondering when you'd call." His voice is deep and smoky, amusement lacing through his words.

Cocking my brow, I cross my ankle over my knee. "Have you now?"

"Word is out you're sniffing around the people who have shares in Cornwall. I figured I'd be next."

I chuckle. Unlike my other deals, I didn't hide my interest in Cornwall from the public. I wanted my grandfather to sweat.

"Fair enough. So, I think we can cut the bullshit then. You know what I want."

"My shares." A silence fills the line before Kingsley adds, "What can you offer me?"

Okay, two can play this game. I'll see what his opening bid is. "Word on the street is, you're trying to negotiate a deal with Fleur Entertainment...the only industry you're not in yet. I can give you an entry."

"How so?"

"I own half the banking relationships of their company, which I'm sure you're aware of."

More silence as he ponders my offer. Twisting my lips into a grin, I wait for a counteroffer. I'm giving him the family discount. With Robert Kingsley being Emily's dad, I have to resort to more highbrow methods of getting what I want. After all, he'll eventually be my father-in-law.

Emily may not know it yet, but she is marrying me one day.

My fingers tap the handrest as I imagine my pixie in a beautiful white dress, walking toward me with her heart in her eyes. My chest flutters with joy.

"No. I don't think so."

Frowning, I sit up. "What do you mean, no? What's your counter?"

"No counter. I'm not interested."

I narrow my eyes as I try to read into his tone. Cursing myself for not arranging for an in-person meeting so I could see his face and analyze his tells, I force myself to take a deep breath and calm the fuck down.

"Don't lie, Kingsley. There must be something you want."

He chuckles, his voice hoarse and grating to my ears. A muscle tics in my jaw as the hairs on my arms rise. The next words out of his mouth are his counter, despite what he says, and it's going to be something I won't like.

"I want you to break up with my daughter."

The adrenaline churning through my body is suddenly annihilated by a flood of dread and disbelief. The newly beating organ that is my heart, chugs to a stop as my lungs are robbed of breath.

No.

What he is asking is the one thing I can't give him.

"No. I'm not breaking up with Emily."

"Adrian Scott or Adrian Callahan or whatever you go by now, I still remember you all those years ago, the boy hopelessly in love with my daughter, standing next to her at the recital. In addition to the love I saw in your eyes, I also saw a fire, an ambition, a hatred so deep I felt it that day standing in front of you. I know why you're intent on buying Cornwall Holdings. It was too obvious once I realized who you were.”

He laughs softly and I can imagine him shaking his head in some fancy office. “A man with such vengeance simmering in his veins cannot provide happiness to my daughter. You’ll snuff out her aura with your toxicity. How about I give you an offer instead? You break up with Emily, and not only will I sell you my holdings in Cornwall, I’ll also keep your secret from your…grandfather.”

There comes a time in every chess player’s life when he loses the game to a worthy opponent.

Checkmate.

“No, breaking up with Emily is not an option.” I get up and pace around the desk as I crack my knuckles. The fury, which has briefly abated since my wondrous weekend with my pixie, is now back, the firestorm raging hotter and fiercer. “It’s. Not. A. Fucking. Option,” I growl, my voice seething.

More chuckles. “Don’t be so rash in deciding right now. Think about it. Is your revenge against your grandfather more important than your relationship with my daughter? You know what my offer is. Come find me when you decide.” With that, he disconnects from the line with a *click*.

“Fuck!” I swipe the papers and my phone off my desk, the crashing sounds jarring in the large space. “Shit! Fucking piece of shit!” Tugging my hair, I pace the floor, which is now littered with the evidence of my frustration.

Knock. Knock.

“Sir, do you require assistance?” Kim’s muffled voice calls through from the other side of the closed door.

Thumping my fists on the desk, my knuckles raw and red, I inhale a deep gulp of oxygen, an attempt to quash the rising wrath inside me. “No. You can go back to your duties, Kim.” I shudder from the exertion as my mind runs through the various options to circumvent or take down Kingsley.

“Yes, sir.”

Damn it all.

Thwack. Thwack. Thwack.

My knuckles feel the pain of every throw and jab, despite wearing thick gloves.

Thwack. Thwack. Thwack.

Right hook, jab, left hook, undercut. I dole up combination punches upon combination punches, unleashing my fury on the unfortunate victim in front of me. Parker, in this case.

Fuck Kingsley. Fuck my grandfather. They can all rot in hell. My vision is a sea of red and I advance toward my enemy, destroying him with my fists, the thundering pulse in my ears, the war chant. My surroundings blur into a sea of black and white. I faintly notice people yelling at me, a few jabs skimming the side of my rib cage, but I pay them no heed. Nothing will distract me from my goal, from obliterating whoever stands in my way.

Thwack. Thwack. Thwack.

My arms burn with fatigue as I throw out punch after punch, the exertion tiring my body, but my mind is red hot and clear.

Suddenly, strong arms appear from behind me and wrap around my chest, dragging me back on the boxing ring. I flail my arms behind me, eager to hit the new enemy who's attacking from behind. The fucking sneak.

"Adrian!"

I land an elbow and hear a satisfying *oomph* as the arms loosen briefly before tightening again, holding on to me with all his might.

"Adrian, snap the *fuck* out of it."

A haze of tan and black appears in front of me and before I know it, my head snaps to the side as someone delivers a harsh jab across my jaw, knocking out my mouth guard. I stumble, momentarily disoriented, a loud ringing reverberating in my ear. The pain, a late guest to the party, swipes through me and I collapse on the floor. I shake my head, my vision blurry before stabilizing and I wheeze, my body desperate for oxygen.

"Shit. Did I hit him too hard? I don't think I did." The voice is muffled, like I'm underwater.

"No, I think he's just in shock."

I feel a pair of hands on my shoulders, shaking me gently. Rolling on to my back, my eyes slowly refocus on the concerned face hovering above me. Dark-brown hair, blue eyes, sharp jaw with scruff. James.

"Hey, man, you okay? Parker didn't hit you too hard, did he?"

A tickle sparks inside my chest, morphing into full-body shudders as I laugh, the sound seeming strange to my ears. I gasp as the urge to cry mixes in with the imagined humor in my situation, a joke no one understands but me. "He wishes."

Another face appears in my vision. Golden-brown hair, green eyes, shit-eating grin. Parker. "Dude, what's up with you? I tapped out, and you kept on going. James had to haul you back and I think you even landed one on him."

The fog slowly clears from my vision and I sit up. Parker hands me a towel and James tosses me a bottle of water. Tugging the gloves off my hands, I let out a shuddering exhale as fatigue finally creeps in. I towel the sweat off my face, my hair, and my body, wincing at the red welts on my skin and knuckles. Parker put up a valiant effort today.

"Just bad shit at work." I uncap the bottle and take a few large gulps of water, hoping the liquid will quench the beast inside me.

Parker plops himself next to me as he takes a few sips of his own water. James slowly sits across from us, his startling blue gaze pinned on me as if assessing my every flicker and motion. The guys met up with me at Dominick's after work, where I apparently lost my mind in the boxing ring.

"Cut the crap, Adrian. Work doesn't rile you up like this. You aren't the type," James murmurs, his eyes trailing over my face.

"We're a vault. What happens in Dominick's stays in Dominick's." Parker leans against the ropes, looking into the distance.

"What made you decide to give up everything for the woman in your life?"

"What do you mean?" James stares at me intently, a slight furrowing of his brows.

"You uprooted your life for Jess. Moved halfway across the world for a chance to win her over, and it's not guaranteed." I glance over at Parker, whose lips are flattened into a firm line. "And you... you had a lot of shit to deal with, but you went out of your comfort zone and changed your life in order to be worthy of Liz." I close my eyes. "It's a lot of sacrifice for something that's not a guarantee."

"I think it all boils down to whether you think your life will be better with or without Emily." He arches his brow at me, as if daring me to contradict him. I don't—it's obvious the only woman in my life other than my sister is her. "If you get to achieve everything else you want in the world, but she's not by your side, would you be happy? Or would it be better having her by your side but perhaps sacrificing some other things in your life...if that's your question?" James answers. "For me, Jess was worth everything, and she still is. My life is worthless without her."

"We both tried living without our women and let's just say things didn't turn out well," Parker adds. "Liz is worth every sacrifice, every hard change, every risk." His eyes take on a faraway look, a soft curve on his lips, no doubt reflecting on his wife.

I hum noncommittally, my mind still reeling from the call with Kingsley earlier. Revenge has been the main driver of my life for the last decade or even longer, if I were to be honest with myself. Emily gave up on me once those years ago. Who's to say she won't bail on me if things get rough again? Is she worth giving up the fire that has been propelling me forward all these years? Will I grow to resent her?

A million questions swim around in the chaos of my mind, the swirling waters dark and murky. *But she's not like that, Adrian. But are you sure? After all, you're rich and powerful now. Anyone would want to be with you.* The kernel of doubt which has been buried deep and almost forgotten once again sprouts inside me, wondering how to reconcile the woman I love and know to someone who callously tossed me aside all those years ago.

"I need a drink," I mutter as I drain the rest of my water bottle, crunching the plastic in a loud crinkle. We get up and head toward the locker room and showers.

Parker slaps his hand over my shoulder. "The good things in life are always worth fighting for. Whatever it is you're dealing with, don't let her slip away."

My mind visualizes a future without my pixie by my side. It's not very difficult to do, given it'll be something resembling the past decade of my life. I'd continue wandering forward, swiping down enemies, delivering kill after kill, earning money for the sake of doing it. I'd be coming home to the same palatial apartment, my footsteps echoing in the hallways, playing the piano when the loneliness creeps in, all the while missing the energy from her, reminiscing her every grin, every smile, every devious twinkle in her eyes. My heart clenches, the agony so striking it threatens to rob me of my breath. Sweat forms on my brows and my pulse races as an irrational panic floods me.

Before I step inside the room, James murmurs behind me, "Adrian. I treat Emily like my own little sister. Whatever crap you're thinking about, don't hurt her."

Twisting my head, I stare at him, his sapphire eyes the temperature of the frigid ocean. I swallow the lump in my throat and give him a terse nod before walking inside. A new wave of adrenaline courses through me, the impulse to see my pixie, to hold her in my arms so strong it threatens to override any common sense.

My phone pings with an incoming message.

Jack: Have you decided what you're going to do with Emily and the shares situation?

Adrian: No. I haven't.

Jack: Here to chat as usual. For what it's worth, I haven't seen that lovesick smile of yours since you were in high school. It's a good look on you.

I grip my phone tightly as I reread his last message, my heart wielding arrows in a war against the javelins of my mind. The victor isn't determined, but my soul roots for the pounding organ fighting for its life.

My biggest fear is not of me hurting her.

It's opening myself up to be destroyed by her.

. . .

The warm, seaborne breeze whisks across my face as I walk on the sand, my feet feeling every solid grain, every hard pebble beneath me as I carry my shoes and socks with one hand. The beach is devoid of people at this late hour.

An unusual heat wave has hit the shores while parts of the country are experiencing record lows in temperature. The world is coming apart at its seams. Very much like my own life.

After our bout in the boxing ring, followed by a drink at the bar, I went home, where Anna prepared a hot meal of filling beef stew and stir-fried vegetables before she left for the evening. My mind wandered to Emily, wondering what she was doing, if she was at home, a mere forty floors below me. She was noticeably quiet today, with only a few short texts letting me know all is well and she's busy at work. The unease from her terse responses piles onto the pandemonium in my mind, and before I knew it, I found myself driving to our beach, aching to walk along the shores and clear my thoughts.

The skies are especially dark tonight, the moon only the thinnest sliver. Glowing stars scatter across the dark canvas, with the three brightest glints lining up side by side, beckoning to be noticed. Orion's belt—legend has it, Orion, the hunter, fell in love with Pleiades, the seven sisters, and Zeus turned them all into stars and now, the hunter is forever chasing after his loves until the end of time. The myth painted Orion in a bad light, his drive and desperation forcing the sisters into an eternity of damnation in the skies. Another man to be ruined by the enticing draw of love. My aching heart wonders if someday, instead of being the hero in our story, I'd turn into a villain, my dark soul damning Emily into hell with me.

Lost in the heaviness of my thoughts, I pay no attention to the path before me, only stopping when I smell the faint scent of lilies carried by the gentle wind. My feet freeze into place as I look up, finding my pixie in the distance, her hair shimmering as her face turns upward toward the heavens. The soft moonlight bathes over her silky skin, skimming over her curves, currently clad in a long dress, the skirt billowing from the breeze.

She looks ethereal as she stands still, as if she's absorbing the moonlight, imbuing herself with the magic of the elements, with the waves gently lapping in the background.

My heart stutters and restarts, my blood heating in my veins, and I can feel the weight being lifted off my chest. My mind calms as a quiet peace seeps through me, and suddenly, it's as if the path before me is illuminated and everything is clear. Swallowing audibly, the beats in my chest leap as the music thrums inside me and my feet move of their own accord, flying across the sand toward the pixie before me.

Only she can give me peace in my soul.

Only she can make my heart sing.

How could I ever give her up?

Reaching her in a few strides, I sweep her into my arms and her eyes flutter open in surprise. I twirl with her under the diamond skies, with the heavens as our witness. Burying my face in her hair, I hold her tightly against me, not wanting to ever let her go.

"Adrian, how—" she gasps as we spin together, the darkness a blur behind her.

"Shhh...I just realized something," I murmur before softly setting her back on the sand. Cradling her face in my hands, I dip down and seal my lips with hers, relishing in the way she melts under my embrace as if she, too, were waiting for me to find her here.

My lips suck and trace hers, the kiss devoid of the usual hunger but infused with tenderness, with love. The darkness inside me fades away, leaving behind a soft glow, the warmth provided by her presence. My pulse drums in a strong rhythm as a torrent of emotions rises inside me and I pour my heart out to her with each swipe of tongue, each taste of her sweetness, each tug of her lips. We part for air and I pull away, watching her brown eyes glimmer in the dim light, her eyes wide with surprise.

"I love you, Emily," I whisper, finally saying the words I've been carrying inside me for some time…a sentiment I perhaps have never stopped feeling even after the time and distance separated us.

Her eyes flare, the pupils obliterating the irises, and her lips part. She places her hands on my chest and I clutch her to me and squeeze, desperate for her to understand the truth behind my words.

Perhaps Adrian Callahan has long disappeared, but Adrian Scott loves you all the same.

A flurry of emotions flashes through her gaze as if she's fighting a war with herself. She stiffens and I feel an almost imperceptible tension rolling off her body.

"You don't need to say it back," I murmur, taking in her quick shift in stance as anxiety. Suddenly, I don't feel so afraid anymore. I'm lain vulnerable in front of her, my deepest fear, and yet, peering into the abyss hasn't broken me and I'm still standing.

Emily swallows, her delicate throat rippling, and she bites on her plump bottom lip. I smooth one hand over her face, memorizing every curve, every freckle, every little detail that is her. She stares at me in silence, her eyes peering into my soul, as if searching for something. After a few moments, she shakes her head softly as if bewildered, a wet sheen gathering in her eyes. She clenches her jaw, her caramel gaze suddenly filled with resolve, as if she somehow made a decision.

She breaks out into a wide smile, her muscles softening, the invisible ropes coiled around her body just moments ago seemingly spliced open. She curls her hand around my neck and brings my face down to her level. Leaning in, she tugs my bottom lip in her mouth, her teeth nipping the tender flesh, awakening my senses, sending blood straight to my cock, before smoothing the pinch with a gentle lave of her tongue.

Releasing my lip, a teasing grin forming on her face, she backs away slowly. "You mentioned you want to fulfill my wishes and dreams with me. You still game for that?"

Wordlessly, I nod, transfixed by my pixie, who's reaching for the ties of her dress on her shoulders. A few easy tugs later, the fabric slides into a puddle on the sand and she stands before me, clad in the thinnest black-lace lingerie known to man and my cock hardens to full staff, threatening to break free of the confines of my trousers.

She curls her finger toward me before reaching behind and unbuckling her bra. Seconds later, the panties also join the clothes on the ground. She stares at me, her mouth parted before her teeth clamp down in a soft bite. Her beautiful tits, a nice handful, glow under the moonlight, her nipples pebbled into hard points, begging me to taste them, to suck on them. Her hips flare out in the most enticing way, and a thin strip of hair covers the pussy I crave to devour. My mouth dries instantly, my hands automatically tugging off my tie, and I hurry to divest myself of the rest of my clothes. My skin is on fire, and I want to pounce on the woman before me, my vixen, my lover, my all.

Emily lets out a small giggle as she spins away, darting toward the soft waves. My lips curve into a grin as I remember sitting on this beach a long time ago, laughing at her dreams of skinny dipping, wondering how a goody-two-shoes like her is hiding a sinful streak inside her all along.

Laughing, my chest light while my heated blood rushes in my veins, I chase after her, reaching her a few seconds later as she dips her feet into the chilly waters. Her shrieks brighten the stillness of the night and I sweep her in my arms as we brace ourselves for what will no doubt be an icy awakening from the Pacific despite the warm weather.

A frosty wave washes over us as we clutch each other, my larger frame wrapping over hers, taking most of the icy burden on my back as she trembles in my arms. Concerned, I peer down at her, only to find her eyes twinkling back at me, her body shaking in laughter.

"Out of all times to tackle skinny dipping, you just had to pick wintertime, huh?" I rumble and swipe away a wet strand of hair plastered to her face.

"I saw an opportunity, and I took it." She wets her lips and my eyes zero in on the movement. "Plus, I wanted to see how serious you were about fulfilling my wishes and dreams."

Another wave laps at our waists, but I barely notice, my eyes focused solely on her, the woman I love with every inch of my heart, every ounce of my soul. Her smile slowly fades as she takes in my expression. Sliding my hand behind her neck, I stare into her eyes, imploring her to believe the next words out of my mouth.

"I meant every word, Pixie. I don't need wishes and dreams for me. I just want them for you because you deserve everything." My voice is thick and I slide my thumb across her cheek, wiping away the tears falling from her eyes. "I love you," I murmur before tugging her flush against me so no more distance lies between us.

Hoisting her up, I trail my lips down the curve of her chin, over the tender skin of her neck, my tongue lapping at the fluttering pulse, earning myself a moan and a whimper from her. She wraps her legs around my back, her hips automatically gyrating in an erotic rhythm. Tilting her head back, she bares more of her neck and chest to me. I suckle her delicate collarbone, tease the gentle divot, then I bend her farther back, exposing her swollen tits.

"You'll be the death of me," I mutter, staring at her erect nipples, budding like the eraser tips of pencils, perfect in shape and size. "Fuck me." I close my lips over one of the beckoning points and she cries as I suck hard before licking the tip with my tongue. God, she's the sweetest thing I've ever tasted, and I just want to keep going back for more.

She clasps my head against her as her hips move faster, her wet pussy rubbing against my dripping dick with the expertise of an erotic dancer. "Life," she pants, her hips twerking against mine, angling the tip of my cock past her clit with each undulation. "I'll be the life of you. Not death. Never death."

Emily slips her hand between us, grasping my hard rod in a vise, and I grunt as sparks fly inside me. My balls are aching and heavy and I grip her ass tighter, massaging the firm globes. She slides my cock into position, the tip teasing her wet hole.

"I want to spray my cum all over every inch of you," I whisper, circling my dick over her entrance. Every movement is tortuous for both of us. She claws my back and whimpers, her sounds lusty and desperate, driving me wild and crazy. "I want to mark you up and fuck you so you'll feel me everywhere...so everyone will take one look at you and know you're mine."

"Fuck yes," she gasps as she wiggles against me, her body aching for it. "I need it, Adrian."

"What do you need?"

"Your big, hard cock. Oh my God, I'm so wet. Please, Adrian."

I grunt, barely holding on to my sanity as her crude words caress over me in the most sensual foreplay. I flick her clit with my dick, and she trembles, the sensations driving me insane with lust. She whines, digging into my back. "Fuck me, Adrian. Slide it in. Fill me up. Mark me up from the inside."

"Shit!" I slam inside her, her tight walls welcoming me in a lover's embrace. We groan at the sensations and my balls draw up, ready to burst at the first glide. I bite my lip, the pain a temporary distraction as I rear back, withdrawing almost to the tip before slamming back in. I clutch her round ass to me and hoist her up and down, bouncing her on my dick in an erratic rhythm.

She moans with each movement, her carnal cries louder and louder with each thrust. Her tits shake in front of me and she throws her head back, her arms curling around my shoulders. The waves crash upon us again, the chill of the ocean doing little to douse the inferno between us. If anything, it spurs her to move faster, to move harder.

"Fuck yes. Ride my dick like you're my whore," I grunt, my mind delirious with pleasure. I quicken my hips, our skin slapping against each other's in a harsh rhythm, my ass clenching with each stroke.

"Fuck, yes...yes..." she chants, her eyes rolling back, her lips parting, and her legs begin trembling. Her tight channel grows slicker, the muscles spasming as her body locks in tension.

Curling one arm around her waist, I slide my free hand between us, pinching her hardened clit and she screams as spurts of liquid flow out of her, her pussy strangling my dick in a death grip. Molten lava floods my veins, barreling to my balls and my dick and with a few more vicious thrusts, I let out a roar as I succumb to the explosion, the pleasure so intense, my vision temporarily blackens out. My cock spasms inside her, each spurt of cum drawing a whimper from her as my hips move on their own accord, extending our high, eking out every droplet of sensation.

With the heavens as a witness, I press a deep kiss on my pixie's lips, pledging with my heart and my soul I'll somehow conquer the demons inside me and find a way for us to be together, if she'll have me once more. I'll pave a way for Romeo to be with his Juliet, to twist the play's tragic ending into one of hope and happiness.

The morning light seeps in from the window, cloaking the spacious room in a dim, blue glow. My eyes feel heavy from the deepest sleep I've had in ages. Slowly, I blink, my mind still fuzzy from slumber, and I try to reorient myself in this unfamiliar space. High ceilings, a neutral palate of blacks and grays, thousand-thread-count sheets feeling like silk on my skin—Adrian's penthouse. Warmth glides through my chest as snapshots of last night flitter through my mind.

Finding the courage to go to the beach once more, letting the memories wash over me.

The way he looked at me, as if I'm the air he needs to breathe.

His large body wrapping around me as he cocoons me in a feeling of safety, as if he'll take all away all my worries.

My earlier conversation with Kristi floats to the forefront, and a nagging pinch pulls me further away from the haze of deep sleep into wakefulness. My mind was a convoluted mess of emotions when I went to the beach last night, my heart telling me what I felt with him couldn't be fabricated. Perhaps our reunion may have been engineered. Perhaps he did hold hatred in his veins for me at some point, but his anger toward me has faded, like marks on the sand, washed away with each gentle caress of the waves. When he stared into my eyes, his blues impassioned and intense, and he told me he loves me, my soul leaped with joy. This feeling couldn't be fake. I refuse to believe it.

Turning my body toward the pillar of heat next to me, I glance at his sleeping profile. I admire the sharp planes of his face, softened in slumber, the lines on his forehead melting to the background, the long, thick lashes having no business being on a man's face, the strong nose, soft lips capable of delivering such scorching kisses, the strong jawline. My heart flutters and the niggling unease dissipates as love washes over me.

"I love you too, Adrian," I whisper to his sleeping form before pressing a kiss on his cheek. He grumbles and tugs the comforter up, and I giggle softly. The man looks like he hasn't slept in ages and no doubt the two rounds of sex last night after we got back home from the beach didn't help either.

Getting off the bed, I stretch my arms before walking into the large master bathroom to wash my face and wake myself up. I have my brunch with Melanie and Sarah later. Both Melanie and I took today off from work, and Sarah is theoretically unemployed at the current moment. After a quick splash of water on my face and pulling my hair into a ponytail, I tiptoe back out to the bedroom, finding Adrian still slumbering peacefully. Careful not to wake him, I jot down a note, telling him I'll be meeting the girls for a quick bite so he won't worry when he wakes up.

I quickly go downstairs to my place—there are definitely advantages to living in the same building—and take a shower and finish getting ready. After applying some light makeup and fastening my damp hair into a bun, I glance at the mirror, satisfied with my appearance. I throw on a thick taupe sweater and black leggings and head out the door.

Thirty minutes later, I arrive at Le Cirque, because Liz has requested Melanie to bring her some pastries tomorrow at school, all the while muttering how bummed she is since she couldn't make it to our meeting today. Spotting the girls at a small corner table on the spacious patio, I wave and walk toward them.

"Bonjour, mon ami," Antoine strides up and whispers in my ear as he snakes a hand around my waist and pulls me in for a brief hug.

Laughing, I give him an air kiss in greeting. "Morning to you."

His perceptive eyes skim over my face before he smirks. "Hm. I like this look on you."

"What are you talking about?"

"The mighty has finally fallen. You're in love."

I wave him away. "Oh, shut up."

Antoine laughs, his eyes crinkling at the corners. "Don't bother denying it. I'm French. We have a sixth sense for such things."

"Fine, fine. I'm in love now. You happy?"

"Yes," his eyes turn serious, "this look on your face is what I've always wanted for you."

My gaze softens as I place my hand on his arm. "Thank you, my friend." I nod to the girls at the table. "I'm sure you've already said hi to them."

He nods and grins. "I had the kitchen prepare a bag full of freshly baked breads and cakes for you girls to take back...and an especially large package for Liz. Tell Parker not to steal all of them for himself."

I snort before turning away to walk toward Melanie and Sarah, who are huddled over the table, whispering.

"Thank you, Antoine!"

"Tell Adrian I'll have his head if he hurts you," he hollers to my back, his words dissolving into a few deep chuckles.

The girls get up and envelop me in the warmest hugs before we sit down.

"We ordered for you already, since you always get the same thing," Melanie comments as she places her hands on the table expectantly, her brows cocked up.

Sarah follows suit, her hands clasp together on top of the table like she's conducting an interview.

"What?" I murmur and take a sip of the latte before me.

"You and Adrian. Spill. A few text messages and brief phone calls won't suffice," Sarah says, her cheeks twitching, as if she's fighting the urge to laugh.

"God help me against single women who aren't currently getting any." I roll my eyes and smirk, my comment earning me a napkin tossed in my face.

"I seemingly remember not very long ago, somebody proclaimed she is going to be permanently single, and long-term relationships aren't for her, and it's better to leave any entanglements at a high than stick it out for the lows. Oh, how the table has turned." Melanie narrows her eyes and shakes her head in mock disapproval, her classic ponytail swishing behind her as I hand her napkin back to her.

"Fine. Fine. You got me. I'm the world's biggest hypocrite, okay?"

Sarah pats my hand, her eyes brimming with laughter. "You can totally ignore us, Ems. We are just dirt jealous of you."

Melanie snorts before snickering. She leans forward, her voice in a hush. "But seriously, how are things going with you and Adrian?"

My heart tugs as my mind flits back to the sleeping man I left on the bed a while ago. "Things are going great...I think."

"You think?" Sarah furrows her brows.

The little sprout of unease resurfaces, the devil whispering in my ear.

"He makes me feel like I'm the only woman in the world for him. And to be honest, he was the only man to ever make me feel this way...even back in high school. It's as if I've been waiting for him all this time, hoping our lives will intersect again, and we'll find our way back to each other."

"How romantic," Melanie breathes, her eyes dreamy.

"And you did...so that's good. Then why the uncertainty?" Sarah's amber gaze sharpens as she picks up on my discontent.

I bite my lip as the servers stop by and place an assortment of savory crepes and pastries on our table, the smell of creamy eggs and melted cheese wafting in the air.

"Ems?"

I cut into my crepe, slicing through the buttery-soft salmon. Taking a deep breath, I brace myself and ask, "What would you think if you found out the person you love orchestrated your entire reunion without you knowing?"

Silence fills the table and I glance up, finding Melanie and Sarah staring at me with wide eyes.

"What do you mean?" Melanie bites into a *pain au chocolat*.

I explained to them what I learned from Kristi earlier on. "Jess told me to trust my gut because I've always had a good sense about these things. But I don't know…" Shaking my head, I sigh. "It's easy for me to get a read on these things for other people, but somehow when it comes to me, I'm as good as blind."

"How do you feel when you're with him?" Sarah asks.

"It doesn't feel fake. At the beginning, I knew he hated me. I could feel it in my gut, could see it in his eyes. But recently, all I can feel from him is affection and love. The darkness is still there, but it never felt malicious toward me. But he never told me about this. He kept everything to himself like a closed book, and I couldn't help but wonder…"

"Why don't you ask him? Maybe there's a reasonable explanation for everything."

"It's complicated. Kristi is tying my promotion to making this project a success. So, when she told me the truth of what she knew, I promised her I wouldn't jeopardize the relationship between him and I and I wouldn't say anything…"

"Because deep down you're scared there's something nefarious going on and if you ask him, everything will be over," Sarah finishes the sentence for me, her eyes softening in sympathy as she reaches over and squeezes my hand.

"Oh shit," Melanie murmurs as a pinch of sadness slithers through me. "Maybe being single has its advantages," she mutters, visibly deflating.

Taking a deep breath, I let out a full exhale, the weight on my chest easing slightly. "Never mind this, girls." I shake my head. "Nope, I'm not going to think this way. Emily Kingsley won't succumb to overthinking. I'll focus on the present, which is a gorgeous billionaire is hopelessly in love with me and giving me the best sex of my life, and what happens tomorrow will happen then and when the contract is over, we can air out any lingering confusion, right?" I grin, the effort feeling a tad forced.

Melanie doles out a terse nod before lifting her glass up for a cheer. "That's the spirit, Ems, the firecracker we all know!"

We clink our glasses together and Sarah adds, "Not that this means much, but my *gut* tells me this is all real for him, too. He looks at you the same way he did all those years ago, Ems." She smiles, her warmth infectious as she takes a sip of her drink.

• • •

Kristi: I know it's your day off today, but do you have time for a quick call?

Frowning at the message on my phone, I pause as I step inside the foyer of Adrian's penthouse using the key he gave me the night of the blackout. He should be at work today, but I thought I'd surprise him with a home-cooked meal waiting for him when he comes home. They say the best way to keep a man happy is through his stomach. No harm in trying, I suppose, even though he knows better than to expect daily meals from me. This is reserved for special occasions only.

Wrangling the bags of groceries I picked up on the way back from brunch with the ladies, I press her number, then hit the speakerphone before walking over to the kitchen and setting everything on the granite countertop.

"This is Kristi."

"It's Emily. You wanted a call?" I take out the packets of short ribs and store them in the large double-sided fridge.

"Sorry for bothering you on your day off. The P&L forecast for the upcoming year is due today to the partnership board. We were so focused on your progress with the Scott case I forgot to ask you for your budget for the next year."

Nodding to myself, I continue unpacking the grocery bags as I respond, "No problem. What do you need from me?"

"The jobs you have in the pipeline and where I can find those revenue and expense estimates."

"I have three projects that are signed and finalized. You can find their files on the top right of my filing cabinet in my office. I labeled them with a green marker. Two projects are close to being signed—we're in final stages of negotiations. My assumption is, we'll probably need to do a price cut to win them. So, you can probably estimate collecting sixty percent of the billable hours in the high-level quote. Those files are in red on the bottom right."

Putting the vegetables in the sink for washing later, I add, "Kristi, I have two nonprofit jobs I want to add to the plan. The revenues will be minimal and there will be additional expenditures, but I believe they'll be good exposure for our firm."

"You know you won't get to sign these jobs until you make director, right?"

I crack my neck, relieving the tension accumulating in the muscles during the conversation. "Kristi, you still have my back for the promotion, right? That was what we discussed."

"If you continue to keep Scott happy, I'll make the play for you, but don't forget that's the condition."

I exhale, the motion doing little to relieve the heaviness weighing inside my chest. I haven't told Adrian about this because I'm afraid he'll take this the wrong way, but it feels underhanded to keep this from him. "Yes, I remember. And like we said last time, he's very happy. Please budget those two jobs for me."

A few seconds of silence pass by as if she's mulling over my metrics. "Fine. Don't disappoint me, Emily."

"You can count on me."

The call disconnects and I shake my head, wondering when I'll be able to do the work that drew me to this profession in the first place. I take out a cutting board and hum under my breath, determined not to let work worries get in the way of my day off.

Riiiiing.

The sudden blaring of the cell phone shocks me in place. Glancing at my phone, which is quiet, I frown just as the ringtone is abruptly silenced. My breath catches in my chest and the earlier unease uncoils itself inside me. Quietly, I walk around the marble island, turning a corner toward the living room, and I see Adrian sitting on the sofa, staring at the phone in his hand. He's clad in a navy sweater and sweatpants, his back muscles bunching up, rippling against the fabric.

"Adrian? I thought you were at the office?"

He fiddles around with the screen on his phone, his tone nonchalant. "No. Didn't end up going in."

Slowly I creep toward him, my heart pounding against my rib cage, guilt blooming in my gut. "H-How long have you been sitting there?"

He straightens up and takes a deep breath before turning around, his lips curving into a small smile. "I came downstairs just now." He takes a few steps toward me and wraps his arms around my back. "What are you doing in the kitchen?"

"I'm preparing a casserole for dinner. Thought I'd surprise you when you get home."

He chuckles, the vibrations felt through the layers of our clothing. "Emily Kingsley, the housewife, huh?"

Pushing off him, I swat playfully at his chest. "Don't you dare get used to it. And who said anything about marrying you?"

"We'll see about that." He smirks, but the warmth doesn't quite reach his eyes, a glacial blue so penetrating it's almost unsettling.

I blink a few times and look away. "Ha. Why don't you exercise or something? Don't disrupt me in my flow." I twirl around and walk away, my heart still racing as if I'm a thief who had a close brush with law enforcement.

He didn't hear my call with Kristi, did he?

· · ·

I wake up the next morning at the sensation of something slithering across my arms. Blinking my eyes open, I turn instinctually toward Adrian's side but feel something tethered to my wrists. Glancing up, I see black silk restraints wrapped around me, binding me to the bedposts. I tug, the straps unforgiving.

"Good morning, Pixie. I see you are awake." A husky voice caresses my skin and I pull myself up, finding Adrian lounging on the sofa facing the bed. His torso is naked, the morning light illuminating every slab of defined muscles. A pair of sweatpants is slung low on his waist, his Adonis belt proudly displayed. My pulse picks up in rhythm as I wet my lips.

"Adrian?" I cock my brow and watch as his irises turn dark at the edges, the intention in his eyes shooting a shard of pleasure straight to my clit. "What's this?"

He slowly stands, his abs rippling with the motion, and my heart skips a beat. Striding over slowly, he keeps his gaze on mine as my breathing ratches up and my skin feels flushed.

"I keep thinking about your research on me when we met in your office that first time. When you said I was known to be 'depraved' in the bedroom." He flips the comforter off my body, exposing my nakedness to the cool morning air. My nipples turn into hard points and the ache between my legs intensifies. "I realize I've never shown you that side of me before. So, I thought I'd give you a small glimpse, but if you're uncomfortable, just tell me no."

Adrian's eyes are cobalt in the dim light, his gaze intense as if he's bottling something inside him. At my silence, he slowly crawls up the bed, his movements as sleek as a panther, and he spreads my thighs, angling my core, already wet with arousal, toward him. His nose grazes the sensitive skin of my inner thigh and I shiver from myriad sensations.

"You smell so sweet, so delicious," he rasps as he inhales my slick folds before swiping his tongue from clit to the puckered rosebud of my ass.

I arch my back and let out a moan, clamping my legs around his head.

"So wet for me." Another swipe.

"A-Always," I breathe, my body warring with the impulse of getting closer to those wicked lips of his or pulling away from the onslaught.

"Mine." He pulls the swollen clit inside his mouth, sucking it like it's the best delicacy on earth. White hot shards of pleasure spear through me and I thrash on the bed, my body thrumming with lust. I tug at my hands, unable to move them, the restriction heightening the sensations in my body.

"Do you love me, Pixie?" He lightly taps my clit with his tongue as he slides two fingers into my tight channel.

"Shit," I moan, my hands clenching, wanting to claw at him, to draw him up to me.

"Do you?"

His question hits me belatedly, and for a brief moment, the pleasure dissipates. I realize he's never heard me say those words to him. Not since we were in high school. Another wet glide of his tongue over my swollen lips has me letting out a keening cry, the sparks returning in full force. "Y-Yes. I love you, Adrian." My words are breathy, but I hope he knows they are sincere.

Smack.

He slaps my pussy, the sting jolting me off the bed before he soothes it with another tortuous swirl of his tongue, the pleasure blending with the pain in the most erotic cocktail.

"That's for abandoning me all those years ago," he growls as he delivers another smack as the previous sting fades to nothing. My hips arch up and I let out a throaty moan.

"That's for you haunting me for all these years." His tongue flickers the bud rapidly, as if he's possessed, and he slides another finger into my wet core, curling them so it hits my G-spot.

The sensations are too strong, the sharp pinch of pain and heady flames of pleasure blurring together, a combustible cocktail as the pressure builds between my legs at an intense speed. I mewl, my words incoherent, my body twisting on the bed, unable to escape his punishments or his attentions.

He slowly climbs up my body, his lips trailing kisses along my stomach, his tongue swirling over my pebbled nipples before he settles his imposing frame over me. Dark sensuality drips from his entire being as I inhale my favorite scent of mint and musk. His eyes, burning brightly, bore into mine before he leaves a smattering of kisses over my jaw, the whorl of my ear, before finally whispering, "Damn right, you love me."

Slamming his lips with mine, he thrusts inside me in one strong glide, bottoming out. His mouth sucks and swallows, his lips tangle and duel, his kisses obliterating all rational thought as his hips piston inside me, each smack of his skin against mine loud and crisp.

"O-Oh my God," I cry, my body shaking with each punishing thrust. He dominates me, his hips moving against mine in a frenzy.

Adrian swallows my cries and pleas with possessive suctions and licks. He grabs my tits, thumbing the nipples as his thrusting speeds up, his cock jack-hammering inside me like a weapon, as if he couldn't get close enough, get deep enough.

"This pussy is mine." *Thrust.* "Only mine." *Thrust.* "Oh fuck, you're going to make me come so hard," he rasps as he stokes the fire between us.

I tug at the hand ties to no avail and fall mercy to this un-leashed beast. His eyes turn feral, his pupils blown, his pants heavy, and he moves within me like he's trying to purge something out of himself. He twists my nipples, the sharp pain sending me off the cliff, and I let out a scream, my nerves exploding into a thousand pieces. I shudder against him, my walls throbbing and clamping his dick like a vise, riding out my high.

"Fuck, yes," he pants as his frame shudders against me. I shake underneath him, my orgasm dragged out by his pleasurable aggression. He releases my tits and hoists my hips higher, throw-ing my legs across his shoulders, bending me to his will. His lips twist up in a snarl and he overpowers me. The sight of him being so untethered turns me on as heat gathers between my legs once again.

Changing his angle, he slides in deeper, his balls hitting my ass with each slap as my entire body shakes and shudders. My teeth clatter against each other as more wetness seeps out of me, my body completely at his disposal. My nerves are frayed and raw, my clit too swollen and sensitive and I attempt to arch away from the onslaught, even though my body still craves him.

"I can't, Adrian. T-This is too much!"

He drives into me, angling his hips at the end of each thrust, hitting a spot so deep inside I see stars.

"You can, Pixie. Oh, fuck you can. Look at your pussy gripping me like it's addicted to my cock." As if to prove a point, he hits the magical spot a few more times and my mouth falls open, my hands clenching and my muscles bunching as the heat rises once again and dots appear in my vision. My eyes begin to roll to the back of my head and my body arches up, my muscles tensing once more, my legs shaking as unbearable heat gathers at our point of connection.

"O-Oh Adrian," I cry out as he slams into me in rapid succession, and the sparks overflow once again, short-circuiting my system and I'm thrown into a space between reality and ecstasy, unable to move other than to ride out the pleasure flowing through my veins—the highest of highs. My vision blacks out and I grip the bedsheets with my hand, my pussy clamping and shuddering with each wave of orgasm.

"Emily," he roars, his hips trembling, and he comes, unloading powerful streams of cum, each throb of his cock sending more aftershocks inside me.

Panting, I slowly come down from my high as my soul settles back into my body. He buries his face in my neck as he reaches up and releases the ties on my wrists, the blood flooding back into my hands in pinpricks. Shaking, I wrap my hands around his back, relishing his large frame completely overtaking my petite one. Angling my head to place my lips next to his ear, I whisper, "I love you, Adrian."

He tenses for a moment, the muscles on his back flexing, before he relaxes and murmurs, "I love you always, Pixie." He lifts his face and my breath catches in my throat.

The beautiful blue eyes, icy cold once more.

He blinks and smiles, the expression rigid, before he withdraws from me, swings his legs off the bed, and heads to the restroom.

The earlier unease flares back up, the pleasurable hiatus slowly slinking away.

CHAPTER 43

Adrian

Buzz. *Buzz. Buzz.*

I silence my phone without checking the caller ID. My arm wraps around the warm body of my pixie, who's curled into my side during her sleep after she all but passed out after our last bout of lovemaking. The sunlight streams in from the windows. The soft glow filters through the curtains, illuminating her smooth skin, caressing each and every one of those delectable curves. Her forehead is unblemished, her brows unfurrowed. She looks so peaceful and happy resting next to me, her lips curving into a soft smile, the tiniest flush lingering on her cheeks.

My heart constricts as I recall her conversation with her boss. I decided not to go into the office yesterday, hoping to surprise her when she came home so we could spend another wonderful day together, creating more memories, filling in gaps of time lost when we were apart. Instead of the elation I hoped to receive, I instead learned about her deal with Kristi, how her promotion at work is contingent on pleasing me, on keeping me happy because I'm no doubt their biggest and richest client.

I guess I only have myself to blame. After all, I kicked off this chain of events, painstakingly arranging every reunion between us, forcing her to spend time with me, so I could make her fall in love and then break her heart like she did mine in a way I once thought was irreparable. Little did I know, my heart never forgot about her, my hatred was just a way of keeping a place for her in the once-dead organ, which resurrected with every interaction with her, the scars mending and disappearing with every kiss, every embrace, and every smile from her.

And now, I'm faced with the reality perhaps my plan backfired. Not only did I fall hopelessly back in love with her—though one could argue I never fell out of love in the first place—I have to face a distinct possibility she may be using me to further her career or maybe she's with me because I'm part of the upper echelons of society now, just like how her mother and even the asshole, Ryan, have changed their tune about me, Adrian Scott, the billionaire. Perhaps the reality I thought I was experiencing was just another layer of pretense.

She didn't even say she loved you until this morning.

"Adrian," Emily murmurs before she snuggles closer to me, her hand caressing the hard planes of my chest as if she wants to ensure I'm still there with her.

And I realize I'm torn between life and death, suspended in purgatory, unable to leave her, yet unable to give her my all. Eleven years ago, she was with me out of pity, because I was too poor. Now, she may be with me because of her career or other reasons. But my heart is starving, famished, and ever since she reappeared in my life, I've been feasting on the pieces of her love, my hunger never satiated.

I chuckle soundlessly as I realize I'm the pitiful animal caged in the trap I engineered.

"Is everything okay?" She clutches the blanket to her chest as she sits up, a frown marring her beautiful face.

I turn away. "I'm fine."

"Something is wrong. I can tell. Will you talk to me?"

I scoff before swiping my hand through my hair. Her hand clutches my forearm. "Adrian. Please don't retreat into your cold, hard shell again. What's wrong?"

"Are you with me because I'm rich and can help you get a

promotion?" Gritting my teeth, I turn to face her, finding her skin leaching of color.

My heart plummets.

"N-No. Of course not. I mean, my promotion is contingent. No, this is not how you're supposed to find out. My feelings for you are real—"

Buzz. Buzz. Buzz.

My chest clenches, my lungs constricting. Swallowing the lump in my throat at her incoherent protests, the hole in my heart widening with each second, I reach for my phone again, glancing at the screen. *New Hope Hospital.* My muscles tense as I answer, my conversation with Emily momentarily forgotten.

"This is Scott."

"Hi, sir, this is Jenny from New Hope Hospital calling. Your father was just brought in after suffering from a heart attack. We have in his charts to call you as his emergency contact."

My pulse races and my lungs feel like they've been robbed of breath. "Is he okay? What's his condition?"

Emily frowns as she squeezes her hand on my arm in support.

"The doctors are still with him right now, so we don't have the prognosis yet."

"Call or text me with any updates. I'll be there in a few hours."

I disconnect the call and quickly dial another number. "Kim, get the jet ready and have Pierre come pick me up as soon as possible. Call Dr. Cross. Dad's in the hospital. Have him go to New Hope asap. No, I don't care if he may be with other patients or balls deep in some pussy. Get him there."

Tossing my cell phone on the nightstand, I get off the bed and head toward my walk-in closet, throwing on random articles of clothing as my mind races with many scenarios. Despite my opinions and perhaps some underlying resentment of Dad and how he handled those years when Mom was sick, he and Millie are the only family I have, the people, other than my pixie, I care most about.

I can't bear to lose yet another loved one.

Sweat beads on the back of my neck as I pull out a bag and start tossing a few essentials in there, knowing I could have someone buy me whatever I need later. Gritting my teeth, I curse under my breath.

Delicate arms encircle my waist and the scent of lilies hits my senses. Emily presses her warm body behind me, her curves molding against my muscles in precisely the right way. The tension leaks from my body in those few precious seconds and I uncoil under her embrace.

"He'll be okay, Adrian. He has the best doctors. Things will turn out okay." Her voice chokes up as if remembering how she held me in her arms the night Mom passed. She squeezes me tighter. "We have to have faith. Do you want me to go with you?"

Snapping out of the moment of reprieve, I shake my head. "No. It's fine. Stay here. There's nothing you can do, anyway."

"Adrian, about our earlier conversation. I know it's not the time to discuss it right now, but it's not what you think it is."

I stare at my overnight bag, unable to look at or answer her.

A few minutes later, my phone chimes, a text from Pierre indicating he's downstairs. Emily walks me to the private elevator bay, her eyes brimming with concern. She stands up on her tiptoes and leans in for a kiss, but I shift my face at the last second, an involuntary motion acting as the guardrails around my heart, and her lips land on my jaw.

She pulls away, a slice of hurt intermixing with concern in her eyes, but she blinks and forces out a smile. "He'll be fine, Adrian. I'm here. Just call me at any time."

Giving her a terse nod, I step into the elevator, not turning around until the doors slide closed.

. . .

Emily

Unease weighs on my chest, so heavy, I'm finding it difficult to breathe.

Other than the worries I have for the health of his dad, a slither of dread winds itself inside me, unsettling my senses. Ever since the hot sex this morning—it was delicious and I can't wait to explore this side of him—he's been acting distant.

He must have heard some parts of my call with Kristi. There's no doubt about it, but how much did he hear, and what conclusions did he draw in that sharp mind of his?

All the wrong conclusions, I'm sure.

A pit of nerves gathers in my stomach, a heaviness settles on my chest as worries and unease pollute my mind.

I cringe internally. This is neither the time nor place. His dad is in the hospital—there are much more important things to worry about.

Typing out a few emails in my office, my mind distracted, I bemoan how I should've taken today off as well. I'm obviously unfocused and horribly inefficient.

Riiiiing.

My phone's shrill ringtone interrupts my inner chaos and I answer without bothering to look on the screen.

"Hello?"

"Emily, have you heard from your brother?" My mother's saccharine voice comes through the other line. Damn it, I should've checked caller ID.

"I haven't. Steven is a grown man, I'm sure he's very busy." Angling the phone on my shoulder, I type out a reply to another project proposal on my computer screen.

"This is what happens when you have children. When they all grow up, they don't need you and then they gallivant to God knows where and ignore you, leaving you to fend for yourself in your elderly years."

I fight the urge to roll my eyes. As much as she tries, there's only so much Mother can change. Apparently, guilt-tripping is on the menu today. "Mother, I really don't have time for this."

"One more thing, Emily, and don't say I don't tell you things. In the interest of honesty, I want to let you know your Adrian called your father the other day."

I stop typing and my mind focuses on the conversation for the first time. "What?"

"He wanted to buy the Cornwall shares your father holds. Your father didn't tell me much, but it didn't seem like the conversation went well."

The roar of my pulse thrums in my ears as I attempt to take calming breaths. "What on *earth* are you talking about?"

"Your father holds the next largest set of shares of Cornwall. It's pretty obvious Adrian has been trying to purchase controlling interest in the company. If he has our shares, his ownership would tip over fifty percent."

"Did Father sell to him?" My heart is in my throat and I feel nauseated. I remembered the look on his face when he told me Cornwall was his grandfather. He'd do anything to get his revenge.

Would he be with me in some scheme to get those shares?

The nausea churns as if I'm floating on rough seas in the middle of a storm.

"I don't know. Your father wouldn't tell me."

"I-I have to go, Mother. I have an incoming call," I fib, desperate to think in peace.

Disconnecting from the call, I bury my face in my hands, wondering how my life got here. My emotions are a tangled mess, my worries smothering me, rendering me immobile as unease settles in my gut. Doubt and uncertainty mix inside me in a heady brew, its toxic fumes seeping into the crevices of my heart. Glancing at the clock, I notice Adrian should've arrived an hour ago.

With trembling fingers, I dial his number, hearing the steady beats of the ringtone.

"You've reached Adrian Scott. I'm unavailable to answer right now. Please leave your number and message."

"Adrian, it's me. I'm worried about you. How's your dad—"

My phone chimes with an incoming text.

Adrian: Dad's condition is stable, don't worry.

I let out a deep breath, a layer of concern melting away.

Emily: And you? Do you want to talk?

I want to ask him about what Mother just told me. I want to tell him about my conversation with Kristi. I don't want him to misinterpret anything. No more secrets.

Adrian: I need some time to think. Please give me time.

What? I breathe out and stare at his response as bone-chilling fear seeps into me. I quickly dial his number again.

It goes straight to voicemail.

Panic and dread swirl inside as stark desolation cloaks me, the pinpricks of its embrace digging through my skin, leaving sharp wounds behind.

So many secrets. So many lies. Not enough time to disclose them all.

Tears slip down my cheeks and I wonder if we'll survive this or if this is the end of our story.

CHAPTER 44

Adrian

"**Y**our father is fine. Thankfully, the heart attack was mild this time. Based on preliminary exams, we think additional damage should be minimal. Given this is not the first time he's here, we performed an angioplasty and put a stent in the artery where the clot was. We have him on some beta blockers and thrombolytics for blood clots. We'll keep him here for two nights to monitor and wait for the other scans and tests to be completed. Then, we'll figure out next steps for him." Dr. Xavier Cross, one of the best cardiothoracic surgeons in the country, a long-time friend from Cornell and asshole extraordinaire, stares at me with concern in his hazel eyes, his normally cocky face devoid of the usual arrogance. We're standing in front of Dad's private room, where he's resting inside.

"Thanks, Xav." I rake a hand through my hair as he slaps me on my back.

"Of course, man. I have your back. I don't just leave the bed of a supermodel for anyone, you know," he says as he winks, his usual wry grin decorating his annoyingly smug face.

"One more word, and I'll rescind my donation to the new wing."

He clasps his chest in mocked horror. "You wound me! After all these years." His face smooths out and his expression is one of seriousness once more. "All jokes aside, we'll take care of him here. I need to head out for another consult, but we'll be in touch."

I give him a nod as he strides away. A yawn catches in my throat. The adrenaline from the day's events is finally running out, and the beginnings of exhaustion are making an appearance. Quietly entering the spacious room, I'm hit with a sense of déjà vu. Despite the elegant furnishings of the private quarters reserved for people who are able to pay for them, the smells are still the same— the sterile antiseptic, the bitter undertones of soaps and cleaning agents, the stale, recirculated air. Illness doesn't discriminate between the poor or the rich, but money does help. Whereas Mom didn't get the best treatment in the timeliest of fashions, Dad is whisked away to a VIP room, attended by one of the top surgeons in the world, and his prognosis is much better because of it.

Sitting down, I take in his still figure, the slight rising and falling of his chest, feeling different, yet somehow the same as the boy in the hospital room all those years ago. The same helplessness, the same worries, the same anger at why this keeps happening to my family.

I take out my phone then type a message to Millie.

Adrian: Don't worry, Dad is fine. The doctor said it's minor this time so we'll video chat with you when he wakes up. No need to fly over here.

Millie: Okay. Let me know if anything changes and I'll be on the first flight over.

Letting out a sigh, I scroll to the most recent message from my pixie, a message I've left without replying because of the barrage of emotions assaulting me for the last few days.

Emily: Please talk to me. I want to tell you the truth...about everything. It's not what you think it is. I'll give you space, but know that I'll be waiting for you. No more secrets this time. I love you.

Turning off the screen, I close my eyes, wondering how everything got so confusing. Before Emily came back into my life, my days were simple, if not monotonous. Anger and a thirst for revenge were my main drivers each day, the main forces behind me getting up at the crack of dawn, toiling away until daylight fad-ed into dusk. The thrill of winning each deal, destroying people who've wronged me, raking in more money than I'll ever be able to spend fed the beast inside me, staving off starvation for yet another day.

But now, the heady promise of revenge doesn't seem to entice me anymore. The beast craves something else. The deep, black hole inside me wants something only Emily can provide.

Her love. Her kisses. Her warmth.

I'm an addict, struggling at the edges of sobriety all these years apart, and as soon as she came back into my life and I'm infused with a hit so strong, so exhilarating, my heart won't take anything less for an answer, my soul won't be satisfied with the meaningless highs that sustained me the last eleven years.

And now, I'm afraid, even if she's with me for all the wrong reasons, I won't be able to part with her because a life without her, even if it's not all of her, is dreary and pointless.

My chest aches as my mind is filled with thoughts of Emily, her twinkling eyes when she laughs at me, the smirks on her lus-cious lips, the seaborne breeze fluttering her silky strands, and her scent of sweet lilies, always bringing me peace.

"Ugh. I feel like I've been hit with an anvil," Dad groans as he shuffles on his bed.

I get out of my chair and walk over to him, helping him up to a sitting position before brightening the lights in the room.

"Take it easy, Dad. How are you feeling?"

"Ugh. I'm fine. A little loopy from the meds, but okay." He turns his head to face me, his penetrating eyes on mine. He looks gaunt, but the spark is still there. "What did the doctor say?"

"Dr. Cross was here just now. He said it was mild this time. Likely no additional damage." I let out an exhale. "You have to take better care of yourself, old man." I clasp his hand in mine and squeeze.

Dad chuckles and sighs. "You've been taking care of this fami-ly since you were a kid. Being in here brings back memories of your mom." He stares at the ceiling, his eyes vacant, as if remembering the past. "I know back then, you must have despised me for how weak I was when your mom was dying. I probably didn't give you a good example of shouldering the responsibilities of love. And that's what it is, really. Love is not only a heady emotion but also comes with large burdens. As the vows say, in sickness and in health, I regret how I wasn't strong enough to be your and Millie's shelter during the storm."

He clears his throat, his voice husky, and he turns to me. "But I'm damn proud of how you turned out, son. And I know your mom is up there, happy at what a strong man you've become. So perhaps, our love story had a tragic ending, perhaps I wasn't a perfect man, but ultimately, I don't regret loving your mom, having you and Millie, and if I had another chance to redo everything, if your mom would still have me, I would've chosen her all over again."

My vision blurs and I bite my lip, holding back the torrent of feelings inside me. "Didn't you say back then, if you had to choose all over again, you wouldn't go after her?"

"Son, I was overcome with grief then. But in reality, life is unpredictable. We don't get to read books and only choose the good chapters without the bad ones. Your mother and I had many good chapters in our story and we got the two of you. A few dark pages don't ruin the entire book. It may have been bittersweet, but it was still a book very worth reading and very memorable."

I lean forward, clasping his hand in mine. I whisper, "What if you're scared to read the book? What if the book isn't going to be what you originally thought it was?"

He smiles, his face looking so much older now. "You'll miss out on a lot of good chapters, son. We can't live our lives in fear. You may very well be holding the best read of your life in your hands. Don't miss out on it. If you love her, give it your all while you still have a chance."

My eyes burn as a muscle in my jaw twitches. I swallow the lump in my throat before standing up. Letting out a ragged sigh, I rake my hand over my face. "Thank you, Dad."

As I leave his room, my phone buzzes in my pocket.

"Parker."

"How's your dad doing? Anything I can do for you or your family?" A quiet hum filters through from his background. Most likely he's on the road.

"His condition is stable. Thanks for your concern. We have it handled."

"Just let me know. I'm always here for you. It was the same back at Cornell, and the same today."

A warmth unfurls in my chest at his words, at his friendship, something I've missed when I spent the past decade in the shadows building my empire.

"You should call Emily, you know."

I stare at out the large window in the corridor into the quiet courtyard. Birds flit across the skies. A few people are sitting on the bench chatting. "What do you mean?"

"Liz got off the phone with Emily just now. She said Emily sounded terrible and worried since wasn't able to reach you. Are you two okay?"

"If one day you found out Liz got together with you for all the wrong reasons, or perhaps kept secrets from you, what would you do?"

The sound of the blinker comes across the line as Parker contemplates his answer. He murmurs, "Talk to her...I wouldn't give up on her, on us. Because, your hypothetical situation...I've lived it. I lied to Liz before, Adrian. We spent agonizing time apart because we didn't talk to each other, and I didn't tell her the truth. But the thing is, despite all of these 'lies,' it doesn't change the fact that she loves me and I love her. And with this love, we can overcome anything."

My heart thumps with the rightness of his words.

"Whatever you're thinking, know there's always two sides to a story and what you think you know may not be the entire truth or the truth at all. Talk to her. If you love her and if she loves you, which I'd bet my fortune on, you two will get through whatever it is you're going through."

A sudden resolve laces my veins, the antidote to the unease earlier. As I walk down the corridors of the hospital, the weight on my chest lightens. My mind catches up to the fact I've have the muscle strength to carry the burden all along. My mind is clear, as if the swirling fog has suddenly been blown away, revealing clear skies and warm sunshine.

I finally know what to do.

. . .

Two days later, I stride up the halls of TransAmerica. Dad is back home resting with around-the-clock staff taking care of him. He complained this was overkill, but I couldn't care less. The receptionist, a thin woman with blonde hair and a stern face, stops me.

"Sir, who are you here to see and do you have an appointment?"

"Robert Kingsley and tell him it's Adrian Scott. He'll see me."

Her eyes widen a fraction as she recognizes my name and a quick call later, she ushers me inside the elevator and leads me to a large corner office and knocks on the door.

"Come in."

Striding in, I see the man who'll one day be my father-in-law, sitting in his leather chair, his piercing hazel eyes trained on me. Standing next to him is his wife, her hair perfectly coiffed, dressed head-to-toe in luxury.

Her eyes widen when she sees me and she breaks into a wide smile. "You must be Adrian Scott. I recognize you from the tabloids. I've been asking our Emily why she hasn't brought you home to meet us—"

"Mrs. Kingsley, you may not have remembered, but we have met before." Glancing at her, I pin her with a cool stare. I knew she never approved of us in the past and from her shocked expression, it appears she doesn't even recognize me.

"I'll remind you. I used to go by Adrian Callahan. We met at your daughter's piano recital our senior year."

She gasps, her hand flying up to cover her mouth. "That poor kid—"

"Is now one of the richest men in the world, which goes to show, one shouldn't judge a book by its cover. After all, what you're holding may be a rare and valuable first edition." I bite my cheek to keep from snapping at her, leashing down my emotions out of respect for her being Emily's mother.

"I-I'm sorry—" Mrs. Kingsley whispers, her eyes still widened in apparent distress. I fight an urge to snarl. *Too little too late.*

"Audrey, Adrian Callahan or Scott, whatever he goes by now, obviously has something on his mind. Let's hear him out," Mr. Kingsley interjects.

She whips her head toward her husband. "You knew who he is all this time!"

He ignores her and motions for me to continue.

"I'll make this quick." I unbutton my navy-blue suit jacket and place my hands on his desk, dispensing with the pleasantries. "The choice is and always will be your daughter. You can keep your shares and you can tell the old man who I am for all I care. I honestly don't give a shit. Emily and I have spent too many years apart, and I'm not wasting one more minute playing these games of yours." Gritting my teeth, I mutter, "So, you can take your shares and shove them where the sun doesn't shine."

Mr. Kinsley leans back, his eyes unflinching and cold in assessment. He cocks one eyebrow. "What if I say no? What if I don't think that is enough for us to give you our blessing to be with Emily?"

"Robert!" Mrs. Kingsley exclaims, apparently horrified that her husband would turn away one of the most eligible bachelors in society as Emily's suitor. He holds out his hand, his eyes staring unwavering at me.

I curl my hands into fists and thump the table. "I don't give a rat's ass. The only reason I'm here is because I know she cares about the both of you, so this is a courtesy." I clench my jaw, attempting to calm the heated passion in my voice. "If you want me to give you my net worth, my holdings, my business, I would hand it over without a blink of an eye to be with her, but know this, if that is the case, that'll be the last you'll see of your daughter."

Spinning around, I take a step toward the door before his voice stops me.

"You know, I never trusted you. I was always worried you were with my daughter for all the wrong reasons. If you had taken those shares and broken up with her, I would have protected my daughter from a heartless bastard."

Mrs. Kingsley's hand flutters to her chest as her husband stands and walks to the other side of his desk before leaning against it. The earlier harshness on his face softens as he lets out a quiet exhale. He continues, "Emily believed in you. She was so adamant you were going to do great things if given the opportunity. I can now see she was correct all along and we were wrong." He stares at me, seemingly scrutinizing something in my eyes before murmuring, "You do love her."

Mr. Kingsley dips his head in a nod, as if coming to a decision. "Those shares you want, if you still want them, you can have them. I was only saying no because I wanted to see where you stand with Emily."

I let out a ragged breath as the victory I've been seeking is well within reach. The blessing from Emily's father. The shares. The things I've fought hard for with blood, sweat, and tears. Swallowing the lump in my throat, my eyes sweep over the Kingsleys, finding Mr. Kingsley looking at me with something resembling respect in his eyes and his wife still apparently shell-shocked into silence.

My voice is thick and heavy and I rasp, "I hope you know, one day, I'll marry your daughter. Nothing and no one can separate us any longer."

With this sentiment, I turn around and stride out of the stifling office, my heart racing, my thoughts jumbled, but my next steps are clear. The final act before the dominoes come tumbling down.

"The infamous Adrian Scott, as I live and breathe, gracing me with his presence on a Saturday morning." My grandfather chuckles, his startling blue eyes without humor as he sits in an armchair on the veranda of his large colonial mansion on top of the hills of Palos Verdes Estates. The skies are gray and cloudy today, with a thick marine layer permeating the air, cloaking the surroundings in a dense fog. Birds chirp softly in the background, hiding amidst a sea of lush greenery. "How did you find me?"

"I have my ways." Smoothing out my trousers, I take a seat in the wicker chair across from him.

I stare at the man before me—a thin face, a full head of white hair, a delicate nose, reminding me of my mom, a frail frame clad in the finest of clothes. He looks so small compared to the gigantic house behind him, the empty, quiet, soulless home where his throne sits. I've never seen my grandfather up close before, always plotting my kill from afar, never revealing my cards until my victim realizes they are taking their last breaths.

"Are you here to convince me to sell my shares to you?" He smirks, as if he has me all figured out.

"No. I don't need to. As of a few moments ago, I own fifty-two percent of the shares of your precious legacy. It's over."

"It's impossible. Kingsley would never sell to you. He sees you for the snake you are. It's a bad business decision."

Chuckling, I pin him with my gaze. "That's where you're wrong. Unlike yourself, some people actually care about the happiness of their children and also, unlike yourself, Kingsley loves his daughter, someone who happens to be head over heels for me." I twist my lips in a snarl. "Your days on the throne are over, old man. You should've taken the out I gave you before."

His face turns mottled and his lips twist in disdain. "I underestimated you, Scott. You're definitely a different type of monster, willing to toy with someone's feelings and sink so low to get what you want. So, what are you going to do with my company? Dissect it? Sell it?"

"For someone like you who doesn't even care about the well-being of his family, of course, you can't fathom love and sacrifice." I stand and button my suit jacket before turning to him. "I was going to chop it up, sell its scraps, and watch you squirm when you see the one thing in your life, which was more important than your daughter, than your grandchildren, crumble in front of your eyes." I take a perverse pleasure in watching the color leach from his wrinkly skin. He shifts in his chair before reaching out to grip a tumbler of golden liquid in his hand, as if needing something fortifying to handle what I'm about to say to him.

"What is it to you?" His eyes turn shrewd and his brows furrow, as if he senses my disdain for him is more of a personal nature. "*Who* are you?"

"But I'm not going to repay hate with hate. Instead, the earnings of your precious company will be held in a trust in perpetuity, to be doled out to financially challenged families dealing with cancer, who are unable to pay for the bills to get the care they need. And Cornwall Holdings will be renamed as Callahan Holdings, after a wonderful woman the world lost too soon. Francine Callahan."

Cornwall's hands tremble, the amber alcohol sloshing out of his cup, making a mess on his trousers. His face turns red as he takes in ragged breaths.

I walk toward the steps, staring out into the gloomy skies, my heart at ease, the fire in my veins finally eradicating. "The irony? Your legacy, the one you worked so hard to protect, the very thing you loved more than your family, will now be renamed, and soon, the world won't remember you, but they'll know the name of your daughter, the very person you cast out without a care, because she supposedly tainted your reputation." I glance behind me, finding his face slowly paling. "The person you killed in cold blood."

"Y-You..." His finger shakes as he points at me. He takes a deep breath before he attempts again. "You snake!" He looks so weak, so pathetic.

"You once told me you wish you had a grandson like me." My lips curl into a sneer before I spit out, "Well, guess what? You got your wish, old man. I mean, *Grandfather*. This is the one and only time I'll call you by that title."

Walking down the steps, my back straight and tall, I pause as my feet hit the gravel. "And by the way, my real name is Adrian *Callahan*."

Without waiting to hear his response, I climb into the back-seat of my town car. I need to find her, my pixie. To tell her my plans for revenge are over. To come clean and tell her everything. To start fresh with a clean slate.

"Pierre, to the beach, please."

As my driver turns around, I stare at my grandfather one last time, finding an old man staring into space, an emptiness in his gaze as he collapses into his chair, his shoulders slumped. He's all alone, with nothing but money he probably won't live long enough to spend, and empty pride to his name.

And I pity him.

• • •

The first rays of sunshine peek through the clouds, cascading over the soft waves in an ethereal glimmer of gold and silver. A light, salty breeze whips at my face, the smell evoking memories of happiness and heartbreak, of youth and innocence, as I take my first steps on to the sand. A few people are ambling along the quiet shores on the secluded beach this morning. My heart skips and flutters, the beats deafening to my ears, as if it knows the identical echoing beats of its other half are nearby.

I breathe through my nose and out through my mouth as I walk toward our spot, hoping I'll find her there, still somehow holding out hope for me, for us, after all these years. The cries of seagulls and screeches of children playing in the sand pierce the stillness of the morning, but I pay them no attention. My thoughts are occupied with fleeting images of Emily's smile, the way she throws her head back in laughter, her impish grin and pinkened cheeks when she opens my notes by her locker. I remember the fire blazing in her eyes when she stood strong and tall before me the first day we reunited at her office, her tears of joy and sorrow when I kissed her soft lips atop the Empire State Building.

Everywhere is her. Everything revolves around her. How silly was I to believe anything otherwise.

I close my eyes and let memories wash over me, my chest warming despite the brisk morning air. A faint scent of lilies wafts over and I take in a ragged inhale before my eyes slowly open.

My pixie stands in the distance, her smooth chocolate locks drifting in the breeze. She's staring into the waves, her body still as if she's lost in thought. Her gray cardigan and long purple dress flutter with each soft kiss from the wind.

My breath catches in my throat and my heart constricts. My eyes burn and the lump in my throat grows. As if sensing my stare, she slowly turns around, her eyes widening when she sees me standing before her.

"Adrian," she breathes, her chest lifting and falling in short bursts, as if she, too, is overcome with emotions.

"It's over," I murmur as I stand in front of her, taking in her frail face, the dark shadows under her eyes.

"What is?"

"I got Cornwall." I reach over and clasp her hand in mine, smoothing my fingers over her chilled ones. Clearing my throat, I say, "I-I've won."

At her silence, I look up, finding her perceptive chocolate eyes pinned on me, a flash of pride and a tinge of hurt swimming in those pools. She dips her head before glancing away. "My father sold you his shares, didn't he?"

I nod, clutching her fingers in a tight grip. I stare at her delicate hands, afraid to look at her as I utter the next words. "Emily, I don't care if you're with me for the wrong reasons, if I'm somehow tied into your promotion at your job, or if perhaps I'm suitable for you now that I'm Adrian Scott and not the poor Adrian Callahan of back then. I—"

Sniffles.

At the sound of quiet crying, I glance up, finding Emily's eyes wet with tears. She drags her hand away from mine. "After all this time," she whispers, "do you really still believe this of me? That I'm with you really only for superficial reasons?"

No.

I want to tell her that, even though I don't know that for a fact. But somehow, perhaps deep down inside me, I've always been unwilling to believe everything that has transpired between us was based on surface-level superficiality.

My gut tells me it's all real. My heart echoes the same.

She curls her hands into fists and takes a huge breath, as if fortifying herself with bravery. "Do you know why I left you all those years ago?"

My heart thuds in my chest at the anguish on her face, a pain so sharp slicing through me even though I don't know the source of the injury.

"Eleven years ago, your father was supposed to get arrested for embezzlement and you were also going to be reported to the headmaster for illegal fighting, which would've gotten you expelled from Warwick. You wouldn't be able to go to college then. In exchange for my parents keeping their silence, I had to break up with you."

Tears stream down her face in earnest as she chokes out a sob, finally letting out years of pent-up pain and sadness. She bites her lip as she stares at me, the truth evident in her eyes. The sorrow in the chocolate pools, which I have seen time and time again before, now makes perfect sense.

The earlier pain is now a crushing agony, her feelings fully transferring to me as if our hearts and our souls are finally fully linked together. I clench my hands into fists as my lungs are robbed of breath. I shake my head, both understanding and not comprehending her words at the same time. *No. This can't be.*

And yet, the truth rings loudly in my ears. The rightness of her words, washing away the soiled past in crushing clarity. Everything makes sense now.

My pixie.

All these years.

And I thought she abandoned me and pitied me.

I spent years hating her, spent years trying to forget her, spent years letting poison seep into my skin, corrupting my heart.

The insults I hurled at her, the hurt I've caused her.

All this time wasted.

My eyes prickle with tears, a thick lump forming in my throat, and I let out a mirthless chuckle at my idiocy.

With a few strides, I reach her and pull her flush against me, curling one arm around her waist, the other cradling the back of her head. She trembles in my embrace as I smooth my hand on her back, blinking back the tears in my eyes.

"Why didn't you tell me?" I rasp. "Even if you couldn't tell me then, you could've told me now. I know I didn't make it easy for you to tell me the truth, but surely there must be a way. Why did you let me continue hating you? Continue doubting you?"

She clutches me tighter, as if afraid I'll let go. "You were still so angry at the past, so intent on taking revenge on anyone who has hurt you before. I couldn't risk you going after my parents. They have their issues, but I still love them. And I also didn't want you to feel guilty about the choice I made."

She lets out a shaky exhale. "I know about the paparazzi, how you've planned everything to arrange for the photo leak, the fake dating. I can only assume your plans for revenge once included me...I just couldn't bring myself to let anyone else get hurt." Emily tilts her face up, her eyes watery as she whispers against my chest, "Tell me, are you still seeking revenge? Were you with me to get your shares?"

I shake my head vehemently and stare at her unwaveringly, pleading with her to understand the truth in my words. "No. What may have started as plans for revenge quickly faded once I was in your presence. Emily, y-you were always the one for me. I never got over you. I *couldn't* get over you. My love for you has never ended."

I slide my hands to her face, using my thumbs to swipe the tears off her cheeks. I whisper, "I-I'm so sorry, Pixie. I would do anything to unwind time, to take back all the harsh words I've said, all the hurt I've inflicted on you." Clutching her back in my embrace, I bury my face in her hair, my heart overwhelmed with both love and regret. Hindsight is twenty-twenty. In retrospect, I should've known. Emily Kingsley was the one person who didn't mind my humble beginnings, the one spot of brightness in my life back then. How could I think anything otherwise of her?

"All this time," I whisper, my voice thick and choking up. "I never knew. You carried this burden by yourself for me and I b-blamed you for everything." My arms tighten around her as I shake against her small frame. "I should've known. Our love was so strong. I should've known, but instead, I let my pride get in the way. I don't deserve you. Will you forgive me? Will you let me spend the rest of my life making it up to you?"

"Shhhhhh..." She hushes me as she smooths her hands on my back, softening the tensed muscles with each pass. My kindhearted pixie, still worried about my feelings even when her heart has been pummeled over and over again. "You couldn't have known, Adrian. I set out to hurt you. To convince you the words out of my mouth were real. That was the only way. Don't blame yourself for it." My heart flutters at the warmth in her words, the consideration, the love, everything I don't deserve. "It all worked out, didn't it? We found our way back to each other. It was my choice...I don't regret a single thing. You reacted the way you did because you didn't have all the facts. If I couldn't have all of my wishes and dreams..." She swallows, pulling away, her eyes welling once again with moisture.

"I wanted you to have yours." Her lips twist in a shaky smile. "And you did it. You did everything you set out to accomplish. I'm so proud of you. My sacrifice wasn't in vain."

I cradle her face, my eyes memorizing every inch of her—the light dusting of freckles on her porcelain skin, so pale they're almost unnoticeable, the warm, golden flecks in the soft chocolate pools of her irises, her beautiful lips, the cupid's bow perfect in every way. My thumbs swipe at tears slipping down her cheeks again and I swallow the thickness in my throat. A small breeze whisks by, and I belatedly realize my cheeks are also wet from tears.

Perhaps these tears are no longer ones of sorrow, but are now ones of joy.

She laughs, the sound lilting and sweet as she wipes my cheeks with her sleeves and I smile at her, my vision blurring once more. Warmth spreads from my chest to the rest of my body and I let out a ragged breath, my lungs finally feeling free to truly breathe. My heart feels whole, the love inside overflowing for the woman in my arms.

"God, I love you so, so much, Pixie. From now on, let me chase after your dreams with you. No matter what happens, let me stay by your side," I rasp. "Promise me, whatever problems we face in the future, let us face them together. No more sacrifices. No more lies."

She nods as she blinks her dew-tipped lashes. She's utterly breathtaking. "I promise."

Tilting her face up, I lean down and seal my lips with hers in an obliterating kiss. Every suction, every swipe, every taste is a vow, one I'll never break. My heart soars and my soul takes flight as the world fades around us. My tongue sweeps inside her mouth, tasting her essence, leaving parts of me behind. She whimpers and stands on her tiptoes while I angle her face to be closer to her, to tell her with my tongue, my lips, and my passion that everything I have is hers. Our bodies meld together, our hearts beating in sync, and for the first time in eleven years, my soul is finally at peace.

My pixie is at my side again and I'll never want for anything anymore.

We part for air and she whispers, "It has always been you, Adrian. I love you with all my heart."

"My soul is yours," I answer as she doles out a shaky smile.

I curl a lock of hair behind her ear as the sun finally breaks through the clouds, turning the sky into a kaleidoscope of golds and yellows, as if nature, like me, is finally waking up after a long sleep.

"I want to tell you about Kristi—" she begins, her eyes darkening.

"Shh..." I place my finger on her lips. "We have all the time in the world. All the time in the world." I have no more doubts in my heart, no more suspicion lacing my blood. Our love is pure, the best thing that has ever happened to me, and nothing can make me believe otherwise.

I know we have many things to discuss, many more secrets to be unveiled, but at this moment, none of it matters because all I know is I love this woman with everything inside me and she also feels the same way. And that's enough.

The music is in the silence between the notes.

Emily's lips tilt up in a dazzling smile, rivaling the beauty of the white-tipped ocean waves before us. I curl my arm around her shoulders and tug her to my side. She burrows her head against my chest as we stand on the soft sand, witnessing nature's symphony, marking the beginning of the rest of our lives.

"**O**n your knees, Pixie," Adrian rasps as I slowly drop to the floor in the living room of the penthouse suite at Kensington Hotel in New York City. Adrian had a business trip to the Big Apple and asked me to go with him for a mini extended weekend vacation. The past nine months have been blessedly beautiful. We also finally aired out all our secrets to each other, what his original plans of revenge were, how he gave them up soon after we started fake dating, and how Kristi made the deal with me to make director, which had no bearing on my love for him. The old wounds took time to heal, the trust slowly rebuilding between us, but we're stronger because of them.

Finally, there are no secrets between us, only love. Deep-seated, wholehearted love.

"Adrian, I—"

"Shut the fuck up and take that dick like a good girl," he commands, his startling eyes growing darker at the edges, but not before I see the spark of amusement shining in them at the reference to the eye mask fiasco during our first trip together to the city.

Biting my bottom lip, I feel myself getting wet from his terse command and boy, does he like to dole those out on a regular basis.

I usually give it back as good as I get except in the bedroom, when I just want to feel completely owned by him.

Taking my time, I unbutton his trousers then painstakingly slide down his zipper, knowing the slowness is driving him insane with need. He groans in frustration as he shifts on the sofa and widens his legs so I can get closer.

"Someone is excited to see me today," I tease him as I rub my thighs together, eager to stave off the aching pressure there.

"Take my damn cock out, Emily."

Smirking, I slowly slide down his pants and boxer briefs and his steel rod springs to attention, curling up toward his stomach. A long vein pulses on the side, and my mouth waters, wanting to lick it. I dip out my tongue, swiping one long stroke from base to the very red tip and Adrian grunts, his hand fisting my hair as he nudges me down closer to him.

"I love your big, hard cock," I moan as I part my lips and take the tip in. "I can't wait for you to split me in half." Inch by inch, he slips inside me until the tip hits the back of my throat. I relax my tongue and breathe through my nose before I swallow, the motion drawing him farther down.

"Fuck. Your dirty mouth." His head falls back as his hips arch up, setting a quick pace while I twirl him with my tongue with each thrust. "My pixie is a slut for me, aren't you? God, you can suck cock like no other."

His praises are arrows of pleasure to my core and I feel myself leaking between my thighs. My lips pump his cock in a hard rhythm as I free my hands to slide the straps of my dress down to the floor, exposing my breasts and lace-clad pussy to the air. I bring my hands to massage the swollen globes, the beaded nipples begging for attention. I look up, finding Adrian's eyes dark, his pupils blown as he stares at me in lust and wonder.

I slurp louder, making sure I take him in as deep as I can, tears clouding my vision. He tastes salty and his dick swells up even more and he jerks his hips erratically.

"Is your cunt dripping for me? Touch yourself. I want to see you come as I make you swallow every drop." His grip on my hair tightens, sending shards of pain to my scalp, and I moan, the vibrations in my throat causing him to shake in front of me.

Sliding my hand inside the lace, I circle my fingers over my wet entrance, and smear the cream on my swollen clit. I flinch from each pass, the sensations too much, and I continue to whimper, chasing each thrust of his cock inside me with each swipe of my fingers. The pressure builds at an intense speed and Adrian fully takes over fucking my mouth like a possessed man.

His face is tense, his eyes dark and trained on me, a muscle twitching in his jaw as he holds my head in place while he slams his hips over and over against my face, bottoming out with each motion. Tears stream down my face in a mess as fire builds between my thighs.

"You're so fucking beautiful. You take my cock so well," he rasps as he hammers inside my mouth and I can taste the saltiness of his pre-cum leaking out of the tip. His motions speed up and he starts to spasm, his eyes rolling back. "Shit. I'm going to come, baby. Come with me, pretend your fingers are my cock."

Whimpering, I hook two fingers inside my tight channel, angling it such so I hit my G-spot. Fireworks spark behind my eyes and with one hand on my aching breast, the other hand thrusting myself into a frenzy, I start shaking, the tendrils of orgasm making an appearance. Adrian groans as he chases his own pleasure, completely dominating my mouth. He lets out a guttural moan, his cock swelling then pulsing, shooting his cum straight down my throat in thick ropes.

"God, yes! Swallow every drop."

His sounds of rapture send me over the edge and I spasm around my fingers, the pleasure exploding between my thighs and radiating over the rest of my body as my mouth falls lax while I shudder on the floor before him.

Before I know it, he hauls me up and pushes my face down on the sofa. My body is liquid jelly, as my limbs haven't regained function. He takes advantage of my malleable state and stands behind me, spreading my legs and lifting up my ass.

"I'll never get enough of you, Pixie. This soaking-wet pussy is mine," Adrian growls into my ear as he slams his hard dick inside me in one full thrust, apparently not satiated from the blow job I just gave him.

"Adrian!" I shriek, trying to claw away from him on the sofa. "I-I'm too sensitive down there, oh my G-God." He thrusts inside me in earnest, his cock giving me no reprieve as my walls throb and clench around him, welcoming him home.

"This is so fucking good," he chants, crowding behind my back, his muscular forearms caging me in, and he ruts into me like an animal in heat. His smell of mint and musk invades my senses and I grip the cushion for dear life, letting him use and dominate me.

More juices flood my pussy as the erotic sounds of skin slapping skin fill the air. He gyrates his hips, angling his dick to hit me deeper, hitting that sensitive place inside me, grazing my clit with each pass. Adrian hoists my legs higher and continues his sensual assault.

"You're fucking wet and dripping for me. Your pussy is sucking in my cock like a whore. I can feel you tightening... You're going to come and make a fucking mess all over the place, aren't you, baby?"

His filthy words add gasoline to the fire and my legs tremble and I start panting, not caring I may be making a mess all over the couch. White dots show up in my vision as the pinpricks of pleasure turn into a firestorm and I spasm uncontrollably, toppling over the edge into the heavens or hell. I let out a lusty cry and my juices squirt out of me.

"Fuuuuck," he groans, jackhammering into me in rapid succession before he too succumbs to the madness and follows me over the cliff. His hot cum floods my insides in strong spurts, the liquid sending tingles inside my channel, prolonging my high. He slows his thrusts, gently riding out the rest of his crest before he collapses over my body, his breathing harsh against my ear.

"Hot damn," he pants and I whimper in response, unable to speak.

"Didn't you say you'll be busy with work? So far, I haven't seen you work yet," I mumble into the cushions a few minutes later.

He chuckles, his deep voice sending shivers down my body. He sits next to me and cradles me in his arms, laying my head on his lap. "Complaining, Pixie?"

"No. But just so you know, I had to take a few extra days off work because you sprung this on me last minute. Why do you need me on this trip, anyway?"

"You'll see." He wipes my sweat-beaded forehead with his hand and kisses my hair. Lifting me up into a sitting position, he reaches over and tweaks my nipples. "God, I want you again."

I giggle. "You're a beast, Adrian."

"Your beast." He massages my breasts and pinches the hardening tips and I whimper in response. Groaning in frustration, he murmurs, "No time for this right now. Get your ass ready. We're going out."

"Where?" I twist my face to look at him, finding his lust-filled gaze on mine, his lips tilting up in a smile. I stand up and frown.

"You'll see." He swats my ass cheek, and the slap reverberates in the room. "Ugh, please get ready, my love. I'm this close to fucking you again."

Grinning, I sashay to the bedroom, relishing in his curses as he no doubt is trained on my wiggling butt as I walk away from him.

• • •

"Are we there yet?" I grip Adrian's hand tightly as he leads me through what sounds like double doors.

"Almost, Pixie. Careful, there are steps here."

After we got ready for a mysterious event, for which he told me to don a cocktail dress and he is decked out in his usual mouth-watering, three-piece suit, he blindfolded me in the town car, saying he has a surprise for me, and now he's leading me to God knows where with the silk scarf still wrapped over my eyes, rendering me completely dependent on him.

A faint scent of his mint mixed with a unique smell of flowers and circulated air lingers in the air. I hear someone cough softly in the background, followed by a quiet "shhhh."

"What's going on?" I ask as I carefully climb up the steps, leaning against Adrian for support.

"Patience is definitely not your strong suit," he teases and we reach a flat surface and walk forward. "In front of you is a bench. I'm going to turn you around and have you sit on it, okay?"

Reaching out, I feel a cool, smooth surface, the texture like leather, and I carefully sit and place my hands on my lap. "Now what?"

"Give me one second."

"Damn it, Adrian, any more of this suspense and you aren't getting any tonight!"

A few snorts ring out in the room, and I hear the soft squeaking of a hinge. Then, I feel his fingers reaching behind my head and loosening the silk tie off my face.

Blinding-white lights flood my vision and I blink, trying to orient myself after half an hour of relative darkness. In front of me is a beautiful, Yamaha black grand piano, the shiny surface gleaming back at me. I gasp as I marvel at the gorgeous instrument—most likely one of their premium concert grand pianos in the CF series— and my fingers gingerly touch the keys. I look around, my eyes finally trailing to the rest of the space and notice I'm on a big stage, with rows and rows of classic red-velvet chairs in front of me, a spectacular circular ring of lights on the ceiling of the auditorium, the place where I've imagined myself time and time again.

Carnegie Hall.

I'm sitting in front of a grand piano in Carnegie Hall.

"Ems! We love you!" Liz screeches from the front-row seat, waving her hands at me.

I gasp as I notice my friends and family in the first two rows. Liz and Parker with little Lucy, Jess beaming next to James with baby Violet in her arms, Melanie wagging her brows at me, Steven and Charles sitting on the side with identical shit-eating grins on their faces. Sarah and Jack are sitting together, Sarah angling her body as far away from her nemesis as possible. My parents are also there, their faces serious as usual, but this time, I detect a hint of pride in their eyes.

The auditorium doors suddenly open and in walks a woman who looks to be fresh out of college, her brown hair in a tight bun with a pair of thick, black eyeglasses framing her face as she scurries over to Steven with a large bouquet of lilies in her hands. She glances up at the stage, flashing a tentative smile before handing the flowers to Steven, who is wearing a small frown on his face. He murmurs something and dips his head into a nod and mystery girl flushes and hurries away. Steven turns around and glances at her retreating backside before shaking his head and facing the stage once more, the smug grin back on his features. He holds the flowers up in my direction and winks.

"You're making us look really bad, dumbass." Jack snickers, directing his comment to Adrian, who is standing next to me, arching his brow.

Sarah elbows him. "Shut up. You're completely ruining the vibe."

"Come on, Siren. You know you love me."

"In your wildest dreams, Jack. Gosh, please sit farther away. Of all the chairs, you just have to choose the one next to me."

The two bicker, and I've never seen Sarah vibrating with such animosity as she glares at the nonplussed Jack, who gives her a wink. These two always seem to be at each other's throats whenever they see each other, which is completely out of character for Sarah. But I can't help noticing the spark of attraction in her eyes when she stares at him when she thinks no one is looking.

Laughing, I glance at Adrian, who is staring at me with tenderness in his eyes. "Adrian, what is this?"

He smiles and reaches behind him to pull out a heavy volume and hands it to me. "You once said you wanted to play piano at the Carnegie Hall, so here we are."

Tears well in my eyes, my love for him growing even more, something I thought was impossible. My hands shake as I clasp the book tightly, finally staring at the lightly worn navy cover, the yellowing pages. "A-Adrian... Is this what I think it is?"

"*Muller Goldleaf Limited Edition Beethoven Complete Piano Sonatas.* This is what you said you wanted the first night we met at the beach. It took me three years to find a copy and another year to convince the owner to sell it to me. I've had it with me for five years, hoping one day I could give it to you."

I bite my lip as I caress the pages with one hand, my other hand swiping the tears off my cheek. "Five years?" I glance at him, finding his eyes shining with moisture as he nods.

"My heart has always been yours, even when we were apart. My soul craves you, my heart needs you to beat, my lungs need you as much as air."

Slowly, he drops down to one knee and my hands fly to my lips, halting my gasp. He reaches inside his jacket and pulls out a dark-navy velvet box and flips open the lid. Lying on a bed of blue silk is a round-cut solitaire diamond ring surrounded by a halo of smaller diamonds. The stage lights illuminate every sparkle, every glimmer. My lips wobble as my heart pounds inside me.

"A-Adrian..."

He stares at me, his eyes burning hot, a vein pulsing on his forehead. Wetness clings to his lashes and he says, "Emily, you've saved me time and time again. With you by my side, my life has meaning, my life has joy. You bring me peace. You've taught me why Romeo and Juliet risked everything to be together. You've showed me how pure and selfless love can be. My life began when I walked into the office my first day at Warwick and was put on hold that night at the beach eleven years ago, only for it to restart once you came back into my world. I live for you. I breathe for you. My heart beats for you. My soul soars only with you. Will you please do me the honor of marrying me and letting me walk alongside you for the rest of our lives?"

My lips tremble as I swallow the lump in my throat. My vision blurs and more tears slip down my face. There is only one answer to his question. "Yes, Adrian. I love you."

He chokes up as he slides the ring on my finger and seals his lips with mine, his kiss soft as he dissolves into low chuckles. "Thank God. I love you so much, Emily. So, so much. You're my center, my compass in this journey through life." His lips find mine again and the kiss turns heated, his tongue dipping into my mouth for a quick swipe as I melt against him, clutching his back.

Applause rings out, cheers echoing in the auditorium, and we part for air. Adrian smiles, a rare, dazzling smile lighting up his entire face, and my heart free falls. I've finally found what lies at the bottom of the abyss.

It's our heaven, our love permeating the air, flowing through its waters.

I grin at him and arch my brow. "And plus, Emily Kingsley will never lead you astray."

Adrian throws his head back in laughter at my reference to what I told him in the halls of Warwick before staring at me with love shining in his eyes. I give him a wink and he chuckles under his breath.

He slides onto the bench next to me and places his hands in position. I flip to the first sonata on the book, staring at the gold-tipped pages dulled by the passage of the years, but no less beautiful.

And we play. Together.

My heart fills with joy and my life is finally complete.

• • •

Thank you for reading THE HARSHEST HOPE. Hope you've enjoyed Emily and Adrian's story as much as I did writing it. Please consider leaving a review on the retailer website and Goodreads (https://www.goodreads.com/book/show/150305720-the-harshest-hope). Your reviews will really help this author out and will allow for more readers to find this book.

Do you know Jack and Sarah are going to star in the next book, THE BRIGHTEST SPARK? Their story is filled with banter, steam, all types of swoon, and features a bad boy with his good girl angel. Don't miss it. Order it here: (https://geni.us/thebrightestspark)

Want to tag along with Adrian and Emily on their steamy trip to Alaska for the holidays with Charles and their friends? Sign up for my newsletter to get TWO EXTRA BONUS CHAPTERS, new release alerts, exclusive bonus material, and more. Just click on the "The Harshest Hope Bonus Chapters" in the website: (https://www.victorialum.com/bonus)

Join my Facebook group, Victoria Lum's Luminaries (https://www.facebook.com/groups/576423100572205) for sneak peaks, exclusive giveaways, and to chat about all things book-related! You can also find me on Tiktok @victorialumwriter (https://www.tiktok.com/@victorialumwriter), Instagram @authorvictorialum (https://www.instagram.com/authorvictorialum/), and other sites at this link (https://linktr.ee/authorvictorialum).

ACKNOWLEDGEMENTS

This writing journey has been wild and I'm so thankful I get to do this once again! I've seen other authors share a bit of their process in the acknowledgements and I want to try my hand at it this time around.

Emily is one of my favorite characters to write (and I have a feeling Steven will be a close second). She's fun, energetic, and positive, but ever since she appeared on the pages of *The Sweetest Agony* with her "I don't care for long-term relationships mentality," I knew she had a heartbreaking story to tell. Sometimes, the people with the most traumatic and painful pasts wear the brightest and happiest masks on their faces.

I've always been a fan of the underdog winning the race in movies and dear Adrian has been through so much in his life, I actually wanted to apologize to him after I finished writing the first act. As my heart tore in half at that point, the two of them whispered incessantly in my mind, begging me to finish their story, even if it was a bigger and longer story than I originally set out to tell. These two are so perfect together and the very definition of love conquers all.

Her story with Adrian spans more than a decade and literally took a piece of my soul with me by the time I finished writing it. My heart ached for them, my soul bled for them, and I'm so very glad they finally found their happily ever after.

My family: To my husband, thank you for being the biggest supporter of my writing, from being my reluctant alpha reader who gives me really good feedback, to being the sounding board for future novel ideas. To my children, thank you for putting up with your mommy working all the time. I love you.

My editors: Becca Mysoor, Grace Bradley, and Amy Briggs, thank you as always for your edits and feedback. I'm growing as an author, and you all play a big part in the journey.

Proofreader and Formatter: Thank you to Virginia Tesi Carey and Elaine York of Allusion Publishing for fitting me into their busy schedules to get this book to the finish line.

My PA: Thank you to Nikki Johnson for helping me with all the admin tasks I'm perpetually behind on and for reminding me of critical deadlines.

Cover designer: To the awesome LK Farlow of Y'All That Graphic, thank you for everything and for bringing my boys to life.

Beta readers: Malia, Jenn, Jess, Fiona, and Isha, I love you girls. Thank you for all your feedback and support as always. The story is better because of you all.

Fellow authors: So many authors have helped me on this journey—it is impossible to name everyone, but I appreciate each and every one of you.

PR Firms: Thank you to Greys Promo and Literally Yours PR for your promotional efforts and helping me get the word out especially since I scheduled this with you last minute!

My Fellow Readers: Thank you for reading my stories. I love chatting with you on Instagram or Tiktok DMs, Facebook comments or messages. Thank you for giving me a chance. Without you, I wouldn't be an author. I have so many plans for future stories, so stay along for the ride.

With love,
Victoria

ABOUT THE AUTHOR

Victoria is a lover of all things romance, including movies, books, and television shows. A hopeless romantic since childhood, she is always dreaming up stories and happily ever afters. Caramel lattes are her fuel in the morning and she can usually be found reading anything she can get her hands on. She lives with her family and a beautiful Siberian husky in sunny California.

Keep in touch!
Sign up for her newsletter below:
Newsletter
(https://dashboard.mailerlite.com/
forms/289149/81041142820374109/share

Follow Victoria on social media:
Tiktok
https://www.tiktok.com/@victorialumwriter
Instagram
https://www.instagram.com/authorvictorialum/
Facebook Group
https://www.facebook.com/groups/576423100572205